TWENTY THREE

By

Murray McDonald

First Published by Kennedy Mack publishing

TWENTY THREE

ISBN 978-1-8381908-0-4

For Cleo

Chapter 1

The day my life ended was not a notable event in the grand scheme of world history. In fact, had it not been for the events that ultimately led to my demise, I'm sure it would have passed with little note.

Being the final victim in a killing spree that rocked what was otherwise a quaint and tranquil vacation destination was my fifteen minutes of fame, my chance to shine in the glare of the world's media. Of course, having only my final breaths to realize that would be the case somewhat lessened the moment. At least for me.

The press would have their moment, flocking their news anchors from around the globe to stand quite pointlessly as close as the authorities would allow to the various crime scenes, hassling the residents and vacationers for even the most mundane tidbits of information that was as meaningless as the anchor's presence.

They say that your life flashes before you as you take your final breaths. I can testify that's partly true, part of my life did flash before me, the realization of the point where fate had intervened and ultimately led to my demise. Each breath I took, each one closer to the end, indicated my time on the island and in this life was coming to a premature end. Peace surrounded me. The tranquility of the island at night was breathtaking. My final breaths were accompanied by the memory of the beautiful vista of the spectacular bay that had otherwise made the last few weeks the best and most exciting of my somewhat ordinary life. The boats would be bobbing gently in the harbor, responding to the lapping waves, the lights atop their masts twinkling against the darkening sky as the last evidence of the day's sunshine finally dipped into darkness. It warranted a drink in one hand, not the gun that was resting in mine.

A darkness was quickly befalling me, the final flashes as my breath slowed, a story that has to be told, a story that explains everything, and I have barely moments to share, if even that…

***

Two Hours Earlier

Deputy Sheriff Kay Miller stared at the laptop. An empty box beckoned for her to fill it with an unknown code. After weeks of intensive investigation, she had a lead. She was sure she had her man, she just had to prove it. She had every resource available to her from the State of Maine and the FBI but could rely on neither. She had taken the law into her own hands. The man had to be stopped, and it was up to her to do it.

Everything was changing; the team was being re-organized. Kay disagreed. She had worked longer and harder on the murders, despite being the newest member of the Knox County Sheriff's Department. It was her first posting, on the largest of the Fox Islands—Vinalhaven Island—a beautiful, lobster rich island haven in the Penobscot Bay off the coast of Maine. Boasting only 1,000 year-round residents it was the easiest of postings in Knox County. While the summer population swelled to nearly four times the norm, the affluent visitors did nothing to impact the already negligible crime rate. For the newest member of the Sheriff's Department, it promised nothing but drunken brawls and the occasional car accident to keep the boredom of routine at bay.

A noise from the front door snapped Kay from her thoughts. She looked at the clock on the laptop's screen. It was just before 9.00 p.m. She wasn't expecting anybody and from recent experience that generally wasn't good news. Unfortunately for Deputy Kay Miller, recent experience was not about to be proved wrong, as the man she had fallen in love with, the first man she had ever loved, fell and slumped into her arms for the last time. It was a love that could never be.

Chapter 2

Memorial Day Weekend – One Month Earlier

"Cold" was the word that described the sea spray, not "cool" as had been suggested, although "freezing" might even have been a more accurate description. Whatever the case, the early summer sunshine was struggling to offer any warmth to Kay's spray-chilled face. The ferry was cutting through the waves with purpose, but they weren't making a lot of headway. Vinalhaven Island, fifteen miles by ferry from the mainland and Rockland, and from as far as Kay knew, modernity, sanity and reality.

A new recruit to the sheriff's office, Kay was replacing the recently retired officer who had served for over forty years, the majority of them on the island. As another wave soaked the ferry's deck, she couldn't help but understand why he'd retired to Florida, where winter sea temperatures were far higher than the water hitting her. There was no disputing the scenery was far beyond that of any pristine white beach. This was rustic, wild nature at its most beautiful. The rugged, rock-strewn beaches gave way to the lush green lands that sprouted from the sea all around them.

The ferry wound its way through a well-planned route, boasting to all how amazing its life was to enjoy such a wonderful seascape trip after trip, day after day. The visitors experienced it twice a year, the residents more so, but none more than the ferry and her crew. Their pride in where they were lucky to call home was evident.

Kay had caused quite a stir at the ferry port. For once, it hadn't been her but more her position. She had driven as advised to the head of the ferry line and was boarded first, as her position in the community dictated. The Knox County sheriff vehicle was always welcome. The large SUV cut in front of the line and was met with blasts of horns from further back in the line, which stretched back to where two ferries worth of traffic awaited. Kay had taken a spot that meant it was likely two fewer cars would be making the trip that day. She hadn't booked and had simply taken one of the coveted Friday Memorial weekend spots. A day late in arriving, her spot had gone to someone else the previous day, not that that was going to appease whoever had just missed the trip they thought for the last few hours of queuing they were destined to make.

Kay shrugged to the loader as she drove onto the front of the ferry. There was no hiding once aboard. The uniform would see to that, still crisp and bearing the manufactured folding creases that would soon disappear, never to be replicated, no matter how hard Kay tried. While she would be easily identified as the space stealer, the unfortunate victim of her theft would be busy searching for accommodation for an unexpected extra night in Rockland before seeking her out in the morning should their anger spill over to another day. She reminded herself how unlikely that was as she looked down at her perfectly creased unflattering gray pants; she was the law.

Kay was so used to skipping lines and getting special treatment, she had forgotten who she was. The loader hadn't been won over by her looks, but by her position. A glimpse in the window opposite as she exited her vehicle confirmed that. She had never looked so…she couldn't even think what the word was. She wasn't unattractive. The uniform hadn't removed her looks, but it had certainly taken the shine from them. Plain. That was the word she was searching for. Her long, flowing brunette hair was tucked up into her hat, her dark brown eyes hidden by her shades, and the sun high above was casting a shadow over her face thanks to the sheriff's hat. Her shirt hung loose, her pants easy fitting. Gone were her customary figure hugging outfits accentuating her womanly curves.

Even her work shoes were doing their level best to make her sexless and all in all, the uniform had done just that, made her as uniform with the rest of society as possible. She liked it. No. She *loved* it. Her teeth, perfect and dazzling white—a million dollar smile she had been told many times—would have to be tempered. Kay Miller, deputy sheriff of the Knox County Sheriff's Department, had a job to do, and she was going to do it to the very best of her ability. She had dreamt of little else, and although it had taken her more years than she'd have liked, she was finally there and would do her best to fulfill her dream.

Unbeknownst to her, less than 48 hours later that dream would crash into a reality that nobody could have predicted. Well, not entirely nobody. One person knew exactly what they were doing.

Chapter 3

Memorial Weekend

Kay had received a warm welcome when she drove onto Vinalhaven as its new resident law enforcement officer. Two of the Town's Selectmen had made the effort to meet her upon her arrival. The Selectmen were the town's executive board, and from her research prior to arrival, Kay knew there were five, three men and two women. Between them they were the elected officials who ran the island.

Whether it was just by chance or a more orchestrated decision, it was the two female Selectmen that greeted her with a basket of food. Sarah and Liz had both been born on the island and were keen to portray just how wonderful island life was. A stark contrast to Kay's miserable childhood, she was relieved when the stories of their younger follies of their upbringing ended. It was the life every child dreamed of and few, certainly few that Kay knew as a child, ever had. Kay had read voraciously as a child, escaping her reality, entering the world the two women had lived. Days full of adventure and excitement, safe in the knowledge loving parents and a warm and secure environment. As far from Kay's life as a child it was possible to get.

A quick tour of her office was followed by her being guided to a small cottage that would be her home while on the island. It was perfect. A whitewashed beach house was the theme, everything was either, white, painted white, or made from reclaimed wood that had been whitewashed. A whitewashed deck faced towards the harbor below, the sun glistening across the water as it began to dip towards the mainland in the distance. Westward facing, it would afford her the most spectacular sunsets.

"It's one of the best views on the island," said Liz, the older of the two, catching Kay's expression.

Kay unleashed her smile. "I believe you."

"I have a feeling you'll be a very welcome replacement for at least half the population." Liz smiled at Sarah, nearer Kay's age, knowingly.

Kay took a second to realize what they meant and blushed when the compliment hit home.

Sarah winked. "More than half."

Kay offered an awkward laugh as the redness travelled down her neck. Both Sarah and Liz, realizing they had overstepped and made Kay uncomfortable, looked at each other while Kay studied the food basket, a bottle of red and white wine atop. She reached out and checked the white; warm. The red would be perfect but she stopped herself. She wanted to be alone, and offering a glass of wine would extend the women's presence.

"I think perhaps we should let Kay settle in," said Liz. "I'm sure she's had a long day."

"Yes, of course," Sarah agreed. "We'll let you unpack and enjoy the sunset in your new home."

Kay closed the door behind the women, hearing them whispering their surprise at how sensitive Kay was through the door. So desperate to discuss Kay with each other, they hadn't even waited until they had walked away, the click of the door closing behind them enough for them to start.

Sure, Kay had issues. Everybody had issues. However, she had coping strategies, and in general in ninety-nine percent of situations she'd not have blinked with what happened with Sarah and Liz. Yet, for Kay, situations occurring in her home were different. That was her safe place, being made to feel sexually desired in her safe place by a stranger was crossing the line of comfort that in any other environment she'd have laughed off, or perhaps even enjoyed. But her home was different, and this was her new home.

She removed her hat and shook out her hair, vowing to apologize in the morning for her crankiness. She didn't want them to think she was some crazy chick. When she took off her shades, the glare of the sun on the water below reflecting against the whiteness of her room nearly blinded her but her eyes soon grew accustomed to the brightness, and a warmth filled her. Despite her awkwardness with Sarah and Liz, it really did feel like home.

A shower preceded the opening of the bottle of red and once dressed in a pair of jeans and a sloppy jumper Kay sat and embraced her new location. As the sun dipped behind the horizon, she looked around the bay. Lights off in the distance began to ignite, twinkling in the twilight. She looked south towards the mouth of the bay before her. Lights shone where earlier trees had sat, homes previously hidden from her revealing themselves in the darkness. A shiver ran down her spine; a chill came over her she took a long pull on her glass of red, emptying the glass. She reached for the bottle; it was empty. She opted for the bottle of white. It was still warm, she hadn't put it in the fridge. It was no longer about the taste, though, it was only about the result. She opened the bottle.

She needed to sleep through the nightmares and the wine was her savior.

Chapter 4

"Someone's pissed," said Frank, checking his rearview mirror as the overlong blast of a horn indicated a less than happy fellow motorist behind.

"Annoyed with the cop taking a spot I'm sure," said his wife, Valerie.

"Can't blame him. We've been here hours and there's only one more ferry after this one."

"Whatever," huffed Valerie, losing interest; something she did increasingly often with Frank. Their marriage was more about being unable to untie the knots they bound on their wedding day than anything else. They'd be far poorer apart; both enjoyed a lifestyle that their partnership allowed. Both personally and in work they were stuck with each other. For richer, certainly being the option they chose, although neither ever voiced it, they both simply had an understanding. Valerie asked little of Frank's going's on and he had no interest in hers. They were happiest when apart. Being stuck in the car for hours together was a recipe for disaster, but so far, the radio talk show had managed to keep them from having to chat with each other. One thing they did share was a love of politics and their new president. A number of talk shows had thrown their support behind the embattled president, whose war on the mass media sparked many a debate. For Frank and Valerie, they were firmly of the same opinion. Their president was a victim, and both had vented their frustrations along with the talk show host. It was the most either had spoken in each other's company in years.

Frank maneuvered onto the ferry and drew level with the police officer who had stolen the vacationer's spot at the front of the boat. The deputy was exiting the vehicle as he stopped and engaged the parking brake. He had to pretend not to look, while being utterly captivated. Frank could sense the beauty behind the façade. She was no ordinary deputy. He stole a look at Valerie, who was too busy checking her make up in the passenger's visor mirror to notice or care about her husband's leching.

"Officer," he said, tipping his imaginary hat as he exited his car.

"Deputy," she corrected absently before walking away, something far more important than Frank on her mind.

He looked over in reaction to a guttural laugh from behind him.

"Jesus, Frank, she's at least twenty years younger. You're fifty-two, overweight, and not even close to her league, even twenty years ago!"

Valerie turned and walked away. Frank stared after her, his eyes burning into her. She waved a hand in the air with a flourish without looking back. She knew him too well. His anger rising, he'd have happily thrown her overboard.

He turned to the deputy. She was watching the interaction with interest. He smiled as best he could manage given his temper. The deputy's mouth didn't move, she watched him stony faced. An awkwardness fell over him and he broke off the gaze and turned back towards Valerie, who was disappearing up the stairs towards the viewing deck. He followed, visions of his wife falling overboard dragging him onwards.

He glanced back. The deputy had not broken her gaze; it was focused entirely on him. He turned and sped towards the stairs.

"Valerie, wait up," he called, loud enough for half the boat to hear. His tone was bright and breezy, his thoughts far from it.

Another torturous hour in his wife's company later, Frank descended the viewing deck to his car. The deputy gave him a wink and broke into a smile, reading him like a book. He opened his door clumsily, dropping his keys as he pulled the door open. It was as though the deputy had seen his darkest thoughts and knew she had forced him to suffer his wife's company for the entire crossing to keep up an appearance.

"Sorry."

Frank jumped when the voice spoke behind him. The deputy was in his personal space.

She smiled warmly. "Sorry," she repeated, "I was miles away earlier when you spoke to me, completely distracted."

The smile completely disarmed him. Her beautiful teeth matched her flawless skin.

"Please don't worry about it, busy time of year for you guys."

"My first day. So sorry if I'm a bit off, my mind is racing with everything." She offered her hand. "I'm Kay."

"Frank." He accepted the handshake.

"And I'm his wife Valerie." She shoved Frank aside and took the deputy's hand in his place.

"Kay," she said again, her smile disarming Valerie as effectively as it had Frank.

"Anyway, nice to meet you both. We'll be docking soon, so best we get in our vehicles. Are you vacationers or residents?" Kay asked, walking back to her truck.

"Vacationers," replied Valerie.

"Well, I hope you enjoy your stay." Kay waved, ending the conversation when she stepped into her truck.

"You're pathetic," Valerie said out of the side of her mouth, while maintaining her smile for the deputy.

"She came over to me," Frank protested, closing his door.

Valerie selected the radio station and turned up the volume, shutting him out with white noise. Their one connection, the one thing that would keep them from each other's throats, had gone. Frank searched through every station they both enjoyed, and none were available on the island. It was going to be a very, very long few days.

"Seriously?" Valerie whined as each station passed with nothing but white noise emitting from the speakers. She hated Vinalhaven, it had taken some persuasion to get her to join him on the trip.

Valerie looked out across the bay as they drove off the ferry, a sense of dread falling upon her. A dread she hadn't felt for fifteen years, the last time she had been on the island, a place she had vowed she'd never return to, and not least because it was where they had met. Frank had begged her to come. An old friend from their time on the island had recently friended him on Facebook and had begged them to meet up. A small reunion was planned, and Frank had decided to make a weekend of it. Although Valerie had initially protested, having had a fling with said friend unbeknownst to Frank before they got together, she couldn't say she wasn't intrigued to see him as well. As the island's familiar scenery and smell hit her, she realized she had made a monumental mistake. Her heart rate raced as memories flooded back. Memories she had fought for years to forget.

Valerie looked across at her husband. A darkness had fallen across his face; he was reliving those same memories. She was not alone, but just like with their marriage, neither dared utter a word. They drove on.

Chapter 5

"What does it say?" Valerie shouted from the shower.

"We're to head up and meet him at the house. The door's open if we arrive and he's out with the dog."

Valerie couldn't help feeling a surge of excitement at seeing Gerald after all these years. He was slightly older than she and Frank, though he had never looked it, and he certainly had known what he was doing. She had never experienced anyone like him before, nor since. Gerald had spent his childhood travelling the world and after years of constantly traveling had elected to settle on Vinalhaven. He had told them all those years earlier it was finally somewhere he could call home.

Gerald had been the handyman come security man on the small island estate where Valerie and Frank had worked and met one another. She never said, "fell in love." She wasn't really sure they ever had been in love. They had both hit thirty, were in a relationship together, and thought they should get married, not because they wanted to, just because it was what everyone did in their thirties back then.

Their room, the best available, of course had the best views, which she deliberately avoided as she dressed. As beautiful as it was, the harbor brought her no nostalgic memories. Carvers Harbor, the main town on the island, was a place she hadn't wanted to revisit, and every minute she spent there, another hazy memory began to force its way back. The ice cream store, the art gallery, the quaint tea shoppe, the lobster boats, the hotel they stayed in built over a bridge where the sea rushed under twice a day to replenish the pond behind...

Where Frank was average and plump, Gerald was tall and dominant. He had wrapped her in his powerful arms, taking her deep with each and every stroke of his powerful loins. Her stomach knotted at the memories, the good ones overcoming the bad. She had been inexperienced, in her early twenties, fresh out of college and in her first real job. Gerald was worldly wise. He made it clear it was nothing more than some summer fun, and had given her no illusions it was anything other than that. Yet it hadn't stopped her dreaming. With the arrival of a new recruit, prettier and more experienced than Valerie, Gerald's eyes wandered, and Frank was the beneficiary of Valerie's newfound love for sex.

Gerald had friended Frank but never her, despite her Facebook page being prominent on Frank's. For all these months the two had been chatting online she had never understood why. She had been more friends with Gerald than Frank had ever been. Not that Frank knew they had been lovers; Gerald had always made it clear fraternization amongst the staff was not allowed and never once alluded to their tryst unless in complete privacy. She wondered if he was still hiding their secret and with him having requested they both come, she wondered if there was going to be some fun. She was sure she'd be able to engineer a couple of hours over the next day or so to get him alone. It wasn't as though she hadn't had her fair share of affairs—she deserved them after having to suffer Frank all those years. He likewise enjoyed his affairs, though he wasn't as careful as she was, or he was just stupid. She feared the latter.

Frank looked at her curiously. "Why are you putting on your walking boots?"

"You've had a few beers, how else are we getting there?"

"There's one sheriff's deputy on the island. The chances of getting caught are nil." He picked up his car keys.

"It's not even a half mile walk to his cottage."

"Exactly, a half mile drive. We'll be fine."

"I'll need my boots to walk back."

Frank raised his eyes to the heavens. He had no intention of walking anywhere. They were on an island with one deputy and no way on or off after the last ferry departed at 4:30 pm, unless by private boat or light aircraft. Even then, once darkness fell, the runway was closed and the rocky outcrops were treacherous for anyone except the most seasoned and experienced sailors in the area.

"We'll be fine there and back."

"For God's sake, Frank, have you not had enough DUIs to learn your lesson?"

He shrugged and held the keys up, motioning for her to join him. Despite her better judgement, she did. Walking a half mile in the darkness wasn't exactly Valerie's favored option. She'd bitch and moan about his driving drunk, but it never stopped her from getting in the car with him.

If they had counted, twelve people on the island witnessed their journey towards the far end of the bay and Lane's Island, a small outcrop, reached by a bridge that crossed a 30-yard gap between the islands. Lane's Island was a private estate with Gerald's cottage guarding the entrance to the estate beyond. A number of lights off in the distance suggested the estate was alive and well. Neither cared, their memories of their time at Lane's Island was firmly in the past, where they both wanted it to remain. They focused on the cottage as they crossed the bridge. A light above the doorway lit up the entrance and another the living room beyond.

Valerie's pulse began to race. From her upper lip she licked the remnants of a glass of wine she had drunk whilst drying her hair.

"Come on!" Frank urged when she hesitated. All thoughts of sex dissipated in an instant as she took a step towards the doorway, a darkness descending on her.

"Maybe…" she started, not sure where she was going.

"Maybe what?" asked Frank, charging onwards towards the door.

Before she could answer, he called back to her, "There's a note on the door. '*With the dog, have left a bottle of wine, help yourselves to a glass,*" he read aloud. *"I'm already a couple ahead!"* Frank opened the door and entered as instructed.

Valerie followed behind, pausing when she entered. Something felt…off. The house was cold, damp. It was late spring; the sun's warmth had been beating down for the last month at least. A scented candle was doing its best to make the house smell homely but the coldness it failed to hide hung eerily. The living room was sparse, with a sofa and a single chair. A fire roared in the fireplace but failed to dispel the dankness. A bottle of wine sat open next to three glasses, two empty and one with the last few drops of a drained glass. Gerald had, as his note said, had at least one already. Frank poured them each a glass and held it up to toast his wife.

"This feels wrong," said Valerie, examining the room more closely. She remembered two decades earlier, when the room had been filled with memorabilia. Nothing remained now. The walls were stark, and only one small light sitting on a table next to the sofa offered any light beyond the roaring fire whose heat failed to warm the small room. The house was cold, unlived in, abandoned. Cold.

"Why did Gerald want us here?"

"What?" asked Frank. "You're asking that now that we're here?"

"It just feels wrong." Valerie shook her head. "I mean, I don't even remember you and him even being that friendly. You've nothing in common with him."

"Rubbish," said Frank with little conviction. Gerald was the cool older dude that all the younger guys wanted to be friends with, be seen with. Gerald pulled the girls, a different one every week, and if Gerald liked you, you were in the in crowd.

Valerie's eyes scanned the badly lit room more carefully. The only thing that sparked any semblance of her recollection was the carpet, and it needed replaced twenty years earlier. Her knees and butt had borne the brunt of many a burn in the short time she had experienced Gerald. There was no sign of the books that once lined bookshelves built into the small nook by the fire. She had lay in his arms and wondered at his trips, the books a journey in themselves and of which Gerald was immensely proud. There was little in the room her memory hadn't captured all those years earlier, early on in her new job. Those were the good memories, ones she had no need to hide.

"Let me see your phone. I want to see the messages you were exchanging," she demanded, a sense of anxiety building.

"Whatever." Frank handed over his smart phone. "It's not messenger though, it's Snapchat."

Valerie ignored the snapchat app symbol—it was utterly pointless, her husband was a technophobe idiot—and went to Frank's Facebook page and scrolled down. His friends there were, not surprisingly, not very many, however, alarmingly, there was no Gerald.

"What's Gerald's name on Facebook."

Frank looked at her with some bemusement and shrugged. "Gerald."

Valerie swiped through his friends list more carefully. There was no Gerald. She opened up Snapchat. There was no Gerald there either. In fact, *no one* was on his Snapchat friends list.

"He's not in Snapchat either. There's no one in there."

"I only used it for him. He was struggling with his internet connection, and Snapchat needs far less bandwidth," Frank explained.

Valerie knew that was rubbish. Snapchat had one function the others didn't; as soon as you read the message it deleted, never to be seen again.

"We need to get out of here now!" she demanded, watching in horror as Frank took a large gulp of his wine. As she stared at him dumfounded at his stupidity, his gaze moved towards the door. It silently swung open, its hinges having been recently oiled. When the door opened the solitary lamp extinguished, leaving only the dancing fiery flames to light the surreal vision that lay before him. Valerie turned to see what had caught Frank's attention. Her scream filled the cottage and a hundred yards in every direction. Unluckily for them, the nearest living soul was over two hundred yards away.

Slumping to the floor unconscious, Frank never heard Valerie's final screams.

Chapter 6

The ringing telephone pulsated in tune with the pain that filled Kay's head. Her eyes failed to focus and she struggled to make out whether it was 6:08 or 8:06. Whichever it was, neither was welcome. She had barely slept after consuming…she realized she had no idea how many bottles of wine. Saturday had been spent unpacking, although that had uncovered the wine she had had the foresight to pack and things had gone from bad to worse. It felt as though she had just laid her head on the pillow when her phone started to ring.

She reached out and tried to silence it. It wasn't ringing. She looked across the room to where she realized the noise was centered, a desk phone atop a small table in the corner. All the way over the other side of the room, out of her reach, it just kept ringing.

Surely it was going to go to an answering machine. She prayed it would, however, it just kept ringing, every shrill tone equating to a pulse of pain. She fell out of bed and crawled across the floor, reached out to pick it up and could have cried when the ringing stopped, leaving her with a dead receiver in her hand and the length of the room away from the comfort of her bed.

She replaced the handset and had made it halfway back when the ringing began again in earnest. She turned and snapped the handset from its holder.

"Hello," she answered, as professionally as she could sound at that time on a Sunday morning.

"My wife, i-it's my wife…" a voice stammered.

Kay quickly snapped out of her haze, putting her game face on. "What about your wife?"

"She's dead. Somebody killed her!"

It was crazy. Her first real day on the job. She wasn't due to start until 9:00 a.m. although, as it had been made clear, her hours were really as required on the island and there wasn't any expectation there'd be much to worry about. But there she was, and her first active duty call was a death.

Strike that she thought. *A murder.* Surely not!

"Where are you?" she asked, trying to maintain her composure which, given how she felt was not easy.

"Frank, my name's Frank. We met on the ferry I think."

"Ah I remember." Frank and his wife, strange couple, no time for each other. "Where are you staying?"

"At the Tidewater but we're at a cottage next to the bridge on Lane's Island."

Kay had taken a drive around the previous day to get her bearings before unpacking. It hadn't taken long. There were three main roads that surrounded Carvers Harbor—Main Street, West Main Street, and Atlantic Avenue. West Main Street ended at the ferry and Atlantic Avenue ended on Lane's Island, one on either side of the mouth of the harbor, while Main Street sat at the back of the Harbor. Atlantic Avenue was the road she needed to take.

"Don't move or touch a thing," she commanded. "I'll be there in five minutes."

Kay grabbed her clothes and was about to don them when a smell assaulted her nostrils. She'd been sweating in her sleep. A two-minute shower took the edge off the odor and still had her on site within the promised five minutes, albeit still buttoning the final buttons on her shirt as she reached the cottage.

A car was parked outside the rather run-down looking cottage, and a light burned in the porch area above the doorway. The window frames badly needed to be repainted and the door would have benefitted from a replacement at least five years earlier. In general it was a sorry sight. A strange place for vacationers to be and certainly not in any fit state to be used as a rental.

Frank was awaiting her arrival, his hands and clothes soaked in blood, dark and dried, not wet and fresh. Whatever had happened, had occurred some time ago.

Kay unclipped her sidearm and approached warily, radioing the mainland as she walked slowly and carefully towards Frank. She looked all around but it was clear they were alone.

"Rockland base, this is Deputy Kay Miller, Vinalhaven Island. I have a suspected homicide, I repeat, a suspected homicide, and suspect in my sights."

Kay didn't hear the coffee being spluttered out, the controller had the professionalism not to broadcast that part of his reaction. *This is Rockland base, please repeat, it sounded like you said homicide?*

"That is correct, homicide, and suspect is in my sights. Please advise." Kay released the transmit button and focused entirely on Frank, who had not moved since she exited her truck. "Frank, I'm going to need you to lie down on your stomach and place your hands behind your back," she requested calmly.

"It wasn't me!" Frank exclaimed, looking back wildly towards the cottage.

"I'm not saying it was, Frank. It's just, as you know, I'm here on my own, and I have to take precautions until I see what we've got."

"My wife's been killed is what we've got, you stupid—" Frank caught his temper when he noted Kay's hand reach for the grip of her gun. Stopping himself before she drew it, he laid down as instructed. Kay kept her hand on her weapon and approached cautiously, placing handcuffs on his wrists and breathing a quiet sigh of relief after she had him under her control.

"Deputy Miller, this is Sheriff Jackson. Did I hear you may have a homicide?"

"I've been advised by a man I've just put in restraints that his wife has been killed. I have not been on scene as yet."

"I know from the notes my predecessor left you've had a lot of fancy training, even some at the FBI, but if you wouldn't mind just confirming she is dead, perhaps its best to minimize your impact on the crime scene."

"Of course, Sheriff Jackson."

"Just call me boss, everyone else around here does."

"Yes boss." Kay's eyebrows spiked at the thought. She had been recruited months earlier by Sheriff Jackson's predecessor, who had surprisingly lost in the recent election. There was still some hint that foul play had been involved as few understood how Jackson had managed to beat the much loved and first Knox County female sheriff. Whatever the case, the new incumbent had honored Kay's offer which, given her experience was no real surprise. A big city cop with detective experience and a number of FBI courses under her belt, she was a real catch and way overqualified for the role. However, the previous sheriff had understood her reasoning and had obviously sold Kay and her experience to the new sheriff, who had quickly confirmed her appointment after the election.

Checking Frank's cuffs were secure, Kay walked towards the cottage. The smell of dampness hit her before she opened the door. The hum of a generator broke through the silence, and Kay noted the electrical lead snaking away from the light that had been crudely erected above the doorway entrance. Another lead snaked from the living area back towards the same hum. She pushed the door open. A body lay on the floor, blood soaking into the carpet around it. The woman was clearly deceased. Judging from the amount of blood there would have been little left in the body. Apart from the look of complete and total shock etched on the woman's face there were no obvious signs of violence. Judging from the blood Kay guessed one knife wound to an area around or into the heart. A closer inspection confirmed that was most likely as only one tear was visible in the woman's dress. Without moving the body Kay could only see the front half of the victim and could only guess there were no other wounds on the back.

She radioed her findings back to the main department headquarters and her "boss" in Rockland on the mainland.

"Okay, don't touch anything else. I'm leaving now with a team. Where is the suspect?"

"Cuffed on the ground in front of the cottage."

"And he's covered in blood?"

"Soaked in it. It's like he slept in it, seriously it's all over him."

A long pause followed, then, *"Keep him there, we're on the way. The mail plane will bring us across. We're rousing the pilot now, so should be there within half an hour."*

"I didn't do it!" Frank protested, struggling to keep his face out of the dirt.

Kay glanced around. It was a very scenic spot. The rustic cottage in its glory days would have been a beautiful home. Surrounded by woodland behind and the beautiful Carvers Harbor and Vinalhaven in front, it was a truly picturesque and tranquil spot. A number of houses were in view across the bridge while the main estate behind lay almost entirely out of view, although glimpses of the brickwork and buildings could be glimpsed through the gaps in the trees.

Kay focused on the homes with line of sight to the cottage, she counted eleven. The three nearest were the largest of the eleven and also obviously unoccupied, with storm shutters closed on every window and door visible. Rich people's holiday homes, they commanded some of the finest views on Vinalhaven, but nobody was appreciating them. Of the other homes, the closest was well over two hundred and fifty yards away she guessed. In the dark, it was unlikely the occupants had seen anything, but she noted their positions to check it out anyway.

"Can you please let me out of these cuffs? I need to use the toilet!" Frank asked, his voice cracking.

"I'm afraid you'll have to wait."

"I can't," Frank whined.

"You're a big boy."

"It's my stomach, it's really hurting …"

Frank groaned, a mixture of embarrassment and pain, and, Kay watched his beige pants darken around his rear.

"Can I please get these off so I can clean myself up?" Frank gesticulated wildly against his cuffs.

Kay felt some compassion. The man had just defecated himself. If he wasn't the murderer, he had just lost his wife and his dignity, but on the other hand, his wife was lying in the same pool of blood he had been in. He was the only suspect she had, and she wasn't going to ruin it because he couldn't wait to use the toilet.

Kay returned to her truck and pulled out a handbook marked "FBI Procedural Handbook," one of many volumes that filled two boxes within her trunk. She skipped through to suspect handling, and a quick scan of the procedures revealed exactly what she expected. There were no situations listed that described hers.

"Sorry, I can't risk you destroying evidence, whether deliberate or by accident."

"I didn't fucking do it!" Frank cried, tears welling in his eyes. While it was the first time he had shown any emotion, he was more upset about messing himself than by his wife's death.

Kay shrugged, showing him the handbook's cover as proof before depositing it back in the trunk, closing it firmly behind her. "I can give you some water if that would help."

"You going to wash my ass for me?"

"No, water, as in a drink of water. We have to maintain the crime scene, and I'm afraid you're part of it."

"But I shit myself out here, not in there!" Frank screamed.

A car was approaching, a local heading across the bridge. Kay walked the first few yards of the bridge to intercept it, waving the car down.

"Everything okay, deputy?" the driver inquired. "The jungle drums are beating back in the town."

"No, not really. I'm going to have to ask you to turn and head back, this is a crime scene and the less we disturb it the better."

"That doesn't sound good." The driver frowned. "I'd be happy to park at the other end of the bridge and stop anyone else from coming. I'm the Chair of the Selectmen, John Gilder. My wife's Jean."

"Oh, yes, she's lovely. I bumped into her yesterday when I was finding my way around the town and island."

John glanced over her shoulder at the man writhing on the ground in the distance, straining to see if he could recognize him, but he was too far away. "Something serious?" he probed.

Being the chair of the Selectmen, John Gilder was the most senior elected official on the island and by default her closest thing to a local boss. Kay couldn't see how disclosing the truth to him could hurt.

"A murder. Looks like the husband may have killed the wife, though he's claiming not."

A loud groan erupted behind them, followed by a noise that implied Frank's bowels were once again emptying their contents.

Gilder's eyes widened. "Dear God, is he okay?"

"A lot better than his wife," Kay remarked in defense of her cuffing a distressed man.

"Yes, of course. I'll get back across the bridge and stop any other nosy busybodies."

"That would be great."

Kay turned back to her suspect/witness/distressed husband and most importantly, increasingly ill looking Frank.

The sound of a light aircraft's engine cut into the morning air, the noise disproportionately intrusive in relation to its size. The small speck grew slightly as it neared but not to an extent that Kay—not the best flyer—would ever dare try it. She followed it as it dropped out of sight behind the trees where she knew just a few months earlier a very similar aircraft had crashed.

Her radio buzzed. *"Deputy Miller, come in."*

"Miller here."

"Slight problem, I'd normally get you to pick us up, there's no one at the airfield."

"I can't leave the scene, but John Gilder is here. I could send him for you?"

"Perfect, can you ask him please?"

"Yes, will do."

"Boss."

"Sorry what?"

"You meant to say yes, will do boss!"

"Oh yes, sorry. Yes I did."

"Boss?"

"What?"

"Sorry, yes I did, boss."

"That's what I said, no?"

"Forget it. Just send John!"

Kay ended the conversation with a grin. Anyone who needed to be called boss that badly didn't deserve to be called boss.

"John!" she shouted across the divide before giving him, his instructions.

John Gilder waved to indicate he understood what she said and made off with a screech of tires, taking his new law enforcement secondment a little too seriously. Another groan from Frank added to his already unpleasant odor and mess. His sweat drenched face was now accompanying a seriously unhealthy gray pallor. He was trying to pull himself into a fetal position.

"Do you take any medication?" asked Kay, becoming concerned he was increasingly unwell.

"No." He struggled through the pain that was eating at his stomach.

A screech of brakes announced Sheriff Chris Jackson's arrival with an entourage consisting of two deputies and a medical doctor. Kay recognized him before he spoke. His posters had littered the county prior to the election. He was a hard-looking man, more akin to that of a criminal than a law enforcement officer. Tall and imposing, he was a man you'd definitely think twice before crossing.

"Well. My predecessor did not do you justice." Sheriff Jackson leered highly inappropriately as he marched towards Kay. "It's a pleasure to meet you, finally!"

Fortunately, the scent of the crime scene and Frank's untimely accident had the sheriff distracted within seconds of his eyeing Kay as no "boss" ever should.

"So, what do we have?" asked the sheriff. "And why the hell is that man lying in his own shit?"

Kay grimaced. "He appears to have developed fecal incontinence."

"Is that fancy words for he shits himself?"

"Yes, a nicer way of saying it, I'm not a fan of profanity."

"Okay," Sheriff Jackson replied absently, not taking note. "And he picked this abandoned dump to off his wife?"

"It didn't look like a dump last night, it was dark when we got here," Frank argued, his voice pained from the effort.

"So you thought it was a romantic spot to off her?"

"I didn't kill her!" Frank groaned loudly as another movement passed.

"Jesus, will someone take that away and process him for evidence?"

The two deputies who had waited awkwardly to be introduced to their new colleague by their boss nodded a professional hello as they rushed by Kay to take charge of Frank.

"Doc, would you mind doing the necessary?" asked the sheriff, motioning towards the cottage. He handed the doctor protective coverings for his shoes and hair along with a pair of gloves. "And please take care not to disturb anything. The State Police Major Crimes detectives are heading our way and I don't want to give them any cause to moan."

The doctor walked as far as the living room door, where he could see the victim was deceased. Her heart had literally pumped every fluid ounce of blood from her body. He could have gone and checked for a pulse, but he'd only have disturbed the scene and trampled through the slowly congealing blood.

"She's deceased," he declared, walking past the sheriff before he had even had a chance to see what was inside.

After a two-minute look at the scene the sheriff was back questioning Kay. "So, what has he said?" he asked, nodding towards Frank, who was bent over in some discomfort while the deputies took photos and samples from him and began to remove his clothing. It was a task Kay was very grateful she didn't have to assist with.

"Boss, we've only got a white jump suit, it's not going to work well with the, you know…"

The Sheriff Jackson shrugged, he didn't care. "Well?" he pressed Kay.

"All he has said is he didn't kill her and wanted out of the cuffs. Beyond that he's been groaning and defecating himself."

"Jesus. We're not playing Scrabble, shitting himself works just fine! No admission of guilt?"

"As I said, I'm not a—" Kay stopped herself. She'd fight that battle another time. "No, he's been claiming innocence."

"You sure he didn't slip up and say she deserved it, or even something like 'what have I done?'"

"No, only that he didn't kill her."

"Maybe you misheard him. Perhaps he said I didn't *mean* to kill her?"

"No, definitely not."

The Sheriff nodded, thinking. He'd obviously hoped to wrap it up before the state police detectives arrived. Without an admission of guilt that wasn't happening, and with the second painful sound of an over revving engine overhead, time was slipping away. The Maine State Cessna 182 bounced and buffeted its way towards the runway a mile away from the scene.

"You go get 'em," ordered Sheriff Jackson, "I'll keep the crime scene secure."

Kay headed to her truck, the sheriff shouting after her, "Do you know how to get there? I forgot you're new to the island."

"I'll find it."

The island was only six miles long, less than that wide, with only a few roads and plenty of signs. Kay could almost see the plane landing.

As Kay pulled away the Chief Selectman sidled over to Sheriff Jackson. "Interesting," he said, drawing the word out as he watched Kay drive across the bridge.

"Not my call, she was already hired." Jackson shrugged, his mind focused on the crime scene. He had been Chief Deputy Sheriff before he stabbed his boss in the back and ran against her. Throughout the history of the department the chief deputy had never run against the sitting sheriff.

Jackson had done the unthinkable. He had not only run, he had beaten the incumbent. It had required two recounts to confirm he had the winning margin, and it had come down to five votes. A legal wrangle had ensued over twenty spoiled papers that clearly favored the incumbent, but the decision stood. Knox County had a new sheriff. An overspill from the presidential election, it was clear that national politics had influenced the local vote, much to the huge disappointment of many. Sheriff Chris Jackson had few friends, but thanks to his political persuasion and protest votes he had won a surprise victory.

"Sheriff?" a panicked sounding deputy called from the selectman's car. His trunk had become their evidence gathering store.

"Don't move from here," Jackson instructed the selectman and he walked over to his deputy. The sight of the suspect in obvious distress, leaning against the wheel of the selectman's car with the doctor showing some signs of concern, was evidently the reason for the panic.

"We need to get him to a hospital and quick!" the doctor advised, making no attempt to hide his concern in front of the suspect.

To emphasize the point, Frank buckled over and emptied his stomach, followed by a painful retching sound as he continued to try and empty what wasn't there.

"Mr. Gilder, I said wait there!" Sheriff Jackson shouted angrily when he caught movement behind him. The Chief Selectman was at the doorway of the cottage and not the ten yards back where Jackson had left him.

"Yes, take him and quick, we need his statement," Jackson said absently to the doctor, tracking back to the selectman. "Did you go in there?" he demanded.

Having just turned 62, John Gilder couldn't have looked any more like a naughty child having just defied their mother than he did at that moment. "No, no, not at all!"

Jackson eyed him suspiciously. He didn't believe him, but if he had gone inside the crime scene would have been contaminated, perhaps beyond redemption.

"So, if there's any evidence found that you were in that cottage it would have to be from before today?" Jackson barked.

Gilder didn't answer immediately, considering carefully how to respond. "I've been in the cottage before. Not recently, but I *have* been in there. There's not many homes on the island I've not been in."

"But you weren't in there today?"

"As I said, no!" Gilder's anger was beginning to rise.

"Last night?" Jackson pressed.

"That's just insulting." Gilder stormed back to his car.

"Is that a no?" Jackson shouted after him, a smile growing on his face. The selectman was an important man on Vinalhaven but in Knox County, containing 40,000 residents, Vinalhaven was a small town with just over 1,000 inhabitants. He could take crap from people with influence but that wasn't the likes of John Gilder. The Mayor of Rockland, perhaps, but not the chief selectmen of a barely inhabited outlying island.

"What did he say?" Gilder called as he neared the car, looking at the suspect Frank.

"He said it wasn't him," replied the deputy, taken aback by the force of the selectman's questioning.

"Not that, the name. What did he say?"

"He said it was Gerald, I think."

Jackson could see the name had rattled John Gilder.

"Who's Gerald?" he asked.

"I don't know, I thought he said something else," John Gilder replied, only his words didn't match his conviction nor the lack of color that had instantly registered on hearing the name. "I need to get back, I have an appointment," he added, clearly flustered.

"We need your car until the deputy gets back."

"I'll walk!" he huffed, stepping aside as the Vinalhaven EMS truck rushed towards them, its siren and lights causing far more attention to the situation than the sheriff would have preferred.

"Sheriff!" the doctor called urgently.

"Yeah?" Jackson looked over, preoccupied with what had just transpired with Gilder.

The doctor glanced down at a catatonic looking Frank. "I don't think he's going to make it."

Chapter 7

Kay arrived at the airfield as the Maine State Police plane was taxiing to the drop off area at the end of the 1,100 foot gravel runway which had been carved out of the landscape, nothing more than a strip amongst the trees with a notice board and a phone. It pulled to a stop, and two men exited and began to unload equipment. Kay parked as near as she could and while one gave instructions to the pilot the other walked towards her.

"Kay Miller." She offered her hand to the man.

"Mark Winters," he said, accepting her hand. "And that's Fitch." He gestured to the back of his partner.

Fitch stepped back from the aircraft and waved to the pilot before turning around to face Kay, walking towards her with a smile rivaling her own. She couldn't help but notice he was very pleasant on the eye.

"Ross Abercrombie, Lieutenant, Major Crimes Unit, Maine State Police," he held out his hand.

Kay glanced at Mark Winters' wicked smile. He sniggered, obviously enjoying the play on his partner's name.

"Yeah, they call me Fitch." He cast a side glance to his partner, the embarrassment at being referred to by the clothing store evident.

"Well it does fit." Kay smiled, flushing at the obvious compliment she had inadvertently given. The brand was famous for their very attractive models, both male and female.

"Anyway, we've got work to do," he barked, the embarrassment still evident and turned to the cases.

Mark shrugged an apology and turned to help his boss.

Kay pushed her two boxes of manuals to the back of the trunk to make space for the detectives' equipment.

"Fitch, which do you want in first?" asked Mark.

Kay spun to him. "I thought you meant they called you Fitch behind your back!"

Abercrombie shook his head. "It's been my nickname since I was fourteen."

"Yeah, when he started looking like that!" Mark added with a hint of jealousy.

He was a good bit taller than her, she guessed 6'2", had dark hair with wisps of gray at his temples, and the weathered skin of a man who liked the outdoors, tanned and rugged. Just her type, although catching a glimpse of the wedding ring on his finger killed any thoughts of anything other than a professional relationship. His colleague, a similar height and build, was also married. They married young in Maine, both looked early thirties and looks wise, although Fitch had the edge, Mark was not hard on the eye either. She suddenly wondered if they were partners in more than one way. After all, you could never assume. By the time they had loaded the truck all such nonsense thoughts were dispelled; she had spotted Fitch checking her out at least four times. He might be married but he certainly wasn't dead down below. She still had it, even in her sexless uniform.

"So, what do we know?" asked Fitch, climbing into the front seat, while Winters climbed into the rear for the short ride to the scene.

"One female victim approximately in her forties, first indications are one stab wound to the chest. Her husband is the only witness and currently the main suspect. We've secured the scene and detained the husband, who unfortunately appears to be having a problem controlling his bowels."

"That's not good," said Fitch, distracted by a helicopter flying overhead. "That's a life flight chopper. They only call them when it's life threatening."

"It's going where we're going," said Kay.

"The wife was definitely dead?"

"Without a doubt. The suspect looked pretty ill though."

"That ill?" he asked, pointing to the chopper.

Before she could answer they cleared the headland and watched the chopper set down on the bridge as close to the cottage as possible, avoiding the trees and the people that surrounded the small cottage. Kay sped up, wanting to get there before whoever was being airlifted was taken away. It was her island and her crime scene.

Stopping halfway across the bridge they all jumped out and rushed towards the unfolding drama. The suspect, Kay informed Fitch and Winters when she recognized him, was on a stretcher being rushed to the chopper.

Sheriff Jackson came to greet the detectives.

"What happened?" Kay asked him.

"He deteriorated quickly once you left. The doctor called the chopper in but it's touch and go." He turned to her companions. "Detectives," he said with an edge.

"Sheriff Jackson," they replied in unison with little feeling.

Kay ignored what was obviously some history between the males, some alpha crap no doubt, who had the biggest whatever. There were more pressing issues. "Did he say anything else?"

"Just that he didn't do it and that it was Gerald, whoever Gerald is."

"Do we know if Gerald owned the cottage?"

"No but John Gilder looked like he'd seen a ghost when he heard the name and then swore he didn't know a Gerald and had misheard what was said."

"Where is he?" Kay asked, noting he wasn't in sight, but his car was.

"Hightailed it out of here shortly after the Gerald nonsense."

"We're ready to go," interrupted the air medic.

"Cool, I'm with you," announced Fitch, stealing Sheriff Jackson's thunder. "Deputy Miller, was it?"

Kay nodded.

"You come with me; you were first on scene."

Sheriff Jackson held up a hand. "Deputy Miller's place is here on the island."

"She'll be back soon enough, don't worry, *Chris*," Fitch smirked. Kay could tell it was deliberate. Jackson bristled at being called his first name, he expected Boss or at the very least Sheriff Jackson.

Kay looked to her boss for guidance. He nodded reluctantly. The state police detectives were lead on the case, he had no say in the matter. Kay sat back into the seat on the chopper and sighed. Her first full day and she was already in the middle of a battle between two egos.

"Was that really necessary?"

"What? That guy is a grade A asshole. Has he told you to call him Boss yet?"

Kay laughed.

"Jeez, that quick? He's even more of an asshole than I thought, and that's saying something!" Fitch turned to the suspect. "Can he talk?" he asked the medics.

"Yeah, we've given him some morphine, he's a bit more settled now."

Fitch nodded to Kay to try and talk to him, given her earlier interaction.

"Frank?"

"It was Gerald." Frank said immediately, keen to talk. "Gerald set it all up. It looked just like it did years ago, it was dark when we got there. It didn't look like it does in the daylight…"

"Who's Gerald?"

"You know, Gerald, it was his cottage. He lived there when we were on the Island fifteen years ago, something like that. Nice guy, the girls loved him."

"Did you see him last night?"

"I don't know, there was someone there, but I drank the wine and then…" he hitched a breath. "Is…is Valerie really gone?"

Kay nodded slowly.

A tear ran from Frank's eye. "So much blood. I woke up lying next to her, blood everywhere. All over me, I called you and then…"

"He called you covered in her blood?"

Kay nodded; it did sound like a crazy thing to do if you were then going to proclaim your innocence.

"Are we sure there wasn't a third party involved?" Fitch whispered.

"Lieutenant Abercrombie, we have a Detective Winters on the radio for you." The co-pilot handed Fitch a headset.

"Fitch, we've got the knife. It was lying next to the wife's body," Fitch's partner Detective Winters reported. *"Twelve inches, very nice indeed, I'd guess a penny shy of three hundred bucks if I was a betting man."*

"Which you're not, Mark."

"Yeah, you're right. The house always wins! We popped his trunk. Box, bag and receipt in his name, purchased a few days ago."

"Okay, so he bought a knife. Doesn't mean he was the one who stabbed her."

"There's more on the receipt and all in the trunk. A shovel, plastic sheeting, a bag of lime, and enough bleach to clean the cottage three times over."

"Yeah, that's sounding a little more definitive."

"It gets better. We recovered her smartphone. It had two webpages open that were of particular interest, one was for Rohypnol, the other arsenic!"

"Arsenic?" Fitch glanced at Frank. The medic looked up on hearing the name of the poison.

"Did you say arsenic?" he asked, moving nearer to Fitch.

Fitch nodded.

The medic's face fell. "Do we know how much?"

"Any idea how much arsenic?" Fitch asked his partner.

"Not sure, hold on, there's a bag of white powder in her handbag."

Fitch covered the mic while his colleague retrieved the handbag. "He seems a lot better," he said to the medic, looking back towards the suspect.

"That's just the morphine. He's basically oblivious to the pain, at least for the moment. Not sure how long it will last. There's only so much we can give him until his body conditions itself."

"Yeah, I know what you mean. The more pain and longer you use it, you can take massive lethal doses of morphine and survive."

The medic nodded. "But arsenic is a whole different ball game." He tapped the pilot's shoulder. "We need to go to Portland!"

The chopper swung left to a southern heading.

"Hold on, he's found it," Fitch listened and ended the call. "He reckons the bag's half emptied and there's about an ounce left, so maybe one ounce?"

The medic's grave look worsened. "You'd better get as much information out of him while he can still talk."

"How long have we got?"

"Let's just say you don't need the hour hands on your watch."

Fitch pushed past the medic and headed to Kay. Even though he had been away for only a few minutes while talking to the medic and his colleague, he could see deterioration in the suspect. His face had tightened. The pain was breaking through the morphine induced barrier.

Kay caught Fitch's eye, and her look suggested she was concerned. Fitch's shake of the head confirmed she was right to be. Fitch leaned over, his lips brushing her ear as he tried to whisper. She had a deep urge to pull away but fought it. His warm breath tickled her neck as he spoke so softly she could hardly hear him. She had to fight every instinct to push him away. She barely knew him, what he was doing was inappropriate, wrong, intimate, but she was relieved she hadn't made it a thing, created a scene as, despite how wrong it felt, for the message he delivered it was completely right.

"Are you sure?" she mouthed to the medic.

He nodded. "The symptoms are consistent."

"Consistent with what?" Frank asked.

"Rohypnol," Fitch replied. "You were given a roofie, that's why you can't remember anything."

"I was drugged?"

Fitch nodded. "It's why you can't remember stabbing your wife. We believe your wife drugged you, so it could be you have justification for self-defense at your trial."

"But I didn't kill her! I would never—"

"We found evidence to suggest otherwise in your trunk," Fitch cut in. He needed to get him to talk and quickly. "We found the shovel, plastic sheeting, and lime. The Rohypnol has screwed with your mind, so maybe you forgot what you were doing and called the deputy by mistake?"

Frank tried to sit up, indignant. "I called the deputy because someone murdered my wife!"

"Frank, everything indicates you killed your wife and given it looks like she was trying to kill you, perhaps—"

"Perhaps what? I stabbed her with a 12-inch knife?"

Fitch raised an eyebrow. "I never mentioned a 12-inch knife."

"It was lying next to her when I woke up!" A grimace of pain shot across Frank's face. "The date rape drug makes you feel this bad?" he asked the medic, ignoring both police officers.

The medic looked to Fitch for guidance, he wasn't going to lie to the man.

Frank caught the look. "What? What aren't you telling me?"

His face was graying by the second. The morphine was masking his symptoms outwardly but inwardly they were continuing unabated. Frank's head shot forward as his whole body convulsed in pain.

A cold skin of sweat broke out as his body tried desperately to expel the poison but it was too late, the dose was too high and the result inevitable.

"Frank, we don't think you're going to make it." Fitch looked into Frank's eyes. "We believe you've been poisoned with a massive dose of arsenic. There's nothing—"

Frank's eyes closed. A tear escaped from beneath the lids as he accepted the words being spoken. Intuitively he had known something was very, very wrong.

Fitch and Kay backed away to allow Frank time to digest the news, at least as far as the confines of the chopper would allow. Kay once again felt the closeness of Fitch disconcerting. She had been nakedly intimate with people with less contact than she was having with the married detective. Every part of his body was pressed against her, their faces pressed cheek to cheek as they talked in a low whisper. Kay felt his warm breath bristle at her hair, sending shivers through her. She wanted to scratch but once again felt such a maneuver would be misconstrued, particularly given the topic.

As uncomfortable as she felt, she felt no discomfort from Fitch. If anything it was the opposite, she could sense his ease at being so close to her, only adding to her discomfort.

"Guys, I hate to break up your…"

Kay pushed Fitch away. She wasn't imagining it, even the medic had sensed something.

"Yeah?" Fitch held Kay's questioning gaze as he responded.

"He's gone."

Fitch moved towards the suspect. The deathly gray and peaceful, relaxed look of the recently deceased was not something you ever mistook, particularly of a man who had so recently been consumed by pain. The skin was continuing to loosen and flatten over his features, his muscles failing for the final time. Whether he had killed his wife or not, Frank's final few hours were not any Fitch would have wished on any but the very worst criminals he had ever met. And even then, only when it involved children. For those guys he was open to any punishment.

"So, what do you think?" asked Kay, staring at their witness, suspect, and only clue to what had happened.

"I think we've got two murders to add to the statistics and fortunately for us, two murderers who will not cost us a penny to convict. More importantly, it's going to do wonders for my resolution rates."

Kay braced herself as the pilot announced their imminent and now unnecessary landing at the hospital. "What's your theory?"

"A roofie in his wine, he relaxed, and she fed him the arsenic in some way. Despite the rohypnol, he realized what she was doing and knifed her. He then passed out, waking up covered in blood with his wife next to him. Still under the influence of the rohypnol, had no memory of what happened, forgotten his plans, the contents of his trunk, and called you, the police, assuming there must have been a third party since having no recollection he did it himself.

"Neat," said Kay suspiciously.

"Everything fits. If the prints match up," he shrugged, "it all makes perfect sense."

The chopper landed and they deplaned to the helipad. Frank's body was loaded into an ambulance and, per Fitch's instructions, headed to the chief medical examiner's office in Augusta, where he would once again be reunited with his wife.

"What do we do now?" asked Kay.

"Get back to the island, check there's no evidence to suggest otherwise." Fitch checked his watch. "We'll close two murder cases before lunch."

Kay watched the ambulance drive away, its lights dark. There would be no need to run any red lights, break any speed limits. Frank was gone. Another life extinguished. Two solved murders on her first full day of work. It certainly would make for interesting dinner conversation.

Fitch radioed for a car and asked for the state police Cessna to meet them at Portland Airport. He wanted to get everything wrapped up as soon as possible. It was the holiday weekend and he had plans that night.

"In a rush?" asked Kay, watching Fitch check his watch every few minutes while they waited.

"Got a date tonight."

"That's sweet, you and your wife have date nights."

Fitch looked at her with some confusion, and Kay stared pointedly at his wedding ring. Fitch's face fell. "Oh, that's a long story," he said without elaborating. His face, however, said more than he ever could. A deep sadness fell over him, the elation of solving two murders and the excitement over his impending date obliterated in an instant. His right hand rose to his left and he began to twist the ring anxiously, pacing. Silence and a deep awkwardness fell between them.

Lieutenant Ross Abercrombie, the confident, witty, and handsome policeman looked like a broken man.

Chapter 8

Kay watched on as Lieutenant Abercrombie worked through the evidence on their return. Professional to a tee, he was even courteous to Sheriff Jackson, which disconcerted everyone involved, none more so than the sheriff. On more than one occasion his colleague Detective Winters had asked if he was okay.

The response was simple. "Yes, fine. We've just got a lot of work to get through."

Fitch was anything but fine but was carrying out his work diligently and effectively.

"What happened while you were away?" Detective Winters asked Kay out of Fitch's earshot.

She considered telling the truth, that she had made reference to his wedding ring, but was embarrassed that she had noticed and quite frankly it was none of her business.

"It was a horrible death," was the best answer she could come up with that may have explained his mood.

Winters studied his colleague and friend, shaking his head. "Nah, its more than that. I've not seen him like this since…"

"Since what?"

He shook his head. "Not my place. But anyway that was years ago, nothing to do with now or this case."

As the sun began to dip, Lieutenant Ross Abercrombie called it a day. "I think we've got all we need. Everything here points to a double homicide with the two victims having killed each other. Anyone disagree?"

Whether they did or not, the tone of the finality of his conclusion had pretty much closed the case. Other than nods of agreement there were no dissenters. It was cut and dried. The crime scene was sealed, the evidence packed and logged, and with the help of Marine patrol, shipped across to the mainland along with the remains of the victim and murderer Valerie. A few congratulatory pats on the back ended the investigation, at least as far as the island of Vinalhaven was concerned. The state police had jurisdiction, and with the collection and removal of all evidence the case was closed.

The sheriff and his deputies hitched a lift with the Marine Patrol. Kay had driven the detectives to the airfield where the Maine State Cessna awaited their arrival. After an awkward goodbye, the departing plane cleared the trees and disappeared into the gradually darkening sky. When the engine noise dissipated, Kay was left alone with her thoughts, silence and darkness enveloping her. She shivered and glanced around. Alone with her thoughts was a place Kay neither enjoyed nor looked forward to. She jumped in her truck and selected the only station she could get a reception, WMCM. She hated country music but nowhere near as much as her own thoughts.

Kay made a short detour to the liquor store to replenish her recently depleted wine stocks on her way home. *I'll have to go to the mainland,* she thought as she exited the store. Buying two bottles had raised eyebrows of concern. She needed that per day. She would be the talk of the island if her drinking habits were ever made public knowledge. Once home she collapsed onto the chair on her deck as the darkness of the night finally fell.

She awoke eight hours later on the same chair in the same clothes. She couldn't remember a thing after sitting down. She thought she must have passed out from exhaustion. The two empty bottles by her side dispelled that myth, along with the headache that soon made itself eminently present. Kay stumbled into the kitchen, rummaged through a couple of boxes, and found some Tylenol. The dosage advised two for adults, she took three.

She checked her watch. Just before 5a.m. and the sun was just breaking over the horizon behind her house. She stretched, appreciating the extra hours of sleep she had managed. Her internal alarm clock was more cockerel than human; if the sun was up, she was awake. She slept very well in the winter months, not so much in the summer.

Kay slipped out of her uniform, something she wished she had done when she got home last night. It was going to need to be dry cleaned, there was no way she could wear it again. Her sleep, however sound, had obviously been fitful, with large sweat stains highlighting the fact. She kicked it into the laundry basket and with a freshly brewed coffee grabbed a quick and welcome shower. Clad in a brand-new terry-towel bathrobe over her soaked and naked body, she stepped out onto the deck into the early morning coolness. She sent a silent prayer that she had donned the robe as at least five lobstermen waved to her from their little boats making their way out of the harbor below and towards the ocean beyond. She sat, tucking her legs beneath her in an attempt to completely cover herself from the cool wind biting against her exposed wet skin. She held the coffee mug in both hands near her chin, hoping the steam emanating from its mouth would warm her face.

She could see the lobstermen mouthing "Morning," their voices failing to carry over the sounds of their engines. Despite the tranquility of the scene, the mirrored water rippling against the small boats' bows, the cool morning air was too biting without the warmth of the sun that would take hours before it arched up and over her house to offer her the perfect swan song to the sun's daily efforts. Kay escaped back into the house. The few boxes she had brought with her remained filled around her.

I can unpack, she thought to herself, although the thought was effort enough since the Tylenol had not fully completed its magic. She lay on the little white sofa contemplating turning on the small TV that harked back to an era where it wasn't the most important viewing portal in the room. The view out her window dominated the room. Somebody understood the priorities in life. The scene caught her breath, memories of her childhood flooding back. She blinked her eyes wildly and rushed to the boxes, anything to avoid the memories.

"No, no, no," she reprimanded herself. "Focus on the present."

Kay broke open the first box and pulled out its contents. Everything was new, labels had to be removed. Nothing from the past, all from the present. She calmed, the memories she fought to forget receded back to where she kept them at bay. She looked at the remnants of the two wine bottles out on the deck. She could have done with a glass or two, but she'd have to wait.

The telephone rang and she checked the clock before even thinking about answering it. 5:40 a.m.

From her limited experience in law enforcement, she had to assume any call at that time on a holiday Monday morning was not going to be a good call.

"Deputy Miller," she answered brightly, surprising the caller.

"Eh, hmm, yes. We've got a problem down at the harbor."

Kay's eyes flashed to the serene vision she had had the good fortune to wake up to. "What problem?"

"Eh, maybe it's best you just come see," said the caller.

"Okay. Where am I coming to and where are you calling from?"

"Oh yes, sorry. It's John Gilder, and I'm calling from the motel."

"Good morning, John," Kay said. "I missed you when I got back to the scene yesterday," she added without subtlety.

"You'd best come quick." He ended the call abruptly.

Kay replaced the receiver and dressed in a fresh uniform. She only had one more. After that she would need to find a dry cleaner and quick, but more importantly she'd need to not drink herself into oblivion in this one.

Kay drove the short distance to the Tidewater Motel, the only motel she knew of on the island. The small crowd that awaited her in the parking lot implied her powers of investigative reasoning and deduction were firing on all cylinders. John Gilder stood at the head of the crowd which, at ten minutes before six, was impressive given the entire island had only one thousand inhabitants. Kay guessed fifty people were there, five percent of the resident population. She guessed that would be the equivalent of a half million people in New York City. She shook her head at the random thought and bounced cheerfully from her truck, heading for Gilder.

"What's up?" she asked.

Fifty hands pointed to the water below the hotel. The hotel sat atop a bridge where the water flowed beneath and to a large pond behind. Kay walked across to the edge of the parking lot, which was a harbor wall. She looked down and glanced back at the crowd—she couldn't see anything. Hands gesticulated for her to look under the hotel. She leaned out as far as she dared and looked where directed. A flash of white hair could be seen in the breakwater. A yellow oilskin broke the surface as she watched the spot. It was a body hooked up to one of the supporting struts.

"It's Walter Spencer. Walt to everyone here. He's—sorry, he *was* the harbormaster," John Gilder explained. "Has been for the last thirty-seven years."

Kay leaned to see more, her body wavering on the edge. She had gone too far, her center of gravity shifted, and she felt herself falling forward to the cold water below. She braced herself for the shock but a firm grip stopped her. John Gilder smiled and pulled her back upright. Kay yanked her arm away, rubbing furiously where he had gripped her. The crowd looked on with some amusement at her reaction, their chatter rising as they discussed her behavior.

"My pleasure, don't mention it," John said to the thanks she had failed to deliver. John looked around to the crowd behind, hushing their discontent with a wave of his arms.

Focus, Kay told herself.

She turned to face John with a smile. "Sorry, gave myself a fright there! And thank you."

John dipped his head in acceptance at the overdue thanks.

"I'd better call it in," said Kay taking another look at the body thrashing around the wooden support as the high tide was abating and the pond's water rushed back towards the ocean.

She jumped into her truck and picked up the radio. It was 6:00 a.m. The Sheriff was going to love her. "This is Deputy Miller, I need to speak with Sheriff Jackson urgently."

"Deputy Miller, it's 6:01 a.m. I am not waking him up unless this is a life and death scenario."

"Death"

"Another one?" came the astonished reply.

"Yeah," Kay replied.

Two minutes later a groggy and obviously recently awakened Sheriff Jackson was on the radio.

"The dispatcher just said you had another body?" he asked obviously not believing what he had been told.

"Yes, we have. A Walter, known as Walt Spencer, we believe."

"I'll be there as soon as I can, get someone to pick me up at the airfield."

"Will do, what about the body?"

"What about it?"

"Should we fish it out of the water, or do you want to see it where it is?"

"Wait a minute, old Walt is in the water? We're not talking a heart attack in his sleep?"

"No, he's hooked up under the Tidewater. The tide's going out so it's going to get messy from what I'm told."

"Hold on, I'll call the detectives and come back to you."

Drumming her fingers on the railing, Kay waited while the Sheriff made the call, watching the crowd watching her.

"I've been stood down," the sheriff came back. *"They're taking jurisdiction given yesterday's deaths."*

"Okay, who's coming?"

"Same asshole as yesterday."

Kay was surprised at the genuine wave of excitement at seeing Fitch again passing over her.

"Oh, okay," she said, maintaining her coolness with the sheriff. She didn't want him to know she—surprisingly to herself—actually enjoyed Ross Abercrombie's company.

"Unless you want some support there for you?" offered the sheriff, realizing he was leaving her high and dry with the 'a' hole from state police.

"No, I'll be fine. Don't worry about me."

"I know there's no need to do that, I've read your file. Big city cop, FBI training academy, you're better qualified than pretty much every cop within a hundred miles of here, if not more."

"It's not all that." Kay blushed at the praise she knew she didn't deserve.

"You're sure you're okay with just you and the detectives?"

"Yes, of course, no problem." She ended the call and rejoined John Gilder. "They're sending the detectives from state police again."

"But there's no reason to think it's anything other than a tragic accident. He stumbled out of the bar at midnight, already drunk before spending the next few hours drinking at a friend's house. He stumbled out of there between three and four, barely able to walk."

"You could have told me that before I called it in."

"You should have asked."

"Which house did he stumble out of?"

John pointed back towards her house, but his finger stopped before and lowered to a cottage that sat on top of a dock, part of the harbor wall only yards from its front door. "The tide was coming in then; it would have washed him towards here and now that it's heading back out, we see can him."

Kay looked at him with some interest. It was very neat and convenient from the same man who had been at the scene yesterday.

"Give me a minute." She walked away from Gilder over to her truck and popped the trunk, pulled the box with procedural manuals towards herself and flicked through them, keeping an eye on what was happening with the body. The water was picking up pace and from her experience was only going to become more violent. She scanned a few of the pages, made a decision, and walked back over to Gilder.

"Okay, we need to get him out of there. That tide is going to rip him to pieces if we leave him much longer."

"You sure?"

Kay looked again, the water was receding and gaining speed, more of the victim was exposed after each wave passed, his body swinging increasingly violently with each one. "Absolutely."

"You heard the deputy!" John shouted down to a large inflatable dinghy with four lobstermen who had been awaiting just such an instruction. They revved up the powerful propeller and made to leave.

"Wait up, I'm coming with you!" Kay ran back to grab a camera from her trunk. She hadn't noticed the rescue party waiting at the base of the harbor wall.

She stepped down gingerly towards the boat, refusing any assistance from the many hands being offered to her. Fifteen minutes later and with more photos than could possibly be needed from every conceivable angle she could get, they unhooked the body and pulled him aboard the dinghy, the lobsterman controlling the vessel with a lifetime of expertise to hold the dinghy steady against the tide while his colleagues unhooked the lifeless and limp body, depositing it in on the wooden floor of the dinghy. The victim's face had borne the brunt of the crustaceans that had attached themselves to each of the wooden pillars supporting the motel above. Scratched and torn, his face was barely recognizable to the men who knew him well, only his distinctive white hair and yellow oilskins a clear indication it was Walt Spencer.

The sound of the light aircraft overhead caught everyone's attention. The Maine State Police had arrived.

"Can you send someone to pick them up?" she called to John Gilder.

He turned to the crowd behind him, sending one of them to the airfield as requested.

"We also need the doctor."

"That's fine, he's here." Gilder looking sullenly at the remains of Walt. "Doc?"

The doctor came forward and climbed down the steps to the dinghy where, once again, his skills were barely required. There was no doubt whatsoever Walt Spencer was dead. It was a very sad but easy call to make.

"Can we clear the parking lot please?" Kay ascended the steps to join John. The crowd had moved towards the wall waiting expectantly to see Walt's being hoisted from below. No one moved.

John turned to the people behind him. "The deputy's right, please everyone, let's show Walt the respect he deserves."

The crowd immediately dispersed. Kay took photos of the crowd as they moved away, not just because they had ignored her request, but because she had read in the manuals that the perpetrator of the crime very often was amongst the crowd of onlookers to see the outcome of their crime. Not that there was any evidence of wrongdoing, she just wanted to have everything the detective may expect of her.

"Deputy Miller?" Fitch stepped from an SUV that had collected him form the airfield.

Kay looked around the vehicle waiting for Detective Winters to emerge, but the door remained closed.

"Just me this time," said Fitch. "Detective Winters had a day off scheduled for the holiday."

"Okay, well good morning, Lieutenant Abercrombie."

"Another morning, another body. Only the one today?"

"So far."

"That's a good friend of ours lying there!" John interrupted indignantly.

"Yes of course. Sorry. Lieutenant Abercrombie, Maine State Police." Fitch held out his hand, waiting for John to introduce himself.

"John Gilder, Chief of the Selectmen."

"Ah, Mr Gilder, I have heard your name mentioned. All good of course," Fitch smiled, charming John instantly. "Now if you don't mind, I'd like to examine the body."

"Of course." John moved away from the area. "I'll be over by my motel."

"The smaller the elected position the more susceptible they are to flattery," Fitch whispered to Kay as John Gilder, a man the state police talked highly of, walked a foot taller back to the motel.

"Did he say my motel?" Kay asked.

Fitch nodded. "That okay?"

"Yeah, fine. Why wouldn't it be?" she snapped.

He raised his hands in defense.

"Sorry, I'm just not used to bodies yet I suppose."

"So what happened last night?"

"Nothing. I went home shattered. Why, what happened with your date?"

Fitch pointed to the body. "I was talking about with him." He grinned.

"Oh, sorry, hmm yeah," she sputtered in embarrassment. "It seems—"

"I canceled the date by the way," Fitch cut in with a laugh, "but carry on."

Kay shrugged nonchalantly and explained the story of Walt Spencer's last known movements.

The smile that had been affixed to Fitch's face dropped. He checked his watch. "Six a.m. I got a call at six a.m. because some blind drunk fell into the sea and drowned in the middle of the night?"

"Well, I only discovered this after I'd called it in. To be fair it was the sheriff who called you, not me. You could have called before making the trip." She smiled innocently.

"I'd have had to come anyway but not at this time in the morning." Fitch looked around to the house she pointed to. "Do we know whose cottage it is and who was there?"

She shook her head.

"Okay, I'll have a look at him first and then we'll take some statements and hopefully wrap this one up before lunch. At least there's a good restaurant on the island, have you been to it? Pepper. It's not normally open Mondays but it will be because of the holidays."

"No, I've not been anywhere yet but I've a feeling if it's good it'll be fully booked."

"I'm sure they are but trust me, they'll find room for us. If there's a chance they'll catch wind of any details of the investigation, we'll be fine. Information on a small island community is worth its weight in gold, and today we're going to have the information every person will be clamoring for."

He knelt down and had a superficial look at the deceased. "Jesus, his face is such a mess, how can they be sure it's him?"

"The long white hair and the oilskins. Supposedly there's no doubt whatsoever."

"Do we know if this is all postmortem?"

Kay pointed to the supporting poles and their visibly crusted coating. "He was being slammed against that for quite some time."

"Certainly consistent with the damage. Those shells and clams are like razors, they'd easily do that."

Fitch began to stand, stopping halfway, and felt around the side of the head under the hair.

"We've got a lump there, pre-death. Something whacked him on the side of the head, probably knocked him unconscious but must have been before he died."

"Good catch!" she said, impressed. "Do you think it means he was—"

"Nah, probably means he fell and hit his head before hitting the water or he whacked it in the water. Doesn't mean anything yet. Let's see if we can get the names of any witnesses." Standing over her, Fitch was easily six inches taller than her in her boots, less so if she wore heels but that would have to be a very special event. Kay didn't do girlie.

Fitch led the way to the motel, while gesturing for the EMS team to collect the body. "Get him on the next ferry, okay?" he instructed.

Some weekend visitors were about to lose their spot on what would be one of the busiest days on the ferry.

"Mr. Gilder," Fitch began, winking at Kay.

"Please, Lieutenant, please call me John."

"Thanks, John." He didn't offer reciprocation but the "Mr. Gilder" had already buttered him up.

"Now if you don't mind, we need everything you know about the deceased's whereabouts last night."

John repeated the story he had told Kay earlier, embellishing the details. The islanders had gathered at the motel to discuss the murders, initially worried that they had a murderer loose, the news that the case was closed and resolved led to a few drinks. Thereafter, John was aware Walt had gone with a few other lobstermen to a cottage that a number of them shared for a few more drinks and a game of poker. Walt enjoyed his drink and was already showing signs he'd had enough when he left the motel. John remembered telling him to "forget the cards and head home."

Kay couldn't help but think that nugget had been added to paint him in a good light. She thought she'd throw him a side swipe to see how he'd react. "Was Gerald there?"

"Who's Gerald?" Fitch asked with mock innocence. He had caught on instantly.

"I don't know a Gerald," said John. The words were issued with defiance, his expression and his actions failing to match. "There was no Gerald I know of there. Sorry, where was I?" said John, flustered and having totally lost his train of thought.

"You had suggested what we now know to have been the right thing that Walt should have done," Kay reminded with an edge, demonstrating she didn't believe that part had happened.

"Yes, well unfortunately he didn't heed my warning and went with the guys to play cards as I said."

Kay wrote down each word he said verbatim, noting the names of each of the men Walt had left with and the cottages address, despite knowing exactly which cottage it was.

"Well thanks, John. If there's anything else you remember, please let myself or Deputy Miller know." Fitch led Kay away. "Let's visit that cottage."

Kay drove the short distance and parked the truck on the dock, having driven down the side of the cottage from the road. Three men awaited them in the doorway of the cottage but Fitch ignored them and walked to the dock's edge. There was a five foot drop to the water below, and stone steps led down from his right to a lower docking level that from the angle of the steps he guessed would be directly below him but was currently under the waterline. He looked to his right and followed the steps up to the corner of the dock. Tracking back to the cottage, which was built into the hillside, a path snaked down the side and up and onto the hillside, a well-trodden path leading off towards the town center just a short walk away. The path would have been far quicker than the road they had just driven and began where the man-made stone dock ended. On one side hillside and the other, the side of the dock, with just enough room to get a truck down the gap, the edge of the dock and the water below awaited any unsuspecting driver. The dock itself opened up in front of the house offering plenty of space for the men and previous residents to store and repair their nets and cages.

Fitch turned and faced the men behind, only ten yards from where he stood. He could feel the history. The dock would have housed men just like these, their boats tied to the docks, horses and carts would have come and gone collecting their daily catch. He'd have guessed the entire structure was at least a hundred and fifty years old. The dock was a masterpiece of stonemasonry, each stone carved and chopped to connect as closely as possible to the next. Each day the dock stood testament to their skills as the ocean tried unwittingly to reclaim whatever man took from it.

He brought himself back to the present. It had been a cloudy, moonless night, three a.m. With Vinalhaven's scant smattering of streetlights, it would have been exceptionally dark out.

"Can you put that light on?" Fitch pointed to the light above the doorway. It hung limply where it should have stood proud.

One of the men moved and flicked a switch to his right. "There!" he shouted.

The light remained dark.

"Were your curtains closed last night?"

"Yeah, think so."

"Can you shut your front door please?"

The man obliged, stepping out along with his two friends before closing the door behind them.

"Okay, and Walt left here when?"

"We're guessing about three, we're not really sure. It was a heavy night since we'd decided to take today off for the holiday, so…"

"Yep," said Fitch. He directed Kay towards her truck.

"Are we not going inside?"

"Not unless we absolutely have to. That place is going to reek of three sweaty, drunk fishermen. Can you imagine?" He waved a hand to the lobstermen. "Thanks guys."

"What was with the door?" Kay asked, carefully negotiating the side of the cottage and the dockside before reversing back onto the road.

"No glass, solid wood. When they shut that door last night, they killed any light Walt Spencer would have needed to make his way home. His only route would have been down the side of the house that you've just panicked your way down in the broad daylight. He was blind drunk by all accounts and quite probably, given the darkness, completely blind. Whether he fell off the dock into the water or made it onto the hillside path, one slip or trip and he'd be hitting something as he crashed into the water. Lump on head and reason for being in the water."

"Case closed?"

"Between you and me, yes, but we'd better keep up appearances and make it look a little more thorough."

"Should we not have talked to those guys then?"

"Oh yeah, we'll talk to them but not when they're expecting. We'll come back when they've not been warned we're coming."

"So where to then?"

"Walt's house."

Kay turned left when they hit the road.

Fitch stared at her until Kay felt his gaze. "What?" she asked, turning to him.

A smile broke across his face, a surprised glance that reminded her of the look men gave you when they had just realized how beautiful you were. "I was just wondering…"

God, thought Kay, *I hope he doesn't come out with a really corny line.*

"...how'd you know where Walt lived?"

"I don't," she replied, surprised how much she had wanted the corny line.

"But you just said okay and started driving, not asking where we're going."

"I'm driving to the Tidewater, where John Gilder will direct us, I hope."

"Oh okay."

A search of Walt's house revealed little other than that he'd been a loner hoarder with a cleanliness problem. The house was disgusting and full of rubbish. Only one room appeared to have been kept neat and tidy. Walt's office was pristine, the walls lined with oceanographic maps of the harbor and islands, while his large, powerful PC sat alone on a paper free desk. The screen offered an option to insert a password, and three failed attempts resulted in a timeout of sixty minutes before any further attempts could be made.

"Seems a bit over the top," Fitch remarked as the computer effectively closed down, a countdown clock the only hint he hadn't caused a more fatal shutdown. "I could understand if he lived with a family and had sensitive information but he was a harbormaster and lived here alone."

"Yeah," Kay replied absently, busy checking through the drawers of paperwork.

"You found something?" asked Fitch, noting her distraction.

"Not sure. Apparently he went on a lot of overseas trips. There are receipts here for at least two a year, always to Thailand."

"As in Bangkok, Thailand?"

"Is there another one?"

Fitch shook his head. "You know a lot of men like to visit Thailand for a specific reason, right?"

"Yeah and it's not the great beaches." Kay was aware of where Fitch's thoughts were going. "Might explain the extra security on the computer."

"Definitely. I'll get this sent to our IT team to see if we can find anything."

"I'm not sure that is related to his death."

"I agree, that seems to be straightforward. He fell while drunk and drowned in the ocean. The autopsy will confirm that."

"And if there is anything of an inappropriate sexual manner?"

"One less deviant for us to worry about, I suppose. Whatever the case, if he went to all this trouble securing his computer, I doubt we'll find anything else here."

An hour later they had confirmed the house was devoid of anything incriminating other than the computer and travel records, and even those were merely incriminating with no real evidence of any wrongdoing.

"Open and shut case, accidental death." Fitch closed the harbormaster's door behind them. He checked his watch and grinned. "And just in time for lunch!"

Kay didn't think being seen dining in the best restaurant was fitting given they were investigating the death of one of the more prominent members of the community. "Are you sure it's not a bit…"

"Insensitive? Nah, if nothing else it'll ease the concern of the locals. Three deaths in twenty-four hours? We want to put it to bed as an accident asap, trust me."

For a man she barely knew, surprisingly the words "trust me" didn't fill her with trepidation as they had every time a man had ever uttered those two words to her.

As predicted by Fitch, the fully booked restaurant magically found a table for them. Within five minutes of taking their seats John Gilder happened to be "just passing by."

"Any news?" he asked, grave concern etched on his face.

"Unless the autopsy finds anything we haven't spotted, accidental death," said Fitch.

Kay studied Gilder's face as Fitch spoke. He was good. His face barely moved but she could sense the relief the news had given Gilder.

Why hide the relief though? she thought.

John Gilder had been quick to arrive the previous day, he'd reacted to the name Gerald, and here he was hiding relief at the harbormaster's death being ruled an accident. Given the previous day's murders, surely that would have been something he could publicly show relief at. She was sure she had never met John Gilder before, but something about him was very familiar.

Kay received a kick under the table from Fitch. She looked up, startled by his action.

"John's saying thanks," he repeated on behalf of Gilder.

"Oh sorry, I was miles away."

"I can only begin to understand how crazy your first two days have been," he replied before walking away, ensuring he made contact with every other diner on his way out of the restaurant, making it known to everyone he was in close contact with the investigation.

"What's up?" asked Fitch, watching her watching Gilder.

"Nothing."

"Bullshit. You think there's something fishy about him?"

"Just…I don't know. We've solved all the deaths."

"But if we hadn't?"

"I'd be talking to him first I think."

Gilder waved back to them before exiting the restaurant. Kay smiled but only with her mouth, her eyes unbeknownst to Gilder continued to eye him warily.

Chapter 9

Ross Abercrombie, Fitch to everyone who knew him, was surprised at the effect the Vinalhaven cases had had on him. Even two weeks later he still thought about the three deaths daily and if he wasn't kidding himself, Deputy Kay Miller. Fitch was a name he never liked. It was the curse of embarrassment every time he met a new person, the look of bewilderment and then realization, the knowing smile as they checked him out. He could only imagine it was how women felt when men objectified them.

He opened his wardrobe and grinned at the life-size A&F poster inside the door. A young man toned to perfection wearing only a pair of jeans stared back at him and he smiled at his younger self. The modeling gig while at college was the only reason he tolerated the nickname and was a secret he held close to his heart. The day of his shoot was the day he met his wife, a day he would never forget. Nobody knew of the poster or of his work with A&F, at least nobody he knew in Maine. His resume only mentioned part-time modeling covering the years he was at college.

Thoughts of his wife filled his mind and he closed his eyes, remembering her infectious laugh, her loving embrace, the giggle of their daughter. A tear seeped from his eye and he let it roll and drop onto his chest. Its warmth evaporating, the coldness of its touch on his chest hitting him, jolted him back to reality. The emptiness of the house, a house that had been a home. The quiet was so deafening he left the TVs on 24/7 news channels to ensure there was always some noise around him. He regretted ever moaning about the constant noise they made. If only. He caught himself, living in the if's was what kept him stuck in the past. At least that was what the therapist said.

The doorbell chiming caught his attention. He wiped at his eye, closed the wardrobe door, and checked himself in the mirror. A slight redness in his eyes but nothing anyone would notice without looking for it.

He walked to the door and opened it. It was Mark, a good friend as well as his work colleague who had helped him through what had been the hardest few years of his life.

"You ready?"

"Ready for what?"

"The boys are playing in Little League tonight. You said you'd come."

Fitch looked beyond Mark to the car by the curb where two expectant faces looked back at him from the rear seat. Mark's twin boys were the same age as his daughter and he couldn't help seeing her face when he saw them. She had always loved Mark's boys and her face lit up when they came over to play.

"Come on, it's their last game and you promised you'd come to one," Mark pressed, noting Fitch's hesitation.

Fitch could see the expectation in the boys' eyes. For whatever reason they got very excited when Uncle Fitch was involved. Yet Fitch shook his head. "I'm sorry, I can't."

"We'll be there for a couple of hours, you know where we are. It'd mean a lot to the boys if you showed up."

"Maybe." Fitch did want to go, he just wasn't sure he was ready.

"I'll take that." Mark beamed. It was more than he normally got; Fitch had no qualms about issuing a flat and blunt "no."

Fitch's landline began to trill in the back of the house.

"Still that old phone?" Mark cracked.

"I never fail to wake up when it rings."

"It's going to be work," said Mark, checking his watch.

"Don't worry about it, whatever it is I'll handle it."

Fitch waved his friend off and rushed to answer the phone. It had been perfect timing. The thought of watching all those kids laughing and enjoying themselves wasn't what he needed or wanted. Maybe someday but not yet.

"Ross Abercrombie," he answered, grabbing the handset for what he thought would be the final ring before the answer machine would kick in.

"Hi, Fitch, it's Jerry here over at the crime lab."

"Hey, Jerry, how're things?"

"'Interesting' is about the best I can come up with I'm afraid."

Fitch took a seat. Jerry's tone was not one that indicated he bore good news. "How so?"

"Those two murders you had over on Vinalhaven, you know the husband and wife killing each other?"

"Not going to forget that one for a while. Did wonders for our stats."

"I'm afraid that may be about to change. The semen we found in the wife…"

Although finding semen during an autopsy was not uncommon, it had been a bit of a surprise given the two had killed each other, but it wasn't enough to impact the overwhelming evidence they already had.

"Yeah, we assumed it was the husband's. Please don't tell me it's not."

"It's not but I do know whose it is."

"Who then, if not Frank's?"

"Some guy with a rap sheet as long as my arm and to be honest some of it is pretty ugly shit!"

"Could still be they killed each other. Might be she had a lover and wanted rid of him and he killed her because of the lover."

"Maybe but that's for you to work out, I just work the evidence. Sorry it wasn't quicker, but you did say there was no rush, although I'm guessing you didn't expect that result."

"Any way of telling how long it was before she died that she had sex?"

"Not really but quite recently, the sample was fairly fresh."

"Whose is it?"

"Gerald Ba—"

Fitch almost dropped the phone. "Did you say Gerald?"

"Yeah, Baker. Gerald Baker, you know him, total scumbag."

"No but the name Gerald means something!"

"There is one other thing, I've sent the sample off to be checked."

"What?"

"The sample had an anomaly, something I hadn't seen before. It may be nothing, but I've sent it off to the FBI lab to confirm."

"But the DNA match is right?"

"Oh, that bit's one hundred percent. Gerald Baker's the guy."

"And the other thing, how long for results?"

"No idea. I did put down it was an active murder inquiry, although not technically true until I spoke with you just now. But

given there's no question as to the DNA match, not sure it'll be quick."

"If I'm asked, I won't alert them to your lie. When did you send it away?"

"Just now when the results came back."

"Can you give me any more than 'an anomaly?'"

"No, and it's probably nothing, just ignore it. The match is definite, there is no question about that."

"Yes, but maybe Frank murdered her because of this Gerald guy, and she killed him because she wanted to be with Gerald?" Fitch thought out loud trying to make sense of what he'd been told.

"Yeah but where's Gerald, surely he'd have come forward?" he asked, although rhetorically.

"You mentioned he was a scumbag, why?"

"Sex offender in and out of prison for the last fifteen years, got out after a five year stretch only three weeks ago."

"Whoa, what?"

"Yep, got his rap sheet in front of me. Guy's a total scumbag and up until three weeks ago was in Maine State Prison. It's the reason I called you tonight and not tomorrow morning."

"I assume he's got a parole officer?"

"Gerald Baker has been reported missing since he got released. Nobody's seen him. There's a missing person note on the file from a nephew who he listed as his address for parole and the sex offenders register."

"Shit, looks like I wrapped up the case a little too quick."

"You're the detective!"

"Yep, Jerry, my problem, not yours. You've already gone above and beyond. Much appreciated and thanks for the heads up."

"You're welcome, I've emailed everything I've got so far and good luck!"

Fitch replaced the handset and looked around the room seeing nothing. His mind was racing. What the hell had just happened? He wanted to call Mark but, in all reality, there was little they could do at that time. He'd call him after the baseball game and arrange an early start. He scanned the emails; all was as Jerry had said. The full extent of Gerald Baker's record was on its way to him, the email was just a summary. A serial sex offender, in and out of prison for the previous fifteen years, before then nothing. It was as though he hadn't existed.

Well, according to Frank, he definitely had existed on Vinalhaven in that cottage. Fitch's simplest double murder had just become his most baffling.

Chapter 10

Two weeks of normality Vinalhaven style, or as Kay discovered, unbelievable boredom. There was literally nothing to do. Still early in the season, the island wouldn't fill up for another month or so. Until then she had to do something to maintain her sanity and finally her package had arrived. Refusing any assistance, she managed to maneuver the heavy and cumbersome package into her truck.

"So what's GPR?" asked the postmaster, handing her a release sheet to sign.

"Sorry?"

"The package. It says on the description it's a mobile GPR unit."

Small towns, thought Kay. Everything was everybody's business, nothing was your own.

"It sees into the ground, a bit of a hobby of mine."

"What, like a metal detector?"

She smiled. "A bit more advanced."

"I get that. Almost thirteen grand, that's some hobby!"

Kay slammed her trunk shut, ending the conversation, the level of nosiness had just gone off the scale. There was no receipt or invoice, the postmaster had obviously googled the price from the information on the parcel. "That's really none of your business," she huffed. "I look for old settlements and artifacts, it can be very lucrative."

She was furious with herself as she drove away. She didn't need to justify to anyone what she did with her own money or in her spare time. She had researched

Vinalhaven's history before coming to the island and found it had been inhabited for many thousands of years. Its relatively small size would mean areas of historic interest in real terms would be easier to find.

Following the three deaths two weeks earlier, the most time-consuming case had been finding a lost child, who it turned out had been left on the mainland in Rockland and was sitting in the police station looking for his family. Their indignation at the incompetence of the sheriff's office quickly dissipated when their negligence at not realizing one of their three children wasn't in their SUV when they boarded the ferry became known.

Lieutenant Abercrombie—Fitch—had called with a couple of updates, which amounted to nothing other than confirmation of what they already knew. Frank had died of arsenic poisoning and the fingerprints of him and his wife were on each other's respective murder weapons. The one piece of evidence that had surprised them all, given the state of the relationship, was the semen, but nobody expected it to be anyone's other than the husband, Frank.

It was therefore with some surprise that Fitch's vehicle blocked what would otherwise have been her rapid exit from the postal office car park. He was not alone, once again accompanied by Mark Winters. It was an hour's drive from Augusta to Rockland, followed by the hour and fifteen-minute ferry All in all, it wasn't a drive she'd expect them to make to just be friendly, something was up. She jumped out of her truck and looked across the small bay to the ferry dock. Cars were lined up to board. They had just arrived at 8:20 a.m. they'd caught the 7:00 a.m. ferry from Rockland, which meant they'd have had to left Augusta before 6:00 a.m., an early start for detectives.

"Hey guys," she said, approaching their car, her fury at the nosiness of the postmaster forgotten.

Fitch smiled. "Hi."

"Early start?" she questioned.

"Late finish actually." He looked over her shoulder at the trunk. "What's with the huge parcel I saw you putting in there?"

"Jeez, can't a girl have her secrets?" she said with a smile.

"Sorry, it's just, well, big!"

Kay laughed. "Okay, you got me. I'm a bit of a history geek. Have you heard of the red paint people?" She turned and popped the trunk, retrieving an old book lying next to the oversized parcel. She held it out. "It's fascinating stuff, anyway…" Kay paused. Fitch was trying to look interested, she could see he was trying, but trying and actually being interested were vastly different. "Sorry, I can see maybe another time."

"Yeah, sorry, it's just that we received some information last night that put a different perspective on things."

"Oh, that sounds…" Kay struggled to think of the right word, "interesting, or worrying all at once."

"You'd be right with both."

A small crowd, Vinalhaven style—more than two was a crowd—were looking on with interest.

"Perhaps we should take this back to your office," Fitch suggested.

Kay looked at the gathered locals and nodded in agreement. "Follow me." She led the detectives back to the sheriff's office within the main town building.

Kay's thoughts had run away with her as she drove towards the office. So many thoughts that she was struggling to keep up with them on the short drive. What had she done wrong? Had her errors compromised the investigation? She was sure she had followed the crime scene manuals to the letter.

It was only when they closed the door behind them in the office that finally Fitch unleashed the reason for the unexpected visit. "Valerie hadn't slept with her husband before the murder," he said evenly.

Kay's mouth dropped, she was speechless.

"Yep, that was pretty much our reaction." Fitch glanced at Mark for confirmation.

Mark nodded wholeheartedly. "Exactly that."

"If not, who? And when?" Kay managed.

"We don't know when, but we do know who," Fitch teased.

"So if the guy's in the database he's got a record?" she said excitedly.

"A long one," Fitch confirmed.

"So who is it?" Kay was fed up with the drip feeding, she just wanted a name.

"Gerald."

"Shut the front door!" Kay exclaimed, she hated profanity.

"Nope. Gerald Baker is his name, and up until three weeks ago he was a guest of the State of Maine for five years."

"No?!?" She looked at Mark to see if it was a wind up. He nodded, a knowing smile confirming everything Fitch was telling her

"Gerald, as in Frank's defense, Gerald?"

"The one and only, Gerald Baker. Convicted rapist Gerald Baker, serial sex offender Gerald Baker."

"No, seriously. I mean that's unbelievable. So do you have him in custody?"

"He's been reported missing since leaving prison. Never turned up at his nephew's house nor met with his parole officer."

"Any other convictions, other than rape?"

"All sexual related in some way or other, but here's the thing: Gerald liked them young, and when I say young, I'm not talking legal young, I mean *illegal* young. Certainly not someone of Valerie's age. He's been in and out of prison for the last fifteen years."

"Yet the evidence would point to a dalliance."

"Dalliance?" asked Mark, his eyebrows raised.

"He tried something else," Kay explained, "namely Valerie."

"Oh, you're saying he fu—"

"Yes, Mark," Fitch cut in, "that's what Kay is saying, although far more politely."

"I'm not a fan of profanity," said Kay.

Mark looked confused. "Profanity?"

"Swearing!" Fitch snapped, losing his patience with Mark.

Kay thought for a moment. "Wait a minute, if he liked young girls he—"

Fitch's expression grew grim. "I never said girls."

"You're saying he liked young boys?"

"Apparently Gerald swung both ways."

"That's not normal, is it?"

"Not my specialty thankfully." Fitch shrugged. "However, it does mean the case is re-opened as of now."

"What about Walt?"

"What's Walt got to do with it?" asked Mark.

"His computer, his trips to Thailand—if he was a sex tourist, let's face it, most travel for the underage variety…" Kay lifted both hands.

"Damn, I hadn't even thought of that. We've never cracked his password but it wasn't really a priority."

"So what are we saying?" asked Mark. "Two or three victims?"

Fitch looked at Kay. She looked back into his eyes—a deep green she noticed for the first time. The man didn't have a flaw. His eyes were every bit as gorgeous as the rest of him.

"Let's stick with two for now. Whatever the case looks like we'll be here for a while." Fitch's eyes twinkled as he spoke, and Kay's stomach fluttered.

"So, two victims, one suspect," concluded Mark.

"Two suspects," Kay corrected with some force. "I'd add John Gilder as a person of interest."

Chapter 11

News of the investigation being re-opened spread like wildfire across the island. Never had so many town officials stopped by to say hello over the previous two weeks. Kay had met them all by chance while walking through the building. Suddenly the sheriff's office was the go-to place. It was one of the larger offices in the town building but was just one large open office with a small interview room and holding cell, should the need ever arise. One door connected directly to the parking lot outside, while another gave internal access to the rest of the building.

"Okay, enough," Kay said after the third official in as many hours checked if she or anyone wanted a coffee. She had many times over the previous two weeks but had had to rely on herself to make it. Kay marched along the hallway to the town manager's office, throwing the door open with more drama than she intended. A large bang announced its connection with the filing cabinet at the very limits of its reach, and Charles Ryan, the town manager, visibly jumped in fright at Kay's entrance. The bang and his reaction released every ounce of steam from her anger.

"Oh, sorry, I didn't mean—"

Charles calmed when he realized the bang was nothing more than the door hitting the cabinet. News of the murders had frightened as many people as it had intrigued.

"No, it's fine, don't worry about it. I hear you've a lot going on."

"Yes, sorry." Kay looked at the obvious dent on the cabinet where the handle had connected. Charles followed her line of sight and shook his head; he wasn't worried about it. "Seriously, that was an accident, I'm so sorry."

"Really it's fine, the dent was always there," he lied.

"Anyway, I just need to know who has access to my office. When I say access, I mean a key."

"Hmm, let me think." He began to count off on his fingers.

"No," Kay said when he got to three. "We need a locksmith. That number needs to be zero beyond me."

Charles' eyes fell on the dent in his cabinet and he immediately lifted his phone. "Consider it done."

"Thanks, and sorry again." She departed far more carefully than she'd entered, registering barely an audible click when she closed the door behind herself.

"Where'd you go?" asked Fitch when she walked back into the sheriff's office.

"Just sorting out security," she said sheepishly.

He wasn't really sure what that meant. "Anyway, while you were gone I called the medical examiner to request a more thorough autopsy of Walt."

"Cool." Given his response she felt she had to explain the security problem. "Security as in making sure nobody can come in here and interfere with the investigation. Lots of people have keys for this office."

"Good call," said Mark, busy laying out the photos from the initial investigation of the crime scene, placing them on one side of one of the two blank walls. The photos of the victims were placed on the other side. He had just secured the final photo when a knock at the internal door interrupted them.

The door began to open.

"Hold on!" Kay barked. The photos would be visible to whomever came through the door.

"I've been asked to replace the lock!" a man called through the door.

Kay opened the door while Mark pinned large sheets of paper over the most shocking of the victim photos.

"I want to change both locks please and all keys given to us, no spares to be kept outside of this office."

"That's against town pol—"

Kay had had enough. "I don't give a damn. I'm the law on this island and you're going to do what I say!"

With his hands up in surrender, the handyman set about his work. Fitch and Mark shared a look but said nothing, filing away the outburst for later.

By lunchtime, they had two new locks and another unwanted visitor. Sheriff Chris Jackson arrived to offer his department's help in any way with the investigation. Why he had felt the need for the trip rather than just calling nobody quite understood, but accompanied by three deputies, it was clear he was in some way telling Maine State Police it was still his jurisdiction, despite their lead on the murder case.

"So, two victims," he mused, looking at the evidence wall.

"Perhaps three," Fitch said, keeping his smile at bay, although Kay could sense he was enjoying the sheriff's discomfort at not being in charge.

"Who's the third?"

"It's not confirmed yet. Until then I'd rather not say."

"But the only other death on the island was Walt?"

"I never said the body was on the island."

Kay had to look away to stop herself sniggering. Fitch was toying with the sheriff, his use of the word body very deliberate; Walt was at the medical examiner's office on the mainland in Augusta.

"Oh, right, okay." The sheriff turned to Fitch. "I've brought two of my men to support your inquiries."

"I've got Kay here, that'll be fine for now."

"But Deputy Miller is—"

Fitch quirked an eyebrow. "Extremely well qualified?"

"I was going to say new to the island and the locals. My men here are well known and know the island well."

"I've spent the last two weeks getting to know the island and the locals," Kay countered. "I think I pretty much know where everything is."

"She's been able to take us wherever we needed to go," Fitch said.

"Fine, but the offer stands if you need more men."

"Very much appreciated, I assure you. Now if you don't mind, we've got work to do."

Sheriff Jackson stood for an awkward few seconds. It was his office, his insignia, that emblazoned its doors and equipment and he'd just effectively been told to leave.

"Deputy Miller," he said with as much authority as he could muster, "if you need anything just let me know," he commanded, closing the door behind him.

When the sound of his engine started outside Kay turned to the two laughing detectives. "You really shouldn't you know," she chastised them.

"He's such a pompous asshole it's hard not to."

Kay grinned, keeping her laugh in. She couldn't be seen to disrespect her boss too much. But as much as she tried, he seemed to try harder to prove he deserved it.

By the end of the day they had worked through the evidence they had already collected and already drawn up a list of actions to undertake. First and foremost was locating and finding out every piece of information they could about Gerald Baker. His rap sheet was extensive but contained a number of holes, none more so than the first thirty years of Gerald Baker's life, the point up to which he had managed to stay under the law's radar.

From Frank's dying testimony, it was likely Gerald had lived on the island, and specifically in the crime scene cottage many years earlier. They agreed that would be their first port of call in the morning, a more thorough look at the crime scene. Meanwhile, Mark and Fitch were going to find accommodation and invited Kay to join them for dinner. She politely declined. She still had her new toy to play with, which was taking up the majority of her trunk.

As she waved them off from the office, she locked the doors, freshly secured against any prying eyes, and headed out into the countryside to try out the GPR machine. First stop was a large field to the east of the airfield she had spotted when driving out there. It had good access, but most importantly few prying eyes to watch over her. With some difficulty she maneuvered the box out of the trunk and unpacked the machine. It resembled a large push lawnmower, only with far larger wheels to cope with the rough terrain. A digital screen sat atop the handle with a ten-inch screen. Kay looked at the manual but having researched the machine thoroughly and watching numerous YouTube 'how to' videos she flicked the on switch and waited while it moved through its initial boot up phase. As advised on many reviews it had an initial charge sufficient to at least try it out. The word "ready" flashed on the screen and began to move the Ground Penetrating Radar device forward. It scanned the ground to a depth Kay decided, allowing her to map what was beneath her. Any old settlements would be easy to see and given some recent and very lucrative finds, there was always a chance she'd hit it big. She looked at her chart, a map of the island with cross sectional areas drawn on where she wanted to survey. Each was cross referenced to a grid map for the specific location. It was going to take months to cover the areas but Kay was more than ready to rise to the challenge. It would be therapeutic given the day job and quite frankly there was nothing else to do in her spare time.

She managed to get the machine back in the SUV, deciding the very next thing she was going to do was buy a ramp.

She pulled up in front of her cottage just as the sun was setting, cracked open a bottle of wine, and slumped into the seat on her deck. Her eyes tracked towards the Tidewater Motel, where Fitch and Mark would be sitting down to dinner. She contemplated changing her mind but after another sip of wine, all thoughts of moving faded.

***

If Kay had ventured out, she'd have discovered The Tidewater was the place to be. Never had the bar or restaurant been so busy as news of the investigation continued to spread and become the only talking point.

Even the state of the lobster catch that day was ignored in favor of the breaking story.

Fitch and Mark were trying to keep to themselves, but their location, faces, and pretty much everything about them was local knowledge. Never had so many people come to introduce themselves during dinner. Fitch couldn't help but think as another local stopped by that Kay had been very wise to give the restaurant a miss. If they had had a room service option, he'd have done the same.

"Hilary Cantrell," said an older lady. "Pleased to meet you both."

"I'm Lieutenant Abercrombie and this is Detective Winters," said Fitch, slightly more politely than he had to some of the previous locals. His mother had raised him to respect his elders and Hilary was most definitely in that bracket.

"Terrible news." She shook her head. "I mean, a young couple in their prime, awful."

Fitch had been very dismissive of the others, whose interest had been that of rubberneckers, eager to know what was happening. Hilary was showing genuine concern, like she—

"I remember when they worked here," she said.

Fitch's interest was instantly piqued. "Frank and Valerie?"

"Yes, who else would I be talking about?"

"I thought you might have meant Gerald."

A glint of recognition flashed across her eyes. "Who's Gerald?"

Fitch didn't believe her for a second, the glint of recognition had been replaced with…well, he couldn't quite see. Hilary was good. She could control her emotions, but he had an eye and a BS detector that was honed to perfection.

"Gerald Baker." Fitch hadn't wanted to publicize the name, but it was very interesting that John Gilder hadn't told anyone. If he had Fitch would have assumed Hilary would have been prepared for hearing the name. And given Hilary had just admitted she knew the victims he wasn't holding back.

She was *very* good. By the time he said Gerald's surname any look of recognition was gone. "No, never heard of him," she lied confidently. Fitch knew it but would never be able to prove it.

"So you knew Frank and Valerie?"

"Yes, they worked on Lane's Island. Oh, it must be fifteen to twenty years ago. I didn't know them well, only in passing, you know what I mean?"

"Not really. Did you work with them?"

"No, no, I used to be a schoolteacher, although I did do some private tuition over the summers."

"Gentlemen, how's the food?" interrupted John, who had been watching from across the restaurant with interest. Fitch had wondered how long he'd take to interrupt.

"It's fine, thanks. I was chatting with Mrs. Cantrell."

"Oh, Hilary. Terrible news isn't it?" said John ignoring Fitch's pointed rebuke.

"Oh Charles," John called across the restaurant. "Have you been introduced to the detectives?"

Hilary stepped aside to allow Charles Ryan to join the discussion.

"Charles Ryan, town manager." He offered his hand.

Mark took it. "Mark Winters, and this is Ross Abercrombie."

"I thought one of you was called Fitch?"

Fitch blushed slightly and nodded.

"Oh I get it. Yeah, I do get it." Charles smiled. A wink from Mark was enough to rid Fitch of his blushes.

"Guys, I was chatting with Hilary." Fitch's temper was beginning to fray as what seemed his first real lead was being sabotaged, and if he was paranoid, he'd have thought deliberately.

"It's getting a bit late for me, perhaps I can stop by tomorrow to talk," Hilary suggested.

"That would be good," Fitch agreed. "You know where we are?"

"Yes, I'll see you tomorrow."

Charles Ryan said his goodbyes and helped Hilary to the door.

John watched them, waiting until they were just out of earshot to say, "Poor thing, she's never been the same since the fall."

"Sorry?"

"She had a bad fall a couple of winters ago, started losing it shortly after. She was one of the brightest people I've ever met but now she's not quite all there, if you know what I mean," said John, spinning his finger next to his temple.

"She seemed pretty lucid to me," Fitch remarked.

"Yeah, she has her moments, bless her, but you can never really trust what she says."

"She really didn't say anything," said Mark, as confused as Fitch at John Gilder's comments.

He raised his hands in defense, realizing he had overstepped. "Just giving you guys the heads up is all." He waved over the waitress, a young woman who had just come on shift, pleasant on the eye with a pair of shorts that would have struggled to cover her appropriately with twice the amount of cloth. Her plunging neckline left little to the imagination, and John's eyes lit up as she walked towards them. "If only I was twenty years younger," he said quietly for the benefit of the detectives.

"You'd still be twice her age," Fitch whispered under his breath.

Mid-sip of his beer, Mark expelled his mouthful across the table. "Sorry, choked a bit there," he covered, throwing an evil eye at Fitch, who was struggling to hold his laughter.

"Wow, we've got ourselves some talent!" the waitress said excitedly. "I'm Mandy. What can I get you fellas? And don't worry if it's not on that menu." She winked.

John exploded in laughter. "She ain't kidding. You fellas enjoy your evening!"

"He's a joker that one." She winked at Fitch. Clearly there was another menu on offer.

"Two beers," he said.

"For just now that is." She winked once more before walking away with more swagger than was appropriate given there were a number of children in the restaurant.

"Well, she's up for it!"

"Full on or what!" Fitch exclaimed. "She'd eat you alive!"

"Maybe it's just what you need." Mark instantly regretted the words. Fitch didn't respond to the comment but excused himself before the beers arrived, claiming he was tired and needed some sleep. Mark checked his watch; it wasn't even 9 p.m., and given he was a married man with young kids away from home for the night he kicked himself for losing his drinking buddy. When the beers arrived, he drank both before ordering two more. Something the next morning he would very much regret.

Chapter 12

Kay woke to the ringing telephone. Again. She was in bed in her shorts and t-shirt, she had at least made it to bed. It was light outside, but her alarm hadn't yet woken her since it was before 7:00 a.m. She had yet to find a call at that time in the morning would be anything but bad news. Did the people on the island not sleep?

"Hello," she answered, popping the first of three Tylenol.

"We need you to meet us over at the Tidewater asap!" said Fitch.

"Okay but it's pretty early." Kay glanced at the clock, it was only 6:12 a.m.

"We've got another body."

Kay sighed. "I'll be right there."

The water barely wet her, such was the speed she was in and out of the shower. Within five minutes and with her hair damp beneath her deputy hat she was in her truck and racing the short distance to the Tidewater Motel. Fitch and a forlorn looking Mark Winters awaited her. A woman barely clothed in tight shorts and a low-cut top was slinking out of the hotel behind them. She looked sheepishly across to the two detectives.

"Should we not stop her?" asked Kay, pulling to a stop next to the detectives.

"Oh no, don't worry about her, she's got a very good alibi." Fitch eyed Mark with disdain.

"Oh, I see. But I thought…" Kay stopped herself, it wasn't her place to judge, certainly not openly.

Fitch climbed in the front while a silent and less than comfortable looking Mark fell into the back.

"So, it's not here?"

"No, it's at Booth Quarry. John Gilder got a call from a friend this morning. They knew we were staying at the motel so called for us directly. You know where it is?"

"Yeah, not far."

On an island the size of Vinalhaven, that was effectively meaningless. However, Fitch wasn't in a challenging mood, he was too annoyed at his colleague to worry about what "not far" on an island six miles long meant.

Within five minutes they were pulling to a stop and Fitch remarked, "It really wasn't far."

Kay killed the engine in front of a small waiting crowd. The people of Vinalhaven were early risers.

Another truck pulled to a stop next to them, a small zodiac with an outboard hitched to the back.

"That's for us," advised Fitch. "Gilder arranged it, said we'd need it."

Two minutes later it was apparent why. The quarry was approximately one hundred yards by seventy yards, the water cool but crystal clear and inviting. A small outcrop of rock jutted skyward in the middle of the pond, the naked body of an older female splayed out for all to see.

"I'd say from the color of her skin, we don't need to rush," Mark muttered through his hangover and fake shame. Fitch knew the shame was only that he'd been caught, not that he'd done it.

Kay asked the small crowd to disperse from the immediate area, as pointless as it was. They had to try and protect any evidence at the scene. She taped off the entrance to the parking lot and the narrow pathway to the quarry side while the detectives and the boat owner struggled to get the boat into the water.

"You ready?" Fitch called to her.

"You want me to come out there?"

"Yeah. I'm not sure Mark will make it in his state, his sea legs aren't the best."

The quarry was like a mirror, not a ripple on the surface.

"You are joking?" Kay said.

"Kind of, but he's looking a little gray around the gills. Best he doesn't throw up on the body. He can keep the hordes at bay."

Without uttering a word in his defense Mark walked past her, a resigned look of penance to pay, and he'd take it like a man.

"I've no idea what he's playing at," Fitch fumed when Mark was out of earshot. "His wife is lovely. I mean seriously, what the hell!"

"You never know what's going on behind closed doors," Kay commented.

Fitch shrugged and extended his hand to help her into the boat. She shook her head and barely avoided falling into the water as the small boat rocked wildly when she stepped awkwardly into it. Fitch caught her as she was about to topple, his hands firmly grasping her waist and holding her midair. Kay pushed against him as he brought her towards him. As far as she was concerned too close for comfort.

"Thanks," she said, brushing herself down.

"You're very welcome." He frowned, unsure as to what else he could have done. It was almost as though she'd have preferred to go into the water headfirst.

Kay sat rigidly while they rode the short distance, circling the outcrop, taking numerous photos before setting foot on the rock. The outcrop was roughly five yards square, the floor area of a large lounge, slightly sloping, and rose just a few feet to its highest point before slipping back into the water.

The first thing they both agreed on, she was most definitely dead. The lifeless eyes stared back at them, she was as they had gathered from the quarry side, completely naked and appeared from first glance unharmed in any way, not a blemish on the old, pale skin.

"Oh no," Fitch mumbled when he saw the old woman's face. "I know her."

"You do?"

"She spoke to us last night, Hilary something. She knew Frank and Valerie. She was going to tell us more, but John Gilder interrupted, and we were going to talk to her today."

"Gilder again," Kay noted.

"Hmm, perhaps you could look a bit closer there." Fitch pointed to the area between the elderly lady's legs.

Kay donned a pair of gloves and bent down closer. "I'd say that's semen. You got a sample tube?"

Fitch handed her one from his bag and Kay scooped a small sample, careful not to disturb anything else. "What are you thinking?" she asked, handing him the tube.

"I'm thinking Gerald Baker. You?"

"She's definitely not his normal target. I mean she's what, late seventies? Baker's priors all involve very young women and girls but yeah, I think we need to find Gerald Baker and have a proper chat with John Gilder."

"Sounds like a plan. I'll get the crime scene guys on the way and I suppose I'd better call the FBI."

"The FBI?"

"Standard procedure when we've got a suspected serial killer."

"We don't know that yet," Kay countered. "This could be unrelated."

"Three murders in two weeks, both women raped."

"Whoa, you're jumping the gun a little. There's not a mark on this woman and there's no evidence she or Valerie were raped."

"She had a twelve-inch knife plunged into her after she had sex, doesn't take a genius to conclude it may not have been consensual."

"True," Kay conceded, "but she didn't have any signs of struggling or restraints being used, and we don't know if one directly followed the other. And here it certainly doesn't look like she was forced. There's not a mark on her."

"For God's sake she's a frail old lady in her seventies, Gerald Baker is a big, powerful guy in comparison. How would she have stopped him?"

"We don't even know if it was him…"

"Well there is that," pondered Fitch. "Okay, I'll hold off the FBI call at the moment but if this result comes back with Baker, I'm making that call."

"Of course. I just don't want us to jump the gun and panic the island right before summer."

"Two weeks and they've got to you already," he muttered.

"Sorry?"

"The islanders, you're one of them. Gotta protect the summer season!"

"Without it, the island would be ruined."

"Is it worth risking innocent lives?"

"Is it worth destroying innocent livelihoods?"

"Touché."

They collected as much information as they could before heading back to the shore. The crime scene team was on their way and would deal with the detailed collection and recovery of the body to be sent for autopsy.

"Well?" asked Mark, helping Kay from the boat. Her reticence for help was outweighed by her almost disastrous entry.

"You're looking better," she said.

"Yeah, I…uh, well, I suppose I—"

"You threw up didn't you?" Fitch said.

Mark nodded. "Feeling much better now though."

"I hope you threw up away from here!" Fitch laughed.

"Of course," he replied. "So what did you find?"

Kay explained on the way back to her truck. Mark agreed the FBI was one step off, they needed to confirm there was a link before they made the call.

"Mark, you stay here and protect the scene. Kay can take me back to town and then collect the crime scene team, who should be landing within the hour."

"I'll stay here, Mark should be with you."

Fitch turned to Mark. "Do you know your way around this island?"

"Nope. Even if I did there's no way I'm fit to drive."

"And that, deputy, is why you're taking me to town and we're leaving Mark here."

Kay's face flushed red; she hadn't meant anything other than she felt a detective was too qualified to guard a crime scene. Fitch had apparently taken it another way but to explain herself would just make it worse. Without a word she climbed behind the driver's wheel and headed for the sheriff's office.

"Thanks," Fitch said to Kay's wheel spin as she left to collect the crime scene team.

Fitch opened the sheriff's office door. Despite his lack of key Sheriff Chris Jackson sat waiting for him. Fitch checked the door, it hadn't been forced. He walked across to the internal door to the rest of the town building. It was still locked and hadn't been forced.

"How'd you get in here?" asked Fitch.

Jackson grinned. "It's my office."

Fitch had to play the politics; Vinalhaven was the sheriff's jurisdiction. As much of an asshole as the guy was, he deserved the respect of his office, or at least that's what everyone said. Yet that had been before Chris Jackson was elected sheriff. Up until then every sheriff was a hugely respected individual.

"It's just…nothing, it doesn't matter. How can I help you, Sheriff?"

"Was anyone planning to tell me about the new murder?"

"I'm sure Deputy Miller would have. She's just been a bit busy but to call it a—"

"Whatever," the sheriff said dismissively. "Anyway, I've called the FBI. Figured we'd need the experts, given it's grown beyond you guys."

"Says who?"

"We've got three murders, and from what I gather from John Gilder, this Hilary woman knew the other two victims."

Fitch shook his head in disbelief. "Is John Gilder running this investigation now?"

"Of course not," Jackson replied, a slight hesitation in his voice.

"So why the hell after speaking with him did you call the FBI before talking to me!" Fitch picked up the phone on the desk and punched in a number he knew from memory. "Behavioral Analysis Unit 2 please…thanks…,Hey Janice, how you doing? It's Fitch here…yeah, yeah maybe, bit early to tell, you know what the local guys are like, bit jumpy and this one's a newbie…of course…if I need you I'll call."

Jackson sat and listened to the familiarity with which Fitch talked with the FBI team. They knew him, and from the conversation it seemed very well. He had to bite his tongue at the references to himself. He had jumped the gun, he had assumed from what Gilder had said the link to the other two murders was confirmed, and it clearly wasn't.

"For your information, we don't yet know if it's a murder scene. We still have to confirm that's the case. Now unless there's anything else I don't have time to make calls I shouldn't need to."

For the second time in twenty-four hours Jackson was being dismissed from his own office.

"Oh, and I'll have that key you somehow managed to get a hold of."

"This is my office!"

"This is my investigation. You want me to think you've got something you're trying to hide?" Fitch held out his hand and the key was deposited with a huff. "And who else has one? We were assured we had them all."

"Charles Ryan, I guess. He left a copy for me in his office."

"I met him last night. He helped Hilary home. Is he in?"

"He wasn't when I swung by but that wasn't long after eight. I was on the first ferry."

Fitch was already unlocking the internal door while Jackson was still talking. He rushed down the corridor towards the Town Manager's office. It was empty. He radioed Kay as his cell began to ring.

Mark's name flashed onto his cell screen. He hit accept as Kay replied to his radio message.

"Yeah?" she said, still not in a talkative mood.

"Charles Ryan," he began.

"How'd you know that's why I'm calling?" Mark asked in one ear.

"What?"

"You radioed me, what do you mean what?" said Kay.

"No not you! I was saying what to Mark."

"So, why'd you radio me?" asked Kay.

"Charles Ryan," Mark said, *"he just appeared…"*

"I'm talking to Mark. He called me at the same time I radioed you," Fitch said to Kay.

"Oh, okay."

"Can you tell him I want to talk to him?" Fitch said to Mark.

"I'm not there yet, I'll tell him when I see him," said Kay, thinking the message was for her.

"I can try, not sure he'll listen though," Mark said.

"Not Mark, Charles." Fitch sighed. The three-way conversation was becoming ludicrously complicated and confused.

"What?" asked Mark.

"Enough of this. Kay, I'm hanging up now." He ended the chat with Kay leaving Mark on his cell. "Mark, tell Ryan to come see me."

"Oh, he'll be coming. Just might take a little time and he'll be in a zipped-up bag."

"What?"

"He just surfaced in the quarry, popped up like a fart in the bath."

"Shit, you're kidding. How'd he die?"

"No idea, but he's butt naked just like the woman."

"So we've got another two victims at one scene. I'll be with you in five."

"You don't have a car, it's at the motel. Kay's just pulling up, I'll send her to get you."

"Oh right, okay." There was some awkwardness between them. Fitch wasn't sure why but there was something, and no matter what he said or did it seemed to make it worse. It was silly, almost teenage in its awkwardness.

Chapter 13

Charles Ryan was exactly as described by Mark, butt naked and not a mark on him. He was a fit looking guy in his early fifties. If he had been the man who had been intimate with Hilary, it was a strange match, but given she was as naked as he was, it didn't take a leap to conclude there was a high probability they had been with each other. The fact she could have been his mother, and given their visible age difference in bodies some could argue grandmother, didn't mean it wasn't possible.

"Do you think there's a chance they went skinny dipping and got into trouble?" Fitch posed.

"God knows, but there's no obvious signs on either body of any trauma," Mark replied.

"She was old, perhaps the strain of sex gave her a heart attack, he went to get help and struggled with the cold water? I mean, it was cool last night."

"Plausible, except for, well, Charles Ryan, was he not…" Kay hesitated.

"What?" Fitch prompted.

"I'm guessing you're thinking gay," said Mark.

"Well yes. I'm not the best at spotting that but let's just say I met him yesterday and nothing, I mean nothing, that's not…" she stopped when she realized how conceited she sounded. "Not that I'm anything special but—"

"Kay, you're hot. If he didn't react, it probably means you're right," Mark cut in bluntly. "I can't say I disagree, and I need to say he reacted very differently to Fitch last night."

Fitch whipped his head around. "What? What are you talking about?"

"When I introduced you as Fitch at dinner last and he got it, you didn't notice the smile he gave you?"

"No."

"My friend, you out more gay guys than anyone I know, yet somehow are blissfully unaware of it."

"So what are we saying, they were both murdered?"

"Just because we think he may have been gay doesn't mean he was, maybe he was bi. Quarries are dangerous places. I suppose it's a plausible story."

"Yeah, but let's face it, we thought Frank and Valerie was clear cut and look how that turned out. Let's wait for the evidence this time. Until then we will go with potential tragic accident but keep the case open until the evidence proves it."

Kay remained silent; she was surveying the scene closely. "Where are their clothes? How did they get here?" she asked more to herself than to the detectives.

"I'm sure we'll find them soon enough. We need to get the bodies processed and we'll have a good look around."

A paramedic who was loading Hilary into the ambulance heard them talking and joined the conversation. "Hilary lived just over there on Schoolhouse Road. This is practically her backyard."

All three looked to where the paramedic was pointing at the bottom end of the quarry. Dense bushes and trees lined the side of the quarry and there was no way to see beyond.

"How far?" asked Kay.

"A hundred feet from the quarry on the other side of the trees. Hers is the first house off Schoolhouse Road, first left out of here."

"You knew her well?"

"She taught me for a few years, everyone knows Hilary."

"Some more than others," Mark mumbled, earning him a scowl from Kay.

"Thanks," said Fitch, ignoring his colleagues. "What about Charles Ryan, did you know him?"

"Of course. He is…sorry, *was*, a really nice guy."

"How nice?" asked Mark.

The paramedic looked around, not wanting to be overheard spreading gossip. "Well, I heard you talking earlier and let's just say it was something most of us thought but Charles never came out." The paramedic smirked. "We all just assumed but maybe he was into other things."

"Other things like what?"

"Well, like Hilary. Maybe he was into older ladies, you know, like moms. I mean if he was with Hilary it's pretty incestuous since she raised him like her own son. He was her nephew, his parents died when he was only a baby."

"Hilary was his aunt?"

"Yep, Charles was her sister's son," he confirmed, closing the doors of the ambulance and ending his insight into what was destined to be the next big scandal on Vinalhaven.

"Kay, do you want to take me around and we'll have a look?" Fitch asked.

"Sure." Kay walked to her truck, Fitch following closely behind. A brief, once again silent trip delivered them to the front door of a small cottage with a large expanse of grass at the front and a field of trees behind. An old Buick was parked near the front door. Fitch checked the hood of the car for warmth; it hadn't been used anytime recently and from closer inspection, in a long time. An old-style women's bicycle was leaning against the side of the cottage.

"She probably doesn't use the car in the summer," Kay guessed as they neared the front door. It was closed but not locked, opening to allow them entry.

"Hello!" Fitch called, announcing their presence. "Police!"

Unsurprisingly, there was no response. The door opened into a lounge. Bookcases stuffed with books lined the walls with a large fireplace dominating the room. Two easy chairs and a small couch filled the floor space along with two side tables. There was no television, only an old Bakelite radio on the fireplace.

"Old school," Fitch remarked.

They walked on and into a large kitchen. The window looked out onto the trees, and they could just see the water of the quarry beyond.

"He wasn't kidding when he said it was like her backyard," said Kay.

Fitch nudged her with his elbow, looking towards the table, a large, solid wood table with plenty of seating filling the left half of the room. A bottle of whiskey and two half-full glasses sat on the tabletop. The door that led to the backyard sat slightly askew, a shirt blocking it from fully closing. They followed the trail, opening the door and tracking the clothing across the yard to a path that disappeared into the tree line that they both knew led to the quarry beyond. The trees were in full bloom and the quarry was barely visible despite being so close.

Fitch shook his head in bewilderment. "I'd have bet my house he was just helping an old lady home last night. A lady I'd add who looked like she needed help walking because of her age and for no other reason. I'd never have thought they'd be doing this, and they were family?"

Fitch glanced at the trail of clothes stretching back to the cottage. A shiver ran through him, it certainly was beginning to look like an inappropriate relationship that had ended in tragedy.

"Could it be that simple? She had a heart attack and he was overcome by the cold water going for help?"

Kay shrugged. She didn't want to speculate given the Frank and Valerie case. They had both learned a lesson not to assume. As the saying went, assume makes an *ass* of *u* and *me*.

Kay stepped towards the tree line and the beginnings of the, overgrown and ill-kempt path that had obviously been used less than it had in the past.

"Are you thinking what I'm thinking?" asked Fitch, startling Kay. She hadn't heard him approach so close that he was almost touching her. He too was staring at the path.

"That it's not been used much," she replied warily, taking a step to the side.

"Well yes, but more than that. How does a frail old lady get through that path naked without so much as a scratch on her?"

Kay stepped half back, following Fitch's gaze. Branches and bushes encroached across the path, the gap barely visible in the daylight, never mind at night.

"Quite simply she couldn't, it's not possible."

"Yet the clothes lead to this path."

"But there's not a mark on either body to indicate they struggled through this path."

Fitch stepped into the path and within ten yards was stuck, a thorny bush having hooked its tendrils into his clothing, and he had been negotiating carefully with the full assistance of the morning sun. "Umm, think I might need some help."

Kay assisted, but not without the back of her hand and arm bearing witness to how impossible the path would have been to negotiate at night and naked without any marks on the bodies.

"So where does that leave us?" asked Kay as they fought their way back to the garden.

"Well, I suppose…" Fitch glanced around the garden and the area for inspiration, "…they got here and realized it was impossible to get through and walked around the way we came?"

"By car, the half mile drive we just made?" asked Kay. "Naked and inebriated along a public road, for a midnight swim?"

It was Fitch's turn to shrug, he had nothing else. Beyond that they were back to murder and a staging to make it look innocent. "If you hadn't been on the island for years, I suppose you may not have known the path was overgrown and impassible, staging at night you might simply have assumed it was as it had been years earlier."

"And Gerald Baker hasn't been on the island for years?" Kay added, reading Fitch's thoughts.

"In and out of prison for fifteen years, what he may have known as a well-used path no longer exists but at night, staging the scene, he didn't check if it was still usable."

"So we're saying it's murder?"

"Still, they may have been desperate for that swim and made the walk around the road. We need to process the evidence, at least know what the cause of their deaths was before we can make a call either way." Fitch concluded. "In the meantime, I'll get our guys processing the house."

Neither uttered a word on the drive back to the office, their minds working overtime trying to process the evidence. When they arrived, one thing was clear; the paramedic had already let the cat out of the bag. The incestuous aunt and nephew were the talk of the island. As far as everyone was concerned, it was a done deal. Hilary and her nephew's relationship was far more scandalous than the thought that Vinalhaven had potentially had five murders in the space of two weeks.

Chapter 14

Two Days Later

The only anomaly in the evidence that pointed to anything other than the simplest of conclusions was the lack of scratches from the path. Evidence within both Hilary and Charles's house highlighted without question that the two shared a highly inappropriate relationship and had for a very long time. And from Hilary's perspective, one that in Charles's youth was criminal and suggested she should never have been allowed anywhere near children and certainly not fit to be the beloved teacher that she had lived her life as.

Hilary's autopsy concluded she had succumbed to a massive heart attack as assumed, while Charles had died from drowning, again confirming their theory that he had gone for help and succumbed to the cold and drowned.

Yet the lack of scratches screamed that something just wasn't right with the overall scene.

"How long for the DNA on the semen and the toxicology report?" asked Fitch, looking at the wall of evidence that faced them.

"Same as the previous twenty times you asked," Winters replied wearily, "a few days."

"Without the DNA there's nothing to indicate a third party was involved. It's as clear a tragic event as you're ever likely to see from an evidence perspective without an actual witness."

"Yet," Kay corrected.

"Exactly," surmised Fitch. "Yet it's just too neat, if not for the lack of scratches from the path it would have been perfect. Two people died in tragic circumstances, two people with a very questionable relationship…"

"Questionable relationship?" Kay echoed. "Like a husband and wife who planned to kill each other, yet the DNA identified a third party we weren't looking for and no other evidence suggested existed."

They all looked at the wall again, knowing the anomaly in any other circumstance would have been explained away by them walking around the road rather than cutting through the trees. But the three other deaths had been initially closed due to the apparent overwhelming evidence that they were cut and dried.

The more they dug into Walt's background the less pleasant it became. A number of his trips to Thailand coincided directly with men who had over the years been uncovered as pedophiles, not only confirming the suspicions that had been raised as to his favored destination, but the likely reason for the trips. With every flight manifest they checked over the years, more and more of those who had travelled had subsequently been convicted of pedophilic involvement. Although Walt had managed to sail under the radar, given his seat assignments it was clear he was travelling with a group. One good thing had come from their digging; it was clear there were at least another ten men who cross-checked against the flight manifests who had never been on law enforcement radar. Walt's death was going to result in those ten men being put under a level of scrutiny that even the most innocent and law-abiding citizen would struggle to pass. Walt's death was going to save at least some children from a hideous childhood.

"Despite everything to the contrary I am inclined to declare the deaths murder. If the semen result comes back as belonging to Charles, we change to tragic accident, but I don't want to make the same mistake again."

Kay and Winters shrugged their agreement. "Makes sense," they said in unison.

Fitch sat staring at the evidence wall. "At the moment we have a scandal. When we declare it murder, we're more likely to have panic."

"Or ridicule. You ruled the double murder scene a closed case and Walt an accident. Now you're declaring a tragic accident a murder scene," a scoffing voice came from behind them.

All three spun to see the face of Sheriff Jackson standing in the doorway, an unwanted intruder to their deliberations.

"This way we get the FBI involved and get ahead of the case. If we wait a few days awaiting confirmation of a third party, some leads may have gone cold."

Sheriff Jackson quirked an eyebrow. "Would that be the same FBI I tried to involve two days ago when the leads would have been even fresher?"

Fitch was incandescent. Mark spotted the flare of anger and placed a calming hand on his colleague's forearm. Jackson was equating his attempt to sideline and outmaneuver the state police department due to personal issues to a well-run investigation that had diligently studied the evidence and come to a justifiable conclusion.

"For all we know if the FBI had been here working the case—"

"They may have concluded it was a tragic accident and laughed at you for calling them in," Kay cut in, resulting in an instant change of mood from her boss. His look of triumph was replaced by fury at his staff member siding with his foe.

"A word, Deputy Miller!" he barked, and headed for the door. "You work for *me*!" he hissed when they were outside, spittle exploding across Kay's face.

She pulled out a handkerchief and wiped her face deliberately, ensuring she removed every trace of Sheriff Jackson's DNA from her before looking him straight in the eye. Kay was a woman with issues, of that she was fully aware, but when backed into a corner, she was not a woman who backed down. If someone barked at her, she roared back.

"Let's be very clear," she stated firmly. Jackson went to speak, and Kay held up her hand for him to stop. "I will *not* be spoken to like that by *anyone*!" She pushed forward as she spoke, her inner strength greater than Jackson's outer bulk. He stepped back under her offensive. Her 5'5 against his 6'4 should have been a one-sided conflict, but Kay was overpowering the far larger Jackson with her conviction. "Do you understand me?"

Jackson's face said yes but his pride said otherwise. He disengaged and headed back into the office, his office, the Sheriff of Knox County's office. The two state police detectives had smirks on their faces, both struggling to hold themselves together having watched the interaction. Jackson grabbed his jacket and stormed out of his office, the door rattling in its frame such was the force of his exit. Kay stepped back to allow him past. "Keep me updated," he growled.

Squealing tires punctuated Jackson's humiliating retreat. When Kay stepped into the office, Fitch and

Winters were on their hands and knees buckled over with laughter.

"You two don't help you know," she scolded, a smile breaking out across her face. "He is such an ass though! I really can't believe he won the election. I mean, seriously. The sheriff before him was lovely, she had an amazing reputation."

"The more you see him in action the more you question the result," said Fitch. "Perhaps we should investigate whether there was something amiss?"

"What, blame the Russians!" scoffed Winters. "Like they give two sh… sorry…" he directed a sheepish glance at Kay, "care about who's sheriff of a two-bit backwater county in Maine."

"There are five murders. Maybe it's all connected. Maybe our victims were Russian agents and they are removing them because they knew too much?" Fitch mused.

"You think?" Winters was excited that his wild theory may have been right.

"Of course not. I was joking. Seriously, Mark, sometimes I worry about you."

"Guys, we maybe going slightly off track here." Kay hooked a thumb at the wall where five victims' photos were mounted.

"Yes, yes, of course." Fitch reached for his cell. "Time to call in the cavalry!"

Twenty minutes later after giving a quick précis of the scenes, followed by a number of monosyllabic responses to long questions, a less than happy Fitch ended the call.

Kay and Winters looked on expectantly.

"They think it's too early to link the incidents," said Fitch. "There's enough doubt that they're separate until proved otherwise."

"So they're not coming?"

"Not until we can categorically link all five murders. They are too busy for hunches."

"I thought you got on well with them the other day."

"That's what got me a twenty minute call and not a twenty second call," said Fitch. "Perhaps you can call in a favor? You've been to the academy."

"I attended a few courses. My experience with the FBI has been somewhat over embellished."

Winters winked at her. "I'm sure you stood out among the class."

"Why?" asked Kay innocently.

"You know." He smiled.

Kay looked to Fitch for help.

"He's saying you're hot, that's why you'd stand out," Fitch explained, his face reddening with embarrassment.

"Five hundred law enforcement professionals taught by a female lecturer? I don't think so."

"Okay, so we're back to being on our own with five deaths?"

"Basically yes. We're back to where we were. We need the DNA results to link Gerald Baker to Hilary and Charles and we also need to find a link to Walt."

"But without the FBI's help we're going to struggle to crack Walt's computer, which may be our only way to link him with the other murders."

"Although there is still the chance he did simply fall in the water drunk and drown?" Kay offered with little conviction.

Two skeptical faces stared back. Walt's death, they were all convinced, was linked to the other deaths—his pedophilic trips were beyond question. With Gerald Baker's history of pedophilia and the coincidence of his being on the island at the same time Walt died, it was too much not to conclude a link.

"So what now?"

"We wait for the DNA to prove Hilary and Charles were murdered."

"And in the meantime?"

"Keep trying to find the elusive Gerald Baker."

"The same Gerald Baker that we can find no sign of ever having been on the island in the last ten plus years, and certainly anything since the second he left prison a few weeks ago?"

"The same," replied Fitch with as much frustration as the others felt.

Chapter 15

Four days of waiting for the phone to ring with the DNA results was causing increasing tension within the office. Tempers were fraying at the lack of progress across the three currently separate investigations. Winters and Fitch were barely conversing. Mark's continuing playing away from home with Mandy, the waitress at the motel, was causing a friction that Kay wondered if they would manage to get over. Words had been said over the previous day that had resulted in her having to intervene before it became physical. Ever since, barely two words had passed between the two detectives.

"Seriously, guys, you're going to need to see a relationship counselor if you don't kiss and make up," she snapped when Fitch asked her to give Winters, who was sitting next to him, an instruction.

Before they could reply the phone rang. None of them reached to answer, all froze where they were, staring at the phone. Kay broke the spell and reached across the desk, lifting the handset and placing it to her ear. She listened intently, her face passive.

Mark and Fitch shuffled closer, their chairs colliding as they tried to listen in. They looked at each other and as men can do, the anger and upset between them dissipated in an instant and they were friends again.

"You're sure?" said Kay, confusion evident in her voice. "I'm sorry but I'd like you to re-run that test. And is there any news on the toxicology tests?" Whoever was on the other side of the phone call was clearly unhappy, but Kay stood her ground. "Yes, I'm sure, thank you."

Kay replaced the handset, her expression troubled, pondering what she had just heard.

"Well?" Fitch blurted when she failed to speak.

"It's not a match for…"

Fitch and Winters sat forward in their seats, hanging on her every word.

"Charles Ryan—"

The men jumped out of their seats and high fived, somewhat inappropriately considering they had a murder to solve.

"—or for Gerald Baker," Kay finished, deflating the elation that had filled the room.

"What do you mean not Gerald Baker. Who is it?"

"My predecessor, Deputy Larry Beaumont."

"What? Wait, sorry…what?"

"They're saying it's a one hundred percent match, no question."

"That makes no sense. We must have used evidence bags he had contaminated or something. He's an old man who was medically retired and moved to a retirement community in Florida a few months ago." Fitch shook his head. "And he'd certainly have been spotted had he been on the island, everyone knows him."

Kay shrugged, "I'm only telling you what the evidence says."

"They're re-running the tests though?" asked Winters.

"Yes, but they're not happy about it, moaning about the cost and time and the detrimental impact to other cases, and most importantly they say they don't make mistakes. And we are still waiting on the toxicology results."

"Well they must have made a mistake because that makes no sense whatsoever!" Fitch challenged.

"However, whether right or wrong, it didn't match with Charles Ryan," said Winters. "So we have another double murder and it wasn't Gerald Baker, which means another suspect as well."

"As Kay said, the toxicology results aren't back yet, so murder may be jumping the gun" Fitch cautioned. "It may still be innocent…somehow?" he questioned his own response.

"But if they are murders, it means they aren't linked. Unless they were working together?"

"Which we have no evidence to support or proof that they actually were murders," said Kay in summary.

Fitch frowned. "So we still have two very suspicious deaths, and the chance of a tragic accident becoming less and less likely."

"And no help from the FBI," summed up Winters.

"Nope, it's down to us. I'll contact the major and ask for more help to be sent. We need to get all over this now that we have one confirmed double murder scene and another scene of two deaths that is at the very least suspicious but apparently unconnected."

"And another that remains questionable."

"I suppose I should call Jackson and update him on the DNA match to Deputy Beaumont," Kay said to resigned groans from the detectives. The dynamic was going to change dramatically with additional resources coming from both the sheriff's office and state police as the investigation team was going to have to be ramped up dramatically.

"Dinner tonight?" Fitch asked Kay as he had every night he and Winters had stayed at the motel.

"That would be nice," Kay replied, surprising both men.

Winters threw Fitch a wink. Fitch rolled his eyes but not before his neck blossomed red once again.

"Excellent. Say seven at the bar?"

After one phone call to their major, Fitch and Winters updated her before saying their goodbyes, they were heading back to the motel to get ready. Why they needed to get ready she had no idea, she had no intention of getting ready and had assumed they would just have gone to dinner straight from the sheriff's office.

Men, she sighed. *Complex creatures or just too basic for their own good.*

Another far more basic creature barked a hello as the phone call she was making was answered.

"Sheriff Jackson!"

Kay updated him. For once he was quiet, the news of the match rendering him speechless. He argued how ridiculous the result was, he'd known Larry for over thirty years, considered him a friend, and had spoken to him only a few weeks ago.

"I'll call him and clear this up right now!" he barked when his argument was met with Kay's seemingly unwavering response.

"That's not a good idea, Sheriff. The detectives are in charge of the investigation, we really shouldn't interfere," she said in a conciliatory tone. As much as she didn't like him, she couldn't fault his defending of a man he considered a friend. In fact, it was the most honorable act she had witnessed since she had met him.

"Yes, of course, you're right."

"There's a Maine detective who is on vacation in Florida just an hour away, he's visiting him this evening with local police officers. Hopefully that'll clear the matter up and we are re-testing the result so it may be irrelevant in any event."

"Oh right, okay. Well I'm sure it's just a mistake." His lack of conviction matched everyone else's belief that it was highly unlikely the match would be proven wrong. A mistake was one thing but a mistake identifying one individual who recently lived on the island against any other person on the planet was infinitesimally small.

"I'll update you as soon as I hear anything," Kay promised.

"Thanks, and you'll have additional resources arriving on the first ferry tomorrow morning."

Kay replaced the handset. It was going to be a very different office moving forward, but with two confirmed separate crime scenes and a third suspected, it was more than necessary. Surprisingly, with five people dead under mysterious circumstances panic had not set in amongst the islanders. She couldn't help but think if she hadn't had to be on the island, she wasn't sure she would be. Not a helpful thought when those same islanders relied on tourist dollars, dollars that could easily be relocated if it wasn't reported soon that there wasn't a marauding band of killers targeting the island.

She looked at the clock. 6:00 p.m.. She had time to have a shower and change before meeting Fitch and Winters. Why the thought even crossed her mind she wasn't sure. Well, deep down she knew, but there were far more important things to be focusing on. She picked up the handset, replacing it before dialing.

Tomorrow, she thought. What was one night of letting her hair down.

She locked the office door behind her and was showered and wearing a figure-hugging floral summer dress when she walked into the motel bar an hour later, turning heads in her wake.

Winters saw her first; Fitch's back was to the door. Winters stopped mid-sentence, the sight of her brunette hair free and flowing like a model on a tv hair conditioning ad swept towards them.

"Holy sh…" he whistled, his wandering eye caught by Mandy the waitress, whom he had enjoyed most nights while on the island.

Fitch turned at Winters' reaction, first questioning and then shock.

"Whoa!" He rose to greet Kay. "You sure know how to make an entrance." He beamed, his pupils widening in an attempt to take as much of her beauty in at once as he could. She was stunning and far from the plain Jane façade she hid behind her bland uniform.

"May I say without sounding inappropriate you look…" he truly was lost for words.

"Amazing. Holy shit. I mean, I knew you were hiding the goods but…" Winters missed the subtlety of words Fitch was searching for.

Fitch threw him a scowl. Kay smiled awkwardly as Fitch pulled out a chair, offering her a menu after she took the seat.

"Would you like to order a drink?" asked Mandy, appearing by the table and eyeing 'her man' with a gaze that warned he had best to be very careful.

"I'll have what they're having," Kay answered, spotting the bottles of beer.

"Would you like a glass?"

"No thanks, the bottle's fine."

Mandy glared at the smile erupting on Winters' face. She could read his mind. Beautiful *and* she drank beer from the bottle. If Kay liked football, he'd have his perfect woman. However, as much as Mandy was irritated by Winters' interest in Kay, Kay had no interest in Winters. Or any man she would tell herself, however, she wasn't sure that was entirely truthful. Fitch intrigued her. The more time she spent with him, the more questions there were to answer and so far, none of the questions being raised were ones that stopped her wanting to know the answers.

Kay's beer arrived and Fitch's cell buzzed, bringing the evening to an end before Kay even managed a sip. Deputy Larry Beaumont hadn't been seen for weeks, and the mail piled up behind his front door indicated he hadn't been home since at least a couple of days after Gerald Baker was released from prison, if not before.

Chapter 16

Five minutes later they were reconvening in her office in all their finery. The timeline was worrying; the deputy and Gerald must have crossed paths in the past, must have known each other. Neither had been seen in weeks and both were at the center of a double murder and possible rape, supposedly separate crime scenes.

"There's no such thing as coincidence and this is way beyond that," said Winters, looking at the evidence on the wall.

Kay stepped toward the wall. A rough tracking of the timeline showed at least a ten-year overlap from what they knew as to when the two men had been on the island.

"I agree," said Mark, receiving a slap to the back of the head from Fitch. His eyes weren't looking at the wall or the timeline, they were fixated on Kay's body in her dress.

Kay turned on hearing the slap, her look questioning what was going on. Two sheepish faces stared back at her.

"Grow up," she commanded and Winters grinned, while Fitch's face blossomed a deep red. "Focus, guys." She turned back to the evidence wall. Angry whispers between the two erupted behind her as the two men quickly sorted out whatever was going on.

The timeline they had pieced together from what little they knew had an overlap in the nineties and early noughties for the two men. It was tenuous but at the same time compelling, and it also fit with the time the first two victims had spent on the island.

"So, do we really think they are working together?" asked Fitch.

"Some elaborate plan of revenge from twenty plus years ago?" questioned Kay, looking again at the crossover. "Although without further investigation, it may be there is something more recent."

"A cop of forty years and some pedo teaming up?" Winters shook his head. "It doesn't sound plausible."

"Unless?" Fitch prompted.

Kay and Mark turned to him, interested in his angle.

Fitch paused; he wasn't keen to say out loud what he was going to say. He held back. "Well, I don't know…"

"Let's not forget we've got a well-loved teacher, pillar of the community who we've just discovered was diddling her orphaned nephew inappropriately from a young age as well, who's to say…?" Winters also stopped short of saying it out loud, cops didn't like to think they had not spotted a dirty cop.

"Well you both knew him," Kay said pointedly, seeing both didn't want to say.

"Larry was a nice guy, always smiling, always helping. I'd never have guessed anything was amiss."

"But he remained unmarried?"

"As are you," said Winters.

"Yet surprisingly you *are* married," Kay retorted.

"Guys, let's not forget, his DNA was found at the scene."

"It wasn't exactly left there by accident," said Kay.

"Exactly," said Winters. "Larry would have known he was leaving evidence behind, it makes no sense."

"And you don't think a career sex offender would have been just as aware he was leaving semen in Valerie?" Kay noted.

"Good point," said Fitch. "None of it makes any sense."

"So we have two scenes where semen has pointed to a third party, who would have known better than to leave that evidence behind. And neither of those third parties have been seen in weeks?"

"Basically," said Fitch, with Winters nodding by his side.

"And let's not forget about Walt," said Kay, "along with his rather questionable history that we need to know a lot more about."

"We need to know a lot more about all of them," Fitch added, "including the victims."

"Agreed," came a voice from the internal doorway, startling them all. "There's something off here," Sheriff Jackson said. "Very off."

Kay's anger rose instantly. She wasn't entirely sure if he was referring to the murders or their discussion. Before she could respond, Fitch was racing towards the sheriff. Apparently Kay wasn't the only one to have read more into what the sheriff was saying.

Winters managed to grab Fitch just in time, his outstretched fingers getting enough of a hold as Fitch exploded towards the sheriff, who raised his arms in mock surprise.

"What?" said Sheriff Jackson.

Kay glared at him. "You never said you were coming tonight."

"Do I need permission?"

"No, but I'd have—"

"Dressed for the occasion?" Jackson eyed Kay with disapproval.

"We were off duty having dinner when we got the news about—"

"Don't defend yourself to this asshole" Fitch snarled, while Winters struggled to restrain him.

Jackson stalked towards Fitch. "Who are you calling an asshole!" he demanded.

Winters got between the two men. Jackson was a towering figure, but Fitch was a powerful guy, well-built, and more than able to handle himself.

Kay could see it was only going one way and realized she was going to have to intervene. Whatever was going on here there was history, a history that was deep rooted and steeped in unbridled hatred.

"Let's dial it down a bit, guys," she said, stepping between the two. She only realized her intervention was too late when the first punch thrown sent her crashing to the floor. At least she succeeded in one thing, it ended the fight before it started.

All three men leapt to her aid, feeling awful for their behavior, none more so than Fitch, who had thrown the punch.

Chapter 17

Kay stared into the mirror. The redness on her jaw was clear to see, and there was little to no likelihood it wasn't going to bruise.

"I'm so sorry." Fitch's hundredth apology was muffled by the door between them.

"Fitch, it's fine, I'll be fine." Pain accompanied each word spoken. "Please, go back to the hotel. We can pick up where we left off tomorrow. Well, not *exactly* where we left..." She almost laughed but the action was too painful and a small groan emitted instead.

"Oh no, I'm so sorry." Fitch banged his head against the door, distraught at having caused her pain.

"Come on." Winters guided him away from the restroom door, an arm wrapped around him. It was a toss-up as to who had fared worst as a result of the punch, Kay or Fitch. From the state of him, Winters was guessing Fitch. He was inconsolable.

Kay had taken the hit well. Despite going down she had been back on her feet straight away and it hadn't been a light punch. Fitch had put his weight behind it, he had meant to take Jackson down.

If nothing else the incident had cleared some air that had needed clearing for some time. However, the air between them would never be fully cleared, there was no chance that would ever happen, but at least for the short term it appeared the two men would tolerate each other's presence. Jackson was good enough to accept Fitch's apology, both for the attempting to hit him and for hitting his deputy.

Ensuring Kay was okay, Jackson had excused himself and left to secure a room for the night. Winters struggled to remove Fitch. He wasn't going to leave until Kay came out of the restroom. Since Kay wasn't going to leave the restroom until they had left, they were at an impasse, hence Winters physically removing Fitch from the sheriff's office.

"Kay, are you sure you're okay?" he called before shutting the door.

"Yes," she called back as loudly as her aching jaw would allow.

She heard the door shut and relaxed. It wasn't the first time she'd been hit, but was for the first time in a long time. Her biggest worry was whether her jaw had been broken again. A third time would be harder to fix, or at least the doctor had advised her the previous time to try and be more careful.

She checked the mirror again. The skin around her jawline was red and she could feel a swelling forming, but it didn't feel like bone, only swollen tissue. It certainly wasn't like the last time, involving a surgical intervention and her jaw being wired for weeks. She breathed a sigh of relief. She'd have some bruising but nothing make-up wouldn't take care of.

She opened the bathroom door and revisited what had taken place in her mind. The level of anger didn't match the scenario. There was definitely something there they weren't telling her, history between the two that was barely below the surface of civility. She'd speak to Winters, she knew Fitch was a closed book, the man was so uptight he'd... Kay almost laughed at her own thoughts, and would have had it not hurt when she did. He was wound up so tight he had nearly knocked her out. Yet despite his actions, she was even more intrigued by the enigma that was Maine State Police Lieutenant Ross Abercrombie, reluctantly known as Fitch.

She locked both doors behind her, not even taking a parting look at the evidence wall. After the day she'd had, she'd definitely had enough, and morning would be more than soon enough. She had a bottle of Pinot Grigio in the fridge with her name on it. Actually two, but she'd kid herself only one was needed for the beginning.

Her cottage was in darkness when she pulled up, like most evenings, but there was something not right. Kay hesitated before opening her truck. She put her hand on her hip. Her thin summer dress was not the reassuring feel of cold metal she was hoping for. She checked her glovebox, knowing there was nothing there. Her pistol was in the cottage, along with her uniform, radio, and every other piece of equipment she'd normally be wearing. Numerous items, her belts, badges, shirts, vests etc…instead she was wearing exactly two items of clothing, a thong that she'd lose if she wasn't wearing it, and the light summer dress. She was to all intents and purposes naked, given the sheerest covering of fabric possible.

She flicked a switch and illuminated the swivel light on the side of her door. Its beam shot out into the darkness, offering a spot by spot view of the surroundings. She angled the light around and caught the side of the cottage, the whiteness of the paintwork blazing in the gaze of the beam. A shuffling to the right of the beam caught her attention and she swung the beam sharply towards the noise. Movement beat her but there was definitely something there. She swept faster but the side of the cottage obscured her view. Whatever it was had bolted down the side out of view.

Kay had two choices: get out of the truck and tackle whatever was there or head back to the tidewater and get assistance from at least two if not three other law enforcement officers. She could hear them, *of course we'll come and escort you home, after all it is dark out there.* She'd never gain their respect if she didn't do what a male officer would do.

Kay climbed out of the truck.

A chill wind caught the back of her neck, her hairs instantly rising. The chill passed through the fabric sending a shiver across her body. She shook it off but the chill added to her unease. She wanted to be inside with her pistol in her hand.

"Who's there?" she called.

A blast of the chill wind was all she received in response, pushing her onwards down the short path to her front door. She reached for the key, she had no pockets. She could have screamed at her stupidity, the keys were back in the truck. A gust of wind caught her dress and sent it upwards, and she had to catch it at the back to maintain her dignity, although in the pitch darkness she wasn't sure from whom.

Kay was about to walk back to the truck when she tried the door. It swung open, offering no resistance. It wasn't locked. She racked her mind, had she locked it? Did she always lock it? Her mind was playing tricks, the darkness, the chill, her potential concussion from being nearly knocked out. It all added up, even down to her trying the door. If she didn't sometimes leave it unlocked why would she have tried it?

She stepped into the small hallway, flicking the light switch and illuminating the area. Her holster and pistol were exactly where she had left them. Nothing had been disturbed. Everything looked fine. She turned to close the door behind her, relief that the darkness was simply playing with her, and spotted something laying on the porch. She bent down for a closer look. A cell phone? The back of a phone. She picked it up, the screen below shone in the darkness, the cell was on. She stepped back into the light and the screen lit up, it was recording what it was seeing, her feet as she walked into the light from the darkness of the porch. She slammed the door shut and threw the bolt to secure it before grabbing for her pistol.

Chapter 18

The banging on the door was loud enough to raise the dead, which was exactly what was needed. Winters had been there for ten minutes and had woken all but one person in the motel trying to get a response from the one person he was attempting to wake. Fitch.

He was about to opt for more drastic options when the door cracked open and a gray and unkempt Fitch looked out. A sorry sight and certainly not worthy of his nickname.

"About time…oh hell, you look like shit," said Winters.

"Uh-huh." Fitch was in no mood to argue, whatever he needed to say to get Winters to leave he'd do.

"I'm afraid we've got another victim." Winters sighed, a look of despair in his face.

Fitch woke instantly, throwing the door open to let Winters enter and update him properly. His hangover instantly lifted. He still felt awful he just had to prioritize what was important.

"Who?" he asked. Kay wasn't present and he hadn't missed that fact. With a thousand people on the island there was a one in one thousand chance it was her, but given what had happened the previous night, he had already convinced himself if it was going to be her, the worst time it could possibly happen was after he had almost knocked her out. Hence, the most likely candidate in his mind was Kay. It was the type of luck he had. He'd already experienced something like it.

"Old Judge Francis Wright," said Winters gravely.

Fitch steadied himself against the doorframe. "Oh thank the lord," he uttered, surprising Winters at his apparent relief a judge had died.

Fitch straightened, realizing his reaction was inappropriate. "I of course mean that's terrible, but I just thought it may have been…"

"Someone less deserving?"

"No, I was just worried it may have been—"

"Jeez, who died?" Kay said, seeing the seriousness of their faces as she approached them in the motel corridor.

"Apparently nobody we should be bothered about," Winters grumbled.

"That's not what I said!" Kay's appearance had awoken Fitch from his cloud in an instant. The redness on her jaw was visible, a slight tinge of purple beginning to invade. It was going to be a seriously impressive mark of his assault. "Kay, I'm so sorry about—"

"Forget it. It was a bit raw for makeup." She motioned with her hand towards the bruise, careful not to touch it.

Fitch's face fell from his already despairing look of contrition.

"Sorry, I was just explaining why I hadn't put makeup on, I wasn't meaning to make you feel worse. It was an accident, I know you had no intention of hitting me." She stepped between the two men and put her hand on Fitch's shoulder. "To be honest I was sort of hoping you'd swing for him."

Fitch didn't buy it. He raised his hand tenderly towards her damaged jawline, Kay pulled back.

"Come on, buddy," said Winters. "I think we should move on, we have got a new victim after all."

Kay spun around. "What? You weren't joking, there is another victim?"

Winters nodded. "Retired judge, Francis Wright, although his nickname, ironically, was Judge Wrong."

"Murdered?"

"No idea. Motel owner just gave me the news. He knew we were here and let me know the judge's nurse found him. He was in his eighties, so if I had to guess, probably not."

"But you did say victim," Fitch said.

"Well, you know, victim to the island, whether killed or not, I suppose?" Winters shrugged.

Kay sighed. "So where is he?"

"Not far from your place. His house is one of the larger on the island overlooking Lane's Island."

"Let's go."

"Would you mind giving me five minutes to get ready?" Fitch asked sheepishly, having only recently stirred from his slumber.

"Of course, we'll see you in the car." Kay flashed him the million-dollar version of her smile.

"Whoa, he'll need more than five if you throw him come ons like that!" smirked Winters, punching Fitch playfully on the arm.

Fitch quickly closed the door without another word.

Kay turned to Winters in disgust. "Really? Do you think that was appropriate? I'm right here and do not appreciate the innuendo, thank you very much." She marched off.

Winters was left standing on his own in the hallway bewildered. He thought it was one of his funnier lines and couldn't quite understand why the two were so touchy, unless they really did like each other. He grinned. It was past time Fitch moved on.

Winters joined Kay in the parking lot and jumped in the back of her truck. Fitch arrived moments later, his hair still wet from his Olympic record setting speed shower.

"Jeez, you knocked that one out quick." Winters smirked. He was on fire.

"Grow up, Mark," Fitch snapped, climbing into the passenger seat, avoiding Kay's gaze.

Kay herself was doing her best to avoid both of their gazes. She couldn't help herself, Winters' line was funny, perfectly timed, and Fitch's angry reply only made it all the funnier. She broke into a bout of giggles, struggling to contain herself during what she knew was a completely inappropriate moment.

The more she giggled the angrier Fitch got at Winters, who himself was bent over double in the back of the jeep sharing Kay's amusement.

Fitch composed himself. A man had died and they were laughing like schoolchildren. It had been a stressful period of time, too many deaths in such a short window.

He turned to Kay. She had always been so earnest, it was so unlike her. Her face glowed as she giggled. Her smile was infectious, her eyes sparkled, and a warmth shone from her. He felt her warmth, it was a feeling that felt alien to him. Fitch shuffled uncomfortably in his seat; he hadn't felt anyone breaking through his exterior since…that night. He closed his eyes to shut out the image that was building, soaked in their laughter, imagined the joy they were feeling. He blocked out the memories and lived for the moment. His lips quivering, he broke into a smile, gradually embracing the giggles before all three of them let go in uncontrollable laughter.

A knock on the window was barely audible, and Kay turned to find John Gilder staring back. She wound down the window.

"A man died and you three are sitting here, I don't even know what…"

"Sorry, you had to be there," Winters offered as a justification.

"What with the dead judge?" replied an indignant John Gilder. "He was a friend of mine!"

Kay pulled herself together and composed herself. "Sorry, you're right, but this was nothing to do with the death of your friend, we're going there now."

"I'm sorry for your loss," said Fitch, managing to contain himself. "We'll update you on our return."

Kay picked up on Fitch's lead. "Yes, I'm sorry for your loss too. I never met Judge Wrong, but I hear he was a lovely man."

Winters' explosion into a new bout of laughter was her first sign she had used the judge's nickname rather than his real name; the second was John Gilders stalking off without another word.

"Racist, misogynist, bastard are only a few of the words you'll hear to describe Judge Francis Wright. Trust me, you'll never hear lovely. Interesting that he wanted us to know he was a friend," Fitch mused as he watched Gilder retreat towards the motel in anger. "Not many would ever want to admit that."

"Was he that bad?"

"Worse," said Winters. "They had a party the day *after* he left the courthouse to celebrate the fact he wasn't there anymore. You'll not find a soul who would have a good word to say about the man."

"Not entirely true," Fitch countered. "There're a few wife beaters and Klansmen who may disagree."

Winters nodded.

"Oh, right." Kay laughed ironically. "Or should I say wrong."

Glaring at them from the motel's main entrance, John Gilder was definitely not amused that they were not treating the death of Judge Wright with the honor he felt appropriate.

Fitch sat up straight and composed himself. "I suppose we should go see what finally killed the old bastard."

After five previously questionable deaths, the sixth was to become, without question, their first clear cut murder, despite the scene being the most innocent.

Chapter 19

It was an imposing home and certainly one of the most impressive on the island. Huge windows filled the frontage, taking full advantage of the spectacular views afforded its exceptional positioning. This was a house that had been built for one purpose—to take advantage of its location. Two massive storm doors took center spot, the owners fully understanding that there was a downside to the unencumbered views from which the house benefited.

The views south towards the ocean and Lane's Island Reserve were breathtaking and the sight of Gerald's cottage, the scene of Frank and Valerie's demise, sitting just across the bridge was missed by none of them.

Kay pulled to a stop.

"Was it really only a few weeks ago we met for the first time?" asked Fitch.

"Oh sweet." Winters laughed. "He's keeping track of when we all first met."

Before he could respond to save his embarrassment, a woman rushed towards them, tears streaming down her face, the storm door flapping in her eagerness to exit the house.

Kay jumped out and embraced her. The woman was in her fifties and inconsolable, her body heaving as she struggled to catch her breath.

"He…he…he's just sitting there, not moving," she sobbed, each word accompanied by another attempt at a deep breath.

Fitch and Winters caught up with Kay and did their best to help comfort the woman but there was no consoling her. Kay led her to the truck and asked her to sit for a moment and try to calm down.

Meanwhile, Fitch and Winters donned white coveralls and gloves and headed towards the house. Fitch pushed open the door and led the way. The solid oak storm doors ensured little light invaded the hallway but a light to their left directed them into the great room where sitting unceremoniously all but naked for all to see was Judge Francis Wright. His robe was unsecured and had fallen open, leaving nothing to the imagination.

"Well that's not an image I ever want to keep in my head," Winters remarked.

The judge's head was propped against the side of his armchair, a deathly stare thrown to the floor by the wide-eyed corpse.

"I think we can safely say there's no need for a paramedic," said Fitch. "You can tell them not to rush."

While Winters called it in, Fitch circled the body. No obvious signs of a struggle or a reason for the death was evident. It was going to be one for the medical examiner to call.

"Is it okay to come in?" Kay called.

Having made his call, Winters guided her to the body. "Be warned, we've got little Judge Wrong on full show."

"Ignore him!," instructed Fitch with a sigh. "How is she?"

Kay glanced at the corpse, his naked body exposed for all to see, and then out towards the truck where the carer was staring out to sea and unaware of Kay's gaze. "Something's off. Call it women's intuition, but if I didn't know better, I'd say we're being played."

Fitch looked at her curiously. "Played how?"

"I don't know, it just didn't seem real. The whole struggling to catch a breath, panic, I mean, it's not like she just found him, she called it in half an hour ago. It was just a bit over the top. She's his carer, a professional carer, not his wife or daughter. And even then, from what she told me, just for the last few months."

Fitch looked at the woman. Her gaze was fixed in the opposite direction, apparently not wanting to look back towards the house and scene of the death. "Maybe she's never found a dead body?"

"I asked how much experience she's had. Over twenty years working in care homes and with the elderly. So it's not that."

"So what are you saying?"

"I'm saying it stinks and I think she's good for it."

"No visible signs of death. Even if there were, we've got five deaths prior to this one. Are you saying she's involved in any of them?"

"No, this is different. I think she's using that as cover. I mean, why would she leave him like that? Why would she not cover him up? Because it fits with the story she heard about Hilary and Charles, both found naked. She's a carer, she knew he was dead, and being an old man, there's every chance he simply died of old age, so why not pull his robe over him, maintain his dignity?"

"She was worried it was a crime scene," Winters stated.

"He was a horrible person," said Fitch.

"She's singing his praises out there. Wonderful man, never got on so well with a client, couldn't have been nicer to her, she'll miss him, his stories and his jokes," Kay said.

She walked around the great room, thinking through the scenario and the conversation she had had with the carer. She paused. "She said she came into the house as normal, went straight to the kitchen to prepare his breakfast, went upstairs to give it to him in bed as normal, and found he wasn't there. She searched the house and found him in his favorite chair in the great room."

Fitch shrugged. "All of that sounds completely plausible."

"So where have you been in the house?" she asked.

"Just this room so far," said Winters.

"I'd have thought you'd have gone to the bedroom. Old man found dead in the morning, usually in bed, no?"

"Yes," said Fitch, seeing where Kay was going. "We came in here because the light was shining from in here."

"So what? The carer put the light on," reasoned Winters.

"No. I asked her what she touched in the room she found him as it was a very important part of the investigation, anything that she may have touched could be crucial. I was very precise, as was she. She definitely did not turn it on because, and I quote, 'not even the light switch because strangely they were already on.'"

"And?"

"Well I did the same as you, came into the dark hallway and immediately followed the light."

"But she's been working here for months, maybe the light's always on." Winters posed, playing devil's advocate.

Kay shook her head. "Remember, she told me it was strange they were on, yet she never investigated."

"The doors were shut?" Winters looked to the hallway. "Oh, there are no doors," he noted. "It's open plan."

"Exactly. Yet in her own words it was strange. It hit me as I walked into the house, and when you put it all together, I just don't think it adds up." Kay motioned to the carer. "*She* doesn't add up."

"Mark, run a check on her," said Fitch. "Contact previous employers, see if there is anything there. In the meantime, other than your hunch, Kay, we've got an elderly man dead with no sign of any trauma."

"No sign being the key words," Kay emphasized.

"I'll keep your suspicions in mind," said Fitch. "Let's get the doctor in here and get a professional view. In the meantime, let's have a look around and see if there is anything at all that appears suspicious, otherwise it is going to go down as a death by natural causes, no foul play."

A squeal of tires outside caught their attentions. Sheriff Jackson's truck came to an abrupt halt behind Kay's truck. He jumped out and bounded towards the house, ignoring the occupant of Kay's vehicle.

Fitch rushed towards the front door.

Kay sighed deeply. "Oh no, not again."

Fitch beat Jackson to the door and raised his arm to stop his entry.

"What the hell are you playing at, Fitch?" Jackson shouted in anger, coming to a stop on the steps.

Fitch raised both hands in conciliation. "I'm not stopping you coming in. Well, I am, but only because you have no protective gear on."

Jackson looked down at himself. "Oh, yeah, okay. Give me two minutes."

"God, I thought you were going to start all over." Kay took a breath of relief from behind Fitch.

"It's early yet." Fitch winked. "So, where we? Oh yeah, unless we find anything untoward, death by natural causes."

Winters nodded, while Kay folded her arms and stared at her truck and the carer looking out to sea. "This isn't connected to any of the others," she said firmly. "It's not going on the wall with the others until you prove otherwise."

Fitch was concerned Kay was losing perspective. "Let me have a chat with her," he said, leaving Winters and Kay to bring the quickly approaching white image that was Jackson up to speed.

"Why the hell didn't you call me?" he fumed at Kay.

"Honestly, I forgot you were on the island, it all happened pretty quickly."

"Hmm," he eyed Winters. "But you did remember tweedle dumb and tweedle dee I see."

"Detectives Abercrombie and Winters are the ones who informed me about the body."

Jackson turned to Winters questioningly.

"John Gilder at the motel informed me. Actually, he tried you, but apparently your bed hadn't been slept in. He assumed you had gone back to the mainland."

Jackson's face dropped. He, like Winters, was a married man. Unlike Winters, however, he was an elected official and claimed to be a staunch Christian, pro marriage and pro life. Whatever his nocturnal goings on had been, it was unlikely they fit with his public persona.

Jackson quickly changed the subject. "So, the old coot, Judge Wrong, is gone?"

"You weren't a fan?" asked Kay, surprised.

"I may be an asshole at times, and I know I'm not the easiest guy to get on with, but Judge Wrong? Shit, that man was in a league of his own."

As the others had done before him, he followed the light from the dimly lit hallway into the great room.

"Whoa, so that's a sight you want a warning is coming," he said, dramatically recoiling from the naked corpse. "I see we have a true 'little man syndrome.' Explains a lot," he laughed.

While Jackson had a look around, Kay and Winters turned their attention to the view out the window, watching Fitch's interaction with the carer with fascination. The carer was undoubtedly distressed by Fitch's questioning and ended up with him spending most of his time consoling the woman.

"So what's the thoughts?" Jackson asked, then "Who's the lady?" when he saw where they were looking. "To be honest, I thought Fitch could do better."

"The carer," Kay replied, ignoring the jibes. "She called it in."

"Poor woman, finding him like that." Jackson motioned to the judge.

"Hmm, we'll see."

Fitch finally managed to disengage himself and rejoined his colleagues in the house, his face impassive.

"Well?" Kay pressed.

"No question," he said confidently. "She did it."

Chapter 20

Jackson looked at the body of the judge and back to his law enforcement colleagues. "What do you mean she did it?"

"It doesn't add up. What she says, the body exposed, her behavior, it just all seems…off," said Kay.

Jackson shook his head. "We've had six deaths in the space of a few weeks, four definitely suspicious, another questionable. Finally, we have a nice, simple death of an old man and you guys have this one pegged straight away as a murder?"

"Have a chat with her," Fitch urged.

"What will she tell me, she killed him?"

"No, but you'll see this isn't a simple death of an old man."

"He's old and he's dead, not a mark on him. No sign of any struggle. Doesn't come simpler. There are more signs of violence on Deputy Miller than the judge," Jackson said scathingly.

Fitch's face dropped. The bruise on Kay's jaw was blossoming in line with his remorse every passing minute. "That was an accident, and if remember correctly I took that hit instead of you," said Kay pointedly to her larger and imposing boss.

Buoyed by Kay's defense, Fitch replied confidently, "We'll see what the autopsy says. In the meantime, I don't want *her*," he pointed to the carer in Kay's truck, "to leave the island."

"An autopsy? Oh for Chrissakes, you guys have lost it. You're all spending too much time together." Jackson left without another word.

They watched him walk down the path, his cell phone affixed to his ear and he was gesticulating wildly as he climbed into his truck.

"Well, that was helpful," said Fitch.

"Maybe he has a point?" Winters said hesitantly. He hadn't thrown his weight behind the murder theory as yet.

"Don't you fu—"

Kay raised a hand. "Guys…guys, let's keep it calm, okay?"

Fitch nodded to Winters. "Go get the doctor." Turning to Kay, he said, "You and I will have a look to see if there's anything suspicious."

After an hour of searching the house, nothing appeared amiss, no clear evidence existed to suggest that Judge Wright had died of anything other than natural causes. From his preliminary exam the doctor found nothing untoward, and unless the autopsy found otherwise, it did seem as though the judge had simply died of natural causes.

"Can we get the body on the next ferry and up to Augusta please?" Fitch said to the paramedic team as they carried the judge's remains out of the great room on a stretcher.

The paramedics looked at the doctor, who asked, "Why Augusta?"

"The medical examiner," said Fitch. "For the autopsy."

"But there's no crime here and no suspicious circumstance," the doctor said with some confusion.

"I think you'll find that is for me to decide."

The doctor looked increasingly uncomfortable and stuttered, "Hmm, well…I-I believe it is for the sheriff to decide in Knox County. Only then would the state detectives become involved…no?"

"Well, technically that's true. However, given we are on site and attended this scene…" Fitch shrugged.

"Does that mean you have the lead here?" asked the doctor. It was becoming increasingly clear who Jackson had called when he left the house. The doctor was stuck in between two egos and unfortunately for Fitch, one had clear legal jurisdiction.

Fitch glanced at Winters and Kay, unsure. He only ever went to scenes he had been requested to attend by local law enforcement. Although requested here it was not by a law enforcement agency, it was by a member of the public.

Winters shrugged and looked at Kay.

"I'm new here, don't look at me!"

Fitch pulled out his cell and dialed a number. "Hey, Bill," he began.

Kay looked at Winters questioningly. "Bill Hutchison maybe," Winters whispered. "He's the medical examiner for Knox County."

"Bill, I understand you're busy and a hunch doesn't cut it but come on, we've got five suspicious deaths here. Surely that in itself warrants an autopsy for the judge." Fitch listened, and when he spoke again his voice sounded more and more exasperated. "Well no, I am not saying we believe they are linked."

Kay could fill in the pauses given Fitch's responses.

"Well nothing is absolute until it's definitely ruled out, obviously."

Kay guessed the question had been 'so you're saying they're not linked?"

"I'll call you back." Fitch banged the end button to expel his frustration. He turned to face his colleagues and the doctor who were waiting for his update. "He'll do an autopsy, but only if we say we believe the judge is potentially linked to the other cases."

"Which we don't. We're one hundred percent certain he's not and his carer in some way or another is involved."

"Can someone decide please!" asked one of the paramedics, still holding the stretcher.

"Take him to the funeral home in Rockland," instructed the doctor. "They can store the body there in their morgue while the detectives work out what's to happen." He washed his hands of making a final decision on the spot.

When the paramedics looked to Fitch for confirmation, the tiniest of nods was the best he could muster. It was more than adequate for the straining paramedics to get moving to release them of the burden of the judge's weight.

Kay huffed in frustration. "She's going to get away with murder."

"No she's not, we just need to find something," said Fitch.

"And quick," advised the doctor, closing the door behind him.

"Let's dig into her history, check with previous employers," said Fitch.

"In the meantime, what do we do with her?" Kay asked, motioning to her truck.

"Unless we can find evidence otherwise, nothing. The sheriff has ruled it natural causes."

"Then how do we justify asking for her previous employment and details?"

"She doesn't know what Jackson ruled as yet. Kay, are you fine with asking her for the information?"

"Sure, no problem. Leave her to me."

"Okay. While you talk to her, we'll wrap things up."

Kay walked out to the truck. The carer, she noted, was no longer staring out to sea, she was watching Kay and her colleagues' every movement with great interest.

"Hey, how you doing?"

"Fine, thanks," replied the carer. The tears and redness were gone from her eyes.

"Good. You're looking better as well." Kay smiled sympathetically. "I just need to get a few more details, if that's okay?"

"Of course, what do you need?"

Kay unbuttoned the breast pocket of her shirt and retrieved her notebook and pen. "I need to make a note of your previous address and employ—"

"Why would you need that, is there a problem?"

"No, just standard stuff," Kay said nonchalantly, trying to cover the anything but usual request given the sheriff's finding.

The carer shuffled across the seat towards Kay, brushing her out of her way as she exited. "The sheriff ruled it natural causes. You don't need anything else from me. Any other 'standard stuff'"— she made air quotation marks with her hands—"speak to my lawyer."

"Oh, you have a lawyer?"

"Yes, and a very expensive one. Very good at winning harassment claims, among other things."

"Other things? That sounds interesting."

"Am I under arrest or are you going to detain me?"

Kay stepped back. "Not yet."

Fitch and Winters had noticed things hadn't gone according to their plan and decided to hang back and watch from the steps rather than further inflame the already heated situation.

The carer ignored their presence on the steps, barged past them, and closed the storm doors, shouting "Get off my property!"

Kay had followed the carer and stopped short of following her back into the house, instead staring wide eyed at her brazen performance. An audible click from the storm doors hinted they had just been locked.

"Did she just say *my* property?!?" the three of them echoed in unison.

Chapter 21

Thoughts of the judge and the carer dissipated quickly on arrival at the sheriff's office. Two Maine state detective vehicles and a Knox County detective car awaited them, along with six eager faces.

"Looks like we're going to need a bigger office," Fitch quipped.

Kay was on her cell, having had the exact same thought. "Hey, Maggie, would it be okay if we requisitioned the town hall for the foreseeable future?"

"Uhh, I'm not sure, Kay," Maggie replied hesitantly. *"Normally Charles would deal with those types of requests."*

Given Charles Ryan, the recently deceased town manager, was unreachable, that wasn't really going to help Kay.

"Maggie, Charles is gone and you're covering his role. It is your decision to make." Maggie was a great number two, however, she was not going to succeed Charles, mainly because she had made it abundantly clear she had no interest in doing so.

"Please run it by John, he's the elected official who can make that decision," Maggie politely and somewhat apologetically advised, ending the call.

"What's wrong?" Fitch asked when he saw Kay looking at her cell after the call had ended.

"Maggie, the town clerk just said something that may help us," she said.

"Are you going to tell us or just leave us hanging?" prompted Winters when Kay didn't elaborate.

"It was John Gilder who told you about the judge?" she asked.

He nodded. "Yeah."

"What exactly did he say?"

"He said...let me think, 'I've just had a call Judge Wright has been found dead.' To which I replied, in retrospect maybe not my best timing, you must be wrong."

Fitch rubbed his forehead in despair.

"Yeah, he didn't appreciate it and then became a bit more officious and said can we please deal with it."

Kay smiled. "So the elected official of the island asked you to deal with it."

"Does he have power over and above the sheriff?" asked Fitch, seeing where Kay was going.

Kay shrugged. "I'm used to cities and police departments. All these elected officials from county, state, and whatever is beyond me but it's certainly an angle to try."

Fitch was already calling the doctor, not wasting a moment. He wanted the body to go straight to Augusta and not stop at the morgue. Any delay or diversion could impact any potential incriminating evidence.

While Fitch tried to change the judge's destination Kay called Gilder. It wasn't a request as such, there really was no alternative. The town hall was to become the investigation epicenter and all other events and meetings would have to be rescheduled with immediate effect.

Kay and Winters left Fitch to what had become a heated discussion and after brief introductions commenced the move from the sheriff's office on one side of town to the slightly larger town hall on the other.

Fitch joined them mid-move. "Didn't work," he grumbled, having gotten nowhere with the doctor. "As far as the doctor is concerned it's for the medical examiner to make the call, not him. Anyway, perhaps we should focus on the murders we definitely do have in the meantime and get these guys to work."

After a few hours of maneuvering desks, chairs, and tables through the tight corridors, and with the assistance of the local cable provider, the town hall had become to all intents and purposes the new sheriff's office.

After the cable employee hooked up the last desk phone and left with their thanks, Fitch called the team to order.

"Okay, okay, settle down, people. You can sort your desks and wi-fi connections soon enough. First things first, let's get a rundown, a quick summary of where we are and what we know. Kay, do you want to kick off?" he asked.

Kay stood and proceeded to run through the events of the Memorial Day weekend and the deaths of the first two victims, husband and wife, Frank and Valerie.

Fitch took over when she got to the part where his involvement in the investigation began. "For those of you haven't heard, which I doubt you haven't," to which he received a few laughs,"—Frank's last few hours had become somewhat of an urban legend, "I'm afraid the story is nowhere near as hideous as the reality. This was a truly horrifying death you would not wish on your worst enemy."

Fitch detailed the crime scene, running through the numerous photos displayed on the wall and how they had initially concluded that the victims had murdered one another.

"As you know, it took some time for the semen sample results to identify a third party that has subsequently re-opened both cases as homicides with one suspect at large, one Gerald Baker. Given the time between our initial findings and the appearance of the evidence linking Baker, we're in catch up mode here. We have the evidence from the scene but we're two weeks behind Baker than we would have been otherwise. But before we delve further into Baker, let's cover the other scenes. Kay?"

"The following day, I received another early morning call. Another body had been found…" Kay proceeded to run through the scene as she had found it, pointing out the relevant photos from Walt's honorary portion of the wall. "Initially," she continued, "we considered the death an accident, but the more we discover about Walt, the more we believe his death should remain within the scope of our investigations."

A few of the officers looked on questioningly, wondering what it was that had been discovered.

"We'll come back to the links as we see them," Fitch said, wanting to keep the process moving. Hands were being raised but he waved them down. "Let's get through the crime scenes. Please take notes of any questions you want to ask. As you'll be aware, a few days ago, Hilary Cantrell and Charles Ryan were found dead in Booth's Quarry. Initially it also looked like no other parties were involved, but just like our first scene, not all was what it seemed. More and more questions were raised, and with them, revelations were uncovered, right up until last night when we received the results of a DNA test done on the semen found at the scene."

Fitch had them in the palm of his hand, they hung on his every word. Knox County was a small population of people who pretty much knew everything about everybody. These officers and deputies were about to find out previously unreported information and ultimately the reason all six had been told to report to an island where they were to be stationed for an indeterminate amount of time away from their family and loved ones, to solve what was quickly becoming the biggest case in the state of Maine in as long as any of them could remember.

"Retired Deputy Larry Beaumont was a match for the semen at the scene." Fitch paused and let the still confidential information sink in. From the surprise on their faces, it was clear Sheriff Jackson had managed to keep the news to himself.

"We have been unable to trace Beaumont, and from what we can gather, he has not been seen for some weeks. This coincides with the disappearance of Gerald Baker. I should also point out we can find no evidence that either man has been on the island."

"Other than their DNA," said Kay, "which is pretty good evidence they were. However, we can find no other evidence."

"Yes, we have their DNA but that is it, nothing else to prove they were here." Hands shot up. "Okay, one at a time."

Fitch pointed to one of the Knox County detectives, a recent graduate and whom he knew to be the son of a former head of the sheriff's CID division.

"Detective Kyle Moore," he announced helpfully. "I heard Judge Wright died, is there—"

"We do not believe there is any connection to these cases," Fitch cut in.

"Natural causes?" Kyle asked as a follow up.

"Let's just say we are confident his death is completely unconnected."

As the questions moved back to the main cases, Fitch, Kay, and Winters answered numerous other questions, none, they were relieved to note, were any they had failed to anticipate.

"In summary, we have three separate scenes. One double murder and another double death scene, suspicious but not yet confirmed as murder, and a third questionable death. All apparently are unconnected. However, all of them have one thing in common, one that, to be honest, fills me with disgust. Somewhere in each of them it would appear we have a pedophilic angle. Gerald Baker was a convicted offender, Walt Spencer associated with a number of convicted pedophiles and if we ever gain access to his computer we assume we will find evidence that he has to date successfully hidden. Finally, Hilary Cantrell was Charles Ryan's aunt and it is clear she was abusing him sexually from a young age. Three separate scenes, all unconnected but with one common thread. Although there is no reason to believe that thread links them, Hilary was a victim, while Gerald Baker is obviously the suspect, and Walt remains only under suspicion, we have no concrete evidence. Hence the FBI do not see fit to link them unless we do find more of a common thread."

Kyle's hand shot up. "My dad served with him and I knew him growing up. Most of the kids around here called him Uncle Larry."

"We've had that mentioned a couple of times," Winters noted.

"Yeah, but he was the uncle you wouldn't let babysit your kids, if you know what I mean." Kyle frowned. "My dad just used to laugh it off and say 'different times.'"

"We certainly hadn't heard that," said Kay, glancing over at Fitch and Winters.

That nugget of information had just given them a potential connection between Larry Beaumont and Gerald Baker they had been missing.

Chapter 22

They had spent the rest of the day allocating tasks and running down any potential leads that may have led them to the whereabouts of Larry Beaumont who, despite his previous law enforcement status, was now a suspect wanted for questioning in the suspicious deaths of two citizens he had spent his working life protecting on Vinalhaven.

Sheriff Jackson had arrived back on the island for a flying visit following his unannounced departure that morning after scuppering Fitch's autopsy plans.

He walked into the room to high fives and 'hey Boss' from his two detectives who had recently been allocated to the team.

"Are you bringing your investigatory genius to the effort?" Fitch asked with disdain, his best attempt to be civil.

"No, I think you've got more than enough of my resources. Between Kyle and Dan, you have the A team!" He high-fived his guys, then turned back to Fitch. Kay had stepped out from behind Fitch where he previously hadn't seen her. Her arms were folded firmly.

"And Kay, of course, goes without saying." He smiled and moved to high-five her, she kept her arms folded.

"Still got it with the ladies I see," Winters cracked, laughing.

Fitch threw Winters a look that could kill. "I've got calls to make," he said meekly before walking away like a wounded animal.

Kay watched him walk out and noted that the interaction had not buoyed the sheriff. He too looked somewhat crestfallen by Winters' attempt at humor. Whatever history existed between the two men was clearly unresolved and serious.

Winters followed Fitch, he absolutely had repair work to undertake, leaving Kay with Jackson.

Jackson regained his composure and the arrogance returned. "I've got a trunk full of paperwork for you," he said. "Forty years of Larry Beaumont's work with the sheriff's office, the majority of it on the island. Whatever you guys need here, you let us know and you'll get it ASAP."

"Thanks," Kay replied. She wasn't sure she had seen the sheriff so helpful before. Whether it was for her, a show for the detectives, or even some conciliatory reaction to whatever the hell had just happened, she didn't know or care. She had the information for the task she had been allocated—going through Larry Beaumont's service history. Kay was the only person on the team who hadn't met, served with, or known him.

She followed Jackson out to his SUV, which he had parked next to hers to transfer the boxes of files. She opened her trunk; her GPR machine was taking up the majority of the space available.

"What's that?" asked Jackson, instantly intrigued.

"Oh nothing, it's just a hobby of mine." She guided him away. "I've got plenty of room on the back seats."

Sheriff Jackson stood firm. "But what is it?"

"It's like a modern metal detector," she said vaguely.

"So you're a treasure hunter?"

"Historical hunter, I look for old settlements and see how people used to live."

"So not for treasure?"

Kay smiled. "Well, you never know. People have found millions of dollars' worth of gold and silver."

She had been through it enough times to know she was going to have to bore him with the science to lose his interest. She pulled out her maps, charts, and a couple of old books on the history of the islands. "Have you heard of the red paint people?"

"No," Jackson replied with little interest.

"They were living here around five thousand years ago and—"

"Sorry, maybe another time. I need to catch the last ferry."

"But look," she showed him her charts, pointing, "I've found numerous sites that need to be excavated."

"I'm sorry, another time," Jackson insisted.

While Kay meticulously tidied away her charts, maps, and history books, Jackson loaded up her back seat with files, happy to keep himself separate from Kay while she was in history buff mode. By the time she got around to helping him, he was done.

"Okay, all done, I'll just say goodbye to the guys, and I'll get going," he said hurriedly. "When I've got more time we'll get back to those red people."

"It's the red *paint* people." Kay grinned, knowing it would never happen. She had tried with Fitch on a few occasions to no avail. Given their relationship, or whatever they had, he at least had reason to show interest.

With her car packed and Jackson gone, she headed back in to say her own goodbyes. She was going to spend the evening poring through the life and times of Larry

Beaumont with a bottle or two of France's finest, or more likely California's finest, fermented grape juice.

"You all set?" asked Fitch. He acted as though nothing had happened with Jackson.

"Yes thanks. You okay?"

"Good thanks," he replied nonchalantly, turning to the team. "Kyle, Dan, you are on Frank and Valerie. I want you to go through their lives from birth to their last breath. Ignore our previous research and start from scratch. We can compare what we had once you're done." He shifted to Winters. "Mark, get our guys doing the same on Hilary, Charles, and Walt. I know we've already done a lot, but likewise, let's start from scratch and see what we missed. My gut is telling me all of these cases are connected and whoever is responsible is playing with us."

"On it," came a chorus from the team.

"Excellent. Back here tomorrow 8:00 a.m. we will have a catch up session. Get some rest tonight, guys, this isn't going to be a simple one."

Fitch grabbed his things and walked out the office. It was only a short walk back to the Tidewater Motel, but it wasn't something he had done before, always hitching a ride with Kay.

"Winters," said Kay, "are you going to tell me what the hell is going on?"

Winters shook his head. "Fitch isn't just my boss, he's my best friend too. Just give him the night to himself and he'll be fine tomorrow."

Kay moved to rush after Fitch. Male bravado wasn't going to cut it with her. The man was hurting and she wanted to help.

She was stopped mid-step. Winters clasped a hand around her arm, pulling her back from the door. "Kay, seriously. Please don't go there. Trust me, I'll keep a close eye, I'm just getting the guys going and I'll catch up with him."

"You're sure? You'll keep an eye on him?"

"Yes, I promise. I've been doing this for years, I know what to do."

Kay swallowed hard. If he had been doing it for years, he wasn't solving the problem. "Okay but if you need me, call me," she insisted.

She climbed into her truck and breathed deeply. She hadn't had a moment since she had arrived at the Tidewater Motel that morning to catch her breath. She looked at the cell phone sitting on her passenger seat. With everything else that had happened, she had forgotten all about her nocturnal visitor, and the need for a detour on her way home.

Chapter 23

Kay pulled her truck to a stop. A car was parked in the driveway, indicating there would be at least someone home, although given the distances to travel on the island, that was less meaningful in Vinalhaven. She retrieved the phone which had auto locked shortly after she had seen all she needed to see and walked towards the front door of the house just a few hundred yards from her own home. The door was opening as she approached, and Kay rested her hand on the grip of her sidearm.

"Oh please, *please* don't tell my dad. I am so sorry!" blurted the young man who stood in front of her.

Kay smiled warmly, it wasn't the first time she'd had a young admirer become infatuated with her. It wasn't his fault, his hormones would be all over the pace. And ultimately it wasn't as if he was being nasty to her. Quite the opposite, he was complimenting her. Although it was something most women yearned for, it wasn't something Kay had ever bothered too much about, perhaps because the compliments had always come and she never had to look for them.

"Not this time, but go get your laptop," she ordered without further preamble.

"Officer Miller, isn't it?" asked a man appearing at the door questioningly, watching his son scurry towards his room.

"Yes, good evening." Kay recognized the man but couldn't remember his name, or even if she had known it.

"Jim Kingsley, I'm Brian's dad." He held out his hand.

"Kay Miller." She clasped his hand and shook. "I don't think we've met?"

"Apologies, I know. Sorry, I've been a rotten neighbor, a lot going on at the moment."

"Not to worry. In any event, I've not been here that long."

"To be fair, I've only just got back on the island a couple of days ago."

Kay looked longer than she should have at the man. He was older than she'd have thought for a fifteen-year-old's father. She racked her brain but couldn't place him. Generally she was good with faces.

"Is there something wrong?" he asked.

"Not at all. It's just been a long day."

"You're thinking I'm a bit old to be Brian's father?"

"No, God no. I would never!"

"We had him later in life, a true blessing from God."

Kay managed to keep her face impassive. "Children are," she said as generally as she could muster.

"Anyway, apologies. Is Brian in trouble?" he asked.

"No," she had planned for the question, "we're just checking with younger islanders if they had any interaction with Miss Cantrell recently."

"Oh, I hadn't heard that…"

"Yes, we—"

"Which you'd think was strange, given my ex, Brian's mom, is a teacher at the school."

Brian reappeared in the hallway behind his father and heard the interaction. His world was collapsing around him, he was going to be exposed as a stalker to his father.

Kay put on her best poker face, behind her impassive expression fighting to think of a counter to Brian's father's revelation.

"You wouldn't have, given we just started. Brian is first on my list. Well, that's not entirely true, he was on my way home and thought I'd just see if he had any—"

"You'd better come in then." He ushered her in, friendliness replacing the defensiveness.

"Ah, Brian you're there," he saw when he turned to let Kay in. "Good lord, son, you look like you've seen a ghost. Are you okay?"

"Yeah, Dad, fine!" Brian answered, his face betraying his words.

"Are you sure, son? I know Hilary's loss has hit a number of students but I'm so sorry I didn't realize it had hit you as well."

"No, Dad, I'm fine. Seriously, I'm fine." His panic eased and he managed to muster up some confidence in his voice.

"As long as you are sure. I could sit with you, if that would be easier?"

Kay gently tugged at the father's elbow, leaning in when he turned to her. "Jim, I really don't think that would be helpful, you know?" she whispered.

Jim pulled back, clearly not happy with what Kay was referring to, and led her away from Brian into their dining room. "Look, I've been on the island for thirty years. I've known Hilary nearly all my adult life, and I'm not buying into the nonsense rumors I've been hearing."

"Trust me, sir, they are true. And if you wouldn't mind, I literally need just five minutes with Brian."

Hearing torrid and unpleasant rumors being gossiped throughout the island was one thing, having a law enforcement officer involved in the crime confirm them was an entirely different matter.

"Really? It's not just gossip? I mean, I always thought Charles was," he paused, "you know. Well, we all thought he was gay."

"There is suggestion that was the case, but of the other, we have categoric evidence of inappropriateness of Hilary's behavior, of that there is no doubt. I'd also add there's no indication anyone else was involved. However, where young people have been exposed to her, we'd rather make sure."

"Of course," he said absently, his mind elsewhere.

Kay studied him with interest "Is there anything you want to share or tell me that you think we should know?"

Jim looked surprised but Kay read him easily. He was feigning the surprise, he'd just remembered something he probably had forgotten long ago, and she was sure it had to do with Hilary.

"No, " he shot back, an angry undertone slipping into his voice.

Kay stopped herself from pushing him, there apparently was something to discuss but he wasn't ready to share. It was something she'd have to revisit. However, thanks to her peeping Tom, or in this case Brian, she was going to have to interview every kid on the island as part of her cover. She had enough to keep her busy.

"Perhaps another time. Would it be okay to speak with Brian now? As you can imagine we've got a timetable."

Jim shook himself out of his pent-up memories. "Of course." He gestured for Brian to enter.

"Thanks, Dad." Brian pushed past without reference to the laptop he was carrying.

After the door to the dining room shut, Kay dropped the smile and spoke low and menacingly. "Okay, you little…" She bit her tongue and composed herself. She needed something from Brian. Placing his phone on the dining table she continued. "What on earth did you think you were doing!"

He followed her every move as she deposited the evidence he knew would have exposed him. "I am so sorry, I don't know what I was thinking."

"Open your laptop. I want to see every photo you've uploaded from your phone, whether here or on some cloud somewhere."

Brian blanched. He grudgingly placed his on the table, hesitantly opening it for her to see a password was required to gain access.

Kay glared at him and then the blinking password box. Brian failed to move. "Should I call your dad in and we can all do this together?"

Brian entered his password and the computer screen came to life. Kay reached over and took control, scouring through his photo album and making him enter any cloud passwords required to access other areas.

"I haven't uploaded any of them," he protested throughout her checking.

She noted he wasn't being monitored by his father, given his bookmarking of his favorite porn channels and sites openly with no attempt to hide. He was a fifteen-year-old boy, there was no way on earth she'd let a child of hers have free access in a way this boy obviously had. From what she had seen, women in uniform was obviously his thing. She deleted his bookmarks for good measure. He had cultivated thousands of links, she could only guess over a few years of puberty.

She pushed his laptop aside and focused on the phone. The photos she had seen before the phone locked were her concern, she wanted them removed for good. "Pass code?"

When Brian looked as though he was going to hold out, Kay tilted her head in a *don't even try it* move.

"651232," he responded.

Kay typed in the code and the screen came to life just as it had been last night after Brian had dropped it on her porch. She went straight to the photos and videos she had flicked through. Brian had apparently been watching her for some time, the photo and video dates stretched back to not long after her arrival on the island.

"So let's talk about what you've been doing."

Brian's pale face reddened instantly. "I dunno," he shrugged, "I just, you know…think you are…you know, beautiful." He buried his face into his chin.

It was Kay's turn to blush. It was very hard to get annoyed at someone who was telling you they watched you because they thought you were beautiful.

"That's very kind of you," she admitted, "but you do realize nothing will ever happen, right? You're a young man and I'm old enough to be, well, technically your mother. And it really isn't appropriate to be sneaking around people's homes, you could get into a lot of trouble."

"I know I was being really stupid," Brian sobbed. "I really am so sorry!" he blubbered.

Kay glanced at the dining room door; she didn't want the parents to become concerned. She put her arm around Brian. "I'm not going to say or do anything, this will just be between us. Now come on, pull yourself together. I just don't want you to get hurt, and sneaking around a house at night you may get mistaken for a burglar or worse," she warned kindly. "You just never know."

The moment she mentioned keeping it between them, Brian's tears began to slow. "I really am so sorry, I don't know what I was doing," he said, reaching out for a hug.

Kay withdrew from the attempted embrace. He was a besotted fifteen-year-old boy, she wasn't going to give him mixed messages. "No, Brian, that's not appropriate," she said calmly. "We don't have a lot of time and we need to delete all these photos. I also want to confirm there are no others and that once deleted they are permanently gone."

Brian nodded and wiped his eyes. Went through the phone with Kay and watched as she deleted the pictures one by one.

Kay hit the delete button again and again—the evidence of her drinking habit, her biggest concern, empty wine bottles, and a clearly inebriated Kay in various poses was not an image that would do her career prospects and standing any good. Beyond that, given a few of the time and date stamps of the images it could seriously impact the investigations that were underway and would call into question Kay's capabilities during the evidence collection and potentially cause some very tricky legal concerns when they caught the murderer. While two pictures in particular had concerned Kay, fortunately she didn't think Brian had noticed anything since Kay was wrapped in only a towel in the photos.

Nevertheless, she had to make sure those two photos were gone for good.

"Everything okay in there?" came a voice from behind the door, Brian's father.

"Yes, Dad, we're just finishing up," Brian said brightly. His mood had lightened dramatically since he found out he wasn't going to be exposed by Kay as a stalker creep to his parents.

Kay hit delete on the final photo and checked the memory and trash for any photos or videos she may have missed. "And you absolutely do not have any copies?"

"I never uploaded them. They were only ever on my phone."

"Okay, one last check. Log on to your cloud service on your laptop again."

Kay searched through and noted the last upload of photos; they were prior to her arrival on the island.

"Now, Brian, you seem like a really sweet boy, although I do think you may have a bit of an unhealthy obsession with porn."

He shrugged. "I'm fifteen."

"Just as long as you know that stuff isn't real life. Girls don't generally like to be treated like that."

"No?" He smiled innocently, definitely interested in where Kay was going with her talk.

She quickly realized that herself and changed tact. "Look, I'm not here to counsel you, although I think given your behavior you do need some."

Kay shut the laptop. The photos were gone, she no longer needed his compliance. Kay dropped her pleasant tone. "But I'd have to expose you for that. I'm not going to do that this time. I'm going to give you one warning and one only. With the current situation on the island, it would be completely understandable for me to shoot anybody sneaking around my home at night."

Brian stared at her in horror. "You'd shoot me?"

"I'll shoot anyone I find snooping around my home." She looked directly into his eyes, her face emotionless and impassive. Kay stood and patted Brian on the back. "Be safe."

She exited the dining room and barely missed knocking over Brian's father, who had been hovering near the door.

"Everything okay?" he asked.

"Yes thanks. Brian's fine, nothing at all to be concerned about."

"Oh, thank the lord. As a parent you do worry you may have missed something." He sighed in relief. "It's so hard nowadays, you never know what they're up to."

Only that your son is a creepy, porn obsessed stalker, Kay thought, keeping her smile in place.

"Yes, I agree," she said aloud. "As long as you have strict oversight of his online activity and monitor his browsing etcetera, you'll be fine."

Kay looked past the father and could see Brian's eyes widen; his world was about to be turned upside down.

"What about trust? We feel that is very important."

"I've worked a lot with teenagers in the cities," Kay said with a wink. "Believe me, hormones and trust aren't good bedfellows. If you're not monitoring his activity already, I'd get on it straightaway. I mean, he's a fifteen-year-old boy, you wouldn't let him roam around bars, sex clubs, strip joints, and drug dens, would you?"

"Of course not, we're a good Christian family!"

"Well if you're letting him roam free on the internet, you pretty much are."

It was Jim's turn to look to his son, whose genuine look of horror told the father all he needed to know. "I'll call my friend, he's a tech guy."

Kay winked at Brian. She had her photos and privacy back, Brian had learned his lesson, and she was certain he wouldn't be anywhere near her house anytime soon given the devastating blow she had just dealt his online activities.

Jim walked her to her truck. "Thanks again for the advice," he said, "but I do think we need to talk more."

"Okay, anything in particular?" Kay dug her keys from her pocket.

"You made me remember things I had forgotten long ago, things I'd probably rather not have remembered but…" Jim scratched at his chin awkwardly, not comfortable with where the conversation was headed.

"Okay. And you think they may be relevant?" asked Kay, trying to keep Jim talking.

He looked across his driveway at his home and Brian, who was watching them from the doorstep. He scanned the area to see if anyone was around. "I think so," he said quietly.

Kay glanced at the back seat of her truck, the pile of paperwork to go through to try and chase down her predecessor. If she found him he could help solve a crime and potentially prevent others. "I've got a lot on just now but if you think it is pressing…?"

Jim shook his head. "To be honest, I probably need some time to get my thoughts together, a day or so?"

"Sounds like a plan." Kay waved a goodbye to Brian. He did not return her wave or smile.

Chapter 24

Kay pulled the last box from her truck and heaved it inside, dropped it on the hallway floor, and leaned back against the wall, slowly sliding down until her legs were splayed on either side of the box. Her head jerked backward, as she subconsciously fought the exhaustion, unfortunately a little too forcefully. The resulting thud was the perfect wakeup call when her head met with the immovable force, the wall.

With her mind more alert she glanced towards the small kitchen. The stainless-steel fridge reflected the hallway light and shone it back.

A sign, just one, she thought to herself.

Not yet deciding whether she meant glass or bottle she pushed herself from the hallway floor. It was a herculean task, but she managed, the enticement of the cold glass of wine that lay ahead was all her body needed for the final effort required to shift her mass and get going.

Cold glass in hand, Kay arranged the boxes by date, planning to start at the beginning of Deputy Larry Beaumont's career and work forward. A large swig of wine rewarded her arrangement of the boxes in the correct order. Her rewards were going to be easily achieved and having had a recent delivery, perhaps she would have to up the ante somewhat. Otherwise she'd be out of it by the end of the first box.

The first two boxes covered Beaumont's life before Vinalhaven and were, in essence, nothing of any interest. A young deputy going about some very routine policing. No names stood out or incidences of any note.

The third box and by coincidence, corresponding glass, began to show some interest. Life in Vinalhaven from thirty years earlier was as dull as she could have imagined it would have been, few reports were filed, week after week updates simply read, "no incidents to report." It appeared monthly updates were held with the selectmen, again little to nothing was ever noted. The most exciting incident was a parking brake had failed on a car while it waited for a ferry. It had rolled into the sea and blocked the ferry from Rockland docking for a number of hours.

It was towards the end of the third box that Kay's interest was piqued. An incident of drunk and disorderly conduct by one Gerald Baker. No arrest was noted, only a mention that the aforementioned had partaken of a little too much and had become embroiled in a disagreement in the local bar. However, the real point of interest was the reason for this disagreement: "tourist was concerned at the interest Mr. Baker was showing in his daughter. Baker laughed it off, the daughter was only fourteen and had been 'hanging around his place despite his complaints.'" Apparently, that was enough for Beaumont to let Baker out without any follow up.

Baker's name had continued to appear thereafter in the next two boxes. Despite being a repeat offender and some questionable complaints against him, Beaumont would let him go the next morning, his record unblemished bar a note to cover Beaumont should complaints ever be forthcoming. What was very interesting was the weekly update that covered each of the filed events, a simple line referring to dealing with drunken behavior, no further action required. No mention of names or complaints leveled against the same individual time after time.

Over time the records from the island would have been archived and with no reports of crimes or arrests, these files had probably never been checked before. They would simply have moved from one storage cupboard to a larger one. What Kay was finding was a history of questionable behavior being covered by the local deputy, there was without doubt a history between the two that stank to the point of Kay having little doubt she had found the link they needed.

Such was Kay's intrigue, it was only her fourth glass that accompanied box number six. She was noting the names as they were mentioned, mostly they were innocent, but it was notable how the same people kept appearing. Walt Spencer, the harbormaster, had been noted a few times alongside Gerald Baker's activities. Likewise John Gilder, although only once negatively, otherwise all references were as a result of his selectman standing. Two other names kept appearing, Victor and Clyde, lobstermen. However, a quick search of the internet showed both had died a number of years earlier, presumed lost at sea after their boat sank in a storm. Neither body had been recovered. Before Kay could begin to think that perhaps they hadn't perished at sea, she noted both would be in their late eighties had they managed to survive what appeared from the reports, an un-survivable event.

Beyond the bar, one other establishment had resulted in numerous mentions, its existence alongside Gerald Baker certainly adding to the mix. Reynard's Orphanage on Lane's Island. Another search of the internet updated Kay that the home had been owned by a trust, used as a retreat for orphans from across the state. A sort of Outward Bounds adventure center. Ten years earlier it had closed and had been replaced with a retirement community. One vulnerable group to another with very different requirements. Kay could only assume there was more money to be made from the elderly, or perhaps they were less hassle. She'd had no incidents in her few weeks from the retirement community, whereas it appeared Deputy Beaumont had been kept fairly busy by the orphanage.

Being a short-term center, the orphans did not interact much with the local community, did not attend the local school or church, or any local facilities. From what Kay found they pretty much kept themselves to themselves. Issues appeared to revolve around runaways and the occasional shoplifting by orphans from the island's stores.

Runaways were by far the vast majority of reports being filed by Beaumont. The majority were found and returned. A small number each year had not been found but on further investigation, all those who hadn't had been subsequently spotted, either on the ferry or within Rockland on the mainland or nearby, thereby eliminating them from Beaumont's area of responsibility. They were passed to state police and beyond as runaway orphans, not entirely top of anyone's agenda or concern to track down. With hundreds of thousands in the system and millions of runaways reported each year, Kay gathered it was fairly easy for the missing runaways to get lost in the mix. While she had no idea what a normal number of runaways from an orphanage would be, she assumed it wouldn't be a small number.

Quick research showed permanent runaways was not a normal occurrence. The state of Maine would have expected a handful across the entire state and not just from one location. The questions began to mount for

Kay as she poured another glass. Why hadn't what was equivalent to the entire state of Maine's missing "orphans" tally for the year not sparked concerns from Reynard's, a relatively small facility in one of the most secure and safe locations in the state?

It took her less than ten minutes to uncover a scandal that had for the previous ten years, and thanks to Beaumont's "filing," gone unnoticed. The runaways had been listed as missing from their main facility, not from Reynard's, where they had only been housed temporarily. How could it have been missed, or as Kay was beginning to think, how had they managed to cover it up? She thought back to the reports, in each instance the case had been closed for Reynard's due to sightings on the ferry and the mainland. In other words, every single instance of a permanent runaway had eliminated Vinalhaven as an issue as the child was no longer there. They had apparently escaped, not one of the permanent missing had not been spotted this way. Eliminating any suggestion the child would be found on Vinalhaven, they were the mainland's problem thereafter.

"Oh my god!" She drained her glass with one gulp. The scale was significant, the state missing child ratio was almost entirely covered by the Reynard runaways, despite it housing a tiny fraction of the state's orphans at any one time.

Kay checked the stats for the previous ten years. It had dropped, but according to the records that happened a couple of years before Reynard's closed, somewhat undermining her theory. The number of runaways had remained relatively similar, but with the vast majority returning within 96 hours, that number was somewhat irrelevant. The issue was the number of permanent runways, or more correctly, missing children not accounted for.

Kay's heart jumped when she found a reporter had investigated the concerns a number of years earlier who had apparently stumbled on the same data and put two and two together, just like Kay. However, it was quickly undermined by quotes from numerous officials, including Deputy Beaumont. The reason was as a result of the trust placed in the orphans at Reynard's, it was a far more open facility being on an island and as such security was more lax. If the kids wanted out of the system, a trip to Reynard's offered them the chance. Deputy Beaumont advised that it was something that had gradually become apparent and they had put additional security in place. Kay noted the date, two years before the facility closed. It was only after the article had run that the numbers reduced and not long after that the facility changed to an elder care facility.

She was definitely onto something and was tempted to call Fitch there and then. Box ten and glass eight scuppered any thoughts of calling Fitch. Kay's heart stopped when she opened the first file, its summary read "MVC multiple fatality"—a motor vehicle crash. The first item was a photo of a twisted, mangled car and the tree it had struck. The report detailed Beaumont's findings at the scene and listed the fatalities, a mother and her young child. Specifically, Fitch's wife and daughter.

Chapter 25

Kay's eyes were instantly drawn to the clock. 06:34. The trill of the phone reverberated louder as the timing of the call registered. Another of those too early to be good news calls summoned her awake. She half opened her eyes and awaited the dull thud that would generally accompany an early morning wake up, but it didn't come. An empty blister pack of Tylenol by her bed suggested preventative action had been taken. She answered the phone and Fitch's dull tones brought her fully awake. Before he could ruin the morning, a thought brought a smile to her face, an action that would also have involved preventative measures between two consenting adults.

Her memories began to fire, the file lay by her bedside, MVC multiple fatality – Abercrombie. Her mind cleared.

"Good morning," she said, "or I'm guessing not?"

"Not, but we're not far. I'm looking at your house right now."

Despite the drawn curtains, Kay pulled the sheets over her half naked body. "What?"

"This one looks fairly cut and dried, suicide."

"Where?"

"Gunshot to the head."

"No, where are you?"

"Oh, we're at the Kingsley household."

Kay's heart stuttered. Brian was fifteen, she had gone way too heavy on him. Young, naïve, and at an incredibly impressionable age, his blood was on her hands.

"I…I just spoke with them last night, I can't believe—"

"You spoke to them last night?"

"Yes. Oh god, this is my fault. I went too heavy on him. I caught him sneaking around my house taking photos." Kay started hyperventilating as the gravity of her actions hit home. He was a young boy with a healthy interest in women and was struggling to learn how to deal with it.

"Why didn't you say anything yesterday? That's a pretty serious situation to keep to yourself, don't you think?"

"I didn't want to make a deal of it, you know? No point ruining his life over an adolescent crush. But I never thought—"

"Kay, no, you've got it wrong. It's the father, Jim Kingsley, who shot himself."

Kay recovered instantly, the weight of blame lifting. She had had a perfectly pleasant conversation with Kingsley and had kept his son's behavior from him. There was nothing she had done that would have led to the man taking his life. She paused, that wasn't entirely correct. His mind had wandered to memories he had obviously suppressed, he was supposed to be getting them together and follow up with her.

"I spoke with him too, he remembered things from his past that he was going to share with me. He said he just needed to get them together." She paused. "It is definitely a suicide?"

"About as textbook as I've ever seen."

"Too textbook?"

"Come see what you think."

"Give me five."

Kay jumped in the shower and threw on a uniform, thanking the lord for her hat. Otherwise five minutes would have been an hour. She checked the mirror and noted the yellowness edging towards purple on her chin. Another two minutes of makeup application was required before leaving.

She bypassed her truck and walked across the street, it was quicker. Both Fitch and Winters were waiting for her. Winters handed Fitch a ten-buck note. "He said you'd make it in five, I said not," he explained at her quizzical look.

Kay smiled at Winters' faith in her. "I'd have been here two minutes ago had it not been for my extra make-up regime." She pointed to her chin.

Fitch wordlessly handed back the ten bucks, adding one of his own.

"Perfection doesn't need time," Kay quipped, trying to take the edge off the dampener she'd just thrown, blushing slightly when she realized how conceited that sounded, particularly when she caught a glimpse of Brian Kingsley, a very different looking young man than the one she had talked with the previous evening. He was broken, his arms dangled limply, his head angled downwards, his eyes bloodshot from the tears that stained his cheeks. She brushed past the detectives and took him in her arms. "I'm so sorry, Brian."

His full weight collapsed against her, his body heaving with each grief-stricken breath.

A car skidded to a halt and a woman barely waiting for the car to stop jumped from the passenger seat. "Oh, Brian!" she cried, roughly replacing Kay with herself. Kay stepped aside and the mother took control. She stroked her son's head soothingly. "I'm so sorry," she repeated over and over.

Kay stepped away and turned her attention to the driver, an older man. He had exited his vehicle but made no attempt to join in comforting his grandson.

Fitch and Winters had also turned their attention to the new and apparently reticent bystander.

"Are you okay?" asked Fitch, striding towards the man. Kay, a few steps behind was also keen to understand the dynamic.

"All a bit awkward," he said quietly. "I'm his mom's new boyfriend and he doesn't know about me. They've not long split, you see."

"Ah okay," Fitch said. "Well if you can just stay here that would be great," he added loudly to cover the man's hanging back.

Fitch turned and found Kay by his side. "New boyfriend apparently," he said quietly. From his expression he was obviously thinking the same as Kay, up close the guy looked even older than from a distance.

"Fair enough." She shrugged. "The father was no spring chicken, she obviously likes the more mature gentlemen."

"Each to their own, I suppose," he said halfheartedly. "Anyway, let's go inside and see what your FBI training can tell us."

"I took a couple of courses, jeez! Will everyone stop making out like I'm some sort of Feebie guru!"

Fitch grinned. "It's more than anyone else within the vicinity."

It was a warm, genuine smile, one that she could see him giving his daughter every time he saw her. The thought gave Kay a lump in her throat about a young, beautiful life lost before it began. The coroner's report had found the cause of her death to be massive internal bleeding. The tragedy of it brought a tear to her eye. She could only imagine the pain that Fitch had gone through, having gone through some of it last night herself.

"What?" He noted the change in her expression, a look of deep pity towards him, something he had experienced a lot over the previous five years. He knew exactly when somebody had found out about his loss. That look was universal, the *oh my god, you poor man, how did you cope*, look.

"Nothing," she said, shaking her head, "just thinking about the scene."

"Bullshit. Winters told you, didn't he?" Fuming, he glared at Winters, who was blissfully unaware of Fitch's rage towards him.

"Told me what? What are you talking about?"

"About my wife and daughter."

Fitch made towards Winters, his smile replaced by pure unrepentant rage. Kay grabbed him by the arm. "Whoa, okay you got me. Nothing to do with Mark though, it was in the files."

"The files?"

"Beaumont's files. The ones you tasked me with going through."

"Why the hell would my wife's crash be in Beaumont's files?"

Kay looked at him quizzically, he wasn't making any sense. "Why wouldn't it be?"

Fitch's fury was morphing into utter bewilderment, completely confused by what Kay was saying. "Beaumont worked nearly his entire career on this island and certainly the last thirty years, why on earth would he be anywhere near my wife's crash in Appleton, on the mainland?"

"I don't know why. All I know is I have a file in Beaumont's records that has your wife and daughter's crash report. It looks like he was first on scene."

From the look on his face, it was clearly news to Fitch.

Winters had spotted something was up and joined them.

"Who was the first officer on scene at my wife's crash?" Fitch asked Winters.

Winters looked at Fitch and then Kay, surprised the topic was being covered. "State Trooper William Turner," Winters replied without pausing for thought. "But why?"

"Kay found a report on the crash in Beaumont's records," Fitch cut in.

It was Winters' turn to be astonished. "What?"

"I don't get what the big deal is," said Kay. "Maybe Beaumont accompanied Turner?"

"There's not a word written or a person involved in that accident that we haven't memorized or spoken to at length. As you'd imagine we had a very vested interest."

"I'm so sorry," Kay offered her somewhat belated condolences.

Fitch pulled himself back to the present. "We have a distraught family we have to deal with here and now."

His eyes were filling up, the pain as fresh as she'd imagine it had been five years earlier. He wanted to change subject and focus.

"Yes, let's do that. I'll give you my three cents' worth." Kay smiled. Fitch returned it, warm but pained. She wanted nothing more than to wrap him in her arms and give him the comfort she knew would do little for his pain but would show he wasn't alone in his grief.

However, wanting to move on as quickly as possible Fitch turned and led the way. Kay followed him into the house and the bedroom where the suicide had occurred.

Jim Kingsley was sitting on his bedroom floor, his body propped against the wall. His head was tipped forward, his right hand by his side, a pistol apparently having fallen from its grip.

"It's a .22, small, lethal, and fairly quiet," Fitch said. "Combined with the cushion," he pointed to Jim's lap where a cushion with scorch marks indicating it had been used to muffle the shot, "it would have been relatively silent."

Kay looked for an exit or entry wound but couldn't see any visible marks.

"Roof of the mouth, no exit. Bullets just rattled around, I'd guess a pretty much instant death."

Kay nodded. It was a clean and relatively painless way to go. "It also covers the letting your kid find you, I suppose, which I have to say was my first thought. You wouldn't want your kid seeing the back of your head splattered across the wall. But you'd barely even know he was dead and not just sleeping."

"Yep, and the gun appears to be his. There's a gun safe in the closet, door is open, not forced."

"Suicide note?"

"On his laptop." Fitch pointed to the screen. "It was plugged in to ensure the screen was on when he was found."

Kay read the note, it was not offering much other than how much he loved his son, how sorry he was, and what Brian was to do. Interestingly, he was advised to call the state police office and not 911, which would have gone straight to Kay through the Knox County sheriff's office.

"Why the state police and not 911?"

"No idea. It's a bit strange, but then so is putting a gun in your mouth and pulling the trigger, particularly when you've got a kid." The sadness in his voice said it all. Kay remained silent, allowing Fitch time with his thoughts. She surveyed the rest of the room, nothing appeared out of place.

Well?" asked Fitch.

Kay could only imagine he had had many dark thoughts over the previous few years, losing the perfect life and being left alone to drown in your sorrow was not something she would wish on her worst enemy, never mind a guy like a Fitch. He appeared to be one of the most genuinely nicest guys she had ever met. If he had a flaw, outside of his grief and resultant baggage, she was yet to find it. If Hallmark had made a card with the perfect man, it was Fitch's image that should be adorning it.

"I have to agree with you, suicide, unless anything else comes to light."

"Forensics should be arriving shortly, they'll confirm one way or the other. In the meantime, let's keep our minds open but I don't think we need to interrogate the son, unless forensics picks up anything suspicious."

It seemed a sensible approach. Brian was in bits and probably in no fit state to be interviewed in any event.

Fitch informed the mother they were free to leave but asked that they remained on the island until they had spoken to Brian. She had accepted the restriction without concern, she just wanted to get her son home to her new house on the other side of the town. Apparently, Brian was about to find out the mom's driver was more than just a driver.

Kay's cell rang as she helped Brian to the car. She gave him a supportive hug as she deposited him in the rear. His mother mouthed a thank you as Kay took the call.

"You have got to be shitting me!" came a shout through her handset, loud enough for the mother to hear. She shut her door more forcefully than required and the car pulled away.

"Sheriff Jackson, I really do not appreciate your tone or language," she chastised.

He ignored her. *"There's another death?"*

"I'm afraid so. A suicide, it would appear."

"Who?"

"Jim Kingsley," replied Kay, to silence. "Sheriff?" she prompted after a few seconds.

"Are the two state geniuses sure it's a suicide?"

"It appears to be, there's no suggestion of foul play."

"Well, let's not get carried away with conclusions, we've been there before."

Kay ignored the jibe. "What was strange," she went on, "was he asked the son to contact the state police and not the sheriff's office. Any idea why?"

"Not at all, why?" He sounded overly defensive.

"Did you know him?"

"Are you interrogating me?" Jackson asked aggressively, before barking, *"Keep me updated."* He hung up.

"Charming," Kay said into a dead line.

Fitch and Winters were by her side when the call ended.

"My illustrious and inspirational leader," she said, placing her cell in her pocket. Neither needed to be told; they had heard Jackson's dulcet tones clearly despite the phone not being on speaker.

Winters scowled. "That man is such a—"

"Profanities are not allowed, remember?" Fitch interrupted, realizing the impact Jackson had on her. Nobody liked to be in the position of being at odds with their boss.

"I was going to say idiot, that's okay, is it not?" said Winters. "You know me, I don't effing swear." He grinned.

The sound of a plane overhead drew their attention. The forensics team was arriving.

"Mark, can I leave this with you?" Fitch asked.

"Of course, but where are you going?"

"With Kay back to her house."

Winters smiled. "You two behave now," he warned, resulting in what could only be described as an adolescent level of awkward silence and blushing. Never had a nail been hit so firmly and beautifully on its head.

Chapter 26

Kay asked for a couple of minutes before Fitch entered her home. A quick sweep for any incriminating bottles, glasses, or underwear that may have not made it to the wash basket needed to be dealt with. A quick check of the bathroom for anything embarrassing was completed in record time. She breezed back to the front door as calmly as she could.

Her efforts to present the perfect home were irrelevant. Even the stunning view from her lounge window, one that would be hard pressed to be beaten anywhere in the world, was ignored. Fitch was lost in the file. He was reading each line over and over again, ingesting the new detail that surrounded the death of his wife and child. Vacation cover explained away Larry Beaumont being on patrol in the area where the crash had taken place. What wasn't was the fact that Beaumont had been first on scene yet had not been mentioned in any other reports or why his file had never been added to the rest of the reports. It remained off the system and only in hard copy.

"Why was it not filed?" Fitch muttered.

Kay debated leaving the rhetorical question hanging, however, given her own nocturnal activities she felt the need to answer. "It appears Deputy Beaumont had a history of covering himself with unfiled reports." She pointed to the pile she had found the previous night. "And we've got our link. Beaumont covered Gerald Baker's behavior numerous times."

Fitch's head shot up. "We have? Why didn't you tell me earlier?" he demanded.

Kay stepped back, taken aback by the aggression that had seeped into his voice. "It's barely 7 a.m., Fitch. We've just been at the scene of a suicide, consoled a child, and you've just discovered a new report from your wife and daughter's fatal crash five years ago. Tell me, when during any of that was an appropriate moment to run through what I uncovered last night?"

Fitch recoiled at his own behavior. The thought that Beaumont had found his wife and child and from what he could gather from reading between the lines, been with them in their dying moments, was eating him up inside. Why had he hidden his involvement? Why had he been kept out of the subsequent reports, of which there were many? His wife and daughter had crashed on a straight road, on a beautiful day, on a near empty road, and both died as a result. After extensive investigations of both his wife's toxicology, cell phone, and the vehicle, the conclusion had been his wife must have fallen asleep at the wheel and veered off of the road before striking a tree.

There were too many questions that remained unanswered. His wife had tried to call him numerous times prior to the accident. She hadn't left a message, she'd just tried his number repeatedly over a short period. Something must have been wrong. His daughter hadn't been strapped in her seat, from the report it suggested she had been in the front seat, something his wife never allowed. His wife was paranoid about driving, she'd never have driven while tired and she was a painfully careful driver, barely ever going above 50. The speed at point of impact was estimated at 80. None of it made sense. Despite his protestations, the investigation had been closed, with driver fault listed as the cause.

The full force of the memories rushed back, the unanswered questions, the lack of any reason as to what had happened hit Fitch like a train. Tears flowed from his eyes. "I'm so sorry," he managed as he looked down at the file, photos of his wife's crumpled car embedded in a tree.

Kay was unsure to whom he was apologizing, her or his family. She didn't know what to do as this powerful man began to heave, the full weight of the tragedy of his life weighing down on him. She had a rule never get close in the workplace. She was already having thoughts about the man she knew were inappropriate. Following the revelations, she had discovered they were even more so. Yet she couldn't just stand there and watch him. She walked across to him, sat, and took him in her arms. His head accepted the shoulder she offered, his body pressing against hers as the tears dripped onto her shirt. He held her as close as any man ever had, and it felt good. She knew it was wrong, but even as his heart spilled for his family, she felt the comfort from his presence, the strength and safety of being with him, wrapped in his arms.

She could only imagine how his wife must have felt in those arms. Invincible, untouchable, and very much loved. She had been a lucky woman. The years she had with Fitch must have been very special and brought her immense and complete happiness and peace of mind. Kay took comfort from the thoughts and suppressed the more inappropriate thoughts of how good his body felt against hers and how incredibly good the man smelled.

Fitch felt Kay's arms wrap around him, holding him close, and the memories of his wife flooded back. Five years was a long time, but he remembered every moment of their life together as though it were yesterday. The emotion he felt when his daughter ran to greet him from work, jumping into his arms and wrapping her tiny arms around his neck and kissing him on the cheek, telling him how much she had missed him and loved him. In those five years he had set up numerous dates, never once following through, always finding a reason to cancel. His mother's hugs had given comfort, but Kay's aroused a very different emotion, something that brought memories of his wife flooding back all the more.

He felt himself molding into her body, two becoming one. The more he needed her strength, the more she gave. She stroked his back tenderly as he cried, tears that he hadn't let go since the day he had been told. He hadn't been stroked like that since. His mind tried to block the memories that were flooding back. He hadn't opened himself up like this to anyone. He simply hadn't allowed himself to, everything was still so raw. The closeness and comfort felt good, her smell, freshly showered, reminded him of the precious and tender moments he had all too long ago enjoyed.

Kay felt a change. The weight was easing. She looked down and found herself staring deep into Fitch's eyes. He was staring back, his eyes reddened from the tears wide and pleading, inviting, questioning. It was one of the moments in life where words were unnecessary. Their gaze translated and transposed their emotions better than any words ever could. Fitch tipped his head upwards and Kay's moved down, their lips touching gingerly at first, their mouths finding a natural rhythm, as though past masters.

The moment their lips touched Kay felt an instant change in the embrace, Fitch no longer needed her strength and support, instead she felt the strength switch, she was in his arms, his body held hers and supported her, giving a feeling of comfort and security she hadn't felt for many years, if ever. She opened her mouth and welcomed him deeper, her fingers teasing at his dark, wavy hair, pulling him gently into her.

The heat between them was electric. Neither dared speak, break the spell of comfort and security that both had fallen spellbound to. Fitch gently maneuvered himself beneath her, laying the full length of the couch, her body ending up on top while never parting their lips. Kay felt his embrace strengthen, pulling her against him, she felt him beneath her, pressing harder and harder. It felt so good she didn't want the moment to stop. His hands traced gently down her shirt, her back tingly as his fingers caressed her skin, her breath catching as they traced the length of her back and beyond before gently pulling her against him.

It was clear there was nothing that could stop them, nothing that they wanted to stop. Two consenting adults who had found each other at a time they needed. Kay could sense he needed the okay to move on. She needed to give him a signal. Neither were going to talk, they didn't want to break the spell, the magic of the moment both needed so badly. She took her right hand from his hair and ran it down his face, his neck, and could feel the muscle beneath his shirt as she tracked her hand down his body. She had one target, unbuckling his belt. Her signal she wanted him.

Much to her own surprise she undid his buckle with ease. They paused, their mouths locked, catching each other's breath as the signal sent by Kay was registered, accepted, and the repercussions ignored. The moment, infinitesimal in real time, passed and they eased back into the moment, the decision made and accepted and any awkwardness over what they were doing dissipated in an instant.

Kay's hand moved beyond the belt, undoing the button and slowly sliding Fitch's zipper down. He hitched a deep breath as her hand pulled aside his pants, his anticipation building. Her hand moved back teasing the elastic waist of his boxers, peeling it back slowly, allowing her access. His hands fumbled with her belt and zipper as she pressed onwards. His tongue stopped and Fitch stopped breathing when her fingers felt under waistline of his boxers, brushing against him as he began to push her pants down, his eagerness growing with every movement of her fingers tracking deeper and deeper into his boxers.

She could feel him twitch under her, as desperate for her as she was for him. She had never felt desire like it. She wanted him more than she had ever wanted anybody, which for Kay was a groundbreaking moment in her life. A tear escaped from the corner of her eye. It was not often in her life she had experienced that level of joy.

Fitch had moved beyond her pants and was pulling at her underwear when reality bit and the spell between them was shattered in an instant.

"Hello!" came the shout from her front door, which she hadn't locked and was opening.

Both stopped instantly and jumped to action, pulling desperately at their clothes to avoid being caught.

"Are you guys here?" Winters was coming in.

They were two consenting adults, both single and free to act on their attractions. But just as their actions had gone unspoken, so was their desire to keep their actions a secret.

By the time Winters made it into the lounge, both were sitting innocently on separate sides of the small room, Fitch looking at the file, while Kay sorted the pile she needed to discuss with them that she'd discovered the previous night.

"Everything okay?" he asked, concern in his voice.

"Yeah, of course. You all finished over there?"

"Yes, all finished. You sure you two are okay? I'm not interrupting, am I?"

"No why?" asked Kay, trying to sound casual.

"I *am* a detective you know," said Winters with a smile.

Kay and Fitch glanced at one another. They had not spoken or looked at each other since Winters had interrupted them.

"I don't know," Winters elaborated, "funny atmosphere, like you've had an argument?"

"Jeez, you are good!" said Kay, a smile breaking into a laugh that Fitch was all too happy to join in with.

"You two can be weird," Winters said dismissively. "Anyway, what'd you find?"

Kay's laughter stopped instantly, remembering what she had found. "Lots, and I mean *lots*," she said, patting the bundle of files.

Chapter 27

The new team had met slightly later than planned by the time they had wrapped up at Jim Kingsley's suicide, locking and sealing the property to retain the scene until the coroner confirmed one way or another that it was death by suicide. Nobody who had seen the scene had doubted that was the case, however, it had not stopped the word getting out of another death on the island. Seven deaths, although a cause for concern, they were not all, or at least not officially, a result of foul play.

To date, only Frank and Valerie's deaths were classified as a murder enquiry. Hillary and Charles's deaths remained suspicious, with Beaumont wanted for questioning. Walt Spencer's death remained an accident, but his background was questionable, while Judge Wright and Jim Kingsley's deaths were both assumed straightforward old age and suicide, respectively. Still, Kay had a woman's intuition screaming at her with regard to Judge Wright.

Kay and Fitch hadn't had a minute alone since Winters' interruption to discuss what had so nearly happened. They were each avoiding eye contact like teenagers who had been caught doing something they shouldn't, despite being free and unencumbered to do as they pleased. One of them had to grow and deal with it or it was going to become a thing. Kay glanced Fitch's way, but he was deep in conversation with the Maine detectives. She couldn't wait anymore. She stood and walked towards the small group, she'd ask for a minute and take him outside to talk. What had happened between them wasn't just a stolen kiss, it was far more.

Before she could reach him the door to the hall opened, followed by the unwelcome sight of her boss. That was the last thing they needed in the mix.

Fitch caught Kay's eye as he too turned to see who had entered their space, and the briefest of smiles disappeared instantaneously. Fitch broke off from his group, grabbed the file he had not let out his sight since he had read it that morning, and made like a guided missile towards Jackson, only with a far more explosive expression.

Jackson's demeanor changed when he noticed Fitch make a beeline for him. His confident arrogance dissipated, replaced with what Kay could only describe as genuine concern. She could have sworn Jackson's hand twitched towards his holster, but out of the side of her eye she couldn't be sure. By the time her eyes checked, Jackson had folded his arms defensively awaiting Fitch's fury which, from Fitch's expression, was imminent.

Fitch threw the file on the table nearest Jackson. "Care to explain that?" he said, his volume menacingly restrained.

Jackson's eyes darted to the file, not wanting to take his eyes off Fitch for too long. "No idea. What is it?"

"It's more evidence of at best your incompetence in closing a case that required far more investigation."

Sensing he was out of imminent danger Jackson stepped towards the table and read the file cover. Beaumont's name and the date stood out. All color drained from his face.

Kay had worked her way quietly toward Winters who was like everyone else in the hall, transfixed at the interaction.

"What's Jackson got to do with that file?" she whispered. She knew Fitch had updated Winters on the file, and both had been as baffled as the other as to its existence and non-existence five years earlier.

Winters turned, realizing they hadn't completed the gaping hole in the story. "Shit, I mean, sorry," he apologized for the swearing, "Jackson was a state trooper before joining the sheriff's department. He was lead on the investigation into the accident."

"Oh, I see," said Kay. "Well, I do and I don't. It seems a little more than that."

"Yes, there was some other stuff going on. Jackson took a shine to Annie, Fitch's wife. Everyone did, she was as beautiful inside as she was on the outside, but Jackson didn't know when no meant, no, not ever."

"And he investigated the crash?"

"They settled that off the record. It must have been about six months before the accident."

Jackson flicked through three pages of the file then lifted his head to face Fitch, "I promise you, I have never seen this before."

"You fucking handed them to Deputy Miller!" Fitch yelled, uncharacteristically both swearing *and* shouting.

"I just delivered the boxes we dug out from storage. I promise you, Ross, I've never seen this report before."

"Winters," Kay said urgently, "what did you say was the name of the trooper who was first on scene?"

"William Turner, why?"

Kay didn't answer, she shot across the hall to get between the two men. "The first trooper on scene, William Turner, was he known as Billy?"

"Yeah, Billy to his friends but William at work," replied Jackson.

Fitch looked at Kay for the first time since earlier that morning. "What's that got to do with anything?"

Kay looked him deep in the eye. She didn't need to say a word, he nodded and followed her, as did Jackson, back to her workspace and the files she had separated from Beaumont's history.

"These are unfiled incidents on the island that Beaumont kept a record of," Kay explained. "Obviously he wanted to make sure he covered himself if required. In here we have questionable incidents, generally involving minors but not always. A few names crop up a few times. One of those names is a man called Billy, referred on one of the occasions as being law enforcement who 'should have known better.'"

"He was…one of those guys,," Jackson said hesitantly. "You know…"

"You wouldn't trust with your wife?" asked Fitch pointedly.

"No," said Jackson, "your kids. A wife would have kicked his ass."

Kay once again got between the two men. "It's pretty simple, can we just ask him?"

"Not possible. He died a couple of years ago," said Fitch. "Cancer I think. But what are you saying? We've got some sort of pedo ring going on here?"

Kay shrugged. "I'm not sure, but we've certainly got connections to look into and leads to follow. In the files we've got clear connections between Beaumont, Baker, Walt Spencer. and this Billy guy. Slightly less clear is a link to John Gilder but he's in there a couple of times."

"You really do think he's mixed up in all this, don't you?" said Fitch.

"Gilder? You think *Gilder's* involved?" Jackson said with surprise. "The guy's a nobody, a small-time politician in an even smaller town. But can we rewind a little? Beaumont was mixed up with Baker?"

Kay nodded. "Yep, and responsible for covering up some quite inappropriate behavior. He kept the files but never processed them, if anything came back to bite, he'd have been covered. He certainly knew what he was doing. Nowadays they wouldn't have got away with it but back then, as you've both mentioned, things weren't quite the same when it came to inappropriate behavior. 'Me too' wasn't a thing. As for Gilder, he's not all he seems. Call it women's intuition or whatever you want but he's mixed up in it all, I'm sure of it."

"Whatever there is, most importantly, we have a link between Beaumont and Baker. That gets us the Feebies." Fitch lifted the handset of the phone.

"And what about this?" asked Jackson, holding up the file Fitch had challenged him with.

Fitch replaced the handset without dialing the number. The voices from the other detectives faded as his head filled with haze and the room began to spin. He reached out for the table to steady himself, but it wasn't enough. Kay was first to move and guided his slowly collapsing body into a nearby chair. His tanned and chiseled face paled and loosened as the realization that he had always been right hit home. His wife and daughter had been killed. Murdered. Otherwise why had Beaumont covered himself and why had Turner kept Beaumont out of it? It wasn't a straightforward crash, just as he had always contended.

"Re-open it," he said.

"What are we re-opening?" asked Winters, having rushed over to see what was wrong with Fitch.

Jackson handed the file to Winters, who read the front cover then hissed, "Oh fuck!"

Kay considered chastising him for his language but figured under the circumstances, it was almost justified. Not that profanity ever should be.

Chapter 28

The sun setting over the ocean cast an amber glow across the town. As the light faded and color gave way to darkness, silence fell. It had been a long day with a lot they still had to unpack but that would wait for another day. The FBI with all of their resources were arriving the following morning and would help uncover the mysteries of what was quickly being heralded as Death Island.

Kay had spent the day bringing the team up to speed with her findings and revelations left behind by Beaumont. She had gone through the last few years of Beaumont's files, but it appeared his winddown to retirement had been just that, a complete wind down. From the files, nothing of note had happened for the previous three years. However, with twenty-seven years of questionable material to work with, the number of questions they raised were going to take some time to work through and were going to upset a number of islanders. But that was for another day. Kay switched off the desk lamp and surveyed the town hall which had become their interim investigation center.

Everyone was still at it, except for Fitch. Following the re-opening of his wife and daughter's case, he must have read the file twenty times, restarting each time he finished. Winters had tried to intervene but was swatted away. Kay had considered trying but given their relationship was at a different level of complicated, she thought it best not. Jackson had hung around far longer than normal, assisting his guys. There was clearly some guilt he was going to have to offload. But digging in and helping had certainly helped his standing with Winters, who had made a point of thanking him before he left. Fitch had raised his head in acknowledgment, which was a breakthrough in relations.

Kay glanced out the window and saw it was fully dark. "Guys, do you think we should call it day?"

"I think a few drinks at the Tidewater are called for," said Winters.

Only two disagreed, Fitch and Kay. As the others readied themselves to leave, Kay waited for Fitch. He didn't move. He sat staring at the file.

When Winters came towards them, Kay waved him away, mouthing, "I've got it, go."

He looked questioningly but Kay insisted, waving them all away. They echoed their goodbyes and left Fitch and Kay alone, the first time since they had been since that morning.

"Fitch?"

Fitch kept staring at the file. A tear dropped and darkened a small circular section of the cardboard cover. "I'm sorry, we can't."

She took his head and cradled him. "I never expected to. I stayed for you, not for that."

His body relaxed and his head fell against her, the tension easing. He'd definitely been beating himself up as much as he had been ingesting every crumb of detail from the file. "I've never felt a connection with anyone since, and then this."

Kay pulled a nearby chair over and sat with him, taking his hand in hers. "Do you want to tell me about them?"

Fitch raised his head, checking she was being sincere. "They were my world, my reason for being."

Kay remained silent, the darkness bar one small desk lamp shining a light on the file was filling the space. They were completely alone, nobody else existed in that moment.

"Annie, that was her name. It was Anne but she hated it, thought it sounded old. She was the most wonderful human being. She'd have given her last dollar to help someone out in need. She was so beautiful." Fitch smiled, taking out his cell and showing her his favorite photo of them both. "And Charlie." He gave a short laugh.

Kay's heart stopped as she stared at the photo he was showing her. They were two of the most beautiful people she had ever seen. Her eyes instantly watered but she kept her composure; he needed her to be strong. She bit at her lip to control her emotions. "Charlie?"

"Yes, the file says Julie, but it was Julie Charlotte Abercrombie. She was named Julie for my grandmother, Annie conceded that, but she absolutely insisted she'd be Charlie to us. She, like her mom, only ever saw the good in people. She had just had her fifth birthday and Annie had taken her to my parents in Appleton about thirty miles away to tell them all about her party. We had an inflatable castle in the backyard and every kid in the area wanted to come. She was a magnet, everybody loved to spend time with Charlie." Fitch's voice broke.

"Okay, I think we need to get you back to your room." Kay struggled, her own voice cracking, the emotion bearing down on them both.

Fitch nodded, he was exhausted. The emotion had taken its toll on him.

Kay drove him to the Tidewater and, avoiding the prying eyes at the bar, smuggled him in via the back door. She laid him on his bed and sat by his side. She stroked his head gently and kissed him on his forehead as the slow, deep breaths of sleep befell him.

After she closed the door to his room the tears flowed. The sadness of his life and his family tragedy hit her like a train. She gathered herself together and made it back to her home. The first bottle of the night was gone before she even made it to the lounge.

By bottle three the tears finally stopped, which coincided with her consciousness.

Chapter 29

NO, Kay screamed in her head, the trill ring pounding her delicate state. *Not again!* She willed her eyes to open and see what unearthly hour this assault on her senses was happening. One eyelid lifted, the second followed in an instant. She grabbed for her cell phone, six missed calls. She looked at her alarm, it was switched off. It was 9:15 a.m. She was over an hour late and the FBI would have arrived at 8:30 a.m.

She swallowed four Tylenol and ran to the shower as a knock at her door suggested the concern for her had gone beyond just calling her. People had a habit of dying on the island.

"Kay!" The voice was Fitch's and was followed by another knock. "Are you okay?" His voice was full of concern. A louder knock. "Kay, are you there?"

"Give me two minutes!" she shouted, half in and out of the shower. She let the water soak her, wash away the sweat and alcohol that had glazed her body following another restless night's sleep. Since joining the Knox County sheriff's office she had mastered the two-minute shower, something she never thought possible. She grabbed a towel and with water still dripping from her opened the door to a worry struck Fitch. The worry left in an instant at the vision of a beautiful woman freshly out of a shower standing before him. He saw beyond the bruised chin, the ugliness of its color disappearing in the glow of her beauty.

"Can I borrow your towel for a sec?" he said, a wicked grin appearing on his face.

"I've seen that movie," Kay laughed. "Give me two minutes and I'll be ready to go."

"No rush." He checked his watch. "The FBI guys wanted to get checked into the motel and are grabbing some breakfast. We're getting started at 10 a.m."

Kay paused halfway down the hallway and turned back to face Fitch. Was he saying what she thought he was saying? No rush as in "we've got time?"

Their eyes met, he smiled. Kay moved her hand towards the tuck that was holding her towel in place, one small tug and it would drop to the floor. Fitch followed the movement; she could see his pupils dilate. His mouth moved but it wasn't his voice she heard.

"Is everything okay?" asked Winters, appearing by Fitch's side.

Kay stopped the upward movement of her hand and rushed back to her room. Another fraction of a second and Winters would have had more of an eyeful than Kay would ever have wanted to give him. However, she felt no embarrassment. It was clear from Fitch's expression and actions that he was definitely not regretting the previous day.

"Just give me two minutes!" she called.

"With you looking like that I might not last two, just pre-warning!" Winters shouted. An "oomph," suggested Fitch had just hit him somewhere.

Kay smiled as she quickly dressed, noting she selected underwear not normally matched with her uniform. Whether it was deliberate or she just felt like a change she wasn't sure, but at least she wouldn't be caught in a compromising situation wearing grandma style underwear.

"I preferred the other look," Winters cracked when Kay rejoined them at her doorway.

"Enough, Mark," Fitch snapped.

Winters shrugged. "Spoilsport. Do you want to hitch a ride with us, Kay? I've got some gossip from the bar last night, for you both."

Kay glanced at Fitch for confirmation, who shrugged. "If you need your truck, we'll drop you off."

The five-minute ride to the town hall was filled with Winters updating on the gossip he'd gleaned from the other detectives at the bar. Jackson, it appeared, was just as hated within the department as he was outside. His insistence on being called boss, his running against the previous well respected and loved sheriff had made him no allies.

"They all think he's just as much of an 'A' hole that we do," he concluded.

"I don't know all the history, but he was a state trooper before the sheriff's office?"

"Yeah, he was a sergeant, Troop D, covering the Augusta area to Knox County. He was the crash reconstruction specialist in the team, so when the accident happened, he was given the case," Winters explained, Fitch having left it for him to answer. "Fitch wasn't happy with the conclusion of the case and made it clear. Jackson was pressured to reconsider the findings, but he always has been an arrogant son of a bitch. He said there was no point and filed the report, closing the case, against the wishes of even the colonel. We're not the biggest force and we look after each other, a tight knit team. It was clear from that point Jackson wasn't a team player, his time with the state police was done, ambition drove him to the sheriff's office and well, you know the rest. He's done the same there."

"Maybe he'll end up governor next," Kay joked.

Neither Fitch nor Winters laughed, it was a thought both had had themselves.

"He's an ambitious guy," Fitch said sternly.

A woman stood outside the town hall, rushing to them as they arrived. Late fifties to early sixties, she was immaculately presented. If Kay had had to guess, she'd have said it was an Armani suit but the handbag she knew was Hermes. A Black Range Rover was parked in the parking lot, and there was little doubt that was also part of her wardrobe. This woman oozed money and wanted people to know it.

"Lieutenant Abercrombie?" she asked as Winters climbed from the driver's seat, her voice clipped, well educated, privately schooled.

Fitch exited the passenger seat. "That's me."

The sly smile indicated she had been made aware of his nickname.

Fitch blushed slightly, much to the amusement of both Winters and Kay. Kay hadn't witnessed it as many times as Winters, but it was interesting to see the reactions as the penny dropped.

Winters nudged her. "Never fails."

"I'm Claudia Wright, my uncle, Judge Wright, died yesterday."

"Yes, of course, please come in." He guided her towards the main doors. "I'm so sorry for your loss."

"Oh please, he was a cantankerous old bastard. Nobody liked the man and the world's probably a better place today without him," she said with a wave of disdain.

"Okay, so how can we help you?"

"I am here with regard to his will. Myself and my daughter were his only family and his sole heirs. At least that was, I was informed yesterday afternoon, until his cleaner had his will changed recently. Do you know she's getting the lot!"

"You mean his carer?"

"Whatever. He changes his will and the old goat dies of old age. Don't believe a word of it, I've been waiting years for the old bugger to die."

"I knew it," Kay blurted. "I knew there was something not right there."

"Damn right there's something wrong here. Every year for the last fifteen years my daughter has spent the summers with him. She was the only person in the world I know who could tolerate him and she was the only person in the world I think he ever cared about. He was putty in her hands."

"She must be a very special girl."

"Simple is a better word, but enough about my failings. There is not a chance on this Earth he'd have given that house to anyone. He knew she loved the house and he promised my daughter it would be hers."

"We had suspicions but I'm being blocked from investigating it further without any evidence. The change of will and the house is probably all I need."

"I don't care about the *house*!" she shrieked. "My grandfather helped build this country, my uncle inherited a lot of money from his father, we're talking hundreds of millions, and that was thirty years ago. This is not just stealing a run-down old house in the middle of nowhere. We're talking one of the biggest con jobs in history!"

"We'll get right on it," said Fitch.

"She's having him cremated today, did you know that!"

"No, we didn't," Fitch replied, his anger building. The doctor and mortuary knew he wanted an autopsy.

"My legal team are in Rockland blocking that. Even if they need to throw their bodies in front of the incinerator, they'll keep that body out and trust me, for the money I pay them they'll sacrifice a few of their lawyers."

"I have no doubt," said Fitch, hitting redial on the doctor's number from the previous day. "I know you're busy and yes you do have time to talk to me," he said when the doctor answered. "I'm with his niece right now, and if that body is anywhere other than the medical examiner's in Augusta in the next two hours, I assure you, I'll be arresting you as an accomplice…No, I don't care what the will says. You knew we have suspicions, suspicions which have massive consequences have come to light…Good, I'm pleased to hear it."

Fitch ended the call.

"She had added into the will that he had to be cremated and then buried within 48 hours, a nice way to cover any wrongdoing." He turned to Kay. "She didn't even bother going to the ceremony, just insisted it was done this morning, as soon as possible, as per his wishes, she claimed."

"Pick her up?" asked Kay.

"Definitely. If she did plan it all, we're talking murder one."

"Excellent," replied the niece. "Thank you!"

"Don't thank us yet," cautioned Fitch. "If she's good it'll be hard to prove, and given the history we tracked yesterday, we've every reason to believe she's very good. We believe she's done this many time before."

"You have evidence of that?"

"She's been the sole beneficiary at least four times from preliminary checks," said Kay. "We know she did it. Proving it is going to be an entirely different thing."

"Let me be clear, I don't care if she killed him, I just need enough for a judge to veto the new will." She walked off, triumphantly updating her lawyers on her phone.

"Rich people," Winters snorted.

"It's all about the money." Fitch sighed. "Anyway, go pick her up before she smells a rat and runs."

Kay and Winters were returning with the carer as two identical and pristine sedans of what could only be the FBI pulled to a stop in front of the town hall.

Four agents disembarked the vehicle, three men and one woman, all wearing almost identical navy suits, each removing their sunglasses as they walked towards the building.

"Do you think they realize how cliched they look?" asked Winters, helping the carer from the car, her hands cuffed behind her back.

"Blissfully unaware?"

"I'm going to sue the both of you!" insisted the carer as they marched her towards the town office.

"So you keep telling us," replied Kay, disinterested.

"It's my house fair and square. What can I do? My clients love how I care for them!"

"What about the money? You don't want that as well?" Winters teased.

"Money? He's got a pittance of a pension, there was never more than four hundred dollars in his account when I went shopping."

They both listened with interest, noting the annoyance in her voice. She was unaware of the potential windfall she'd have received had she succeeded.

Kay cracked a smile. "His niece paid us a visit earlier today. Wealthy woman, serious money. Looks like you may have picked the wrong mark this time."

They entered just behind the FBI agents and joined the introductions. The woman was the lead agent, Special Agent Jo Gonzalez. Mid-forties with a serious expression, she introduced her three colleagues, two younger, Steve and Bryce, and one a similar age to herself, Evan. All were more interested in the woman in cuffs than the swapping of names.

"What did she do, shoplifting?" Gonzalez grinned. It was apparent the FBI were not taking the situation particularly seriously.

"First degree murder," replied Fitch.

"You've solved the case and she's the killer?"

"Actually, it's the only death we have that had no link to the others. Judge Wright."

"I thought that was old age?"

"According to the doctor. However, we're confirming that now. We've good reason to believe she's done it before. This may be her fifth murder in as many states."

Gonzalez addressed her guys. "Evan, Steve, do you want to take over there?"

Fitch nodded to Kay and Winters, who were looking more than a little perturbed at the loss of their collar. The nod was a sign he wanted them to give the carer up, he wasn't going to fight the FBI.

"What's happening?" asked the carer as the two agents walked ominously towards her.

"You're going to be a famous serial killer," said Kay.

"Serial killer? What the hell are you talking about? I worked with old people who were dying."

"Yep, thanks to you." Winters passed her across to the agents.

"Do you have somewhere we can hold and interview her?" asked Gonzalez, scanning the hall.

"Across the corridor to the other wing. There's a holding cell and interview room in the sheriff's office," Kay answered, reluctantly handing them her key.

Fitch was right behind the FBI agents. "We'll be back in five," he said to Gonzalez, leading Kay and Winters outside.

He was careful to make sure no one could hear them before speaking.

"Apologies. I spoke with the mortuary in Rockland. The niece had six lawyers there to stop the cremation, and we're not talking small town lawyers, we're talking New York big firm partners flown in by private jet. Whatever this case becomes we do not want to get tied up in the work that much legal power will rain down on us. Trust me, the further we can keep away from that case the better."

Kay said, "I take it the FBI doesn't know any of that?"

"Not a clue. I thought they might bite when we mentioned five murders in five states, though."

"And given the killer is female, all the more headline and promotion worthy," Kay remarked.

Fitch grinned. "Exactly."

"And one less case for us to worry about," said Winters.

Kay and Flitch shared a glance. It was the one case they weren't worrying about that they had just lost.

"Good point," Fitch conceded.

Oh god, Kay thought as Fitch's words hit home. They were able to share thoughts in a glance. She hardly knew the man, but they were reading each other's thoughts. She needed to step back, get some space and a sanity check. She felt the discomfort of the underwire in her bra. What the hell was she doing? Everything was moving too fast, and more importantly, the revelations of Beaumont's report and the crash had changed everything. She focused on the picture in her mind of the photo Fitch had shared with her of his wife and daughter. He was off limits; she had a job to do and the victims deserved her full attention.

Chapter 30

The news of a significant arrest caused chaos on the island. The ferries, quiet for the time of year, filled instantly, though unfortunately not with the well needed tourist dollar but the tightly controlled local affiliate press dollar. The big spending nationals left it to their affiliates to travel that far. The news trucks and paper journalists flooded the island. Islanders themselves were caught unaware, assuming the story was about the multiple local deaths. Nobody knew the judge's death was even in question.

The otherwise unreported spate of deaths were about to go national. The journalists realized there were two major breaking stories on one sleepy and unheard-of island in the northeastern corner of the U.S. The nationals press was dispatching their own news crews to headline the story but in the meantime the affiliates had their scoop. Sleepy Vinalhaven was about to go under a spotlight unlike it ever imagined possible.

"We're trying to work here!' Fitch barked, his temper fraying. Having been handed the Judge Wright murder the FBI had all but cut themselves off. An arrogance and superiority had descended immediately as it was assumed the locals weren't up to the job. With the realization that the suspect had been operating for over twenty years, the number of victims was likely to be well beyond the five that had already been uncovered. Despite being there to assist with the multiple murders, they had set up camp in the small sheriff's office focusing entirely on the judge's case. It was not what Fitch had expected but wasn't surprised.

Special Agent Gonzalez looked out onto the parking lot again, sneaking a look through the blinds at a makeshift podium, along with a crowd of reporters and news crews awaiting her update on the case.

"I understand, but what am I going to tell them about these cases?" she asked again, further infuriating Fitch. The last thing they needed was a press conference highlighting the multiple deaths.

"You called the news conference. As far as I am aware not for these cases," Fitch reminded her, not wanting to be party to the show.

"Yes but they are going to ask about…" Her attention was interrupted by something outside. "Ah, excellent, the sheriff's made it. Don't worry." Gonzalez's gaze tracked his truck as he drove around the back of the lot and towards the rear where some spaces remained.

A laugh from the office accompanied her comment. "Yeah, that's not a comment we hear often," Kay said to Gonzalez's questioning look.

"Or never," said Winters. "He's a bit of an asshole."

One of the two detectives the sheriff had allocated himself to the team snorted. "A bit?"

"What? He's doing the conference with you?" Fitch asked in astonishment.

"Yes, we always like to engage with the locals when on their turf."

Fitch, already angered, instantly raged. "*He's the one who…*" Faces outside swung towards the raised voice from inside the town hall.

Kay placed a calming hand on his arm. "The sheriff stopped us getting an autopsy after the death. It is despite him you have the case," she explained more calmly.

Jackson entered the room. "What time are we on?" he asked with excitement, his smile ear to ear.

"We're not, you're out," Gonzalez barked, furious he hadn't been truthful with her. She had called him earlier to offer him a place next to her on the podium. He had accepted, not once mentioning he had hindered the case.

"What? Why?"

Although his lack of conviction was underwhelming, he could see by the faces in the office he'd been called out on his bullshit.

"Deputy Miller," said Gonzalez, "you sniffed the carer out, care to join me?"

"No."

"Come on, the camera will love you!"

"No."

"What, you're not even going to tell me why not?"

"No." Kay shook her head firmly. Her face was read by all who could see it, this wasn't a 'no, no, I can't, but if you push I will,' move. This was a categoric, absolute, unequivocal no.

Gonzalez looked at Fitch, who in turn looked at Kay's immovable expression. She was working on a few leads from Beaumont's files and although she wasn't quite ready to share, the implications were massive and she needed to nail them down asap.

"Oh, for the love of God, come on!" He gestured to Gonzalez.

They watched from the hall as the press conference was aired live on WABI TV5, the local station, the nationals picking the show up with the breaking news of a serial killer having been caught in an attempt to steal a judge's home from his heirs.

Kay instantly could see why Gonzalez had been so keen to hold the news conference. The woman was telegenic. She had to move closer to the screen to check this was the same person who had left the office just a minute earlier. Gonzalez was a natural in front of the cameras and Fitch complemented her perfectly. It was like a press conference in a movie, the two perfect main characters leading the charge, updating the press.

"I'd like to thank Maine State Police Lieutenant Ross Abercrombie for the sterling work of his team and that of Knox County sheriff's office in assisting us in securing the arrest of a suspect in what we believe to be a truly despicable crime. While I'm not going to give you too many details as we are at the early stages of the investigation, what I *can* say is that we have arrested a fifty-two-year-old female following the death of a local resident. It is believed that the suspect engineered the death of the resident following the alteration of his will in her favor. We believe this is not the first time this suspect has used this modus operandi and today we are launching a cross state investigation of at least another five cases and we believe there may be many, many more."

"Assisting!? Really?" Kay growled. "Try handing in a box, wrapped in a bow with a tag!"

"Keep watching!" cautioned Winters, breaking into a grin.

"Special Agent Gonzalez is too kind." It wasn't Fitch's first rodeo, and he wasn't about to be upstaged by the FBI after handing them the easiest serial killer slam dunk in history. He had his own agenda. "The moment we discovered the scale of the crime, we just had to involve the FBI."

"Thanks, Fitch." Gonzalez took back control, dropping the bombshell of the nickname that so easily fitted Ross Abercrombie. A buzz went around the reporters and crew as just as had happened throughout his life, they all got it. The pause from Gonzalez as a result of her faux pas allowed Fitch to continue.

"Yes, it's not often you have a female—"

"Serial killer," Gonzalez jumped back in, her frustration growing as Fitch was obviously trying to take the credit. "We have had others but they are rare and we believe the scale of the crimes she has committed will require a significant national effort to track down her previous victims and patients. Now I'll take—"

"Oh sorry, when I mentioned the scale," said Fitch, "I was also referring to…" he left a pause, but Gonzalez was stumped, she didn't know where he was going. The FBI, as they do, had steamrolled in. Once they had taken over the case they had shut Fitch, Winters, and Kay out. The suspect herself had no idea what she had done beyond securing an old house, and she was in no position to update them. The niece had other priorities and a meeting with the FBI had been arranged for the following day, once she had dealt with 'her urgent legal matters.' Assumptions had been made and not checked or covered with Fitch, Kay, or Winters, who had given them the case. Fitch knew the point he was making would cause problems in the short term, but it would also ensure the FBI realized it was a team effort and they weren't dealing with a bunch of backwater cops.

The pause was perfect. Reporters noticeably leaned in to catch the scoop. Fitch looked at Gonzalez but with nothing to say she gestured for Fitch to continue. He smiled a thank you, knowing she was smiling back a less than complimentary response.

"Judge Wright was a well-known and respected member of the legal community. He served the State of Maine for over fifty years, first as a lawyer and then as a judge."

Gonzalez relaxed slightly, thinking that there was nothing they had missed, the realization that they had just taken over and crowded out the locals on what was definitely going to be a career boosting case.

"However, what none of us knew and what transforms the scale of the case is…"

Kay and Winters could see Gonzalez's face drain of color. She had absolutely no idea where Fitch was going. They looked towards her FBI colleagues, each looking wildly at each other for some recognition that one of them knew where it was going, knowing there was going to be hell to pay from Gonzalez. From the limited interaction they had had with her, she screamed ambition.

"…that Judge Wright's father," continued Fitch, "was an exceptionally successful businessman, helping build our great nation along with the likes of Carnegie, Rockefeller, Ford, and Edison, and as such, Judge Wright's fortune is significant. Had the suspect succeeded in her crime she would have pulled off one of, if not *the* greatest thefts in history. Judge Wright inherited hundreds of millions of dollars over thirty years ago, and today it is believed his worth is in excess of two billion dollars."

Fitch let the number sink in, pausing for effect, watching Gonzalez struggle to compose herself. "As a result, we handed the case to the bureau," he concluded. "Questions?"

Hands shot up and mouths opened at once, an incomprehensible barrage of questions thrown in unison.

"One at a time please," said Gonzalez, having pulled herself together.

For the next fifteen minutes the majority of the answers had to be given by Fitch, since Gonzalez was nowhere near as up to speed on the case as she had assumed. All questions were fully focused on Judge Wright, who had become the only story of note.

As Fitch wrapped up what he assumed was the final question a shout came from the group. "Brian James, *Rockland County Times*. This wasn't the only death on the island was it? In fact, it wasn't even the reason the FBI were here?"

"We're here to talk about Judge Wright, not speculate on other cases."

"But six suspicious deaths linked to two previous residents of the islands? Surely that is worthy of comment?"

"What you've said is incorrect. As I said, we're here to talk about the murder of a well-respected lifelong member of this community," Fitch stated, closing the questioner down.

"Sorry, can I just ask one last question? Stacey Rhodes, *Maine Magazine*," asked a sweet as could be twenty-five-year-old journalist who was clearly seeing an opportunity to boost her profile under the media gaze.

Gonzalez nodded, much to Fitch's dismay, *Maine Magazine* was a lifestyle magazine, it wasn't going to be anything to do with the case.

"I think our readers will be interested in Special Agent Gonzalez referring to you as Fitch?" She smiled.

Fitch didn't justify the question with a response. The laughs followed him as he marched back into the town hall. Close behind the smile Gonzalez had painted on for the majority of the press conference was gone in an instant as she turned her back to the cameras.

"Well I have to give it to you, I've never been that publicly fucked over in my entire life," said Gonzalez, in awe. She closed the town hall door behind them.

"You guys just assumed we had given you everything and ran with the case, not once coming back to, or involving us. You've not even shown the slightest interest in the other cases, which I would point out is the reason you are here."

Gonzalez weighed up the situation. She could read her audience and change direction when needed. She had lost this battle, it was time to pivot. "Special Agent Jo Gonzalez, FBI." She stretched out her hand. "It's a pleasure to meet you."

"Lieutenant Ross Abercrombie," Fitch reciprocated.

Winters burst into song. *"Then put your little hand in mine. There ain't no—"*

"What the hell is that?" asked Fitch, glaring at Winters.

Kay laughed and high-fived Winters. "*Groundhog Day*. It's 'I Got You Babe,' the song that's playing when the day resets each morning."

Gonzalez nodded, impressed. "But I do think we're going to need more bodies."

"Have we not got enough?" Winters asked with a wry smile.

Chapter 31

While the town hall lot was packed with journalists, the Tidewater was packed with islanders, the live broadcast drawing in a standing room only crowd on a weekday lunchtime. Most sat in stunned silence listening to the revelation of Judge Wright's wealth, many wishing they had been more pleasant to the man, before remembering how unlikeable an individual he had been.

One man was more interested in the crowd than the TV screen, studying the reactions of those watching, analyzing their reactions and noting idiosyncrasies. He was particularly interested when the questions turned to the other deaths. While previously he had focused on the entire crowd, with that question he focused in on only six faces. He scanned the bar quickly, noting them all glance furtively at each other for the next few minutes. None looked comfortable. He needed to act and quickly. The problem was far worse than he had imagined, and with the FBI in the mix his timeline was tighter than he had hoped.

Rising from his surreptitious seat in the corner of the bar, he brushed past all six from behind as he left, the crowd's reaction to the final question about the lieutenant giving him the distraction required. He made it out unseen just as he had entered. Nobody knew he was back on the island. He had hired a small yacht in Portland, sailed up the coast and across to the island, and nobody had spotted him since his arrival with the focus on the numerous news organizations that had flooded the island.

Arriving at night and docking on a neighbor's jetty he had kept himself to himself. Although his island home was visible to only two other properties that would be unoccupied for another month, he had kept the shutters down and used no electricity. The yacht was packed with enough food for weeks, negating any need to visit the town. He was completely self-sufficient, and despite never wanting to revisit the island, the beauty and atmosphere reminded him of an idyllic life he had once loved. Memories flooded back, some leaving a very bitter and unwelcome taste. It had been a very fleeting welcome return.

His truck remained in the garage, the hookup ensuring the battery would fire the first time whenever he wanted to re-use the old beast. However, with it came recognition. An old bike resting against the garage wall would be his transport. A baseball cap, jeans, an old hoodie, and a newly grown beard would complete the disguise, ensuring no one would recognize him until he wanted them to.

He had set out that morning, the cycle firing old memories the truck would have sped beyond. They were both a blessing and a curse. Ten small envelopes rested in his oversized central pocket, and he kept placing his hand to ensure none had escaped. Another four had been mailed, he wasn't worried if they were intercepted, the note would have meant little to anyone other than for the intended.

Nothing had changed. Literally nothing. The houses, town, and stores were caught in a time loop, circa late 1980's, modern but not up to date. Even the cars and trucks were dated; the lack of miles they were able to travel on a daily basis ensured they stayed longer in their owners' hands than they would on the mainland.

It was only on return you noticed the subtle differences from the mainland, otherwise reality was normalized as that which you lived. The islanders were blissfully unaware of just how disconnected they truly were.

Following the press conference, he had mounted his bike and followed his route back home, detouring to deliver the notes that had remained in his pocket. He had no idea how the notes would impact the recipients, he just knew they would.

***

A chill ran down his neck as the conference drew to a close. As though someone had walked over his grave, he felt an instant unease and looked around the bar. The area had come alive as the broadcast cut back to the studio in Portland. The TV voices faded, replaced by the cacophony of noise as the chatter and gossip began, heads and bodies bobbed and moved, offering him little reason as to why he felt the sudden unease. He checked back; he wasn't the only one looking around uncomfortably. Others were doing the same, unfortunately it was everyone he had hoped wouldn't be. His eye caught the main door closing, missing who had left so quickly after the broadcast had ended. Five other heads followed his, they all missed who had left but none missed the door closing nor the notes in their back pockets.

John Gilder read his note three times, his heart rate increasing with each pass. He scanned the crowd to the five others. Looks of horror mirrored his own. The unspoken truth was laid out before them, what they hoped was merely coincidence clearly wasn't.

Chapter 32

Special Agent Gonzalez was true to her word. She had reset the clock as if nothing had happened, with no lingering resentment from the press conference. She allocated Steve and Evan to continue with Judge Wright's case, while devoting herself and Bryce to other cases. A call had been made and both teams were to be bolstered with further agents being dispatched from the closest field office in Boston.

"I apologize for getting sidetracked earlier," she said. "So what's the real reason we are here?"

Eight heads representing Maine and Knox County's finest detectives turned in unison to the most junior law enforcement officer in the room, Deputy Sheriff Kay Miller, who was yet to join the group and was shuffling furiously through her work. She waited for someone else to respond. No one did.

They had set themselves up in the far corner of the hall, a semi-circle of chairs surrounding two white boards detailing the names and dates of deaths, another board highlighting persons of interest. Kay rose awkwardly and stepped into the center, rubbing her hands together nervously. Special agent Jo Gonzalez wasn't just an ordinary agent, she was one of the top behavioral analysis specialists in the US, and with more serial killers than any other country in the world, therefore the planet. She had more letters after her name than her actual full name, Josephine Gonzalez. Kay had discovered this after googling her. She wished she hadn't, she'd have been a lot more relaxed.

"Perhaps it's best I run through the deceased one by one, that way you can get a full picture of why we are where we are timeline wise."

"Sounds like a good start," Gonzalez encouraged.

Kay described the scene of Frank and Valerie's death and the initial conclusion that they had killed each other. Fitch felt the need to explain part of that conclusion, given his name was lead on the case. Kay had moved on to the apparent accidental death of Walt Spencer, the harbormaster, with the added twist of his potential pedophilic vacations and locked computer. Gonzalez instructed Bryce to get the FBI specialists into the computer immediately. Bryce noted it carefully in his notepad, before tapping out an email detailing the same as Kay continued.

Kay decided to try and keep to the timeline of events. "About two weeks later we received the call that a third party was implicated on the deaths of Frank and Valerie. A Gerald Baker, a convicted sex offender who had been released on parole a few weeks earlier. He has not been seen or heard from since his release from prison. That put a different spin on events, and we re-opened the case into Frank and Valerie's deaths."

"However, there is still a chance they did kill each other. You could argue that Baker's involvement strengthens that argument," said Gonzalez.

"You could, yes," Fitch allowed, seeing how they could have overlooked the angle.

"But I have to admit, his involvement and apparent disappearance do justify your re-opening."

"Shortly after that revelation we had two new victims, Hilary and Charles. Aunt and nephew who had been, it transpired, having inappropriate relations for a very long time. With no apparent marks on either body, we believed Hilary had died of a heart attack while Charles had drowned, perhaps going for help. We're still waiting for toxicology reports."

"Bryce?" Gonzalez said—no explanation was necessary.

"On it!" He noted in his notebook and typed another email. The bureau would be expediting the results.

"We have received again a rather baffling result from that scene. Former deputy Larry Beaumont's semen was found at the scene, more specifically *in* Hilary."

"So, two double deaths with a third-party semen sample." Gonzalez looked like she was going to continue speaking at length but had only one further comment. "Intriguing."

"We certainly thought so. Fitch contacted your department at the bureau but were told we didn't have enough."

"Who did you speak to?" she asked irritably. "We should have been on this ten days ago."

"I can't remember," Fitch told her he, although he knew exactly who it was. Janice. He wasn't about to burn bridges unnecessarily. Gonzalez was making the judgement with hindsight, not as a result of what they knew at the time. "To be fair we only received the Beaumont result three days ago." He gestured for Kay to continue.

"We sent a vacationing detective to visit retired Deputy Beaumont in Florida, but like Baker, he has not been seen for some time. From the unopened mail at his apartment, it would seem they both disappeared at pretty much the same time."

Gonzalez shifted restlessly in her seat. She clearly felt the evidence for their earlier involvement was strong.

"The next death you are aware of Judge Wright's death. We believe this to be completely unconnected from the other deaths."

"I think with what we know and from our initial conversations we can take him off the board. He is unconnected. If you want my initial feelings on the suspect in that case, I wouldn't be surprised if we are looking at upwards of twenty victims. The carer is one of the coldest killers I've sat with in my many years of experience. Yet she clearly was only interested in reward, she would not kill indiscriminately."

Gonzalez's revelation caught them all off guard. They'd thought the five deaths were a reach, never anticipating the number would be higher.

"Which moves us on to yesterday," said Kay, "and the apparent suicide of Jim Kingsley. I would note that we have nothing to date to suggest otherwise. The forensics team themselves are ninety-nine percent certain it was a suicide."

"Toxicology?"

"It's been ordered." Kay paused, awaiting the inevitable.

"Bryce."

"On it!"

'I want to treat it as murder in this room. Until we prove it otherwise, I want them all treated that way. I don't want to have to backtrack in a week, leaving any potential leads to disappear."

All nodded agreement with Gonzalez's instruction.

"So publicly we believe it was suicide, and in here its murder until we prove it was suicide?" Fitch asked for clarity.

Gonzalez nodded. "Yes."

"The review of Beaumont's files was where things started to come together and give us some inkling of what has been happening," Kay went on. "Beaumont was an unremarkable deputy with little to show for forty years of service. I don't think there was one commendation in all of that time. From going through his files, it would appear that was very much how he wanted to be portrayed, but at every turn he had a file that would cover him for any potential outcry. He logged them, he just never officially filed them."

A quizzical look from Gonzalez made Kay realize she needed to expand.

"Let me give an example. Twenty years ago Gerald Baker was accused by a vacationer of being inappropriate with his twelve-year-old daughter. He alleged Baker had tried to touch her while she was swimming in the quarry. We're talking about a large thirty-plus year old man touching a twelve-year-old girl. Beaumont even noted she was immature for her age, so we are talking a straight up sexual assault on a child. Baker completed the report for the gentleman, calmed the situation down, and the vacationer went on with his life assuming Baker had been dealt with. Beaumont never filed the report, and his interview with Baker appears to have been over coffee, where Baker brushed it off as a misunderstanding. Beaumont's files are littered with similar incidents, Baker features many times, meaning there was without a doubt a significant link between the two men."

"And we have all of these files here?"

"We do."

"But surely they condemn him far more than they cover him."

"They do, but only retrospectively. If you consider at any point if a complaint was raised in any one of the cases, he had his copy of the file that he would then have claimed he had filed."

"He retired without destroying them?"

"He was medically retired, we only just uncovered why. He was suffering from dementia. Early stages but he was struggling supposedly. We can only assume he's left not realizing he had left a gold mine of information for us. Although had these deaths not happened, they'd have stayed in storage, so maybe even then he didn't think about them too much."

Gonzalez looked at the board. The list had ended but at the bottom of the victims board were three letters that had been added. "Who is MVC? Is that a new one? I'm not aware of that name."

"Motor Vehicle Crash, a fatal crash that we didn't want to put a name on," said Kay. "It may or may not be linked, it's an older case."

"Convince me."

Kay looked at Fitch; he nodded he'd take it.

"It's a case that's been re-opened with no specific link here other than Beaumont being at the scene which he then covered up along with the trooper who ultimately filed a what we know now falsified report of being first on scene."

"Sounds a stretch, to say the least."

"From the files and what we know of all those protected by Beaumont we have suspicion all were involved in some sort of pedophilic ring. It is only a hunch at the moment but..."

Gonzalez sat up. This case was getting juicier by the minute. A pedophile ring being systematically murdered would be front page and headline news, and combined with the billion-dollar killer, she had hit gold! "So you've linked all of those deaths? Even the victims of the crash?"

"Well no, there are no suspicions on the victims, but it did involve a child. So they were…" Fitch caught himself, he was struggling, the realization that his child may have been abused before dying.

"I think I should explain." Winters stood, wanting to stop his friend's pain. "The victims in that crash were Fitch's wife and daughter."

Gonzalez's head shot towards Fitch, sympathy etched on her face. "I'm so sorry."

"While we don't suspect they had any involvement like the other names on the board, Beaumont's covering of his first-on-scene raises some suspicions as to what he was covering."

"Lieutenant, do you need some time?" asked Gonzalez.

"It's okay. I've had five years and I completely understand I should have no part of wherever that investigation goes, however, I do believe it is a separate case and as such I do wish to continue on this case."

"Let's take five," Gonzalez said. Not waiting for comment, she stood and walked towards Kay, taking her aside. "Do you not see an issue here?"

Kay shrugged.

"Fitch just gave us the number one motive for why you'd kill somebody."

It hit Kay like a steamroller. She hadn't thought about it that way—a pedophile ring abusing and then killing your family, you'd absolutely hunt them down and kill them. "But he didn't know about Beaumont's link to the crash until yesterday, you couldn't fake that reaction."

"You're sure?"

"The man's an open book with his emotions. Trust me, he didn't know. Even then he wasn't on the island for the majority of the deaths. He physically couldn't have done it, never mind mentally. He's a good man."

"I believe *you* believe he is, but do you ever truly know anyone?"

Kay considered Gonzalez's point. "You're right, you never truly can know anyone, but Fitch is innocent, of that I am certain."

"There is definitely a conflict with the link to his wife's crash," Gonzalez pointed out.

"That was five years ago, and victim-wise is an entirely different case. They were victims, these guys are perpetrators."

"Potentially, until proved otherwise," Gonzalez cautioned.

Kay caught Fitch's eye as they both headed back into the hall. Winters was by Fitch's side like the good and trusted friend he was. She could see his eyes asking for an update. She shrugged; she honestly didn't know how Gonzalez was going to play it.

When the group re-convened, Gonzalez stood and contemplated. The silence was deafening, particularly for Fitch, and Kay realized she did not want Fitch off the case, no matter how complicated their relationship or lack of was going to be.

"Fitch, I think there are a few crossovers here that give me some concern," said Gonzalez. "There are many reasons to keep you on the case. You have tried to involve the bureau as soon as you could at every point. You've handed over lead on the investigation by your actions, we've not had to come and take control, and I'm confident we could work together and get a result. But the personal link is troubling."

"I appreciate that, but I wouldn't let you down."

"Oh, I know you wouldn't, but this case is bigger than you. There are many victims involved. We can't risk the case or any potential prosecution because we didn't make the right decision when we should have, and I think we both know the right decision here."

Fitch struggled to disagree. He knew personal life could not impact professional duty. "I understand," he said, crestfallen. "To be honest, I absolutely want to understand the truth behind my wife's crash if there is anything we don't know, but I get that I'm not the person to do it, nor should I be involved in that case. However, I have every faith in the team you have and you as their leader."

"Thank you. I know it's not going to be easy to step away. Let's finish out today and we can talk about handing over your workload tomorrow," she offered as a kind of olive branch. "Kay, was there anything else?"

Kay looked on in stunned silence, the impact and realization of the interaction between Gonzalez and Fitch suddenly hitting her. Lieutenant Ross Abercrombie, Fitch, would be leaving the island, and more importantly, her.

"Kay?" Gonzalez prompted softly, not unaware of the impact of her decision.

"Hmm. Do you mind if I have a minute? Just need to use the restroom." Fitch stood, she waved him back to his seat. She needed time to herself, she'd work out Fitch after she worked out herself. She had never felt a connection with any man that she had with Fitch. She knew it was wrong, knew emotions were heightened as a result of what they were experiencing. In real life, under normal circumstances, she knew she was kidding herself. She had simply never met a man like Fitch. He was a man she could see herself living a long and happy life with. But the history...that was something she couldn't ignore, wouldn't ignore. Perhaps Fitch leaving was for the best. As much as her heart ached at the thought, her head overrode it.

She dabbed her eyes, wiping away tears. She couldn't believe how much of a *girl* she had become around him. She pulled herself together and rejoined the team, avoiding any eye contact with Fitch, just in case the emotions took over. "Sorry, where was I?" she continued confidently. "Oh yes, Reynard's Orphanage, and where I think this may all lead, which was located on the island for many years."

Gonzalez kept her expression neutral but inside she couldn't help but think all her prayers for a career boosting case had been truly answered. She leaned forward imperceptibly in her seat. "Tell me more."

Chapter 33

Kay took a deep breath. "Reynard's Orphanage was a vacation retreat for the State of Maine's orphanages, owned by a trust that opened it around thirty years ago and operated for twenty years. The trust owned Lane's Island, a small island linked by bridge to Vinalhaven. It was there that Frank and Valerie's deaths occurred.

"We're still piecing things together but there is definitely a history of children running away from the establishment. Thanks to Beaumont, it seems, the runaways were filed against their main location and not on the island. It would appear that every orphan who absconded permanently happened to be spotted on the ferry or on the mainland afterwards, meaning they were no longer an island problem."

"Wait a minute, are you thinking what I think you're thinking?" asked Gonzalez.

"What do you think I'm thinking."

"That somehow this pedophilic ring had gained access to the orphanage and drove them to run?"

Kay nodded. "I think we are thinking alike, although I may be slightly ahead of you on those thoughts, given I've had an extra few hours to consider the situation."

"What did those few extra hours add?"

"It's been ten years since the home closed, yet not one of the runaways from those twenty years have surfaced to tell their story, despite the '#metoo' and all the other campaigns."

Murmurs rippled through the team, the impact of Kay's words sinking in.

"So, either nothing happened or…" The full horror of the potential for what Kay was saying hit home. "Jesus, how many?"

"This is where it gets tricky. Shortly after the sale, and rather conveniently given what we are uncovering, a fire wiped out all Reynard's records that had been placed in storage. Everything, paper and computer files alike. Nothing remains. Nothing. I couldn't even find who worked there, not one record remains. All we have are Beaumont's reports, which gives us the runaways' names and their permanent orphanage address. From there we can piece more together, photos, names etcetera."

"This reeks of cover up. So how many are we looking at? Ten?"

Kay had done the calculation already in her head, though she had yet to share it with anyone. Gonzalez and Fitch were both looking her straight in the eye, her gaze switching between both. She dropped the bombshell of the number she had calculated.

"Over one hundred and fifty."

"What the…?" said Winters.

"That's a very big number Kay," Fitch challenged gently.

"Yes. It is just the math though. Approximately nine children went missing a year. Less two years from the twenty, that's over one hundred and fifty."

"We can't assume they were all 'missing,'" said Gonzalez, using imaginary quote marks with her fingers to highlight the word they were using for what could be killed.

"Even ten percent, we're looking at fifteen kids?" cautioned Fitch

"We're getting carried away guys," said Gonzalez. "We have no evidence whatsoever that these kids came to harm. To the contrary, we have statements saying they all got off the island."

"I followed up on a few of those names," Kay said ominously. "Five at random. None of the five were ever sighted again, nor up to twenty years later have they ever surfaced. Anywhere."

"So let's get Reynard's on the board," Gonzalez instructed. "Who is Reynard, do we know?"

"It's a trust so complex it's untraceable. We've no idea who is behind it, and thanks to the fire, it's unlikely we ever will," said Winters, having been tasked by Kay to look into it.

"On it!" Bryce shouted, not waiting for the inevitable.

"Reynard isn't a person's name, it's the name of a fox in old folklore. Vinalhaven is one of the Fox Islands, so I assume it's just a play on that," Kay postured. "I looked it up, I didn't know that."

Fitch smiled proudly at Kay. He had watched her beaver wildly since arriving in the office that morning, he knew she was on to something he just had no idea of the scale of what she had uncovered. Although he, like Gonzalez, cautioned himself it was all supposition, there was no evidence whatsoever that any of the children had succumbed to any harm on the island. Quite the opposite, the only evidence suggested they hadn't.

"Kay," said Gonzalez, "whatdya say we pay Reynard's old place a visit? Fitch, you want to tag along?"

After spending a morning looking at the files and reports, a shiver ran down Kay's spine, the thought was horrifying.

"You look like you've seen a ghost," said Fitch, reaching out to offer her support. His hand gently touched her back, causing her to recoil dramatically.

He removed his hand immediately. "I didn't mean…"

Gonzalez was already leading her out of the room and to the restroom before Fitch could explain himself.

"Do you want to share anything?" asked Gonzalez, her well trained eyes boring into Kay's soul before darting to her jawline and the heavy makeup hiding the purple badge of Fitch's efforts to punch Jackson.

Kay laughed. "Oh! Oh no. That was an accidental punch!"

"Accidental punch? There's no such thing, Kay," she said softly.

Whatever had just happened to Kay in the hall was washed away in an instant. Her cheeks flushed with color and her eyes smiled back at Gonzalez. "I appreciate your concern, I truly do, but it was accidental. I stepped in between two egos at the exact wrong moment."

Gonzalez nodded knowingly. "Let me guess, Fitch and Jackson?"

"Jeez, you are good!"

Gonzalez shrugged. "It's what I do. So, you and Fitch?"

"It's…complicated. Very complicated," Kay said, adding with a grin, "So, you and Bryce?"

Gonzalez laughed. "Touché. That's not complicated. Really, really not complicated." She stopped laughing and changed her tone. "I'm sorry about Fitch, I understand it will affect the dynamic."

Kay nodded. She couldn't speak, not knowing how her emotions were going to react. She was, for the first time in her life, not fully in control of herself.

When Kay walked back into the room, Fitch followed her every move, concerned he had somehow upset her, stepped over a line, or in any way had made her feel uncomfortable. She signaled for him to come to her, taking him outside to talk in private.

"Sorry, I don't know what happened there. I think it was just everything I worked on this morning…it really got to me. All those kids! And of course, knowing you'll not be working with us."

"You couldn't uncover that and not have it affect you, Kay. As for me, you'd be surprised how much happens on these islands that will require a Maine state lieutenant to visit," he said, struggling to smile. He was undoubtedly hurt that his touch had made her physically recoil.

She stepped forward and put her arms around him, pulling him close. He didn't respond instantly, letting his arms hang limply before the smell and feel of her body close to his broke the hurt. He took her in his arms and the feeling filled him with warmth and comfort. Desire was there but not as it had been before. This was a moment for tenderness, and both needed it more than each other would ever truly know.

Chapter 34

Dark gray skies hung low ahead. What had started as a beautiful summer morning had deteriorated as the sun gave way to a front moving in from the south. The darkness ominously beckoned them forward as they drove towards Lane's Island. The sunlight was losing the battle when they crossed the bridge. The town of Vinalhaven stood behind them, the sun still offering the islanders its warmth and light. Ahead lay nothing but darkness and chill and the car instantly cooled.

"Now that's creepy!" Gonzalez exclaimed when the bolt of lightning shot out of the darkness above, illuminating the cottage to their right in full horror style effect.

"Especially given that's where Frank and Valerie died." The hairs on the back of Fitch's neck were standing up. He glanced at Kay in the back. She stared catatonically towards the cottage. Even the crack of thunder accompanying the lightning didn't jar her, nor the sudden downpour of rain, its oversized drops assaulting the windshield with a ferocity that drowned out any talk or thought.

It was a run of the mill summer thunderstorm, a hot, sticky morning followed by a late afternoon air clearing thunderstorm. However, none of them could get over the timing and symbolism given the revelations that had been uncovered that had cast doubt over the history of the small island.

Gonzalez slowed, the ferocity of the rain all but obliterating her view.

"Are you okay?" asked Fitch, turning once again to face Kay behind him. Another bolt of lightning shot upwards, the flash bathing Kay's face in its sudden and brilliant light. Her face was frozen in time, emotionless, lifeless, her death image captured. Fitch reached out and grabbed her hand. It was warm and welcomed his touch and grip. After the flash dispersed her life ebbed back, her soul returned. "Are you okay?" he whispered again.

"Yes," she replied quietly. She tightened her grip in his hand, finding comfort in the connection. Her eyes were staring straight ahead into the seemingly impenetrable rain.

"Five miles an hour and I still can't see where the hell the road is," Gonzalez complained, pulling the car to the side of the road. "We'll just have to wait for this to pass." A third bolt of lightning added an irony to the scene that none of them missed. "Does anyone else feel like we're in some sort of B horror movie?" she asked her passengers.

The comment snapped Kay from her daze. "I'm just waiting for the old creepy gardener to knock on the window and make us jump!"

They all laughed nervously while bracing themselves for the unexpected knock.

Gradually the rain slowed and the darkness moved off. The sun once again logged a victory, pyrrhic as it may have been in the lifelong struggle between the elements. As quickly as the storm had enveloped them it was gone, tracking across the island, wreaking its short-lived commotion.

An imposing white house stood ahead. Sitting atop a small bluff, its unobstructed view south was spectacular. The open ocean dotted with uninhabited islands would offer a tranquility while the view back through the trees towards Carvers Harbor and its myriad of bobbing boats and activity offered some connection to the world.

A number of smaller structures were scattered around the property but none as imposing or striking as the main building. Their car squelched to a stop on the rain sodden drive.

The main door opened and three people stepped out onto the steps at the entrance.

"Somebody told them we were coming?" questioned Fitch.

"Hmmm, small towns," Gonzalez murmured. "There's something nice about the anonymity of big cities, particularly during an investigation."

"Security cameras," Kay noted from the rear of the car. "There are a few on the way in."

Fitch and Gonzalez looked at each other; neither had spotted cameras and they were in the front of the sedan.

"There was zero visibility!" Fitch exclaimed. "How did you see them?

"Guys, I've been on the island for a month, I've driven down most roads before."

"You've been *here* before?"

"Yes and no. I've not actually been in the old folks' home, only done a drive by."

By the time they exited the car, only the soaked ground bore any memory of the sudden storm that had swept across the island. Crisp, clear blue skies reigned again overhead.

An older man stepped forward when they exited the vehicle.

"Laurence Fairchild." He extended his hand. His accent was British, surprising them all given his chino and polo shirt. His perfectly coiffured shock of white hair and deep tan added to his all-American look. He looked like the perfect poster boy for a golfing retirement community, only in Florida, not Maine.

Fitch, Kay, and Gonzalez introduced themselves.

"Well you best come in out of the…" Fairchild looked above, "…sun I guess." He chuckled.

When they reached the top of the steps, he introduced his colleagues. "This is Diane, our matron. That's the English style matron, not your US style." While obviously he expected them to know the difference, none of them felt emboldened enough to question it, although the glances between the three suggested none wanted to look stupid by asking.

"And this is Lottie, my wonderful wife and head of the house." Both women looked to be in their late fifties, early sixties, a few years younger than Laurence. Lottie was dressed immaculately in a summer dress and hat, both of which could have easily paid the matron's salary for a month.

"It's a wonderful house and location," Gonzalez said, making them all turn and soak in the stunning views.

"Thank you, we appreciate it every day."

"It's strange seeing you here," said Lottie with a strong Upper East-Side New York accent. "We were just watching you on the television."

"I can't believe it. That woman, you know she applied for a job with us?" Laurence shuddered. "I'm so glad we turned her down."

"Oh, any particular reason why?" asked Fitch.

"I don't know, we just didn't see a fit." Laurence looked to his matron for her input.

"She gave me the creeps," the Matron said bluntly in a strong Irish accent. "Let's just say I'm not surprised. I was just saying 'I told you so' to Laurence and Lottie."

"Anyway…" Fitch turned to Kay, who was standing near the door as though not really wanting to enter. Uncharacteristically quiet, she was lost in thought. He turned back to the group. "We just wanted to ask about how you came to own the property and whether you had any knowledge of the previous owners?"

Laurence didn't hesitate, no pause for thought to consider his response. "We saw an advert in a property magazine selling the island, along with the orphanage. We had a number of retirement facilities in New York, so plenty of experience. We sold up, bought the island, and here we are."

"So you had no relationship or affiliation with the previous owner?" Kay asked sharply, stepping forward.

Laurence recoiled slightly. Her question had been aggressive despite his willingness to answer questions, and he was taken slightly off guard by the forcefulness of her tone. "Have we done something wrong?" he asked.

"No, no. We just need to understand how you came to own the property," Gonzalez said, stealing the attention away from Kay.

After a furtive look at Kay, Laurence answered, "I believe our attorney commented, if I remember how convoluted the purchase process was due to dealing with numerous offshore entities."

"Thank you," said Kay, her tone conciliatory. She had her answer. "And all the properties on the island are yours?"

"No, four were excluded from the sale, three located on the Eastern shore." He pointed east. "And the old cottage that sits near the bridge, but that was pretty much a ruin anyway. They were supposed to tear it down but it's still there as you know. The other three are fairly small and rarely used, pretty much secluded from us, hidden amongst the trees along the shoreline. It had been a bit of a sticking point on the sale to be honest, but they insisted they were not an option. We worried they'd disturb the tranquility for our residents, but to be honest, in ten years I think I'd struggle to count on one hand how many times we've noticed anyone there."

"Anyone there now?" asked Fitch.

Laurence shrugged. "As I said, we can't really see them from here. If you take the second track on your right when heading back, and then the first right, the three properties are at the end of that road."

"Thanks," said Gonzalez. "And before buying you had no link to the previous owner?"

"We hadn't even visited the island. We lived in Manhattan, and when it became available we just thought, enough of the city life! We've never regretted it one day, although after all these questions…"

Kay remained near the door. It was clear she was keen to move on. From what Laurence and Lottie were saying, it was clearly a waste of their time.

"We've got all these deaths and suddenly the FBI, state police, and the sheriff's office are interested in the old owners?" Laurence was putting two and two together and getting four.

"No, this is not connected to the deaths," Gonzalez lied smoothly. She knew small towns, and once they grasped an angle, it would become the biggest scandal on the island. They needed to shut that down before it started.

"It's not? So is there something else we should be concerned about?'

"No, it's a very old case. In fact, it's to do with an old car accident, completely unrelated."

Laurence looked unconvinced. "And the FBI are interested?"

Gonzalez realized her tactic to keep him from speculating was backfiring, she needed to shut him down. If sharing didn't work, she had another angle. "We are, and if you show much more interest, I'd happily involve you and your solicitor back at the office if you really want to implicate yourself in the matter further."

He backed down. "No, god no. It's just intriguing, my apologies!"

"We really must be getting back. Thank you for your time, and you really do have a lovely home." Gonzalez shook each of their hands before offering a parting caution. "Just to be clear, this is highly confidential and we'll not be discussing it with anyone else on the island, so if we hear something about an old case and the old owners, we'll know where to come first." She smiled.

All nodded before closing the door swiftly behind the three officers.

"Well played, Gonzalez." Fitch then turned to Kay. "Are you okay? You're being very quiet."

"Just listening and learning," she said with a smile, although she was miles away with her thoughts.

"What did you think of the owners?" Gonzalez asked as they climbed into the car.

"I believe them. I don't think they have any idea what went on before they came to the island," Kay replied, the most she had spoken since arriving.

"Likewise," said Fitch, turning to see if Kay had snapped out of whatever was bothering her.

She gave him a wink, all was good. At least on the surface.

"Fair enough. Let's check out the three properties they insisted on keeping."

***

None of them spotted the cyclist off in the distance when they turned as advised, but he spotted them. The slight incline and the vantage point he had as a cyclist had allowed him to see the roof of the sedan before he would have become visible to the occupants. He swerved and deliberately fell to a stop on the bank of the road. He waited for them to change direction, had they witnessed his fall, but after a short while it was clear he had gone unnoticed. He picked himself up and noted a light tear in his jacket, one of his favorites. He swore inwardly, his anger already rising as to why they were driving towards his home. What had that idiot Fairchild told them? He knew it had been a mistake selling to the Fairchilds, but they were the only ones within their extended Society who had the cover story to complete the cash deal as quickly as they needed to ensure the story was quashed. *Story.* He hadn't thought about that for a long time, his anger was sparking memories and potential liabilities, that was one that he had enjoyed closing down a few years earlier, allowing just enough time to pass to ensure there wasn't any link back to them.

Although in his sixties he was fit and active. He brushed himself off, swearing once again at the tear in his jacket, and took the turn to follow the unmarked government sedan. It screamed law enforcement, so why they bothered not marking them he didn't know. As he approached the next turn they would have taken, he took a path into the tree line and dismounted. He tracked through the woods, memories firing as he passed markers that only he and a select few would ever know the meaning of. His anger dissipated as an excitement built, until the voices of the officers began to invade the moment, bringing his anger to the fore. He reached around and felt the pistol, small and easily concealed. It looked ludicrously small in his hands but was more than adequate in defensive situations.

He reached the tree line. The road ahead widened to offer space for the three homes that nestled down by the shoreline. The government sedan parked where the road split into the three driveways to each of the three homes further off in the distance, each buried within their own private woods opening onto the ocean beyond.

He knelt by the tree that he so often admired from his bedroom window, the notches carved in its trunk telling a story only he would ever know. Footsteps approaching had him laying prone amongst the bushes, his vision almost completely obscured by foliage and leaves. He could just about see them; they'd never see him.

"Well?" asked the Latina woman he recognized as the FBI Special Agent from the press conference. He could neither remember her name, nor cared.

"Nothing. Not a sign of life anywhere, all three locked up tight," responded the man who he recalled was Fitch, his nickname from the clothing store Abercrombie & Fitch.

"Nothing in the boat," said a deputy joining them. "I've got the details to check the records. May just be day trippers, hiking and birdwatching on the island though. Part of Lane's Island is a bird sanctuary."

Had she said "on" or "in"? And if she had said "in" did she mean she had gone inside? His hand felt for the grip of the gun, he hadn't expected anyone to go on his boat. He hadn't factored for that nor ensured everything was locked away as tightly as he would normally. He was sure it was, but he hadn't checked. The more he thought, he relaxed the grip on the handle. Had she gone aboard and seen anything untoward she'd not have reported nothing.

He took extra note of her. He had heard about Beaumont's replacement being a young female, certainly a massive improvement in the looks department but nowhere near as helpful, at least to their Society. Beaumont was a true friend of the Society, active even beyond the closure, going above and beyond that what was asked and expected.

He kept himself hunkered down out of sight as the three made back to their vehicle. The deputy opened the rear door and paused. Her gaze circled the area once more, questioning everything she seen. Then she stopped, her eyes fixated on his tree. He reached for the grip, arguing to himself that she couldn't possibly see him, he was completely obscured by the vegetation at the base of the tree. He could barely see her through it, and he was in amongst it. Again, he relaxed. Her eyes were above him, she was focused on the tree itself. He looked closer at her as she stared relentlessly at his tree.

A voice from inside the vehicle broke the spell.

"Come on, Kay!"

Once they were gone he boarded his boat and checked if anyone had been aboard. Without a warrant she'd only have had a quick look from outside, and under no circumstance should she have gone aboard, and definitely not down below. He looked down and instantly relaxed. Everything was fine. He descended the steep ladders, ably assisted by the brass handrails that had to be used in any attempt to get below. It was an older boat, the brass would have been replaced on newer models with cheaper, lighter metals, both cheapening the look and feel of any newer model. He loved the traditional feel the brass provided. His laptop bag was where he had left it, unmoved. He always worried they'd be found, always panicked he hadn't covered himself, but he did it so naturally it wasn't something he needed to check. Even if it had been found, the security was such he shouldn't concern himself. He was a worrier, he always ensured he covered his tracks, always one step ahead.

He'd paid for the charter in cash under a fake name that would check out on the surface. If they dug too deep, they'd find it wasn't real. He had to balance off whether they would do any more than a surface check. The deputy had said herself probably hikers or birdwatchers using the dock for the day.

Even if they did check, digging would take time and he only needed a few more hours on the island.

Chapter 35

"Are you sure you're okay?" asked Fitch.

She had closed her door, her eyes still focused on the large tree across the road.

Kay leaned forward in the seat conspiratorially, her eyes darting to and fro between Fitch and the tree line. "I don't know, I just got a feeling…you know…when it's like someone is watching?"

"Did you see someone in the trees?" Gonzalez asked, turning her head towards the tree line.

"No, just… you know that creepy feeling you sometimes get that something is watching you?"

"Some*thing*? Not some*one*? What, like a monster?" Fitch chided.

Kay sat back in her seat and looked silently out to the trees.

Gonzalez hit the gas and they headed back to the town hall, they had a lot to check up on following the trip.

Kay remained silent for the journey. Fitch tried to engage to no avail, while Gonzalez just played over the conversations in her mind.

Fortunately, the far extremities of Lane's Island were a mere five-minute car ride to the town hall. The silence by the time they parked was deafening, at least for Fitch. Kay exited the car before it had even fully stopped and was at her desk, head down, by the time Gonzalez and Fitch caught up with her.

Winters looked at Fitch questioningly having been ignored by Kay when she stormed into the hall. Fitch shrugged, stopping himself from uttering the word that *the BOAT ?*

he knew would alienate the only other woman in the office and for all intents and purposes his boss. Winters understood and rolled his eyes skywards in a gender supporting acknowledgement.

Kay was disappointed. She thought Fitch got it, got her, they connected, yet he was making fun of her. She touched the small flash usb stick in her pocket she had taken from the boat. She had been extremely careful, noting exactly where everything had been before investigating. She knew she shouldn't even have gone aboard but they needed a break and there did seem something off about the boat, located by the three homes that the Reynard's Trust had refused to sell. It wasn't until she went below it hit her, she turned back to the brass handrails that she had no option but to use to assist her descent into the living quarters, the only marks were hers. She considered her exit, six steps at an incline, impossible to make without using the handrails. They were pristine, polished to perfection, the prints aside. She blew on the cold metal, where she knew she would have to place her hands to exit, pristine, no prints. She went into the small shower room, blew on anything she thought would be touched. Nothing, no prints, the galley likewise. The boat was wiped clean. Not a fingerprint to be found anywhere.

With little time and no justification for snooping, she noted where everything was, carefully replacing everything she checked and wiping them down as carefully as the occupant clearly had. Of course, there may have been a perfectly legitimate reason, Obsessive Compulsive Disorder, requiring the constant cleaning of the occupant's living area. From what she could tell it was one male, and judging by the clothing probably older. She noted the laptop but also knew opening it may result in an inopportune photo being sent to the owner alerting them to a potential theft and the thief, and therefore left it closed. Other than the potential cleaning fixation, and complete lack of any ID or personal paraphernalia, there was nothing of any note. The lack of ID could simply be it was in a wallet on their person. She replaced the laptop in the bag, a clacking noise alerted her something else was in the bag. She reached down and retrieved the item. A small keyring, no keys attached, just a cartoon like animal design dangled from the metal ring, a kid's design, she recognized it. A red fox. A black line at its neck looked out of place, she pulled, and the body split off. It wasn't just a toy keyring, it was a flash drive, the metal adapter with familiar two small square holes hung below the fox's head. The body and bushy tail were separate in her other hand. She knew it was wrong, every thought in her mind told her not to as she pocketed the key ring. She had put everything back exactly where had found it, and clinically wiped down every surface she had touched and breathed on. Apart from the missing keyring, no one would have known she was there.

She had planned to share her find with Fitch, thinking it best to keep Gonzalez out of the loop until there was anything worth risking her career and potential freedom over. The FBI were sticklers for procedure, and she would effectively be admitting to breaking and entering by divulging the flash drive's existence to Gonzalez. Likewise with Fitch but Fitch was, well…up until he'd made fun of her in the car—Fitch.

Kay knew things had changed the previous morning. They had almost crossed a line but fortunately they were interrupted. She wasn't sure how she'd have felt knowing what she knew if they had crossed that line.

While Fitch's wife and daughter may have both been dead for five years, they were back in the picture, and his grief was as raw as it had always been.

She felt the flash drive in her pocket, thought about inserting it into the laptop on her desk, but knew if anyone spotted it she'd give herself away, unable to explain where she had got it and when. It would be her homework when she got home. In the meantime, she fired up the laptop and searched for everything she could find on Laurence and Lottie Fairchild.

Fitch couldn't concentrate, his eyes constantly drawn to Kay and what she was doing. She hadn't looked over once since their return. He felt like a schoolkid with a crush, his stomach churning at the thought she didn't like him anymore. He hadn't meant anything in the car, he just thought it was funny. The thought it was his last day and they were ending on bad terms made it all the worse. Winters would have got it. Fitch hadn't had a woman in his life for five years, he'd forgotten how different things could be construed. He had forgotten how to be in a relationship, not that he hastened to assure himself he and Kay were. It had been so easy with Kay, they had just connected. It had seemed so natural, so like… He caught himself. He couldn't think like that. He glanced over again, the top of her head remained his only reward. He typed in the name of the reporter who twelve years earlier had started questioning Reynard's runaway numbers, resulting in an overnight drop in runaways ultimately across the state due to how the numbers were reported based on the orphan's main residence and not their absconding from the island retreat.

It was over an hour later that he came up for air and realized he hadn't once glanced across at Kay. He looked over excitedly, she was staring back at him angrily.

"What?" he mouthed.

"Apology?" she mouthed back.

Seriously, he was going to have to brush up on his interpersonal skills with the opposite sex. He kicked himself. All she wanted was an apology for belittling her. Which, to be fair, he had done in front of the new team leader. Winters would have laughed it off, but it wasn't about what Winters would have done. He couldn't judge Kay by his standards. It was about what Annie, his wife, would have done. Which was exactly what Kay had done, been annoyed and awaiting his apology, which wasn't forthcoming.

"I'm sorry," he mouthed.

She sent him a smile across the office that could have blown him off his seat. He grinned back like a child, resulting in her laughing out loud. He laughed back. It was all good. Well, that was between them. What he had just uncovered was far from good, it was truly shocking.

Chapter 36

The orange hues of sunset filled the hall. One by one the officers and agents paused, the beauty of the day's end coming to a close sweeping gently and peacefully across them. Their eyes were drawn to the sky's bloody but peaceful battle with darkness that played out endlessly, day after day, the outcome never in question.

"Guys!" Gonzalez, her voice slicing through the peaceful and serene moment. Yeah, it's a beautiful sunset but people are dying. On me," she instructed, bringing the group together like an AA meeting, each waiting to confess their findings.

Fitch was last to the group, taking the last seat available, between Kay and Winters who had kept him a place. He winked his thanks and took the seat.

Gonzalez briefed the rest of the team on the trip to the former children's home, advising that Fitch and Kay were following up on additional confirmation. "I checked the details about the boat from the dock. It's a one week charter out of Portland, paid for in cash by an David Clarke. So far everything checks out. Clarke is a small time landlord, unmarried, and from what I can see a bit of a loner who enjoys the outdoors, sailing, and bird watching. I've got an agent swinging by his residence tomorrow to check it's legit. I'll also stop by this evening and see if I can have a word with him."

"Do you want me to come with?" asked Bryce.

Fitch and Kay managed to stifle their childlike grins, gently nudging each other's knees.

Gonzalez spotted their exchange. "That would be great. Thanks, Bryce, I'll make it up to you." She smiled, knowing exactly what she was saying, then passed the baton. "Kay?"

Kay struggled to remain professional. Gonzalez was obviously playing them at their own game. *Kudos to her,* Kay thought.

"I've being running some background on Laurence and Lottie Fairchild. So far everything checks out. They've run retirement homes for some time, wealthy ex-New Yorkers who purchased the home ten years ago in a cash deal. That's where it gets a little strange. We're talking all cash, no mortgage or loans, 18.5 million dollars."

Kay paused to let the number sink in. It worked. The others shook their heads in disbelief.

"From calls I've made to local brokers, the highest quote based on today's market would be just under ten million for the island and properties. Although to be fair, they had no idea the commercial value of a retirement home, they were basing the sales on residential only values."

"But we're talking an extra ten mil for a retirement home business?" Winters whistled.

"Interesting," Fitch remarked without further comment. He looked as though he was only half listening.

"Apparently, although I have a call into a business sales specialist to check that out."

"You know," Knox County detective Kyle Moore interrupted, "it may not be crazy. I've been getting quotes for a place for my dad. He's not doing too well but it's eye watering what these guys charge. Fortunately with him being a former officer we'll get help from the county, but we're talking over five thousand dollars a month and that's basic."

"Trust me, this place was far from basic," said Gonzalez. "We're talking five-star resort with the world's best views from just about every room. If I retire, I want to go there."

"Well you'd better start saving," Kay advised. "Fifteen thousand per month starting price, for one of only twenty spots."

"Holy shit that's…" Winters paused to work out the math.

"About four million dollars a year in revenue," Kay supplied helpfully.

"Whoa. Worst case you're making two mil a year, so ten mil additional is repaid in five years." Winters blew out a breath. "I'm in the wrong game!" He looked at Fitch, who simply nodded, his mind elsewhere. "Did you hear that, Fitch? I'm quitting and getting into old people's care."

Fitch snapped out of it in an instant at the ludicrousness of what he was saying, "You couldn't even change your own kids' diapers, what are you gonna do with a full-grown man who needs changing?"

The room burst into laughter as Winters twisted his face in disgust. "Nah, forget that. Never happening!"

"Well maybe it isn't strange. In any event, I can find no links between the Fairchilds and the island or Reynard's trust prior to their purchase."

"Let's see what the valuer says and if there's nothing there, we'll leave them be. In the meantime, I'll leave them on the board." Gonzalez turned from Kay. "Fitch?"

"As you know, I've been looking into the report of the runways that we believe ultimately led to the sale and change to a retirement home. The reporter had uncovered that almost all the runaways still missing after a year from orphanages across the state of Maine had run away from one place, Reynard's on Vinalhaven. This had been covered by Beaumont's reporting of sightings either on the ferry or on the mainland, meaning that Reynard's and the island remained untouched by the potential scandal for many years."

"Do we have a number?"

"Not as yet. The Bureau is tracking everyone to find any that have since resurfaced out of state, and there were a few that did run away from other orphanages so we're starting from a number just above one hundred. However, I expect that will fall over the next few days. How far I don't know, but I doubt all one hundred or so decided to hide away permanently never to be seen or heard from again."

"Are you suggesting—"

"I'm not suggesting anything." Fitch shrugged. "I'm merely going through the information I have. We have upwards of a hundred kids who have effectively disappeared from the face of the Earth over an eighteen-year period. It may be every one of them got the hell out of Maine and are living in California. I'm sure many of them are out of state and nobody bothered connecting the dots. They were orphans, the majority aged between 9 and 14, so weren't getting adopted anytime soon."

"Male or female?" asked Gonzalez.

"Fairly evenly split, maybe slightly more females but there are reports suggesting at that age they're more likely to run away, so it pretty much follows the stats."

"I'm getting confused," said Dan, the other Knox County detective. "Are we hunting the killers of the dead," he pointed to the board, "or are we looking into the scandal of runaways at the children's home over ten years ago?"

"Good question," Gonzalez acknowledged. "This case is about the recent deaths but wherever that takes us I'm going to go. I've worked on many cases and none to date have made less sense than this group of deaths." She circled her hand around the photos of the victims.

"And Fitch's wife and daughter, let's not forget them," Kay added.

"Yeah, but they're not linked to this. Beaumont maybe," Winters countered, while Fitch remained silent. "But runaway orphan from years earlier? Come on."

Kay shrugged, not wanting to air her thoughts publicly and risk upsetting Fitch further.

"Before we all come to conclusions without any evidence, let me add some fire to the mix," Fitch pitched in, grabbing all of their attentions. "I tracked down the reporter who broke the story. Took some doing since she retired from journalism a couple of years after breaking the news."

Kay looked at him in surprise. "But the reporter was quite young, wasn't she?"

"Late twenties maybe when she retired from journalism. Packed up and headed off around the world. I couldn't find any sign of her anywhere. She went travelling and then nothing," Fitch paused, "but I managed to find her parents. Strange thing…to this day they never knew why she up and left, still don't and never will."

"What?" Kay questioned. "She's dead?"

"Four years ago. Shot and killed. Carjacking gone wrong apparently. She had just landed back in the US and was on her way to see her parents."

"What the actual fuck is going on here!" Gonzalez exclaimed.

Even Kay didn't feel it was appropriate to complain at the profanity such was the constant surprise in the turn of events.

"It gets better. Or worse, whatever way you want to spin it," added Fitch. "Her parents inherited 8.3 million dollars from her estate."

"She did well on her travels!"

"According to her parents, she worked in bars part-time and taught English as she traveled the world, partying as she went. No career or any suggestion of anything she did where she'd have earned that kind of money."

Kay was first to cotton on. "You're thinking payoff?"

"She headed off just after the trust sold the island for 18.5 million. Five, six years of traveling the world, what would that cost? Not extravagant, just casual, student style with some fun, say around 1.5 to 1.7 million I'd guess."

"From your ten-mil payout. Holy shit!" exclaimed Winters.

"From a business sold for ten million more than it may have been worth," Kay surmised. She glared at the board. "Laurence and Lottie Fairchild are mixed up in this." They had so nearly been removed from it.

"Maybe. There *is* a chance the sale was legitimate, but that number stinks when you look at the big picture."

"So, Dan," Gonzalez responded, turning from Fitch to the detective, "to answer your earlier question, I think this case just got a whole lot bigger. Guys, it's going to be a big day tomorrow and I'm going to need a lot more agents."

Fitch, Winters, and Kay sat silently. Their little investigation was spiraling out of control. Well, their control at least. Gonzalez was firmly in charge, and now there was the addition of missing children and state lines in the mix. With Fitch leaving there was every chance they'd be sidelined, if not removed entirely from the case.

Whether their demeanor welcomed it, or Gonzalez was a mind reader, she made a beeline for them. "Whatever you're thinking about Fitch coming off the case, more agents coming on board, don't worry, you're the core of my team. I need you guys, no matter how crazy it gets here, don't forget that!" She pointed to Bryce, then the door, and was gone.

"Shit!" said Kay. "This is crazy!"

Winters nodded grimly. "My thoughts exactly, although I'm not appreciating the foul language." He smirked.

The three laughed. A nervous, *oh* my god *what's happening* laugh, but a laugh, nevertheless.

"You eating with us?" asked Fitch.

"Not tonight, sorry. I've got a few things I need to do," Kay replied, surprising both Fitch and Winters. The flash drive was burning a hole in her pants, she needed to see what was on it.

"It's his last night," Winters pleaded. "Come on, Kay, a condemned man deserves a last supper!"

"I'm sorry."

Fitch sucked up his disappointment, hiding it badly. Winters put his arm around his friend. "Game and a burger for the boys then!" he said cheerily. "Any of you guys up for a game and a burger for Fitch's last night?" he asked the others in the hall.

"He has to hand over tomorrow, it's not his last night." Kay smiled. "You see the boys tonight and we'll have dinner tomorrow."

"That sounds good." Winters nudged Fitch, who was perking up at the new plan.

"Not you, Mark, just me and Fitch." Kay winked.

Fitch smiled more broadly and inanely than he'd have wished.

Kay made for the door, patting her pocket to check the flash drive was there. She could have gone for dinner and then checked it but her eagerness to see what it contained was too powerful to delay it any longer.

***

He checked his watch; two hours until they were due to meet. He'd made himself a quick bite to eat. Following the earlier visit, he decided against opening up his home and instead kept to the yacht. That way he could keep to the cover story if challenged. He finished eating and after he cleaned, wiped down every item and surface he might have touched. When done, he turned to the small table, retrieving his laptop case from beneath. He opened and pulled out his MacBook. He knew it hadn't been touched, he had ten seconds to enter a password before he received a photo of whoever had opened it. New security had made the app defunct, but he kept operating an older operating system to keep it working. He didn't need others getting involved. If somebody stole from him, he wanted to know who they were, and he'd deal with them. The last thing he needed was to involve the police.

He input the password and awaited a prompt, it never came. The flash drive wasn't plugged in. Nothing new. He reached down into the bottom of the case and felt around, nothing. His heart rate increased. He opened the case wide, nothing. It wasn't there. He checked around the floor, nothing. It wasn't there.

He glanced around the yacht. Nothing was out of place, not a mark left anywhere, everything as clean and wiped down as he had left it. He knew the deputy had been near the boat, though whether she was the one who took it he couldn't be sure. She was an officer not a thief, she didn't have any idea or inclination as to the importance of what had been taken.

He thought back to his bike ride, thinking perhaps he had *not* gone unnoticed. He looked out to the two other properties, maybe they were occupied after all. Someone, someone who knew the importance, had sneaked aboard and covered their tracks. He ruled out the deputy. This wasn't a crime of chance, someone who knew him, who knew he was there, had deliberately removed it. Nothing else made sense. But why? What had they to gain? That in itself didn't make sense, nothing on the flash drive was not accessible to them all, had their livelihoods and freedom riding on the knowledge that if one was exposed, all were exposed. It was a condition of the Society. A cunning and devious group of likeminded people bound by their hunger, predators, preying on the vulnerable. An unsavory bunch, no doubt, but burglary and theft was not their way.

He considered the deputy again. The covering of tracks was so impressive he hadn't realized she had been aboard, but how had she known to be that careful? He was too fastidious. He looked at the brass work that he wiped every time he used it. He walked over to the handrail, placed his hand, and removed it, his sweaty palm showed, its dullness highlighting the shine. She was good, too good for a run of the mill backwater deputy, and was willing to go outside of the law. He had heard her update her colleagues that the boat was clear. Why? With two hours to spare, he needed to understand more about the new deputy of Vinalhaven.

Chapter 37

The loose gravel crunched under the weight of the sedan, announcing their arrival as the still of night fell across the island. Each chuck of gravel echoing under the car created a noise that during the day was all but silent but at night would challenge a twenty-one-gun salute for volume.

The boat bobbed gently in the night, its windows multiplying the darkness emphasizing the lack of life. The homes, likewise, had their windows menacingly dark against the whiteness of the paintwork that was doing everything in its power to shine but barely beating the darkness of the windows.

"I don't think anyone's here," said Bryce.

Gonzalez looked at him with pity. He wasn't the brightest or the best she had worked with. He had other talents, unfortunately none of them work related, but certainly welcome. She'd make use of them later. At the moment she needed him to keep quiet and let her think. She opened the car door and felt a shiver run down her spine. ,She spun to the tree line and the dark, ominous tree that sat head and shoulders above those around it towering ominously over them. She caught a movement by the base of the trunk and her eyes zeroed in on it, her hand reaching for her revolver. Bryce was by her side, his weapon drawn. What he lacked in brains he made up for in bravery. Without a second thought he moved towards the tree, lighting the base with his flashlight, held as he had been taught at Quantico, under his revolver. A rabbit shot out, startling them both, not realizing how close it had come to receiving a .45 caliber bullet through its head.

"This place gives me the heebie jeebies," said Gonzalez.

"The what?"

"Oh forget it," Gonzalez said, then thought to herself, *Millennials..*

"What now?" asked Bryce.

"Exactly. What now?" Gonzalez cast her gaze back to the yacht, its mast swaying in tune with the gentle swell. Stake out the boat or come back in the morning? She looked at Bryce, there was no point gauging his thoughts. "Let's go and hone those talents of yours," she said with a wicked grin.

***

When the car door closed he let out a breath he had been holding for what felt like a lifetime. Somebody was looking for him. Where the rabbit had come from, he had no idea, but had it not he'd have been dead or in the back of the sedan for questioning, trying to explain why he had been hiding in a bush at the base of the tree with a pistol pointed at the FBI. He had no business owning the pistol and his fingerprints would have most certainly caused an issue.

He calmed, breathing deeply. They were gone and from what he had heard would not be back that night. Five minutes earlier and he'd have been on the boat. He had just retrieved his bike when he had heard them approach. Fortunately he had no problem in the dark, no concern for monsters or boogeymen. Not surprising since, after all, he was one himself.

He picked up his bike and hopped on. He didn't have much time, but it wasn't far, and he could go straight to the meeting thereafter.

Chapter 38

Kay settled down on the deck. It was a beautiful warm night, and the stars sparkled above. The chill of late spring had finally relented, allowing the humidity of the summer to prevail. It made for less comfortable sleep but the benefits of sitting out on the deck basking in the evening warmth, staring up at the wondrous sky, the stars shifting as the planet spun below, and the lack of light pollution offered a perspective like no other. It drew her in, the scale and size incomprehensible in its vastness, mind blowing in its depth.

She set her laptop on the small table she had brought out from the lounge. She was reluctant to open it, for the light from the screen would obliterate a vast swathe of universe as only the brightest of stars would be visible outside the light her screen would emit. She reached for the glass instead, glass number two. It had taken one to get herself over what she had actually done. The more she considered her actions the more she realized how crazy she had been. She was with a state detective and an FBI agent and she had broken into a private boat and stolen property. She downed half the glass. The more she thought about it, the worse it sounded. What the hell had she been thinking? Kay looked at the device in her hand. Just over an inch long, the cuteness of the design made it all the more uncomfortable and surreal. She topped up her glass.

She watched the boats bob in the distance, their mast lights telling the world they were there for all to see. She pulled the fox apart, its body slid easily off, exposing the adapter she could place in the USB port on her laptop. She opened the laptop, its screen lit up her face, instantly killing her ability to see beyond the end of the deck, never mind the universe beyond. Another sip from her glass postponed the moment of truth. She entered the password that opened her computer and slid the flash drive into the hole. *Dens*, sprung to mind, the fox's head peeking out of the side of the computer as if coming out of its den. A prompt appeared but she never got to read what it said.

***

It wasn't hard to find most people on Vinalhaven but especially not a deputy, of which there was only one, and who drove a truck with Sheriff Knox County emblazoned along the side in reflective letters that shone under the streetlight that was cast on the driveway of the deputy's home. It also helped he had been in Beaumont's old home many times, so knew exactly where he was going.

His approach to her door went undetected. He placed each foot with extreme caution to ensure any debris likely to crunch or grate was avoided, shadows casting under the streetlight his best guide. No shadows, no noise. He made it to the door and listened intently, holding his breath. No sound came from within. No lights offered any hint she was home, her truck the only clue suggesting she was. He placed his ear against the door. Silence. He ventured up to the semi-circular pane of decorative glass at head height that offered a view outside to those inside, the glass distorted for privacy. You wouldn't know who was there but you'd know someone was. But it worked both ways.

He peered into the glass, his eyes as close as he dared so as not to leave any traces of DNA behind. A tiny movement gave her away. He knew the house well enough to know she was beyond the lounge, out on the deck. He also knew the impressiveness of the view; she'd be looking outward not inward towards him. He was transfixed, trying to work out what she was doing, until finally he realized she was raising her arm, her hand went to her mouth. She was drinking.

He stepped back from the door and pulled out the overalls he had brought for the purpose, a protective suit similar to any forensic officer's, perfect for protecting crime scenes but with one major alteration. His were dyed black, or more correctly, a very dark gray. Black, he found, was too dark and stood out. He pulled the coveralls over his shoes and then his entire body, covering all but his face in the protective clothing. Dark latex gloves, a mask, and goggles ensured no one would know he had been there. He retraced his steps back to the door and tried the door handle, turning it as slowly as it would allow while still rotating. It was locked. He swore under his breath. Who the hell locked their door in Vinalhaven? Beaumont had certainly never locked the door.

A light from the deck lit up the house and he ducked instantly but no movement followed. He was taking too long, he needed to speed it up.

**

As she slid the fox home, Kay heard a noise from behind, startling her. The laptop clattered onto the tabletop and she spun towards the noise. She grabbed for her pistol; her holster was empty, she had left it in the bathroom earlier. She grabbed the wine bottle, the next best thing, and held its neck tightly, its remaining contents slopping across the floor as she stalked towards the door. "Who's there?" she shouted, no idea why she was spooked until she realized why. No car had preceded the noise, no headlights, nothing, just suddenly noise at her door. She had warned Brian, her teenage stalker, so she didn't think it would be him. He had almost wet himself from her warning and had far more on his mind.

"Who's there?" she shouted again but her voice was drowned out by a knocking at the door and the twisting of the handle.

She could see a black mass standing in front of the door. She had the wine bottle in her hand or she could go for her pistol. She glanced towards the bathroom, it was on the other side of the front door, if they broke the door down she'd be caught with her back to the intruder.

"Who's there!" she demanded again.

A muffled sound emanated from behind the door and the black mass in the window disappeared, slumping downwards. She dropped the wine bottle and rushed to the door.

She threw it open and caught Fitch, taking as much of his weight as she could bear as he sank to the floor. "Oh my god, what happened to you?" Holding him tightly she pulled him into the house to safety. She kicked the door closed behind him, the mess could wait

"What the hell?" Kay ran her hand soothingly through his hair.

His eyes opened briefly at the tenderness of her touch. "Sorry," he mumbled almost incoherently. "I'm a bit of a lightweight."

"No kidding, either that or someone's being spiking your drinks!" Kay ignored the puke he had deposited on himself as he had emptied his stomach over her porch and door.

"Let's get you cleaned up," she said, dragging him to the bathroom. It wasn't appropriate to remove all his clothes, but she certainly wasn't disappointed in any she did remove before sitting him under the shower. His boxers left some mystery for her to uncover at a later date, it was the least she could do, although it took every bit of decency she could muster. The man was ripped and certainly still worthy of his name.

"Thank you," he spluttered as the warm water rained over him.

A noise from the deck caught Kay's attention. She propped Fitch against the wall and rushed outside. Her cell was ringing, insistent to be answered.

Winters' name was flashing on the screen. She picked it up and accepted the call.

"Have you got him?" His voice was panicked.

Her laptop caught her eye. The light was spilling across the tabletop, lighting up the vicinity. It had a ten-minute sleep function. The screen was stuck on her desktop, the standard one that the computer used unless changed by the user. It had been less than ten minutes since Fitch had arrived.

Kay was speechless, her tongue caught in her mouth.

"Is he there?" Winters' panic was rising.

"Yes," she replied, looking frantically around the area ahead and behind her, "but so is someone else!"

"What?"

"Come quick!" She hung up and raced to the bathroom. Fitch remained almost catatonic as she grabbed her pistol and rushed back to the deck.

She looked at the laptop to make sure she hadn't made a mistake, she hadn't, she daren't touch it for fear of disturbing evidence. The fox's head, the flash drive she had stolen, was gone. Someone had stolen it.

Chapter 39

Flames danced with the breeze in perfect unison, beckoning the visitors onwards, guiding them with their hypnotic warmth towards the meeting. The doors lay open, welcoming the invited few. For some, it had been many years since they had stepped foot in the building.

"Nice touch" said the man, admiring the torches that had been staked into the ground, lighting the route to the "den." At least that was what it had been called previously. He noted the games room sign above the door disapprovingly. "Where's the head?"

"Storage," replied a man he knew to be the new owner, at least on paper, Laurence Fairchild, his crisp English accent giving him away.

"Get it!" he commanded.

Laurence didn't move. "Long term storage. I didn't think it wise to keep it here," he mumbled. "If I had more notice…"

He waved his hand to stop Laurence's groveling apology. It was sound thinking he couldn't argue with. The carved wooden fox head had stood over the door for years and was the very symbol of their Society. The beauty of the change to a retirement home had resulted in the instant cleansing of the site, dissociating it from its past.

He walked into their old den. It had transformed from the days when he had overseen the facility. No money had been spared on the games room for the rich retirees. An ornate stone fireplace reached up to the ceiling taking up a large portion of the wall where a simple fire had once burned the cold nights away.

Luxurious furnishings and games tables and seats littered the area, giving a luxury lodge feel to what had been an old barn split by temporary partitions offering the Society members privacy when required. The central meeting area had been replaced by a large billiards table.

"No expense spared I see," he said critically.

Laurence shuffled nervously towards a woman shifting uncomfortably in an oversize and expensive armchair, Lottie, he assumed. The rest of the room nodded their welcome. All had attended, none had dared not show. He had always kept them abreast of every action, it was the reason they had all shown, the reason none would have ignored his instruction.

"I'm sure many of you, like me, are basking in some of the wonderful memories we have from our times spent in our den," he began addressing the skulk, as he called them, being the name for a group of foxes.

The reference to foxes was used extensively. He thought of himself as the alpha of the skulk.

"It's been too long since I have seen many of you and sadly, because of recent tragedies, there are some we will never see again."

A murmur rippled through the fourteen pairs of eyes that stared back from behind their fox masks. This was a society where anonymity ruled. Many knew who each other was, always had, having initiated one another to join over the years. But only one person knew all of their identities and their actions over the years.

"There can be no coincidence that we have lost some of our more devoted members. No coincidence. We are under attack, of that there is no doubt."

They looked around at each other, nobody knew if it was from within or outside the group that they faced danger and potential death.

"I see you looking at each other. I know brothers Baker and Beaumont have been implicated but I know them, and I cannot believe they have any part of this. I wanted to assure you nor have I, I feel each loss deeply. You are my family, my kindred spirits on this Earth. We are joined as one until death and beyond."

"How can we be sure it's no one amongst us?" a member asked. "And how else would anyone know?"

"I'm certain it's no one amongst us, we are connected by a bond stronger than blood, stronger than family."

"Yeah, fear," came a mutter from the group.

"*NO!*" he boomed. "Not fear, a common desire. Together that desire drives us, protects us. Alone we are nothing. Outcasts, unwelcome in a world that doesn't understand."

The majority nodded, knowing it to be true. Together they *were* strong, they had been the backbone of the community that had brought them together. Few were island born, the majority had joined the Society and as a result had moved to the island, living in a safe and protected environment, free from the dangers their desires would have caused them had they lived their life hidden and alone. Together they had been strong, they had fulfilled their deepest desires while living under the protection the Society and its members offered them.

"Let us take a moment to remember our fallen brethren." He waited to ensure he had all of their attention. "Frank, Valerie, Walt, Hilary, Charles, Jim…" He turned his focus to Laurence and Lottie. "And let's not forget our very good friend Judge Francis Wright, without whom we'd not be enjoying the opulence that surrounds us!"

"Why risk calling us here together?" asked a masked member. "Surely you're putting us at risk, not protecting us."

"It's important you all know that we are still one, still together. Still looking out for one another as we have been throughout the years. Our time on this island may have been interrupted but we are still watching over you."

"So why are seven of us dead!"

"Someone has targeted us, of that we can now be certain. The circumstances at first did add doubt, but now that doubt has been removed. For those who have attended tonight I will be arranging additional protection. You won't know it's there but rest easy, now that we know we are in danger we will—"

A buzzer sounded, interrupting him. He looked to Laurence, who was already moving towards a cabinet in the wall. He opened the door and revealed a bank of TV screens, security cameras covering the retirement home and its buildings.

"Someone's triggered the perimeter alarm," Laurence, flicking between the camera views at his disposal.

"Everyone relax, I'll deal with this," said the man with a confidence that none dared question. "Laurence, lock the door behind me."

Chapter 40

Kay checked Fitch one last time, ensuring he was in a position where if he threw up again, he wouldn't choke, before chasing after the flash drive thief. Although, given she had stolen it herself, she wasn't entirely sure what legal justification she had for her actions. Whatever the case, she knew she was doing the right thing, the man was clearly involved with the history of the island and the orphanage, why else would he have moored his boat where he had?

He may have had a head start but she knew exactly where he was going, she just had to get there before he set sail. At night with lights off he'd be all but invisible and they'd potentially lose any chance of questioning him or finding out the secrets the flash drive held. Whatever they were, the risk of stealing from a deputy were worth it, to keep them secret, only ensuring Kay wanted to see them all the more.

Worst case, she reckoned she was ten minutes behind the man. With no sounds of cars prior to the theft, she had to assume he had parked a good distance away or come by foot or bike. Whatever the case, that ate into his advantage, benefiting her as she pushed harder on the accelerator of the truck, careering over the small bridge onto Lane's Island. All four tires left the safety of the road, crashing down with a thud after a brief airborne spell. The turn for the sailboat approached and Kay slowed, ready to take the turn at what would still have been too fast. However, a trail of torch lights led off towards the retirement home, beckoning her in a different direction. With everything else going on the trail of burning torches were out of place, like some sort of ritualistic event was underway. She hit the accelerator and decided to follow the trail marked out for whoever was expected. After all, due to the revelations of earlier, Laurence and Lottie Fairchild were not as innocent as they had claimed.

Kay killed her engine before reaching the end of the trail, coasting as far as the truck's momentum allowed. She wanted to surprise whoever was there, not have them scattering before she could identify them. She followed the trail past the main house and down a small pathway to what appeared to be an old barn. The flames of the torches danced to the rhythm of the nighttime breeze, hypnotically beckoning her onwards. Smoke from the flames engulfed her as the path narrowed, leading her on and on. Whether it was the wine she had drunk earlier or some kind of fumes being emitted by the flames she didn't know, all she did know was that she was losing control of herself. The torch flames beckoned her onwards, all thoughts of stealth and surprise abandoning her. Her only thought was to follow the pathway towards the barn. The nearer she got the more she realized her mind was struggling to focus, she circled the barn once, only one door in and out, the two windows on either side offered no view inside, all were blocked by curtains drawn inside.

Kay returned to the front of the barn, where the door opening urgently stopped her in her tracks. One man exited—she guessed it was a man from his size. He was cloaked in a gown and wearing a strange animal mask. Her mind struggled to place it before realizing it was a fox mask. She didn't duck or attempt to hide, she simply froze like a rabbit caught in the headlights of an oncoming vehicle. As surreal as the moment was, she was powerless. The man had her in his sights and she simply waited for him to take her.

As quickly as the door had opened it slammed closed behind the man in the mask, the sliding of metal before a bolt had been rammed home, locking it. There was no going back for the man and no welcome for Kay ahead.

Their eyes met but neither moved, the barn offering one last distraction as flames took hold and traced their way up the old wooden structure. Smoke began to billow into the night sky as flames came to life and shot onwards and upwards, their goal to grow as quick and fast as the old wooden barn would allow. Despite the earlier downpour, the long, hot spring had ensured the wood was tinder dry beneath the surface. The flames found no resistance as the wood offered itself in sacrifice to the flames' quest for life. Kay and the man stared in awe, watching helplessly. The intensity of the fire pushed them back, the heat searing them even at a distance. The fire roared up into the night sky, the screams from inside piercing the air for all to hear. Unfortunately for those inside, the all that could hear, were Kay and the man, who had their own dilemma, keeping themselves alive. As the flames danced into the night sky, a new dance was unfolding below in the woods as Kay awakened to the danger before her.

She knew it wouldn't be long before the visual cry for help, in the form of flames leaping high into the night sky, would replace the quickly dwindling and futile screams of the dying. The cry would be far more effective, and from the actions of the man, he understood that. He made off at a sprint, racing east, Kay assumed towards his sailboat. Slowly coming round from the haze that had all but stopped her in her tracks, she shook off the last remnants of whatever had come over her. She had to get to him before he reached the sailboat. At night with his running lights off he'd disappear into the ocean and beyond in no time.

She cocked her pistol and raced after him. He undoubtedly knew the terrain well, he was darting in and out of trees that Kay was having to feel her way around as they traversed across the small island. When she lost sight of him she suddenly panicked, what if he was no longer running and lying in wait? She had to restrain herself and slow her progress, the choice between saving her life and catching the man a fine balance that she was struggling to contend with. She wanted to catch him more than life itself. She sped up again. The thought of him pulling away from the mooring and disappearing into the night was not a vision she could live with.

Speed prevailed. He had not lain in wait, he had continued unabashed with his escape plan. She caught up with him as his hand was unhooking the final rope that bound him to the land and punishment for all he had done. He paused as she approached, his hand dropped the rope and reached up to his mask, pulling it from his face. Kay looked into a face she barely recognized. A smug smile of recognition from him had Kay raising her pistol. A red rage took over. She lost control and fired but he was ahead of her, his other hand had been pulling his small concealed pistol while Kay was focused on his face. His bullet beat hers to the punch, sending her crashing to the wooden dock, searing pain burning through her chest. She looked up at the man. His face twisted in a sardonic, gleeful grin was not what she had ever imagined would be her final vision. Struggling to breathe, she fought back tears. The pain was nowhere near as painful as the anger that swelled within her. It was not how she had envisioned the end.

Deputy Kay Miller took her final breath and was gone.

Chapter 41

"Fourteen," Winters confirmed. "Definitely arson. Accelerant was used, particularly around the door and windows, the door was bolted from the inside, and the windows wedged closed from the outside. Once it started there was no way out for anyone caught inside."

Gonzalez surveyed the husk of the barn that remained. The fire crew had been on site in less than ten minutes from the first sighting of the ominous orange glow that had lit up the night. While flames leaping far into the moonless sky had beaten the fireman back they had persevered under the intensity of the blaze to bring it under control, though long after the screams had died from within.

The team had convened shortly after the fire was under control. Fitch waited in the car. His drunken state was quickly dissipating, which in normal circumstances may have seen him out of action for at least a day. The scale of the catastrophe was quickly overcoming the alcohol effects, particularly given Kay was still missing. The last she had been heard of was the short phone conversation with Winters, nothing since.

"I-Is she in there?" Fitch stammered, trying to approach the scene for at least the fifth time.

"We don't know, we're not dealing with bodies here, we're dealing with skeletons." Winters guided his friend and boss back from the still smoking ruin. "Please, Fitch, just let us do what we need to do. I care about her as much as you do, we'll find her." He deposited Fitch back in the car. "Can we get another coffee over here!" he called to his team.

All would have easily failed a field sobriety test on arrival but with copious amounts of coffee and a truly shocking scene, the effects of the earlier events that evening, the game and burger that had become Fitch's impromptu leaving party, were all but gone. Only Fitch remained in a state where his presence was a hindrance rather than a help through no fault of his own. Winters knew his limits, and tequila shots was way beyond Fitch's propensity for alcohol. Blackout and throwing up were all but guaranteed following previous history. Winters knew he'd pay for it later; it was unlikely Fitch would forgive him if Kay wasn't found alive and well and his incapacity had in any way hindered the search for her.

Fitch stirred from his stupor. "What about the boat?"

"What boat?" asked Winters.

Gonzalez heard them and leaped to action. "Get in!" she commanded Winters, jumping into the driver's seat.

"The boat at the dock by the houses owned by the trust," she explained hurriedly. "We were there earlier. Seeing what's happened here, it may well be linked."

Gonzalez spared no horses on their race to the dock; she took the junction ten miles an hour faster than physics deemed possible but somehow managed to keep on the road. The tires skidded to a stop on the gravel and the three raced to the dock where earlier Kay had checked out the sailboat. Fitch caught up with them while Winters and Gonzalez caught their breaths from sprinting as fast as their legs would allow them, both bent over gasping for air and looking longingly out to sea. A dark and empty view with no boat to be seen anywhere in the darkness, not even the faintest of running lights gave any hint it had ever been there.

Fitch looked at them both in despair. "Where is she?" he beseeched, his already broken heart struggling to comprehend what was happening. It was only thanks to the effects of alcohol that he was actually functioning.

Winters looked up, his hands still on his knees as he was struggling to breathe. "I don't know but we will find her," he promised. His eye caught, even in the dark night, a noticeably darker stain on the dock. He reached down as he spoke, his finger touching the stain. It returned wet and dark; it wasn't water.

"What's that?" asked Gonzalez watching Winters' face fall.

"I'm guessing blood, and from the size of the stain a lot of it."

"No!" Fitch jumped into the water, sobering instantly. He dove under the surface, desperately searching for whoever's blood it was. The water as dark as the sky above, it was a futile attempt, his hands his only way of seeing in the depths below. The tide was on its way out, whatever had been there even a few minutes ago would already be gone. Winters and Gonzalez pleaded for him to come out but only after an hour did he finally relent and realize there was nothing that could be done on his own in the darkness.

"We need the Coast Guard here with lights and search equipment!" he demanded, having regained his full faculties.

"We've called them, but they won't come until daylight," said Gonzalez, "just a few hours from now."

"She'll be gone by then!" Fitch stared forlornly across the vastness of the ocean.

"If that is her blood, she's already gone." Winters wrapped his friend in his jacket. Fitch shrugged it away, he didn't want comfort, he just wanted Kay to be okay.

Chapter 42

Four Days Later

The team had barely slept since the fire had wiped out fourteen souls and Kay had gone missing. The Coast Guard had searched from sunrise to sunset for three solid days. On the second day Kay's deputy's hat had been recovered by lobstermen out at sea, and although it was a grim discovery, hopes remained high.

Day three saw an end to the search, and any hope of finding her alive. The confirmation that the blood on the dock was hers was compounded by the retrieval of her sidearm thirty yards from the dock, apparently having been dragged by the tide and crabs out to sea. Kay Miller was officially pronounced missing, presumed dead.

The search for the sailboat was as relentless as the search for Kay and would continue unabated until the boat was found. Likewise the search for David Clarke, or whoever the man was who had hired the boat. Being top of the most wanted list by the FBI had resulted in the quick discovery of the alias that led nowhere. David Clarke, who the hirer had claimed to be, did not exist. Footage from the grainy security system at the boatyard showed merely that whoever the man was he knew exactly where the cameras were. The description of the man wanted in connection with over twenty deaths, including that of Deputy Kay Miller, fit pretty much every man in his sixties' who was of average height and build. Even down to not knowing if he did or did not have facial hair, the two witnesses from the boatyard differed completely on the subject.

Throughout the three days Fitch had remained upbeat, sure they'd find her. He had never doubted he'd see her again. The confirmation of it being her blood knocked him over, the sidearm finally and painfully sealing the deal. Deputy Kay Miller, the first woman since the death of his wife who had managed in any way to pierce through his pain, was gone. Winters was worried. Fitch had plummeted to depths he hadn't seen since the crash that had taken Annie and Charlie from him. An extended leave request was turned in by Fitch on confirmation of Kay's death with no end date. It was approved. He was in no state to be at work and certainly was not going to be of any help to the team.

"On me guys," called Gonzalez, taking the stage at the front of the town hall. The size of the team had grown significantly in the three days. A larger team was virtually interacting from across the Bureau's network, outside of the ongoing threat of terror. Gonzalez was leading the single largest domestic operation the bureau had seen for years. The resources at her disposal were eye watering in their capability and reach. Nothing was being spared to hunt down the killer, trace the fourteen victims of the fire, and uncover the truth behind the deaths. Baker and Beaumont had also been upgraded from persons of interest to the FBI's most wanted board.

Winters stood by Gonzalez's side. He was the only link left to the original crime scenes, although Jackson hovered in the background keen to ensure the local sheriff's department who had lost one of their serving officers was not forgotten.

"We believe we have so far identified ten of the victims from the fire, all islanders, two of whom were John and Jean Gilder. John, as I'm sure you are aware, was a selectman on the island for more than thirty years. He died along with his wife Jean. Laurence and Lottie Fairchild, the owners of the facility, perished along with the matron of their retirement home. Although we do not have confirmed identities for the other five islanders, forensics are confirming the five islanders reported missing since the fire against their dental records. We expect to have those results today. That leaves four who we have no clue as to who they were or where they were from. I have a team searching through all ferry passengers and vacationers, we'll be in touch with each and every person until we track down who is missing."

"What if they didn't arrive on the ferry?" came a shout from the hall.

"Well that won't find them, will it?" Gonzalez snapped irritably, she wasn't in the mood for smart ass comments. She pointed to the agent who had shouted. "So if they weren't on the ferry *you* can find who they were."

"But how? If they weren't on the ferry…" The penny dropped, there was no simple way, it could be literally anyone.

"That's *your* problem now." Gonzalez returned to her update. "We still have no idea why these people in particular were in the barn or, if specifically targeted, why. Obviously, we know the Fairchilds were linked to the orphanage, having bought the island, and John Gilder was mentioned in the Beaumont files. We're scouring them for mentions of any of the others. It is likely this will lead back to the orphanage and as such it is highly likely some or all who perished may have some dark past that we may be about to uncover, so let's be wary of how we talk about the victims of the fire. It may come back and bite us."

Another agent called out, "Does that mean this 'David Clarke' is some avenging—"

"Absolutely not. May I remind you we are mourning the death of a colleague at this man's hands?" Winters interjected angrily.

"Exactly. We're dealing with a killer, whether there was reason behind the deaths or not is irrelevant. And as Detective Winters has reminded you, not that you ever should need to be, one of our own was killed by this man."

"Thank you," Winters said loud enough for only Gonzalez to hear.

She nodded to him before continuing. "We're going to update every three hours,. This is fast moving and I want us up to date on where each thread of the investigation is taking us. If there are new areas to look into I want us hitting them hard and fast, I want dead ends cut off and time spent on real leads. I want each team to understand how they overlap with each other. I want results, people, and I want them quick. Whatever you need from the Bureau, let me know, state police, let Detective Winters, know and the sheriff's office, Sheriff Jackson."

Jackson stepped forward to the front of the stage, which since he was in his full sheriff's uniform, and the only uniformed member of law enforcement in the hall was somewhat unnecessary.

"Now go," she commanded. "We'll reconvene three hours from now."

Winters walked over to his team. He had been given lead on behalf of Maine State Police on Fitch's recommendation. He trusted Winters to do whatever it took to get a result. Like the Bureau the team had also swelled in size, but nowhere near to scale; Maine State Police were a relatively small unit. Although the Bureau was very much in charge, the state detectives would offer support wherever possible to break down any state issues. The governor had sent an edict out across the state legislature that whatever the investigation needed, they'd get and quick. Winters had been given no illusion as to his role, which was to ensure that at no time was there any criticism that could be levelled towards the state and the governor for holding the investigation up or not being fully open.

Before Winters could speak to his team, he was interrupted when the TVs in the hall cut to the governor stepping up to a microphone for an impromptu press conference.

Gonzalez rushed across the room. "Why weren't we informed?"

Winters shrugged. "I was aware of it myself." His pay grade didn't allow him to dictate what the governor of Maine did or didn't do.

"We should be there," Gonzalez huffed. It would have been an excellent media shot, her standing next to the governor, a young, no-nonsense man who was being groomed for the presidency.

The revelations that were already out there were wide reaching in the failures that were going to be levelled at the state of Maine, particularly given the runaways and lack of care for orphans who were under the care of the state. Fortunately, it was long before the governor had entered the political arena, and he'd be throwing whoever and whatever under the bus with abandon, safe in the knowledge that none of it would tarnish his name. This was his moment to show true leadership and resolve and he was going to milk the situation for all it was worth. He had been elected on a tough, no nonsense approach and he had the perfect vehicle with which to drive that message home.

"I want to address the reports that are filtering out of the investigation into a tragic fire that has taken the lives of fourteen people," he began somberly. "A tragedy that has also resulted in the death of one of our law enforcement officers, Deputy Kay Miller." At the mention of her name, a grainy and poor photo of Kay was shown behind the governor. It was from her graduation photo from the police academy many years earlier, her head circled amongst the other graduates.

"Could you not have sent a better photo?" Winters asked Jackson, who had joined them for the conference.

"I didn't know they were doing it and to be honest I'm not sure—"

"Shush!" Gonzalez hissed, directing them back to the screen.

"From the initial reports, there have been some serious and criminal failings many years ago, I'm not going to dwell on them now until we know exactly what did and didn't happen, who knew what and when," he continued. "However, these failings involve children," he paused, before continuing, lowering the volume of his voice for maximum effect. "Young, helpless children whose responsibility for their care fell to the state of Maine, through no fault of their own. And from what I can gather, their state failed them."

He paused to let the thought sink in. "Our great state, who we have faith and elect officials to do the right thing, failed them. Well, I want to be clear, crystal clear, here today, inaction to protect the lives of any child, in my book, is complicity in any crime that befell them. I have instructed the AG of that." He motioned behind himself to his Attorney General. "His office will be prosecuting to the full extent of the law each and every person, establishment, or service that we believe were criminally and willfully negligent in any way. Rest assured, the scandal that is coming to light as the FBI and our state police force investigate is beyond shocking, and people will pay for their inactions. I'd advise anyone with any knowledge, involvement, or understanding of what may or may not have happened to come forward now. If not, only God will be able to help you. I vow to use every law at my disposal to make sure you do pay."

It was short, powerful, and most importantly had put on notice every person involved in any way, no matter how trivial, that the level of punishment would be disproportionate to their level of involvement if they thought there was something wrong and hadn't done anything.

A phone number appeared on the TV screen as the governor ended his impromptu briefing, ignoring all questions the press were throwing at him. Gonzalez was relieved to see it was their number. By the time she had read and checked the number was correct, the hall burst into a chorus of ringing phones. The governor had, without a doubt, awoken those who had suspicions out of their long and negligent slumber.

Chapter 43

Fitch watched the press conference from the bed he hadn't bothered to get up from since Kay's death had been announced. He had held onto every bit of hope he could cling to, certain there was a reason she had remained silent for those three long days. The blood and her pistol being retrieved ended that hope. Kay Miller, the first light to shine on his life in five years, was gone. Fitch had spent five years questioning the value of his life. When two of the most wonderful, kind, and gentle beings are extinguished from your life, there is little left to reason. When five years later the flicker of the light you once had is extinguished before it even takes hold, the question becomes somewhat rhetorical.

His pistol by his side, he wondered who would mourn him, who would miss his being alive. His parents would be upset, but outside of them he didn't know. Annie had no family, it was why she had loved his so much and why they were so tight. It was them against the world. The world had won and left him alone with nothing more than fading memories. If he had believed in God, he knew he'd have ended it all years earlier, because any chance of being with Annie and Charlie outweighed any BS that was thrown around when you lose your wife and daughter senselessly, although to be fair to those, it wasn't exactly a daily occurrence for which one prepared.

He turned to his pistol, the bottle of bourbon by its side, half empty. He chastised himself. He had always been a glass half full kind of guy. But then he thought to himself, to be fair, that was before he was lying in bed with a half bottle of bourbon for starters and a bullet for the final course. He took a long swig of the bourbon. It wasn't pleasant, a plastic, bottom shelf variety that had barely made a dent in his loose change. What it lacked in quality it more than delivered in throat burning painful satisfaction. Another long swig and he had drained the bottle. He reached down to the side of the bed where a brown paper bag held another two bottles, a three for two special.

As he neared the end of bottle two, he passed out, his pistol by his side, ready for whenever he could pluck up the courage to use it.

Chapter 44

The governor's press briefing had thrown the doors open. What had been state news quickly became the number one national headline story of the day. The phone didn't stop ringing in the town hall, with the queues averaging a thirty-seven minute wait time to get through. The governor's no nonsense and tough talking had anybody and everybody who ever had dealings with the state of Maine's child protective services in any way rushing to divulge any and all incidences of anything of note they might have experienced. Ninety-nine percent of callers divulged information that was at best irrelevant if not merely utter nonsense. However, the one percent that helped, blew the case wide open.

The missing runaways, emboldened by a governor who had their back, called in. One after another of children, now adults, who had been reported missing for up to thirty years called the helpline. One after another, they told their stories, explained what had happened, filled in blanks, and updated on others who they knew were alive and well. A WhatsApp community of survivors, too afraid and traumatized to come forward, was uncovered. The number that Kay had alerted may be over 150 missing, which on checking had been 158, and Fitch had reduced to just over a hundred, by the end of day one of phone calls had dropped to just 29 children still unaccounted for. Why none of them had come forward previously no one could fully explain, they just felt safer being anonymous, living their lives in the present, not wanting to dwell or be tarnished by a past none were proud of.

The three-hour update came and went, the phone lines buzzed, there was no way Gonzalez was going to interfere with the flow of information. By the end of the day and with 129 runaways having been found alive and well, the mood in the town hall had transformed.

"We have to assume some deaths from the 158 runaways over the last thirty years. I mean, you've got drugs, alcohol, cancer, and accidents in the mix, and let's not forget there would be a propensity for addictive behavior in the children."

Gonzalez looked at Jackson with utter and complete contempt, not even attempting to hide it. "What exactly are you trying to say? That 29 isn't a bad number, that we'd probably have lost them anyway?" she challenged. "And why exactly would they have a propensity for addictive behavior? Look at them!" She threw a hand to the board of the 29 still unaccounted for. A second board was filled with those found, although a number still required to be confirmed but there was no suspicion any were not who they said they were.

"Do you notice anything?" said Winters, his eyes scanning from board to board.

Gonzalez followed Winters' actions and did the same, scanning the boards. "Oh shit," she uttered, seeing what Winters had just spotted. She hadn't been as close to the boards before; it was her first time up close.

"What?" Jackson looked at both boards and was struggling to see the relevance of what they were seeing that was eliciting their concern.

"Put it this way, the answer to your question, if we receive no more calls is most likely going to be six. Six may have died from natural or self-induced measures."

Jackson looked at the boards again, discounting the six would leave twenty-three runways who hadn't been found.

"Get me that list of missing islanders suspected dead," commanded Gonzalez, not taking her eyes from the board.

She scanned down the list when it was handed to her. There was no surprise in seeing the name. She had remembered it, she just wanted to confirm it in black and white. "Brian Vale." She pointed to the name and it suddenly clicked for Jackson.

Twenty-three photos on the board were professionally taken. The other six, along with the other 129 found alive and well, were quick and dirty mug shots, more akin to those stored on an orphan's record. Twenty-three photos, by far the youngest of the 158 were posed, professional photos, stamped in the corner accrediting the company responsible. Brian Vale Photography. The photos spanned fifteen years, it was no coincidence, not a one year change in policy.

"Trophies?" Winters guessed.

Gonzalez nodded, her heart breaking as twenty-three angelic and innocent faces stared back, their silent cry for help being heard many, many years too late.

She took to the stage again and called the group to attention. "Okay, folks, we've had some good news today. We've found a lot of missing kids. Unfortunately, it has probably brought us to the realization that we are indeed dealing with a pedophilic network that operated unencumbered and with law enforcement's assistance for many years. As of tomorrow our focus swings to these twenty-three children. I want anyone and everyone who ever came into contact with them. No matter how irrelevant it seems note it down, report it.

"I want the dead confirmed and the other four we don't know found. I want their backgrounds from as far back as we can find. I think we're looking at a gang who systematically abused and then disposed of the children. I want the 129 runaways interviewed in person, tomorrow. No matter where they are, an agent should be sitting with them by 10 a.m. tomorrow morning."

She waited for a round of yeses, they came back firm and strong. Her team was on the case. "Excellent. Now make it happen, people!"

Chapter 45

Winters had tried in vain that evening to contact Fitch. He wanted to be the one to break the news to him about the runaways. By 10pm and with still no response, he called in his wife Emma for support. If all else failed she usually managed to get Fitch through his darkest periods. She had been closest to Annie, and time with her would be spent reminiscing about Annie, Charlie, and their twins, the same age as Charlie and her best friends.

With the twins in tow she had rushed to Fitch's. If Winters was worried, there would be something to worry about. Winters, his wife knew, was an emotional void. After a few minutes banging on the door to no avail, she resorted to the emergency key, something both she and Mark had promised would only be used in an emergency.

"Well?" Winters said when he answered Emma's call.

"He's coming home with us, the twins are manhandling him into the car as we speak."

"That bad?"

"Worst I've seen him. I'll call you later!" Emma ended the call, needing to help the boys with their Uncle Fitch. They had bitched about the puke, but their mother was a force to be reckoned with. A change of tone to full on serious *don't mess with me* had them covered in their uncle's puke without another whimper of discontent.

It took her three coffees to make any sense of what he was saying, another two before she could actually get a response to her questions. On the sixth he asked where his gun was. "Locked in our gun safe, and I changed the code. And it's not Mark's go to code."

"Can I take a shower?" he asked, resigned to his existence for the foreseeable future.

"Please do," Emma replied instantly.

Showered and smelling more like a human, Fitch reappeared to a plate of food being placed in front of him. "Not hungry," he claimed while devouring every morsel and more when Emma refilled his plate.

By the time he was fit to talk properly it was long after 3 a.m., but Emma was going nowhere. Fitch needed to unload and she was going to be there for him, just as he and Annie had been every time she and Mark fell out, which was often. She was fully aware of her husband's wandering eye, resigning herself to two choices, put up with it or leave him. Leaving him was more hassle than she felt she wanted to cope with with two boisterous twins, but as they grew older, it was a choice that was constantly under review. Fitch was Mark's best friend, but whatever happened between her and Mark, she knew Fitch would always be there for her, just as she would be for him.

"I can't tell you how special Kay was. It was…well, it was like I had got my Annie back, if you know what I mean. We just clicked, you know…?" His thoughts wandered, Emma let the silence hang as Fitch reminisced.

At 5 a.m. she put him to bed, no bourbon and no guns within reach. She made it to her bed and called Mark, finally free to talk. She had not left Fitch's side other than to let him shower, and even then she had insisted he hadn't locked the door and she remained vigilantly listening to every sound from within the room.

"How bad?" he asked. He had barely slept, awaiting her call.

"Two empty bottles of bourbon and his gun by his side," she said flatly.

"I'll be on the first ferry home."

"No, it's fine. I've got him back. We'll keep him busy and occupied, you stay and catch that son of a bitch."

Winters sighed. *"Hmm, it's getting complicated."*

"Complicated how?"

"It looks like we may have a group of pedophiles who have been killed. To be honest it's hard to feel any sympathy for them. The guy we're chasing may have done us all a favor."

"But what about Kay?"

"That's a different story, but when this breaks, I think she's going to be forgotten amongst the bigger story. It'll be something like twenty pedophiles killed by avenging angel, officer caught in crossfire loses her life. There's a danger it's all going to get very political. As much as I want to be part of catching Kay's killer, Fitch is more important."

"For Fitch just now, catching her killer is more important. And what about Kay's family?"

"None. Both parents are dead, no siblings. There're a few personal belongings at the cottage where she was staying while on the island. We have a storage unit key, but nobody knows where it is for. Sad really, she was a lovely woman who it seems had nobody in her life."

"Until she met Fitch."

"Yeah but nothing happened between them," said Mark.

"You are so fucking blind!" Emma was frustrated by how much of a Neanderthal she had ended up with.

"What?"

She sighed. "If you have to ask…"

"But that's not the strangest thing. She left a note that if anything happened to her, she wanted Fitch to get everything."

"As in everything? She left *everything* to Fitch?"

"Well yeah, but everything is what was in her sheriff's truck and a few belongings, a lot of wine—she had a lot of wine—, and a key for what we guess is a storage unit that the FBI cannot track down, so that's all but useless. And there was I believe $426.72 in her bank account."

"But leaving it to Fitch? That's a bit strange."

"There really wasn't very much to leave."

"When did she write the note?"

"I'll get the FBI lab on that first thing in the morning," he responded sarcastically before realizing, *"although that is a good point."*

"So are you staying or coming home?"

"Where do you need me to be?"

"Find her killer, Mark, for Fitch."

"On it," he replied confidently, knowing they were nowhere near solving the crime, or even understanding what had happened on the island all those years earlier.

Chapter 46

Twenty-three names were listed on the board. Beyond that and dates of birth, little was known. Twelve girls, eleven boys, all under the age of 12 at the time they had been reported missing. Three sets of siblings, two brothers and sisters, and one set of sisters. None had been heard of since the report of their escape from the orphanage, other than the mandatory sightings reported by Beaumont or his associates.

The reports from the runaways who had been found began to filter in throughout the morning. Generally they were all older and none had been worthy of a Brian Vale photo shoot. The reports suggested Reynard's was run by a brutal regime, where misbehavior was dealt with by physical and public humiliation. Report after report stipulated physical abuse, beatings, and a lack of any empathy from the staff. However, none mentioned any sexual abuse, only physical abuse, some of which bordered on torture. It was clear all had suffered extreme emotional and psychological issues as a result, many claiming twenty and thirty years later they still had nightmares as a result of the physical pain they had suffered at the hands of the staff. An overwhelming reason for why they had remained hidden was they did not want to relive the nightmare, nor expose themselves to their torturers once again, particularly as members of law enforcement had enabled and protected their abusers. Until the governor spoke, they had no reason to believe they would be safe. One name in particular kept being mentioned, the director of the orphanage during its existence, Andrew Hughes. Unfortunately, despite the overwhelming evidence against him with regards to physical assault against the children, there was nothing they could do. Andrew Hughes, as they already had discovered during previous investigations, had died in a car accident shortly after the sale of the island. Other names being mentioned were no longer able to be prosecuted as name after name matched with those who had been killed in the fire or before or had died over the previous years. Only a few remained unaccounted for. Four names were mentioned that were new to the investigation, four names of abusers, and there were four unknown victims of the fire. Whoever had undertaken their revenge had done so with extreme and clinical efficiency.

"Are you thinking what I'm thinking?" Gonzalez asked Winters as she read report after report.

Winters nodded. "I think so. We've got nobody to arrest or prosecute, they've all been dealt with or already dead?"

"That too. I was actually thinking our avenger and Kay's killer is most likely on this board." She glanced at the 129 found runaways. "From what they went through, I have to say I'd want to kill these sons of bitches."

"But where are the twenty-three, what about them?"

Gonzalez looked out the window in the direction of Lane's Island. "I don't know, but we have a bunch of sadists in control of children, and from what we have been able to uncover to date, would appear were also pedophiles. I fear the twenty-three were abused in a very different way but just as violently, and I fear for them their escape was not physical, it was spiritual. I pray to God I'm wrong, but I do not believe we will find any of them alive. As small as the island is, it will be almost impossible to find them, and that's if they weren't disposed of at sea."

Winters stared at the twenty-three innocent faces, angelic poses that multiplied the horror of what those poor children had had to endure. As he looked through the faces he was reminded of Charlie, Fitch's daughter. Beautiful, innocent, and whose life had been taken long before she had a chance to live. The death of any child was tragic. Tears escaped his eyes as the scale of what they were looking at hit him.

Gonzalez put a comforting hand on his shoulder. She wasn't an emotional person at the best of times but even she was struggling with where the investigation was taking them.

"Anyway," said Winters, "we've got a killer to catch."

Gonzalez gave him a wink of support and headed off to her corner of the hall. Winters pulled out a fresh notebook from his desk and began to put his thoughts down, a technique Fitch had shared with him.

1990 – 2010 Reynard's Orphanage

2008 – exposed by reporter – reporter murdered eight years later

2010 – island sold to the Fairchilds, potential ten million premium. Change of use to retirement home.

2020 – Frank and Valerie (Baker), Walt Spencer, Hilary Cantrell (Beaumont) and Charles Ryan,

(he added Jim Kingsley but circled it, his was still listed as a suicide but his name had been mentioned as staff by runaways, putting him squarely in the mix.)

Clarke, Beaumont and Baker – all on FBI wanted list.

Twenty-three children, believed to be victims of a pedophile ring - presumed dead.

(He listed each of their names in alphabetical order)

129 victims of physical and emotional abuse – alive, reports forthcoming.

Staff and workers named by abused – (he listed their names, noting next to each as he checked against the deceased list all deceased, four names were not deceased, which coincided with four names for four victims of the fire.) Confirmation underway.

Beaumont's files – many staff mentioned, cross check all references.

Annie and Charlie crash (he circled that entry)

Winters stared at his page of notes. The unknown remained what happened to the twenty-three and who the avenger was. He could be any of the 129, or even of the six presumed dead that hadn't been tracked down and had not warranted a Brian Vale photo shoot. In fact, that was most likely. He added the six presumed dead to his list. If they were a killer, they'd be less likely to come forward. That left the plight of the twenty-three. A number of the abused would be quizzed on the faces that matched their time at the home. It was hoped that would shed some light on what happened. As for Annie and Charlie, he circled their names again. Unless they found Beaumont, and he talked, that was going to be a mystery they may never understand.

He tracked back to his 2008 entry. The reporter was murdered in 2016, Annie and Charlie 2015. He circled the reporter's name. It may be there was a link. It was late and he was one of the last of the day crew still in the hall. A small skeleton crew was manning the phones overnight, just in case. He closed his notebook. He had his tasks for the next day: Find Kay's killer and uncover the truth.

However, by himself, he was finding it hard work and far less rewarding. It just wasn't the same without Fitch and Kay. They had been a great team. He double tapped the notebook with his index finger and stood. Mandy had been texting him; he was ignoring her. He had a wife and twins who needed him, a best friend who needed him, and another who needed him to find her killer. Without his team, Mark Winters was finally growing up and taking responsibility for his actions.

He texted Mandy: *"don't contact me again"* before blocking her number. Task number one achieved.

Chapter 47

"The Specials," Gonzalez announced to the team from the stage. "The Specials," she emphasized slowly before pointing to the twenty-three photos on the board. "That's what the other residents of the orphanage called them. The Specials." She stared at the twenty-three faces staring back at her.

"They didn't get punished, they had better rooms, they received better food and clothes than the rest. Everyone was jealous of the Specials. Although one thing none of them could understand, despite their preferential treatment, they were miserable, the most sullen and unhappy residents of the orphanage. I don't think any of you need my help as a clinical psychologist or any of my doctorates to understand why or what was happening to these poor children."

Horror registered on all the faces looking at her. The runaways who had been interviewed about their abuse had remembered most of the Specials, envious of how well they had been treated and irritated by how unhappy they were despite their privileges.

"Oh," Gonzalez swung back to her audience for effect, "and if you thought the preferential treatment was why they were special, it wasn't that. It was that one day they'd be there and the next morning had been adopted by a wonderful, loving family. Just like that, orphan one day, the next gone to a new and wonderful life. We know that wasn't the case because Beaumont covered their tracks. They were runaways, they were never adopted." Again, the audience soaked in and appreciated exactly what was being said.

"This morning I've spoken with the governor and the deputy director. We are officially declaring the twenty-three presumed dead and launching a search for their bodies. Any questions before we get back to it?"

Winters threw his hand up, Gonzalez zeroed in on him. "Mark?"

"I've got a theory on the killer."

Gonzalez nodded for him to share.

"The six who are still missing from the runaways...I'm thinking one of them for the killer. I doubt the killer would have come forward in the 129."

"I like it," said Gonzalez.

"On it!" Bryce was ever ready with his notebook.

"Okay, anything else?" Gonzalez called. Winters raised his hand. "Mark, you've been busy, go ahead."

"I'm thinking there may be a link between the reporter who was killed and Fitch's wife and daughter. The timeline that the deaths happened just months apart."

Gonzalez thought through the idea. "I understand where you are going, but to be honest I don't think it will help the wider investigation. If there were a link to the group, I think you'll find their killer has already been dealt with."

"It might lead us to Beaumont or Baker," Winters argued.

"Okay, but don't spend a lot of time. Get me something concrete and we'll see."

Winters read between the lines; Gonzalez was narrowing down the investigation. She wanted the uncovering of the twenty-three murders of children and hundreds physically and mentally tortured at the island orphanage to be the headline. Someone had killed the abusers and a massive manhunt was underway. Kay's death would disappear between the edits and not make it onto the front page. It was likely her killer would in some way become a folk hero of some description. Opening up old investigations that had been closed was going to water down the headline and complicate the case. She already had the case that would make her the deputy director in a few years, no need to add to the case, or potentially hinder her progression.

Winters nodded, he just needed to find something concrete. Which was something he never would.

Chapter 48

One Month Later

After a month of searching neither a body nor a killer had been found. The news channels had kept the story that had gripped the nation alive for as long as the producers could allow but with no new news to break. The tragedy of the orphans and their avenging angel had dropped day by day until it no longer featured other than local updates in Maine. As expected, Kay's name barely had made it past day two. An avenging angel who was also a cop killer didn't work for the narrative.

The team had dwindled as new and pressing cases ate into Gonzalez's resources. As sexy as the story had been, even the FBI had their limits as to wasting resources. While Clarke, Baker, and Beaumont remained on the FBI most wanted list, only Clarke was clinging onto a position within the top ten. Beaumont and Baker continued to slip daily to the point it was worthy of bragging rights only.

Winters picked up his cell. He had a call to make he really didn't want to, but it was time. He hit the name and waited.

"Hey bud!" Fitch replied. From what Emma had told Winters, he was doing really well.

"Hey, Fitch, how's things?"

"You know, keeping positive, taking the twins to play baseball later."

"Wow, that's great," Winters said, genuinely overwhelmed by how well Fitch was doing.

"So what's up, Mark?"

"Just thought I'd check in and let you know I'll be home tomorrow."

"Cool. We can grab a beer and catch me up before you head back."

"That's the thing, we won't be heading back. The case is being wound down."

"Wound down as in closed?" The change in Fitch's tone was palpable.

"Not closed as such, just not as active as it currently is. The FBI will keep control."

"And Gonzalez, what's she saying?" Fitch asked his anger building.

"She left yesterday. Serial killer in California."

"I'll be there on the next ferry!"

"What do you mean?" Winters said into a dead phone. Fitch had already hung up.

***

He was making another call.

"Fitch?" came a surprised response.

"Is anyone in the cottage?"

"What cottage?" asked Sheriff Chris Jackson, trying to recover from the surprise of Fitch calling him out the blue.

"Kay's. The one Kay stayed in?"

"Hmmm, no I don't think so. None of the guys wanted to and you've got her things that she left you stored there."

"Do you mind if I—"

"You've heard then?" asked Jackson.

"Yeah, Mark just told me."

"I don't have any resources for the island at the moment, didn't really need it given the investigation. So it's all yours."

"You want me to help if something happens on the island?"

"Would you?"

"Let's call it a deal. Free board and if shit happens, I'll cover it while I'm there."

"Deal."

"One more thing," said Fitch. "It's mid-August. I need to get on a ferry today and I'm not currently on duty, so—"

"I'll tell the ferry guys. You have my authority to cross as an emergency. Just head to the front, least I can do."

"For what?" asked Fitch, his anger building at the thought of a trade for his wife and daughter's accident report.

"Helping out on the island, what else?"

"Oh yeah. Thanks, Chris."

Jackson ended the call, which was perhaps the longest and least confrontational he had ever had with Fitch, then called Winters.

"Jackson?"

"Fitch just called me…"

"Shit, I've been trying to call him back, he hung up on me."

"He's heading to the island and going to stay in the cottage."

"Kay's cottage?"

"Yeah, he was surprisingly unconfrontational."

"Shit, he's not in a good place. I knew he was playing Emma. Taking the twins to baseball, that should have been the clue…"

"Sorry what?"

"Just talking to myself. It's fine, leave it with me, and thanks for the heads up."

Winters killed the call and called Emma. "Is Fitch still there?"

"Still? Where's he going?"

"He's coming here!"

"He's watching TV with the twins, hold on." Emma took the phone away from her ear and shouted, *"FITCH!"*

"He went out, Mom," one of the boys said.

"Where'd he go?"

"Don't know but he said he was sorry he'd miss our baseball game."

Winters heard through the handset, and didn't need to be updated. "I think he's been faking his being okay."

"I would have sworn not but—"

"I'm supposed to be finishing up here and heading home, I've been so looking forward to getting home."

His epiphany a month earlier had resulted in the most honest conversation the two had had, probably ever. Mark had accepted he had been less than the perfect husband and that was all going to change. He and Emma had talked more in the last month than they had for a very long time.

"It's not up for debate, Mark. Your friend needs you. We'll be here waiting when you've cracked this case!"

"Thanks, I love you so much."

"Love you too. Now catch that son of a bitch and get back home!"

"Yes, boss!"

Chapter 49

Fitch was thankful for Jackson's assistance in getting onto the island, otherwise he'd have had to wait for at least a day. The winding down of the investigation, along with the notoriety the case had brought, had ensured the slow start to the season was ending with a bang. As soon as the FBI had vacated a room or rented house on the island, it was filled with vacationers or rubberneckers, in many cases both.

It seemed scenes of tragic deaths and serial killer tours were a blossoming business, certainly if the opportunists on the island had any say in the matter. Their tours of Lane's Island were booked solid for the rest of the month. The press had accomplished their part, the thought of a killer, responsible for upwards of twenty deaths, seemed to scare no one. This was a man who had taken revenge for the twenty-three. Kay Miller was merely collateral damage. Even then, a month after her death, you'd struggle to meet any vacationer who could have named her as one of the victims of the killing spree. It was all about the children and the killer of the abusers.

It was an emotional reunion for them both. Fitch, as expected, was wound far too tight to be anywhere near a good place. Kay Miller was preying on his mind, just as his wife and daughter had and still would for the rest of his life. The brave face was nothing more than that.

"So where first?" asked Winters.

"Kay's house. Let's check in on my unexpected inheritance." He smiled weakly. He had taken no pleasure in being left her belongings, it merely emphasized there was a special connection for him to mourn. He had delayed the inevitable as long as he could. It was time to reconnect and solve the case.

Fitch paused outside. The cottage was shining bright in the sunlight, its whiteness a contrast to the dark mood that swept over them both as they opened the door. Fitch recoiled. The smell of Kay permeated the air, it beckoned him, teasing and torturing him with no possible reward. Kay was gone. Winters put an arm around his friend and supported him, steering him away from the lounge area and towards the small second bedroom. Cold, hard, shock treatment, there was no point delaying. He walked him into the room consumed by Kay's GPR machine and a few boxes scattered around, it was a sorry collection of a lifetime of living. Fitch tried to pull back.

"Come on, the sooner we get through this the better," Winters counseled.

Fitch reluctantly agreed. He picked up her history books, smiling. "She tried to get me interested in these damn red paint people." He pointed to the cover of the book. "She was going to find hordes of treasure and get rich, she told me. Evidently she didn't think I was worthy of the history course. To be fair, if the shoe fits!"

"The Feebbies have been through it all, so I'm afraid there is no gold or treasure that she found. I think you got just over four hundred bucks if I remember."

Fitch nodded. "I donated it to an orphanage. Felt like the right thing to do." He was flicking through the red paint people book that Kay had been so keen to share with him. It had drawn him in and was the only thing of hers she had tried to share with him.

"Her notebooks are over there," Winters gestured.

Fitch shook his head. There was something that had drawn him to the book, like a message from Kay herself. "The FBI found nothing in them?" he asked absently.

"Eh, no, I don't believe so."

"Then I doubt we will," he said flatly. "Is there anyone left at the town hall?"

"Nope, last person left yesterday. The investigation is now officially being run from the Boston field office. We handed the town hall back last night, back to just the sheriff's office now."

"So we have free reign for whatever we need to investigate?"

"Yeah, what you got?"

"Nothing yet, just checking the lay of the land. You know, I don't remember this place being this white," said Fitch, changing the subject.

Winters smirked. "I think that's because your eyes were focused elsewhere."

Fitch simply nodded and walked towards the lounge, the red paint people book in his hands.

"What's with the book?"

Fitch shrugged. "I dunno, long story." Clearly he did not want to elaborate.

Fitch entered the lounge, where two boards faced him, intrusions in the otherwise peaceful room.

"I set us up in here," Winters said proudly. "The twenty-three and the key highlights."

Fitch looked at the young, innocent faces and in more than one saw his daughter Charlie staring back. "That one needs to be somewhere else." He pointed to the photos. "That one can stay." He nodded towards the summary board of timeline and main protagonists.

"Actually, if you don't mind, I'm really wiped out. Would you mind if we pick this up tomorrow?" asked Fitch.

Winters was a little taken aback. He had plans made for the rest of the day for them, followed by a few beers that night at the Tidewater, which was being run by new owners. John Gilders' daughter had inherited the motel, but because of the cloud over her father had sold and fled the embarrassment. She was not the only child of the abusers to have sold up and left. The impact had led to a micro property crash on the island, such was the glut of properties available to buy with very few buyers keen to join the scandal ridden community. Vacationing was one thing, living there was an entirely different scenario.

"Where you going to sleep?"

"Probably here. Not in Kay's bed, that would be a bit weird."

"Oh okay, I thought I might take the spare room, once we moved a few things," Winters said cautiously.

"You not staying at the Tidewater? You know, Mandy and—"

"Emma didn't tell you?"

"Tell me what?"

"Mandy's gone. Me and Emma, we talked, properly talked, you know, like adults."

"Really? And…?"

"All good, I just need to finish up here and get home."

"Mark, you're my best friend, you will always be my best friend. If you are here for me, please don't be.

You have a wonderful wife and two boys who miss you like crazy. Get on that ferry and go see them. I'll be fine."

"But we need to—"

"I appreciate everything you have done for me and Kay. Now go, your family needs you, Kay has me and if I need you, I promise I will call you straight away. Go be with Emma and the boys. If you want to truly make your friend happy, that's what you will do." He checked his watch. "You can make the last ferry."

Winters analyzed his every move and word. Fitch was being genuine. He gave his friend a hug. "I love you, man. Call me, no matter when, whatever time, you need me I'll be here."

"Go!"

After the door closed, Fitch sat down and opened the red paint people book. What was Kay trying to tell him from beyond the grave?

He was soon engrossed in the fascinating history of a people that predated native American Indians, who suddenly vanished almost 3,800 years ago, leaving behind a culture and mystery that would never be fully understood. From what he read, their accomplishments were far in excess of any culture of their time—hunting, fishing, and gathering across vast distances, catching huge swordfish long before any other peoples, and for an unknown reason painting their dead red before burial. His mind wandered as he read. Five thousand years earlier those same people had been where he was sitting, looking out across an untouched landscape. The harbor, devoid of its modern-day constructions, would have been a truly beautiful place to call home.

The more he read, the more he understood why Kay had been so keen to track their sites. Arrow heads, trinkets, and sculpted artifacts were created by them, again, long before other cultures. They were an amazing people and therefore all the stranger that they had disappeared almost overnight thousands of years ago. A mystery, not unlike their own that he was trying to crack.

It was only as he read he began to notice the notes, random words lightly written on pages or a word underlined or circled, and little drawings of what looked like symbols from some kind of ancient language, childlike basic shapes and lines that Kay or someone before her had noted on pages. None of them on their own made any sense, just a word written or underlined every now and then a small drawing almost like a doodle here and there on random pages. Fitch grabbed a notepad and went back to the beginning of the book, checking for any he may have missed, then worked through the book systematically writing and drawing on a notepad as he went.

When he reached the end he looked down at the jumble and mess on the pad. There was something there, he was sure. He grabbed another pad and tried to make sense of the jumble of words, completely random amongst the little sketches before him. It made no sense, merely random doodling.

He went back to the small bedroom where the GPR machine stood, taking up the already small amount of floorspace afforded to the room. He pushed it aside. Kay's notepads were where Winters had pointed them out. He picked them up knowing he was wasting his time. If there had been anything there the FBI would have found it. He looked at the other books amongst her papers, all generally related to the native peoples and customs of America. One that did stand out was a book on the native plants of America, mostly because the front cover had a plant that looked like it was growing eyeballs. He grabbed the red paint peoples book and raced towards a section he had remembered, it had been covered within their weapons and how they had dipped their arrows in eye fruit. Fitch had assumed it was a typo and should have read eye of the fruit, whatever the fruit was. It wasn't until seeing the picture on the cover that it did actually mean eye fruit, as that was exactly what the plant was growing, they looked like eyes. He opened the book and read up on the White Baneberry plant, commonly referred to as doll's-eyes.

Oh fuck, he thought, instantly chastising himself for swearing in Kay's house. She didn't approve of profanity.

He hit Winters' name on his phone.

"You need me, Fitch?"

"Quick question. Did you ever get the tox reports on Hilary, Charles, and the suicide…what was his name?"

"Kingsley, and yep, nothing, although there was foul play, particularly on the Hilary and Charles case, we just don't know how they managed it."

"Do you have the contact for the lab?"

"I will have, why, did you find something?"

"Maybe, not sure."

"We had hundreds working on the case for weeks, you turn up and find something in five minutes. Typical!"

"Send me the number," instructed Fitch. He didn't want to get into the long-standing joke that Fitch had all the luck. Prior to his wife, daughter, and Kay dying that may have been the case, he was a lucky guy. But that had more than run out and been paid for five years earlier.

His phone pinged as the number arrived. It was late, but Fitch thought it worth a try.

The phone was answered on the third ring. *"Hello?"*

"Hi, this is Lieutenant Abercrombie. I believe you did the tox reports for the Vinalhaven deaths?"

"Yeah, that was us, is there a problem?"

"Did you check for White Baneberry?"

"Seeing as I have no idea what it is, I'd guess not. What is it?"

"A plant. It has fruit that looks like eyes, and is deadly, although from what I've read nobody in the U.S. has ever died from it, only in Europe. It causes cardiac arrests."

"Okay, you've got me intrigued, leave it with me. Can I get you on this number?"

"Yes."

"Cool, I'll be back to you as quick as I can. It's a big case, yeah?"

"Very," confirmed Fitch, not fully understanding where the revelation was taking him, or what it would mean if he did discover that was the toxin used.

He moved back to the board in the lounge and studied the timeline. A thought crossed his mind but he instantly killed it, it was ludicrous. He picked up his notepad and thought about the notes and drawings he'd found in the red paint people book. He studied them again, they still made no sense. It was a bit of a long shot that Kay's doodlings would have blown the case wide open. He focused on the drawings, something had caught his eye, something he had seen before but he just couldn't place it. He stared and stared at the images, he knew he had seen similar images before, he just couldn't remember where or when. He gave up, it had been a long day. He turned out the lights and laid down on the sofa, the gently bobbing masts below in the harbor hypnotically and rhythmically aiding him to sleep. His mind began to empty as sleep descended, then his eyes opened sharply. He remembered, the trees on Lane's Island, they had caught Kay's attention, the markings on the trunk of the tree.

Sleep could wait, he needed to know what they meant. Fitch grabbed his keys from the table, again stopping, the notepad, the images and then three words, what did the three words mean? Completely random words, always a drawing, and then over the next few pages, three words would have been written then another image, the pattern repeated. The image preceded by three words, but why those three random words? He grabbed his phone and entered one group of the three words, *asleep primal tanks*. Nothing. He tried another grouping, the words so random there was no way to link them. *buffoon generating stone*. Nothing. He typed *three word code* into the search engine more in frustration than expectation. "what3words.com" was the top result listed. Its headline, the simplest way to talk about a location, every three square yards on the planet had been allocated a unique combination of three random words. He opened the website and typed in *asleep primal tanks*. The map zoomed to Lane's Island, not far from where Kay had been murdered. He tried the next grouping, *buffoon generating stone*. The location jumped two squares, just a few feet away from the previous location.

Could it be she had been on to the killer? Tracked him down, and that's why she had been killed? It wasn't that she had just been in the wrong place at the wrong time. Kay had been tracking down the leads and had broken the case. She must have tipped him off in some way, he must have realized she was on to him. That night he had been drunk, whoever it was had come for her. He had been disturbed but she chased after him when he fled.

Realizing she had left him the clues to solve the crime, Fitch raced back through to the second bedroom. Kay had left her belongings to him for a reason. In there somewhere were all the clues to uncovering who the man was. Kay's killer. She had cracked the toxin. Although there had been no doubt Hilary and Charles had been killed, at least they knew how. As for Kingsley, he hadn't killed himself, he had been murdered.

First things first, if he was going to visit scenes connected to the case, he needed backup.

"Don't tell me, you've cracked the case," said Winters, answering Fitch's call.

"Okay, I won't. But I need you here tomorrow first ferry!"

"Unbelievable." Winters sighed. *"See you first thing. Hundreds of agents and six weeks…"*

Fitch spent the next hour going through the red paint people book, symbol then the three words, checking he had them right. They were so random, the slightest error would have him in Outer Mongolia or New Zealand rather than Lane's Island. He was surprised the FBI had missed it, but like everything else, sometimes you had to know what you were looking for and Kay had tried to talk to him about the red paint people and that book, that was his clue she left just for him. She had been obsessed by them, looking for their old settlements with her crazy GPR machine. He switched on the GPR machine, looked through the history of what she had scanned. It was meaningless to him, but he had to assume the FBI guys would have looked and known what to look for.

Fitch could barely keep his eyes open. It had been a long day. He retreated back to the lounge, lay on the sofa, and closed his eyes. He could feel Kay's presence but knew it was just that her smell still lingered in the fabric of the sofa. For the first time in weeks he felt once again close to someone, and just like his wife before them, she would no longer be part of his life. That didn't stop him dreaming. He fell into a deep sleep and reminisced about the warmth he felt in Kay's embrace.

Chapter 50

The trill of the phone ringing woke him with a start from a surprising and restful full night's uninterrupted sleep. He checked his watch, 6.47 a.m.

That can't be good, he thought. Nothing good ever came from early morning calls.

"It's not too early, is it?" asked the caller.

"Depends. Who are you?"

"Grant, from the lab. You called me yesterday about that eye fruit plant."

"Yes of course. What did you find?"

"Hey, you threw me a sideball. I've been up all night checking this out, and you were right. All three had been dosed with the toxin from the fruit. And pretty concentrated too, I'll have to add that to the toxins to check for, it's a new one for us."

"So they all died as a result of being poisoned by that fruit?"

"Yes, although maybe not the guy who put the .22 bullet into his brain, he definitely died from that, but he had the toxin in his blood, so it was maybe used to—"

"Make it easier to stage his death?"

"You're the detective."

"Thanks!" Fitch ended the call.

Kay, he thought to himself, *you were one smart girl.* Even from her grave she was helping them.

When Winters arrived, he was faced with the most upbeat Fitch he had seen in some time.

"So, Sherlock, what we got?" he said sarcastically, embracing his friend.

"My dear Watson, we have the poison and we have it confirmed. It was doll's eyes for Hilary and

Charles and assisted in the staged suicide of Jim Kingsley."

"You're joking. The entire FBI couldn't work that out in almost two months, and you've been back two minutes! So what do you need me for?"

Fitch ushered him inside to the board he had been working on while he waited for Winters to get there. He had written out each set of words against its corresponding symbol.

"What's that?" asked Winters, scanning down the list of symbols and random words.

"If I'm right, and to be honest, I hope I'm wrong, I think it may be where the children are buried."

Winters' head snapped between Fitch and the board. "But that's just a doodle with random words. How the hell does that help us?"

Fitch explained the what3words.com site and got Winters to download the app onto his phone and plugged in the first random set of words. His outpouring of expletives as the map zoomed in on Lane's Island would have had Kay turning in her grave.

Winters counted the images. "But there's only twenty-one images. If you're right that's twenty-one sites, there are twenty-three children."

"I thought of that but that's if they all got their own site. Double burial, there were siblings, remember?"

"We should call Gonzalez, get a proper recovery team out here. This is unbelievable, Fitch, if you did this in one evening. I mean shit, man, that's unbelievable."

"Not me. Kay!"

"What? She had all this and hadn't told us?"

"I think she was just putting it together and she must have tipped the guy off somehow. That night, remember she told you someone else was here before she chased off after him?"

Winters nodded. If he hadn't got Fitch so drunk… It played on his mind daily, Kay's blood was on his hands. Although no one had said it out loud, that didn't mean it wasn't true.

"Hey," Fitch could read him like a book, "none of us could have done anything, okay?"

"So, what then?" asked Winters. "What's the plan?"

"We go check out one of the locations before we call for the cavalry, make sure we're barking up the right tree."

Chapter 51

Fitch instantly regretted his use of the words "barking up the wrong tree." The symbols matched those carved into tree trunks, the trees varied in age, type, and size. One stood high above the rest, bearing all of the images, only they had been carved at varying angles, angles that on checking, directed towards the tree bearing the individual symbol.

The symbols were not easily seen. Carved low and obviously some time ago, they were faint, but thanks to the three words app, they were able to find the tree and then the symbol, not the other way around. Both agreed that would have been almost impossible. They could have looked for weeks before finding the symbols, it would have been looking for a needle in a haystack amongst the woods.

"Have you noticed anything?" asked Fitch when they found the tenth tree marked by a symbol.

Winters looked around the wooded area. "Give me a clue."

"The trees with symbols, well, they seem to be amongst older, bigger trees, like their newer, more recently planted…"

Winters stepped back from the tree and looked down at its base, focusing into the soil and below. "No…you don't think…?"

Fitch stepped back. "Yeah, I do. Time to call Gonzalez."

With heavy hearts they retraced their steps back carefully to the main tree, the one bearing all the symbols. It was overlooked directly by one house. The main view from the upstairs windows would have been that large tree.

"Do you think whoever lived in that house is our guy?" asked Fitch.

"It was Andrew Hughes' house back in the day, but he died in a car crash about ten years ago so he's not Kay's killer. As for this," he waved his hand around the woods, "I'm thinking he's our guy. He was one sick fu—"

"Language," cautioned Fitch. He could sense Kay's spirit around them, she'd led them there and she had died nearby. She would not have appreciated Winters' profanities.

Fitch turned. He had expected a comeback for the comment about him swearing but Winters was staring at the tree, his fingers moving as though counting like a child to make sure he kept track of where he was.

"What?"

Winters raised a finger, he was in the middle of counting.

Fitch waited impatiently. Winters was crowding the trunk, meaning he couldn't see what Winters had spotted.

Winters raised his head and turned with a look of satisfaction. "Twenty-three," he announced. "There are twenty-three symbols on the tree." He pointed a little higher than the others they had noted; two symbols were carved and from the shape of them they were pointing up to the sky, not towards any other trees.

"Twenty-three victims, twenty-three symbols. The sick fucks!" Fitch exploded.

Winters scowled. "Yep."

Fitch dialed Gonzalez's number.

She listened in utter and complete silence as Fitch filled her in, the white baneberry, the confirmation from the lab that it had been used, the symbols and three word location, and the additional two symbols on the main tree.

"Fuck me!" she said when he was done. *"Less than a day, shit—a few hours. Lieutenant Ross Abercrombie, you are wasted at Maine State Police force. You're coming to work for me after we wrap this all up. You hear me?"*

"It was all Kay," he replied, "she left the clues."

"We had them too. We found shit, you found the treasure." Realizing her excitement was inappropriate, she changed tone. *"Well, you know what I mean."*

"We do still need to excavate and make sure we're right."

"I concur, but I'm not a betting woman and trust me, I'd bet every cent I have we've found those kids."

Fitch looked at his phone as Gonzalez spoke, he had another call coming in, it was a number in Virginia, similar to Gonzalez's. "I've got another call coming through, can I call you back?"

"Sure."

He ended the call with Gonzalez, accepting the incoming call.

"Is this Lieutenant Ross Abercrombie?"

"Yes."

"Apologies. I'm not sure what happened, well, actually we got swamped with other cases and this one wasn't chased so it just sort of worked its way to the back of the queue."

"I have no idea who you are, or what you're talking about," said Fitch.

"FBI forensics lab. I'm calling about a semen sample with an anomaly. Oh no, I'm just looking at the date, it's from about two months ago. Apologies again."

Fitch thought back, it was Baker's semen sample. The technician had said there was something he hadn't seen before, an anomaly, but it was definitely Baker's and was probably nothing so even Fitch had forgotten all about it.

"Yeah, I remember now. How can I help?"

"The anomaly, it was the cell structure. It was a bit strange. The match is spot on, the semen was definitely the Gerald Baker guy's, but whether he was actually there to deliver it, if you know what I mean, is another matter."

"I have no idea what you mean, tell me."

"Let's just say you wouldn't have bought that sample in the fresh produce aisle, you'd have bought it in the frozen goods section."

Fitch turned to Winters and updated him. His face mirrored Fitch's, contorted in confusion. "What does that mean?" he asked.

"We need them to check Beaumont's as well."

***

The drone flying high above Fitch and Winters banked and headed back out to sea. It had beamed back all the images it had to. The burial site had been uncovered. The drone landed on the small sailboat sitting two miles out to sea and was packed away carefully. Its price tag was eye watering and it would be needed again.

The sail was raised and the boat headed south for warmer climes.

Chapter 52

Two Weeks Later – Labor Day

It had been a long weekend, almost entirely spent in front of the TV indulging in the excessive amount of sports on offer. Fitch hadn't even bothered heading home. Emma and Mark had insisted he spend the weekend at their house, making it a full on beer, barbecue, and sports extravaganza to bring to an end what had been a truly tragic summer.

It had been a somber affair as the bodies of the children had been extracted from the ground beneath the trees planted above them. The sites of their victims recorded for their ongoing satisfaction, Gonzalez had explained, spitting the words out in utter disgust. Twenty one bodies had been recovered, and one by one given a proper burial. Fitch and Winters had attended each and every one. The island had come to a stop, lobstermen cutting their fishing days short as each child was honored, and forgiveness requested that the island had failed to see their plight and save them. The island was hurting, but the outpouring of love and overwhelming support shown to every child had shown the world the islanders cared it had happened on their watch. The church was standing room only, with a large screen set up outside for the overspill since over a thousand people, every living, breathing islander, believed it was their duty to attend. Elaborate headstones had been donated by the community for each child, including the two young girls whose bodies had not been recovered.

Beaumont's semen had the same anomaly. He too was unlikely to have been in attendance at the deaths of Hilary and Charles, which he had supposedly been. That was a mystery that only the unknown man could probably explain, if they ever found him. However, with only one victim who deserved retribution and over twenty who deserved everything they had received, it was unlikely the hunt would go on much longer. As much as Fitch and Winters pushed for updates on the hunt, the fewer agents there were to ask. The hunt was all but over.

"Chuck me a beer!" Winters turned the steaks on the barbecue.

"Come on," said Fitch, "let's take a bit of a break."

"Hey, just because you're going to be the new boy starting tomorrow, doesn't mean you get to wimp out today. Throw me a beer!"

Fitch reached into the cooler. The ice was just starting to melt and the beer came out sweating, drips of ice-cold water oozing down the side. He tossed the can to Winters and reached down for one for himself.

"You know you're coming with me, I'm going to make it contingent on my going."

Fitch had been ordered to report the following day to the FBI field office in Boston. Gonzalez had made calls and made it clear that Ross Abercrombie was needed at the FBI. Gonzalez was going places, when she spoke people listened. The FBI was going to have to make two places, they just didn't know it yet. Fitch wasn't going anywhere without Winters.

"Best ask the boss about that." He nodded towards Emma. She was a new woman, and the relationship between her and Mark had never been stronger.

"I always know you're safe with Fitch. God knows what you'd get up to on your own," she laughed.

"I'll take that as a yes." Fitch popped the ring on his can just as his phone began to ring. Caller ID told him it was Sheriff Jackson. He guessed the news of his FBI move was getting out. He let it go to voicemail. It rang again straight away, he left it again to voicemail and went on the rule of three. If it was really that big a deal, he'd ring three times. It rang again.

"Jeez, someone's keen to talk to you!" Winters said.

'It's Jackson," he said, answering the call. "Sheriff, how can I help you on this beautiful day?"

"I've got someone here you need to meet," he said so sincerely it was though his life depended on it.

"Can't it wait? It's Labor Day."

"No," Jackson said, his voice unlike anything Fitch could remember. *"And if Winters is there, best bring him too."*

"Are you okay?" asked Fitch, the concern in Jackson's voice spreading through the phone.

Winters looked at Fitch, mouthing, "What's wrong?"

"Just get to my office in Rockland quick as you can. Blues and twos if you can't fly." He hung up.

Fitch relayed the call to Winters, who asked, . "Fly? Was he joking?"

"Deadly serious."

"It's quicker by car. If he said blues and twos it must be something massive. With everything else we've been through, he's never suggested that."

They were both dressed in surfing shorts and t-shirts, hardly the attire for an emergency but they didn't have time to change. They grabbed their sidearms, badges, and hit the lights on their cruiser. They covered the just over forty miles in just under thirty-four minutes averaging around 80 mph. It was a hair-raising ride and the two joked how it felt like a scene from *Hawaii 5-0* in their beach wear.

Fitch skidded to a halt, killed the lights and siren, and rushed into the sheriff's office. He had heard them coming and was waiting in the lobby for them, a look of bewilderment on his face.

"Are you okay?" asked Fitch.

"I'm not sure. I may be going mad, but I need you to meet someone." He led them towards his office. "I've not really talked to them yet, as soon as they arrived, I called you and I've kept out of there," he explained as he walked.

Fitch and Winters exchanged glances. Jackson was making no sense. Somebody was in his office, what was the big deal? *Unless…* Fitch reached for his pistol. The man had turned himself in, that would have Jackson freaked out as much as he was. The man who killed Kay, he may be some sort of folk hero, but Fitch wasn't sure if he was strong enough not to shoot the man on sight.

Fitch relaxed. He could see through the window of Jackson's door it was a woman sitting in his office. Jackson opened the door and stepped inside, the woman stood and faced the three men.

"I thought I'd introduce you to Detective Mark Winters and Lieutenant soon to be Special Agent Ross Abercrombie, also known as Fitch."

She smiled at them, that look spread across her face, the first moment of realization of why he was called Fitch.

"Guys, meet Knox County's newest recruit, Deputy Kay Miller."

Chapter 53

Neither could speak, both stood as though frozen to the spot, time not moving. There was a slight resemblance, the hair was the same color, she was roughly the same height, but she wasn't Kay, the smile wasn't Kay's.

Jackson watched their reaction and felt some relief, he wasn't going mad. The whole craziness that had been Memorial to Labor Day was real, he wasn't in some strange alternate reality.

"But…what…? Where have you been? Did you not see what happened here over the summer?" Fitch splurted. How could she not have come forward sooner? How could she see reports of her death and not come forward to say it wasn't her?

The woman looked confused. "I was told you couldn't take me until now, that you had a funding issue and my start date was changed to now when you had the budget to pay me. Wait, was that not right? Was I supposed to be here already?"

"No, I mean did you not see the news at all?"

"The day after I got the call delaying my start, I received an offer to work security for three months in the South of France on a yacht for a Russian billionaire. I've barely seen or heard a word of English since I left. They flew me back this morning on one of his private jets. Why, what happened? Have I still got a job?"

The three men stared in utter disbelief, their brains rushing to compute and try and make sense of how much of what they experienced over the summer was real and how much was not. None more so than Fitch, whose heart was breaking, but he didn't know for who.

"Guys, you're freaking me out," said the new Kay, and from what they could gather, the real Kay. The paperwork and her old Portland PD badge were on the desk, it was definitely the new Kay's face on the old badge. "It's like you've seen a ghost or something."

Fitch and Winters left the room. The real Deputy Kay Miller was Jackson's problem, not theirs. They walked out into the sunlight in silence, neither able to form any words or make sense of what they had just witnessed. They looked at each other, but neither could speak. There were just no words either could utter to convey how they felt or what they were thinking.

Fitch finally had words worthy of the moment, but his phone chimed before he could share them, a text message from unknown.

§ deputy chef living – come alone. 7.00 a.m. tomorrow 21PS

"What is it?" Winters asked when he saw Fitch's expression.

Fitch just stared at his phone. The timing was too perfect, they had just exited the sheriff's office. He looked around wildly. The office was a one story building surrounded by empty fields and overlooked by nothing. He looked up and spotted a glint in the otherwise cloudless sky. Someone was looking down on them.

He shared his screen with Winters, whose mouth dropped, his inability to speak exacerbated by the content and Fitch pointing out the drone he guessed was far above them.

Fitch opened the 3 words app on his phone and typed in the what he knew to be a completely random combination of words. Whoever was sending it was a heartless son of a bitch. *deputy chef living.* Had he not known better he could have read into the meaning. The location zoomed to Dalton Street in Boston, a quick check confirmed the building, The Four Seasons, One Dalton Street in Boston, the same city he was meeting Gonzalez at 9 a.m. A further check showed the Presidential Suite was on the 21st floor,

"Fitch...21st floor, we found twenty-one bodies. 'Deputy chef living'...you don't think he ate her while alive, do you?"

"No, I don't. The words are random, you don't get to choose them. But yeah, he's definitely playing with us. Why me though, and why alone?"

Winters shrugged. "He feels bad about Kay, wants to apologize?"

"You're forgetting, she wasn't Kay!"

"Shit, you're right. Was she one of them? Is that why he killed her?"

The thought hadn't entered his head. Fitch had fallen for her, he hadn't thought of her as bad in any way. Even meeting the real Kay Miller, he hadn't reverted to thinking she was bad, just that...well, he had no idea what. His mind was still trying to come to terms with what had happened, *was* happening.

"We should call Gonzalez," said Fitch.

Winters' mind, like Fitch's, was fried. He had no ability to think, such were the myriad of thoughts, memories, and conclusions his brain was trying to work on all at once. "Yeah, good shout."

Chapter 54

Three hours and a helicopter ride courtesy of the FBI later, Gonzalez, Fitch, and Winters were staring into space in a conference room at the Boston field office. Gonzalez was as blown away as Fitch and Winters at what she was hearing. She had made to ask questions, each time stopping herself.

She looked at the message again. "He's toying with you. The use of 'deputy' and 'living' and reference to the twenty-one bodies, meeting on the twenty-first floor. We've got the hotel under surveillance. The presidential suite is empty and isn't booked tonight or tomorrow. I suppose the question is do we let you go in alone."

"Definitely. If this means we get some closure on the case, you'd have to throw me in a cell to stop me."

"Okay, good. Likewise, this would prey on me for the rest of my life, I'm desperate to know the full story. We'll mic you up and have a team ready to storm the room. The minute you give the signal, we'll come crashing in and get our man."

"Sounds good."

Winters and Fitch reserved a room at the Four Seasons, the FBI stretching their budget for the expense but only if they shared. Neither slept. The night was spent going over and over the time they had spent together on the island, analyzing every detail, every word the fake Kay had spoken.

"You know, there was one thing I found strange, but it never clicked until now."

"What?" asked Winters.

"Those damned FBI manuals she had in her trunk. Now it makes perfect sense, but I mean, she was supposed to be an experienced city cop, it wasn't normal for her to keep referring to the manuals."

"Normal?" Winters laughed. "That ended Memorial Day weekend. Those first two deaths, that poor guy, shitting himself to death."

"Don't forget, that poor guy was part of a group of child abusers and killers. He was a total piece of—"

Their door buzzed, it was 6 a.m. Gonzalez had told them she'd be there at six. A large team was spread throughout the hotel, and the Presidential Suite had been under surveillance the whole night.

"You don't think you've gone a bit, you know, OTT? I was supposed to come alone, it sounds like we've got the entire field office in situ."

"He's not getting away," Gonzalez promised.

"He's not going to get in to get away," Winters argued.

Gonzalez considered their point. She *had* gone a bit heavy. The room was under surveillance, as was the lobby, and she had an extraction team ready to go.

"Okay, I'll stand a few of them down. Granted, it was looking a little crowded down in the lobby for 6 a.m."

She signaled to her technician waiting in the hallway. He entered and wired up Fitch. It was 6:50 a.m. and Fitch was ready. His sidearm was in his holster on his hip, the man hadn't said he needed to be unarmed.

"Wait…" Gonzalez listened to an update on her earpiece. "It's okay, no, it's okay, a billionaire landing his helicopter on the roof. He owns the penthouse on the top floor."

"61st floor, nice. Must be some view," said Winters, trying to cut the tension that had built up in the room.

Fitch patted his friend on the shoulder, nodded to Gonzalez, and headed to the elevator.

Chapter 55

When the elevator pinged his arrival on the 21st floor, Fitch stepped out, tentative, looking around for the FBI agents that were at his beck and call should he need them. He looked towards the end of the corridor, to a room no one had checked into, nor was due to. He knew it was empty. He checked his watch, 6:58 a.m., he had two minutes to wait. He'd give them their two minutes and then knock, it was the least he could do, although it was looking increasingly likely that the come alone warning had not been heeded. His phone buzzed in his pocket.

It wasn't his alarm, that was still thirty seconds from sounding, it was a text message, unknown sender.

Come in, door's open.

He reached for the door handle with his left hand, his right on the grip of his sidearm. He pushed the door open and found himself face to face with the deputy Kay Miller that he knew, not the new one he didn't. Her face was frozen, an image of her that lit up the suite, the whiteness that engulfed her shining out from the TV screen filling the room. The image captured her perfect smile, her unflattering deputy uniform that Kay managed to make one of the sexiest unforms Fitch could imagine. He smiled as memories of the time they had together flooded back, her smile, her infectious laugh…she was the woman he had fallen in love with, connected with, but had no idea who she truly was. Whoever was playing with him was going to torture him with her. He took a snapshot in his mind of the image on the screen, that was the image he'd hold of her, no matter what was about to happen. He noticed a movement on the screen, Kay's lip quivered, it wasn't a still photo, it was a video. It began to play, and he realized the whiteness surrounding her was her whitewashed beach house. The bruise on her jaw told him it wasn't long after the incident between himself and Jackson that had resulted in him punching her by accident.

The recording began to play. "My dearest Fitch, please take a seat. If you're watching this, it means my time on the island ended unexpectedly, otherwise I'd be there with you…"

Fitch took the seat and watched.

***

Maine State Prison – Four Months Earlier, May

"Nurse, seriously, I'm in absolutely agony here, what is wrong with me?"

It was Angela's third week on duty in her new role, no place for an attractive young blonde woman to be. The prison ward had filled up on the realization there was a looker that had replaced the elderly nurse who normally looked after the ill prisoners. Although "look after" was as loose a term as it could be. She was a woman with little empathy, who even the toughest prison guards were wary of. It was joked that no prisoner ever dared shower in the ward, you never knew whether water would actually come out.

Angela was a very welcome change and had become a hit with every red-blooded male, guard and prisoner alike. Normally avoided, the ward now had a waiting list of fake illnesses growing in extravagance day by day.

She looked at the chart and checked his vitals. There was no doubt the man was suffering, he was definitely not faking. His face was gray and contorted in pain, his body tucked into the fetal position.

She checked the morphine drip he was hooked up to, pressing the button to ensure a dose was delivered as expected. "The morphine drip is working, have you been pressing it?"

"My thumb's numb from pressing it!" he whined.

She noticed the time. "I'll just swap it in case there's a problem." She retrieved a second morphine pack and hooked it up. There was an instant improvement as the prisoner pumped the feed button to deliver the maximum relief the pack would allow. His face and body relaxed.

"There, that's better," said Angela.

"Evening," came a call from the top of the ward, the prison doctor doing his nightly rounds.

"I didn't even realize that was the time," said Angela, much to the prisoner's surprise since she had just checked her watch before replacing his pack.

"So, how's Mr. Baker tonight?" asked the doctor, joining Angela by his bedside.

"Please, call me Gerald. I look around for someone else when you say Mr. Baker."

"Okay, Gerald, how are we tonight?"

"Better now. There was something wrong with my morphine I think."

Angela was standing behind Gerald. Unbeknownst to him she was shaking her head, advising the doctor the morphine was fine.

"Hmm, I have to say it's a strange one alright. The pain comes in waves, morphine works at times and at others doesn't. We need to run a few more tests and get you fit and healthy before you leave us."

"Oh? When?" Angela asked innocently.

"A few days, I believe," said the doctor, looking for Gerald to confirm.

"Two days and counting. I've been fine for almost five years and then this just before I'm due to leave. Three weeks of absolutely torturous pain."

"Well, we'll order a few tests and get some samples, see if we can work out what this is before you head off."

"Please, Doc, that would be great."

After checking on the numerous perfectly healthy and faking it patients the doctor left with a wave.

Angela headed back to Gerald's bedside, pulling the curtain for some privacy. "The doctor mentioned we need to take some samples." She pulled out two cups.

"No problem, do you want me to fill both? I'm not sure I've been drinking enough."

"Oh no, one's not for urine, it's for a different sample, one you'll need a bit of privacy to produce."

"You want me to jerk off a sample?" Gerald asked, making sure he wasn't misunderstanding.

"We need to check your semen, yes. It can tell us if there's anything going on down there, you know, men of your age, prostates, etcetera."

"I thought you just stuck a finger up my a—"

"Please," Angela cut in irritably, "I don't like profanities."

"Would you mind giving me a hand?" Gerald grinned.

Angela turned to leave. "Let me know when you are done."

While Gerald busied himself producing her samples, she replaced the drip which was on her side of the curtain once again, replacing the real morphine drip for her concoction. Each pump delivered another tiny dose of the poison that was coursing through his body, just enough to make sure he stayed alive in complete agony. She always swapped out the drip when the doctor arrived, just in case.

"Done!" Gerald called. "Courtesy of that cute ass of yours. I just thought of that and boom, sample delivered."

Angela felt a small mouthful of sick fill her mouth. She swallowed it down and retrieved the samples. One went in the fridge, the other in her cooler bag filled with ice packs, it would be in her freezer by midnight.

As Gerald pumped at his pain relief, the poison surged through his body. She'd at least ensure he had one more night of sheer agony before unhooking her concoction and replacing it for the morphine for his last day. She didn't want there to be any reason he didn't get released.

Two days later and as planned, Angela was coming off shift as Gerald Baker was released after five years. His nephew due to pick him up was sitting in a coffee shop on the other side of the city awaiting the very cute nurse that had hit on him the night before and who would not be showing up. An uber had been arranged to pick up his uncle. His uncle had no idea what an uber was and was more than happy to accept a lift from the cute little nurse who had been looking after him and unbeknownst to Gerald had led his nephew on the night before.

"I'd imagine the first thing you want is a drink," said Angela, waiting for him to fasten his seatbelt.

He leered at her. "Maybe second. You're a little old for my tastes but five years…"

"Well, that's not on offer here, what is, is a drink." She pulled out a bottle of bourbon she knew was his favorite.

He snatched it from her and took a long, welcome drink from the bottle. The next thing Gerald Baker knew he was sitting in a dungeon-like cellar, gagged and chained to a metal chair. The pain he had temporary reprieve from was back with a vengeance, courtesy of the drip feeding it into his arm. The chains held his arm and body tightly in place. If there was a god, he had abandoned Gerald as he suffered a pain worse than death hour after hour. The drip was sustaining him as much as it was torturing him, and a heavy dose of caffeine for good effect ensured sleep would not come easily.

The blonde nurse was no longer blonde. Her brunette hair, he noted through the pain, improved the already impressive package.

Chapter 56

Four Months Earlier, May

Orlando, Florida, Retirement Community

"Ah, Julie, you're back. Your uncle will be so pleased."

"How's he been?" she asked.

"Poorly. Ever since you were here last, he's been a poor soul."

"Oh, I better get in and check on him then." She unlocked the door to the small retirement flat. "Uncle Larry, it's Julie," she called.

Larry Beaumont was sitting in a chair staring at a TV that wasn't even switched on. "Julie, oh I'm glad you're here. I'm almost out of those pills," Larry said to the niece he hadn't remembered existed when she had walked into his life a few weeks earlier as though she had always been part of his.

"Don't worry, I've brought more medicine. How have you been?"

"Not good."

"Well, don't worry. I'm back now, we'll soon have you sorted out."

Julie cleaned the flat before leaving, making sure she wiped down all the surfaces she had touched. She would be back later but wasn't going to be staying.

She opened the door to leave, announcing loudly, "I'll be back in a few weeks, Uncle Larry."

She knocked on the next-door neighbor's door and asked her to keep an eye on him, she was going to be out of the country for a few weeks working but would be back as soon as she could.

"I wish my niece was as good as you. Your uncle is so lucky!"

Julie smiled. The woman had no idea.

Later that night when the community had popped half a ton of pills for their various ailments, Julie was back, dressed in black, and with the aid of the sleeping pills she had given to Larry earlier, wheeling him to a minivan she had hired under an alias. One of the seedier areas of the city offered her the opportunity to extract the sample she required. A stop at a street worker with a drug problem far in excess of any morals ensured the extraction of the sample required. As the street worker did her thing, Julie was avoiding the numerous offers of curb crawlers who were extremely impressed with the upgrade in talent working the street.

By the time he came to, the drugs that had been disorienting Larry Beaumont for the last few weeks were cleaned out of his system. The pain he felt was as intense as his neighbor's, a man he instantly recognized despite his face being contorted in pain.

"Gerald!" he gasped between waves of pain, not realizing he was gagged. The full horror of his situation slowly became apparent when the woman who had pretended to be his niece had appeared. Her hair had changed; she had been a redhead with short hair, now she had long brunette hair.

"Gentlemen, welcome to retribution!" she announced with a smile. "You are going to tell me everything you did at Reynard's Orphanage, who was involved, and what they did. Thereafter, if you are very, very lucky, your death will be quick. You hold back and it will take me weeks, maybe even months to end your miserable lives."

She pushed Larry across the room and hooked up a second drip, morphine. It would be available to him, the more he talked the more she'd give him as a reward. If he failed to talk she'd up the poison, increasing the pain exponentially, such was the finite balance of the mix she had pumping into them.

Larry talked, he poured every detail he could think of. He wasn't holding back, he had a lot to say and was happy to tell her in reward for easing the pain. He'd do anything to stop the pain. Gerald was struggling in anger against his restraints, suggesting everything Larry was saying was true.

During her questioning, one name was foremost on her mind. When she mentioned the name, Larry grinned. "The one who nearly got away," he had said. "But I got her, yeah she's dead…"

She couldn't control herself. Larry had smiled at the memory of the killing. She hit the pump button for her concoction. What he had told her was supposed to have been rewarded, he told the truth, but there was no way she would reward him for that. She hit the pump button again and again, pumping more and more poison into Larry. His face contorted, his body spasmed wildly, sweat poured from him, his screams of agony almost pierced her eardrums but remained within the soundproof dungeon in the remote house. She watched him twist and writhe, his wrist and ankles breaking as he struggled against his restraints, the pain pulsing through him. His eyeballs began to bulge, red streaks appearing as his veins began to pop. She kept pumping the poison, she couldn't contain her rage. And then, he stopped struggling. His body died. Larry Beaumont had suffered a horrific death, no less than he deserved.

Gerald was harder work. He fought for three days before he could suffer the pain no more. She knew he was broken when the truth of Andrew Hughes, the director of the orphanage, was revealed. He hadn't died in a car crash; he was alive and well, the report of his death thanks to a pedophile ring that looked after one another. Andrew Hughes needed to disappear, and it had been arranged. Gerald didn't know where he lived, only that he was in hiding, but he was still in touch with the group. Gerald had been a hideous man, a truly abhorrent and brutal man. She toyed with shooting him but decided a slow and agonizing death was a more fitting punishment. She loaded his two drips and left. They'd run through his system in twenty-four hours but would deliver pain unlike anything he had ever experienced. Thereafter, chained, bound, and gagged, he'd die of thirst if his heart let him last that long.

She turned the key in the door, exited the dungeon, walked up the stairs, and opened the hatch, locking it firmly behind her before pushing the central kitchen unit back in place over the hatch. The house was a fortress. She had perimeter cameras and security that would monitor for any breaches. She walked to the end of the long drive, her mind clearing as she went. She'd have preferred to drive but couldn't risk it. She wasn't fit to drive, having consumed more wine than she thought possible over the previous few days. She needed it; she couldn't do what she did without it. She turned and walked the two miles into the nearest small town, modifying her plan as she walked. Hughes being in hiding was a problem, she needed to flush him out. With her plan prepared she arrived in the small town and ordered an uber from the coffee shop. She had a plane to catch and a new job starting Memorial Weekend on an island she knew all too well.

Chapter 57

Fitch remained motionless as Kay's image on the screen froze, just as he had. He was frozen, he had nothing. He truly was struggling to comprehend what he had just watched and heard. The woman who was Kay— or was she Angela? Or was she Julie? Who was the real woman he'd fallen in love with and how was she capable of everything she had done?

Before he had a chance to work out how he felt the screen flickered and cut to another image of Kay. This one was slightly different. The smile in her eyes had died, the room she was in was dark, much like the room he was sitting in, and the light that surrounded her was gone. Her image remained still. Again, her lip quivered before she began to speak. The video was continuing, different time, different place. The bruise, he noted, wasn't there.

"I caught up with him as his hand was unhooking the final rope that bound him to the land," she began. "Where he had caused so much pain. He saw me as I approached and dropped the rope. He was wearing a mask, but he wanted me to know who he was, so he pulled it from his face. I barely recognized him but you never forget people like him, monsters remain with you forever. He smiled; he knew who I was. And I knew who he was Andrew Hughes, director of Reynard's Orphanage."

Fitch looked around the room, he was alone. Nobody else was there to help him make sense of the words Kay was saying. It seemed like she was telling him about the night she died, but that wasn't possible.

"I pulled the trigger but he beat me to it. Dropping the rope had diverted my eyes from his other hand. He shot me, and a .22 bullet caught me full in the chest, sending me crashing to the dock. But in the darkness he hadn't noticed I wasn't bleeding, I was wearing a vest under my shirt. He laughed at me wildly, gleeful that he had me in his control. I was struggling to breathe, the power that little bullet packed winded me. Tears filled my eyes, but I fought them back, I had to beat him, I couldn't let him win. The anger consumed me, but I knew with his death my time was done. Kay Miller could be no more. I couldn't be her anymore. That was the point I realized my biggest regret was you, Lieutenant Ross Abercrombie. I knew I would lose you. I had to kill the man but in so doing I was killing us. I almost let him go, let him escape, but he laughed at me, laughed at how pathetic it was that I had failed. Mocked me, mocked us all, laughed in my face, laughed at…" Kay caught herself. Tears were flowing from her eyes, she wiped at them with a napkin.

Fitch's eyes widened. He recognized the napkin, he'd used one himself that morning. It had the hotel's logo. Kay had been in the hotel.

"I shot him. I shot him for everyone. In the process I ended the lie that I was Kay Miller."

Fitch was barely listening. There were two hundred fifteen rooms in the hotel and he'd search every single one if he had to. A noise in the corridor outside startled him and he glanced at the door. He turned back to the screen in time to see Kay doing the same. She was *in the hotel*, beaming this live to his TV. She was alive! He didn't know how to feel, didn't know who she was, his Kay or a deranged, twisted killer. While his mind raced,

Kay continued to pour out her heart and tell her story from two months earlier. Her last night on Lane's Island.

Deputy Kay Miller took her final breath and was gone. She had to act quickly. She fired again, her aim affected by her position lying on the dock. She couldn't make too much of a movement since his pistol was still aimed at her. The bullet caught him square in the chest. He had no vest and his cloak was no match for the .45 round her pistol packed. It tore through him, ending his gleeful grin instantaneously. Her job was complete, she had avenged them all. She hadn't factored in the fire, that had been a stroke of luck, fourteen in one fell swoop. She had circled the building, wedging the windows and dousing them in gasoline before spraying the door with it. Hughes had come out just as she had lit the trail of gasoline that set the barn alight.

She had thought she'd have more time with Fitch; he was an unknown that she hadn't planned for. She couldn't have known, couldn't have known he'd be allocated the case. It was her only regret as she doused the dock in Kay Miller's blood, two pints courtesy of a blood bank in Portland she had engineered for the real Kay Miller to visit.

She dropped her reloaded firearm into the ocean, threw her hat in the quickly receding tide, and boarded the sailboat as Andrew Hughes was slowly and noisily bleeding out on the deck. She cast off and set the rudder for a southerly heading. While she was pushing some packing into Hughes's wound, she pushed hard, ensuring the maximum amount of pain possible. He wasn't going to live long and she wanted to ensure his last minutes, or hopefully hours, were as excruciating as possible. She injected some of her concoction and took great pleasure in the pain it induced, adding to his bullet wound. He was the ringleader; the reason twenty-one children were buried under trees that this monster had planted above them to remind him of the pleasure he had partaken as he killed them in his society's twisted and sick rituals.

The Specials they called them in the orphanage; the other children had no idea what that meant. There was no external bruising on the Specials, they wanted them to look as innocent and as angelic as possible for their sexual fantasies. It was a very select few who warranted becoming a Special, and only Hughes could make that decision. Once a Special was chosen the pedophiles acted out their fantasies, which occasionally resulted in the life being extinguished such was their brutality. The children's lifeless bodies were cast aside as they continued their evening. And if not by accident during their abuse they were dealt with before they were due to return to their main orphanages. The Specials could never be allowed to tell the truth, never be allowed to leave the island alive, never to divulge the true horror of what the orphanage meant for the Specials, the twenty-three.

Hughes lasted three hours. It was better than he deserved. She had lashed him to the deck before boarding the small tender and scuttling the sailboat ten miles south of Matinicus Island. *"joggers bottles shadowless"* if anyone cared to raise the monster.

***

The TV went blank. The woman Fitch knew as Kay Miller, the woman he had fallen in love with, had envisaged spending the rest of his life with, had just admitted on tape to being a ruthless and brutal killer.

Admitting to murdering over twenty people, not just in cold blood but with extreme prejudice, causing as much pain and torture to them as humanly possible, including burning fourteen people alive.

The tape ended, the screen went dark, and a light illuminated on a small table to his left. A flash drive and a sticky note were the only items on the table. The flash drive was a fox's head, the body was missing. The sticky note advised ReynardsSpecials as the password to access its content. Fitch could only imagine the horrors it contained. He'd leave that for others to look over.

His cell rang. It was Gonzalez. She would have heard everything he had.

"Jesus, Fitch, are you okay?"

"No," he said simply, unable to comprehend what he had just watched. There was no remorse for the killings whatsoever in her voice, and the evidence on the tape alone would ensure she received the death penalty. Although, he wasn't sure any jury would deliver that verdict. The avenger that Kay was in reality had become a folk hero, an urban legend. She had killed the worst, the very worst of humanity, those who hurt, raped, abused, and killed innocent children. His Kay was funny, warm, loving, he couldn't believe how she had fooled him, how she had kept the real her from him. He had marveled at how he had pieced together her clues, given it was the clues to her crimes. He was less impressed with his investigative capability; he had, after all, fallen for the killer.

"Do you want Winters to come up?"

"No, she's here, somewhere in the hotel. She used a napkin to wipe her tears, and it was one from this hotel."

"Yeah, but not necessarily today, she must have set the room up for you."

Winters was in almost as catatonic a state as his friend. He had listened aghast as the woman he had known as Kay Miller systematically had described what she had done.

"What I don't get," he said, thinking as he spoke, *"why bring us here to just show us a taped confession? I mean, she could have emailed it…"*

"No, she's definitely here. I heard a noise in the corridor and looked at the door, as did she. This was live, she's in the hotel."

"And on your floor, then. You'd not have heard the same thing at the same time on different floors."

Fitch was having the same thought as the connecting door to a king room that was adjacent to the Presidential Suite slid open.

The woman who entered blew Fitch away. She was as beautiful as he remembered, more so. Her hair and clothing were perfect, enhancing rather than detracting from her natural beauty. She smiled sweetly, he couldn't help but smile back, despite her being a ruthless and brutal killer.

She walked across the room and embraced him. "I'm so sorry," she said. His body remained tense, he did not reciprocate and pulled away. A tear ran from her eye. "You were never part of the plan, Fitch. You were my unexpected consequence and the reason I'm still here."

Fitch opened his mouth and waited for words to come. They failed him, he had nothing.

"You're probably wondering where I've been…"

"Actually no, I thought you were fucking dead, remember? You left us a few clues that you were *dead!*"

She winced at his swearing but let it go. "I meant you'd be thinking that now."

"No, I was thinking you're a ruthless killer but can't abide swearing." He noted her twitch when he swore. "I mean, what the *fuck*!" he added for effect.

"I don't like profanity. It's…I don't know, I just think unnecessary most of the time."

Fitch's phone buzzed, interrupting the discussion of the irrationality of her issue with profanity while torturing and killing people apparently was acceptable.

"That'll be Gonzalez, I liked her a lot." She pointed to his phone, letting him know she knew they were listening.

"Well, it seems her degrees are worse than useless. You were under her nose all along!" Fitch answered the call on speaker.

"She's there?" asked Gonzalez, reacting to the voice they were hearing.

"Yes, and so's Fitch," she answered Gonzalez instead of Fitch.

"Should we come up?"

"Would you mind if me and Fitch talk? I'll hand myself in peacefully, don't worry."

"Fitch?"

"Whatever." He ended the call. As angry as he was, he couldn't help himself, he wanted to hold her. *She's alive*! he wanted to scream from the rooftops, but the reality was she wasn't the woman he thought she was. She couldn't be after doing what she had done. He had no idea who she was, she wasn't deputy Kay Miller in her figureless gray uniform. She was a woman who looked like a million dollars in a dress that looked made to measure, perfect for her. Her hair had not a strand out of place, it was immaculate, and when she moved, it moved in perfect unison, it wasn't tucked roughly up under her deputy's hat.

But her eyes... If eyes were a route to the soul, they stared at him, wide and open, love filling them, looking at him, wishing him to love her back. But he didn't know her. Would never truly know her.

The look he conveyed must have told her that. She looked at him with resignation. She had lost him, the truth hadn't won the day. He didn't and couldn't ever know what she had been through. She hadn't told anyone, not even Nikolai and Maria, the older couple who had saved her from the streets, taken her in as their own, raised her, and given her everything she ever needed. Maria had died two years ago and Nikolai had understood what she needed to do. He knew she had to do it for herself, no matter the danger it had posed, and with Maria gone he had given her his blessing. He had begged her not to go back and meet with Fitch, but knew she had to. Nikolai was an old man, the father and grandfather she had never had, the family that replaced the one she lost, and would give his life for her. Yet she had never told him or Maria everything, only enough that they understood.

Fitch needed more. She couldn't give it. If that meant she'd go to prison, so be it. Nikolai was a wealthy man, she'd have the best defense money could buy. But she wasn't going to lie, she'd tell the truth throughout and accept whatever they threw at her.

"Okay," she said, "let's go."

Fitch stood and looked her in the eye. He could see the pain, see she was holding back. They had connected, a connection unlike any he had experienced in his life, even Annie hadn't read him like she could.

He walked her to the door, stopping her before opening it. "What aren't you telling me?"

She shook her head and opened the door for him. Two FBI agents awaited them. She held out her hands for the cuffs. Fitch pushed her arms down and waved the agents back. He led her to the elevator by himself. She clearly wasn't armed, there was nowhere she could have concealed it in the dress that fit her like a glove. He pressed the button and elevators raced towards them.

Winters and Gonzalez had listened intently. Winters still couldn't understand why she was meeting them there, it just seemed so dramatic and foolish. Why was she giving herself up? She had no reason to, she had got away with it, and from what she had said, had the money to keep away. He thought back to the message that Fitch had received, the random symbol. "Show me the message she sent Fitch again."

Gonzalez showed him the printout she had of the message

§ deputy chef living – come alone! 7:00 a.m. tomorrow 21PS

"That symbol," he said, "it wasn't in Kay's notes, it was one of the two she didn't have that was on the big tree. Not one of the twenty-one."

"So?"

"We never released the symbols or even mentioned them."

"I'm not getting you. Kay knew the symbols were there, she must have known this one too."

"Don't you get it? The symbol and the three words, that's where the child was, it was the location of the Special. Each one was allocated a symbol."

"Oh my God, she was a Special. This is the location of that Special, that Special being Kay."

They rushed towards the elevator as they heard through Fitch's mic that they had left the room and were heading down.

Two elevators showed as being at floor 21, the Presidential Suite when it pressed the button was rewarded with options.

The mic feed cut out as Fitch boarded the metal tube that would take the fake Kay Miller to custody.

Winters and Gonzalez waited as the numbers counted down, struggling to imagine the horrors that Kay had witnessed as a child.

"I'd have done what she did," said Winters.

Gonzalez looked him deep in the eye. "If you repeat this, I'll swear I never said it." Winters nodded for her to continue. "Abso-fucking-lutely, I'm going to shake her hand before we put her in cuffs. Those were sick, twisted fucks that got what they deserved."

Winters cracked a grin. "You've got a right potty mouth on you, Special Agent Gonzalez."

The door pinged open, the elevator was empty. They looked at the screen above them for the second elevator, it remained on floor 21.

Chapter 58

Fitch guided her into the right-hand elevator and hit the hold button as the doors closed. "Okay, it's just you and me, the mic won't work in here. please, tell me why?" he pleaded.

She looked at the man she had fallen in love with, the only man she had ever trusted to allow herself to fall for. But the complexity of that reality was beyond comprehension. It couldn't be, it wasn't an option that they would live out their lives together, a perfect unit, them against the world. In a different time in a parallel universe that may have been possible, but the whole truth was something Fitch couldn't cope with, he'd never get over it. Yet for them to be together, she'd have no option, she couldn't hide it from him.

He could see she was holding back, the pain in her eyes, the tears leaking from her beautiful eyes, it was killing him. He had prayed for her to not be dead for two months and there she was, standing before him, and she was giving him no choice but to take her to prison where, if she was lucky, she'd get to live out the rest of her life.

She looked at him and knew she had no option; it was for him to make the judgment. He deserved the truth, he had opened his wounded heart to her and let her in. Two broken and damaged souls had found solace in one another.

"You never asked me my real name," she said, tears flowing from her eyes.

Fitch stared at her, struggling to understand why that was such a massive revelation. She'd just admitted to over twenty murders.

He shrugged. "What's your real name? Angela? Julie? Kay? Something else?" he asked.

"Charlie," she said to a fresh flood of tears.

Fitch froze, shock replacing understanding. "Charlie? Like my Charlie was called Charlie?"

"My name is Charlotte, but my sister Annie insisted on calling me Charlie," she managed between sobs.

"Just like my Annie insisted…" It him like sledgehammer in the gut. His stomach churned, an instant lump forming as the enormity of what he was hearing registered. Charlie and her sister, his wife Annie, were the two missing children from the twenty-three, the two they hadn't found graves for. His wife had suffered terribly, and he'd had no idea. He didn't know what he'd have done differently if he knew, but he was sure he'd have done something. He couldn't even rule out the retribution that Charlie, or Kay as he knew her, had committed. And he hadn't lived through what they'd had to live through. He listened as Charlie spoke, his mind racing with the possibilities of how and what he would have done.

"I thought Annie died twenty years ago but it seems she escaped just like me. I'm guessing she thought I was dead too."

"So you had no idea she was my wife and Charlie was your niece?"

"Of course not, I wouldn't have fallen for you the way I have if I had known. As far as I knew Annie died twenty years ago, a young girl who I miss every single day. It wasn't until you showed me their photos. I almost died when I saw them, and the realization that we could have been together all those years. Annie disappeared one night after they took her from our room and we never saw her again. We knew as Specials it was only a matter of time. I assumed she was killed. She must have escaped like me and she'd have assumed they killed me too. It was like she died all over again for me."

"But why wouldn't she have gone to the police?"

"The police?" Charlie hitched a breath. "Beaumont helped them. He was one of them. We couldn't trust the police, or anyone in law enforcement or the courts. Did you never wonder why I was so adamant Judge Wright was murdered?"

"Well…I suppose you did jump quite quickly to the conclusion."

"It was his money that bought the place. He was as bad as any of them. We couldn't go to the police, they were protected, nobody would believe us. We'd be dead before the day was out if we reported anything. And the Specials would be gone that same day to cover their tracks. There was nothing we could do, we were powerless. As for Judge Wright, I had plans for him. He was going die a long and torturous death, and that woman stole that from me. I was furious she had let him die so peacefully, not that she had killed him."

"But why wouldn't Annie have told me?'

"You have no idea what they did to us, Fitch. She probably blocked it from her memory. She was happy, the pictures you showed me show that, that was how I remember Annie before we went to Reynard's. She loved life."

"On your tape you said Beaumont had told you he killed Annie?"

"Exactly. I mean, they still got to Annie and got away with it! He must have recognized her and ran her off the road He killed her and they covered it up all those years later. She and Charlie were killed by those monsters to protect their secret. I just didn't realize he meant he had killed her fifteen years after she escaped, I assumed he meant at the time. Remember, that was before I even came to the island. I still thought Annie had been killed as a young girl."

"And if you had known?" he asked, wondering if her thoughts were as dark as those forming in his mind.

"I'd have made him suffer an eternity of pain. You have no idea what we suffered at their hands. Not that he didn't suffer. Oh, rest assured, he suffered." She looked Fitch deep in his eyes and with a sincerity that should have troubled him. However, he took a satisfaction he never thought possible from her words of how she had tortured and killed another human being.

Charlie sensed a slight reticence. "Please remember these were not people like you and I. We are dealing with monsters. These are not functioning human beings who deserve to share the air we breathe. They torture, rape, and kill innocent children for their own gratification. Also, I'd add, I never did any of this sober. Every killing I needed to drink myself almost into oblivion to commit. I've got issues, I know that, but this was retribution, not random. Every person I killed deserved what they got, and although I delivered the verdict and the punishment, it wasn't without the realization of what I was doing. Hence I drank, and I mean a *lot*. I drank a lot of wine, so much wine," her eyes rolled to emphasize that point, "I'm surprised I managed to function some days, but it got me through what needed to be done. None of it was easy but if you are asking me if I regret or feel guilty, I do. But only because I didn't do it many years ago. If I had…" Tears began to flow again. Charlie's sister and niece had died five years earlier at their hands, if she had killed the monsters sooner she'd still have her sister, and Fitch his wife and daughter. For that she was sorry, more sorry than he would ever know.

"You couldn't have known," said Fitch. Somehow the admission that she needed the alcohol to act helped rationalize her actions for him. At least in a small way, she wasn't as stone cold a killer as he had envisioned. "The GPR machine…you weren't looking for the red paint people were you? You were looking for your sister and the other Specials."

She managed a smile. He got her. "Yes, but then I found the tree, the twenty-three symbols. We each had a symbol allocated to us. I couldn't use the machine there. I searched and searched and found each tree, realizing what it meant. It was their markers, their headstones. It was only when I discovered Annie had escaped that I realized we were number twenty-two and twenty-three, the ones with no trees."

"They killed twenty-two but you, number twenty-three, got them!" he said, pride seeping into his voice. The realization the monsters had killed his wife and daughter was still sinking in.

Charlie nodded. Not proudly, sadly. She took no pride in what she had done. It was simple retribution. They had wronged her and her family, she had simply repaid them in kind.

"So what do we do now?" asked Fitch. "I mean, technically we're family. You're my sister-in-law."

"To be honest, my thoughts and feelings are not those I should harbor for my brother-in-law, so I'm not really sure."

Fitch wiped the tears from her eyes. "So what was your getaway, if all else failed?"

"It's sitting on the roof, but only because Nikolai insisted."

"The billionaire's helicopter that landed just before I came up here?"

Charlie nodded. "Nikolai and his wife Maria found me on the streets after I escaped, and they took me in. They were an older couple, didn't have any kids, and raised me as their own. They weren't rich back then. Well, not *as* rich. There's a yacht—actually it's more like a small cruise ship," she smiled awkwardly, "waiting twenty-five miles off the coast in international waters. It sails under a Russian flag so nobody would dare board it if they did chase after me. There's also security on board, but you know that. The real Kay Miller needed to be somewhere out of the way while I was being her. Nikolai made sure she didn't access any English news channels. It apparently wasn't easy; he was stressing constantly."

"You really did plan it all out perfectly."

"Except for you. I never planned for that, otherwise I'd not be here now."

Fitch had heard enough. "Look, we've got two options. Option one, I press the button for the fifth floor and we take the chance we can get you off on mental incapacity. I'm sure Nikolai could afford lawyers who would come up with something clever and I will be by your side all the way. Or option two, I step out, you hit the button for the 61st floor, and we never see each other again."

*****

Winters and Gonzalez waited for the elevator to move; it was taking forever. The agents on the 21st floor confirmed nothing was happening and that they could still hear voices behind the door but couldn't make out what was being said.

The screen went blank. Number 21 disappeared. It felt like an eternity before number 20 was illuminated, the numbers flashing quickly thereafter as the elevator raced down towards them. The number 5 illuminated and the doors opened in front of them.

Fitch stood next to Charlie, his hand in hers, keeping her strong for the fight they were about to undertake.

Fitch leaned over and whispered in Charlie's ear, "Why option one?"

"Because option two meant life without you." She stepped towards the waiting Gonzalez, who stepped back, giving her room to exit.

Fitch hadn't let go of her hand and pulled her back from the door and into his arms, hitting the button for the 61st floor.

"One thing though," he said as Winters and Gonzalez failed to respond before the doors closed.

"What?"

"You need to promise me, no more wine!"

THE END

Please subscribe to updates on new releases and special offers –by visiting

www.eepurl.com/IaKZz